Beyond The Dead

BY: Veronica Talliss

PLAYLIST

THE CHAIN - FLEETWOOD MAC

CONTROL - HALSEY

OCEAN EYES - BILLIE EILISH

THE GHOST OF YOU - MY CHEMICAL ROMANCE

CINNAMON GIRL - LANA DEL RAY

DIE WITH A SMILE - LADY GAGA & BRUNO MARS

JUST IN CASE - MORGAN WALLEN

RIGHT HERE - CHASE ATLANTIC

DARK SIGNS - SLEEP TOKEN

EARTHQUAKE- RYAN TAUBERT

DELUSIONS OF SAVIOUR - SLAYER

THEY DONT CARE ABOUT US - MICHAEL JACKSON

PRAISE JAH IN THE MOONLIGHT - YG MARLEY

XIBALBA - RYAN TAUBERT

ALL OF THE STARS - KENDRICK LAMER & SZA

DRAGULA - ROB ZOMBIE

Trigger Warnings

Gore
Emotional Abuse
Explicit Sexual Content
Cannibalism (Zombies)
Psychological Trauma
Dissociative Disorder
Survival Situations
Dystopian Themes
Gun Violence
Abandonment
Betrayal
Obsession
Torture
Murder/Death
Animal Death (Bear)
Child Death

Please **do not** contuine reading if anything above will trigger you. Your mental health matters. ❤

When two souls are destined to be together, they are connected by an invisible thread. This thread may stretch or tangle, but it will never break.

PROLOGUE

MARCH 7TH 2018

RYDER

She's so perfect. She just spent the last few hours taking my cock like she was an animal who hasn't eaten in months. I missed her so much. Nine weeks away for basic training was too long. I settled in at the hotel after landing and she came to see me straight away. I think *she* missed *me*. My parents died when I was twelve so I know deep down it was because she knows I hate coming back here, or maybe she just wants to spend time with me.

I move a piece of her midnight hair out of her afterglow resting face. Leaving this time is going to suck. Nine weeks was long, but this stretch will be longer, I just know it. The worst part? Not being able to hold her, talk to her or even just check in on her wellbeing. We went from talking every day and seeing each other at school our entire childhoods, to me having to go MIA for long periods of time. Once I'm actually deployed though, I won't so much as have a satellite phone. Just me and my thoughts. No Violet. I have my brothers there but they are guys being dudes. Plus, I'm so fucking sick of hearing about everyone's problems and listening to them jerk off in the bunks above me. I can't have the stupid top bunk because I'm *too tall*. Who knew being 6"7 meant I'd have to listen to that bullshit every night? Sometimes I wish I could escape this life. I wish I could just run away with her, no more so than when I had to tell her I was being deployed the following afternoon.

"I was pretty impressive in basic…so they want me in Afghanistan as soon as humanly possible."

She understood. She always understands. She was the one who said she knew I'd be the best in my class. During my breaks from basic I went and got a few new tattoos too. She loves them. I know she does because after she trailed her fingers across my newly inked arms, we were able to go for round four.

God, she turns me on so much. I'm not the type to have feelings for someone let alone have someone sleepover but she's different. She's so easy to talk to. She cares about me. She listens to me. No one ever listens to me. In the past, girls just see my height and immediately sexualize me and think I'm some fuck machine. I didn't even have my first kiss till I was seventeen. I've never been the relationship type, I'm the kind of guy who you have fun with while he's on leave, and tell your friends about it at girls' night. I'm also the leave me the fuck alone or I'll kill you type. Okay, maybe not murder in cold blood but the sentiment is the same.

Then I met her. My *Ocean Eyes.* The only girl who sees me for who I am and chooses me everything single time. I've never told her how I truly feel and maybe I should, but every time I get close, I can't. I'm scared to lose her, or that my feelings won't be returned. I'm scared that me being away will fuck it up. I told her I would write to her. I know she likes the movie The Notebook so maybe that could be my big romantic gesture.

I flip so I'm lying on my back and looking up at the roof and sigh. Being a soldier is everything I've ever wanted. The thought of helping people and protecting my country would make me proud. Getting to use a gun as catharsis when I'm pissed is also a perk. I want to live a life of purpose. I just wish it didn't include leaving her behind. I kiss the back of her head and pull her closer for a cuddle. I'll just try to live in this moment for a bit longer.

I wake up to Violet pushing her ass against my cock. Moving it in circles, I'm assuming to see if I'm awake. I'm definitely awake. I grab her hips, slowing her down, but grinding her harder. She lets out a soft moan and raises her leg. She lets out a soft moan and opens herself up to me. I pull out my cock and rub the head all over her.

"You're always so wet for me" I whisper in her ear.

Violet comes back from her shower looking like the statue of fucking Aphrodite. Her curves will haunt me like a half-remembered dream, soft and perfect in the edges of my mind. Her eyes hold the depth of rare sapphires, glinting with a light that could cut through the darkest night. Her hair falls in an endless black cascade, carrying the sweet trace of vanilla. Warm, familiar, and enough to undo me with every breath. Now I'm regretting not joining her in there for round number …who knows? I've lost count.

"Your dad kept calling you when you were in there."

Her eyes widen and she grabs her phone off the dresser. "Oh, fuck I'll call him back. Probably wondering where I am."

She lives at home with her mom, little brother and her conspiracy theory wannabe military Dad. Normally I would put an old man like him in his place, especially when he questions my occupation, but I want to leave a good impression on her dad. He's just looking out for his amazing daughter. *I get it.* She's a beautiful soul in a fucked-up world and I *could* be crazy.

I'm just as protective though. Like one time when she was at work and some regular tried to touch her ass, I sat outside her work for almost two weeks straight just to take him out back and beat the shit out of him. She did mention that she was happy he had never come back. I don't know how she manages being a server while also going to college to be a paramedic. I hope I'm back in time to see her graduate, to see her in that uniform saving lives while I stand in the back just watching. She doesn't even know how pure she is, how she was built for something more. Maybe that's what makes me the most insane, because I'd kill to make sure nothing ever stops her from getting there.

"Okay Ryder I've got to run, Dads saying he called Kate and Grace and both of them said I wasn't with them. Traitors. I thought girl code would dictate for them to say that I was with them, but I guess next time I'll have to actually beg them to lie for me. Fuck, I'm sorry I know you leave soon and you probably don't want to hear about my problems but I do want to tell you that I will miss you and I hope you stay safe. This isn't a goodbye, it's a see you later. Come back, okay?"

I smile. "There won't be one day out there that I don't think about you, Ocean Eyes. I can't wait to see everything you've achieved when I get back. I shouldn't be gone for longer than a few months, unless the mission goes sideways but I'm not going to jinx it."

I pull her in for a hug and kiss the top of her head. She's only about 5'9 so she is the perfect height for head kisses. I push her shoulders back so I can look into her eyes and then I give her the kiss my mouth couldn't find the words to say and hope she knows what I'm trying to tell her.

You're **mine** *darlin' and no one's going to ever take you away from me.*

"Hey, can we take a photo? You know… something to remember me by?" She says with that slow, teasing drawl she uses when she wants to get under my skin.

I grin and feel that familiar heat crawl up my chest, as I grab her phone. Pulling her close I hold her just a little longer than necessary, letting her feel the weight of me.

"Alright, smile for me," I say, trying to sound casual, but my voice catches.

"That better be your background the whole time I'm gone, darlin'." I tease, watching her eyes sparkle with mischief.

"In your dreams Kent…" she fires back, her lips curving into that little smirk that always makes my heart warm.

I laugh, handing her phone back, my thumb brushing hers for just a second longer than it should. I watch her climb into that beat-up old Honda of hers, the way she moves…

God, she's intoxicating.

My fingers run through my hair, roughing it up, and I can't stop the smirk from lingering even after she drives off. I head back to my room, heart still racing, and start packing, every thought of her sticking in my chest like fire. It's about a two-hour drive to the nearest international airport.

I arrive and find an empty seat near the plane terminal. As I open my phone to text Violet, I realize she has already texted me the photo.

We look so good together.

I tell her I made it to the airport. She doesn't answer. I assume work is busy so I pull out my notebook and start writing. No time like the present to try and put words to how I feel, I suppose.

Dear Ocean Eyes,

Seeing you leave this morning was hard. Knowing I won't see you for a while is even harder. I wish it was this easy to speak to you in person and I could have told you while we were together, but here goes.

You are fire and light and everything I can't stop thinking about. I see you in my dreams, in every shadow, and every quiet moment. I see the way your hair falls across your face, and the way your eyes catch the world and bend it to your will. Your curves, your laugh, your stubbornness... Christ, I've never wanted anything as badly as I want you. I hold back...not because I don't feel but because I feel too much.

I carry you with me Violet, like a heartbeat in my chest, like a weapon and a prayer all at once. I don't just love you. I ache for you. I ache to see you safe, to see you win, to see you smile knowing the world can't break you. You are brilliant, fierce, unstoppable, and I... I am yours, always. Every step I take, every breath I steal. I do everything I do for you, for us...

So, wait for me. I swear Violet when I come back, I'll make sure you never doubt for a second who you belong to.

With love, Ryder

Now boarding flight 1732 to Toronto

I shut my notebook and tug my suitcase upright. The first thing I'm going to do when I touch down is mail that letter. I just…I hope she feels the same.

No turning back now. See you in a couple months Darlin'.

SIX MONTHS LATER

VIOLET

"I'm so glad you took the weekend off, Vi! We haven't had a trip with the trio, since high school ended three years ago!" Kate says as she drives us home.

She's smiling wide, her long ruby hair catching the sunlight through the windshield. She always talks with the kind of energy that makes you feel like anything is possible. She keeps saying one day she wants to open her own day home. I can see it. Her patience and her kindness make it a perfect fit.

"Hey! Eyes on the road, crazy Kat!" Grace shouts from the backseat, laughing.

Grace has that easy confidence, sun-kissed hair tied in a messy bun, freckles scattered across her nose and always these bright, curious eyes that make you feel lighter just by looking at her.

I laugh, a little breathless, because I've missed them. They've been my anchor since Ryder…disappeared. The last text I have from him says he arrived at the airport and then *nothing*. I've sent a few more texts, but no reply. My mom's been my rock through all of this. She even suggested maybe there was something wrong with my phone; so, Dad and I went to get it checked. Turns out I needed a new number, but when I texted Ryder from that number, I still received *silence,* and now the days have stretched into months, and I catch myself dissociating. I can't help but think back on the moments we shared and the way we were together. I've been keeping busy with school and work, and I'm doing well but my mind always circles back; *why hasn't he reached out?*

"Hellooo, Earth to Violet?"

"Huh?" I blink, snapping out of it.

"Hey, don't think about it. He's probably just out doing sexy soldier shit and will get back to you as soon as he can." Grace teases, and I force a small laugh.

"Guys…it's just weird. I genuinely thought we had something. He even gave me a cute nickname. *Ocean Eyes.* That meant so much. Eyes are the windows to the soul, yah know? I felt like every time he looked at me with those delirious hazel eyes that he was looking into my soul and my soul recognized his. I thought…I thought we were going to be more."

"Girl, I've been telling you since high school, that boy is trouble. Yes, he's sweet, but the man has the emotional capacity of a jar of rocks. He lost his family when he was what, twelve? He probably has no capacity for connection. What do I always tell you?"

"If it's meant to be, it'll be."

"Exactly. Now, let's not pout about a dumb boy."

"Yeah…you're right," I murmur, though my heart aches like it isn't meant to be at all.

Grace grabs my arm and whines, "Yeah, now can you put on that song I love right now, please, please, please?" She folds her hands like she's praying and I roll my eyes but put it on anyway.

We sing along. Laughter fills the car but outside the window, the mountains blur past and my thoughts get louder. He said he'd write and I haven't received so much as a postcard. Maybe the girls are right. He's busy and out in the desert, no service, no mailman.

Fuck, Violet, get a hold of yourself. He will reach out. I know he will.

I join in the singing again as the last hour passes, the golden leaves of Alberta flashing red, orange, and yellow in the autumn sun. Fall has always been my favorite season.

Kate drops me off first. I grab my things, hug my friends, whisper that I love them, and make promises to see them soon. Walking into the kitchen, I see my brother Felix playing in the corner while Mom watches some new Love Island episodes. She loves that show. I smile, whisper my greetings, and head upstairs to unpack and sort things for college tomorrow.

The week ahead of me is jam packed. Back-to-back classes, work, exams. I let out a long breath and pull out the photo I printed of Ryder and I the day he left. I wanted to make a collage of our photos; of all the things he had promised he'd send me but they never came.

I hear footsteps on the stairs and shove the photo under my bottom, as I glance towards my door. Dad enters, sitting beside me.

"Hey, kiddo. I wanted to make sure you were home. I have to show you this but I don't want your brother to see you upset."

"Upset about what?" I ask, heart hammering.

He hands me a letter, addressed to our house. No return address.

Weird

I rip it open.

We are sorry to inform you that Ryder Kent has unfortunately passed away during active duty. Due to the circumstances of his passing, his body will not be returned to Canada. This address was the only one on file. Our condolences.

CHAPTER 1

AUGUST 7TH 2023

VIOLET

This couch always feels too soft. Like it wants me to sink into it and stay there. I sit stiffly, my hands clenched in my lap, the faint ticking of the clock louder than it should be.

"So," my therapist says gently, notepad resting on one leg, "How've things been since our last session?"

I hesitate, then let out a breath I hadn't realized I was holding.

"Work's been… fine. Better than home. My dissociations haven't been as often." *I lie.*

Her eyes soften, but she doesn't press yet.

"There's this quiet when I'm on a call," I continue. "This weird kind of calm. Everything clicks into place. The sounds, the adrenaline, the chaos. I know what to do there. It makes sense. People are bleeding or screaming or barely holding on, but I *know* what to do."

She nods. "And home doesn't feel that way?"

"No." I pick at the hem of my sleeve. "Home feels like holding my breath. Like waiting for something to explode that never quite does."

Probably because I'm living with an actual energy demon.

She tilts her head. "You mentioned your relationship last time and how it felt like you were becoming afraid of him. Have things progressed?"

I shrug. "He's not hitting me or anything. He just makes me feel inferior. Like everything I do is wrong. I save strangers but can't even speak up in my own house without it turning into a thirty-minute guilt trip."

Or constant insults to the point I question my worth.

She's quiet for a moment, then says, "Let's go back to the discussion we were having about your disassociation moments."

My throat tightens. "Yeah."

"You haven't talked about how it's been going. Not really."

I stare past her at the window where sunlight is spilling through the half-closed blinds. Dust motes drift in the air, suspended.

"It normally happens when I arrive at a scene," I say automatically, voice flat. "Training kicks in. This guy was trapped. Middle-aged. His eyes were wild. Panicked but he wasn't screaming. That's what stuck out. It's like he was waiting to die."

My voice wavers for the first time. "We got him out. I held his neck steady while they pulled his legs free. I got blood on my hands. It was hot from the fire."

"What happened when you got to the hospital?"

I blink. For a second, I can't remember. I see smoke. I hear the sirens. Smell burnt plastic.

"Violet?"

I snap back and my chest tightens. I shake my head like it'll clear the memory.

"They took him. I handed him off. He flatlined a few minutes later." I swallow. "I already knew he was gone. I knew it in the back of the ambulance but I kept working anyway. Pretended I didn't. Some people just don't want to live. I saw it in his eyes."

I saw it because I get it.

Silence wraps around us. She sets her notepad down.

"You said earlier that work gives you control," she says gently. "But even there, you're still losing people. That has to be heavy."

I agree.

"You can't control if they live or die but you can help them when they need it most, which is amazing work. You have to remember the things you can control. You can control how you feel about yourself and how you choose to live your life. Remember Violet, you're a compassionate, noble and extremely talented woman, who has a good head on her shoulders."

My throat burns. "I think I should go now."

"I understand, we can keep unpacking this in our next session," she adds, her tone warm but firm. "Same time in a few days?"

"Yeah, thank you Mrs. Finley." I whisper.

She offers a small smile.

"Take care of yourself, Violet."

I stand, grabbing my coat. As I step outside, the early evening air bites at my skin. My phone buzzes in my pocket. I don't check it. I already know it's him.

Heading home feels like walking back into a cage but for now I focus on the sound of my boots. One step at a time. The drive feels longer than usual despite it being the same twenty minutes it's always been. My hands grip the wheel too tight and my knuckles adopt a ghostly white hue.

Fuck.

The music on the radio becomes nothing but background noise, failing to distract me from the knot twisting in my stomach. My fingers tremble against the leather, and no matter how many deep breaths I take, the tightness in my chest doesn't fade.

It'll be fine.

I haven't done anything wrong. There's no reason for him to be upset. I pull into the driveway exhaling shakily as I shut off the engine. The house is dark except for a single light in the front window. My pulse quickens.

Is he waiting? Is he already angry?

I swallow hard and force myself out of the car. I unload my worn-out gear with unsteady hands. My heart pounds louder with every step toward the front door. My fingers fumble with the keys.

"Mommy!"

The voice slices through the night, sweet and full of innocence. For a second, *just a second*, the fear loosens its grip on my throat. I pivot toward the sound, past the looming shadow of the house, toward the only thing in my world that still felt *pure*. The front door creaks open behind me and just like that, the dread comes crashing back. At work, I am needed, respected, and capable. At home, I am nothing. I walk into the living room holding Jane and giving her as many kisses as I can muster. She does this thing where she giggles and tries to push my head away. She is so cute.

Then comes *his* voice.

"You're late."

Jeremy is sprawled on the couch, eyes locked on his phone. He barely glances at me as I walk in. I set my bag down, forcing a neutral tone.

"A kid coded on us. We did everything, but…" My voice trails off. I don't need to say it. He doesn't care.

Jeremy scoffs, finally looking up. "You should be used to that by now."

I swallow hard, trying not to let my shoulders slump. "I don't think losing a child is something you ever get *used* to."

He rolls his eyes. "Whatever. You act like you have to save everyone, but it's just a job. If you were *actually good* at it, maybe the kid wouldn't have died."

A lump forms in my throat.

Don't react. Don't let him see it hurts.

I put Jane down and try to walk past him, but he isn't done.

"Oh, and before you get comfortable, you need to do something with yourself. You smell like shit."

I bite my lip so hard I taste blood.

Yeah, maybe because I just came from a busy day of saving people and I'm covered in blood Dick bag.

Before I can respond, a small voice cuts through the tension.

"Mommy…uppies."

"Okay I guess you can hang out with Mommy for a little bit."

I kiss her forehead, and her little hands wrap around my neck. I hold her tight, breathing her in, grounding myself in the only love that feels real.

I kiss her cheek, my voice softened now. "I missed you, my lovely."

Jeremy stretches, and cracks his neck as he leans back against the couch.

"I'm taking a day off tomorrow."

I frown. "I thought you said we couldn't afford that?"

He scoffs. "I *said* I'm taking a fucking day off." His eyes flick to me like he is daring me to push the subject. "I already told my boss I've got Jane."

I hesitate. "Kate already said she'd watch her for free."

"Amazing, I could use a break, I've been dealing with her almost all day."

I bite my tongue.

Like you ever actually take care of her.

Instead of arguing, I sigh. "I'm taking her to Kate's tomorrow. I don't have the energy for this."

Jeremy smirks like he's won something, "Shocking."

I ignore him and put Jane down, shrug off my jacket and rub my eyes. The exhaustion from my shift is weighing heavy now, and I barely have the energy to stand, let alone cook.

"I'm too tired to make anything. I'll just order a pizza."

"Figures…" Jeremy mutters.

I clench my jaw but keep my voice level. "You got a problem with that?"

"Nah," he says, already looking at his phone again. "Just saying you act all *independent* at work, but you can't even cook a meal for your own family."

I swallow the sharp retort on my tongue.

Not worth it.

Instead, I grab my phone, place the order, and try to push the tension aside. Jane, oblivious to the mood in the room, bounces excitedly on the couch.

" Mommy, can we watch my favorite movie?"

"Sure can," I say softly, forcing a smile for her sake.

She cheers as I start the movie and snuggle my little girl while Jeremy sits on the other end of the couch scrolling through his phone like we aren't even here. I roll my eyes.

A few minutes later, I catch a video while doom scrolling. A girl attacking a homeless man. Not just attacking. Like trying to gnaw at his limbs. I frown, turning up the volume just so I can hear. The video is shaky and filmed from across the street. The girl's movements are erratic and unnatural. The caption reads:

New sickness?

"The hell are you watching?" Jeremy asks, barely glancing up.

"Some girl in the next town over. She's attacking this guy… trying to *bite* him."

Jeremy snorts. "Yeah, and? Junkies do that shit all the time. You should know, you see enough of them at work." The next video pins me in place.

The sky fills the screen, a pale stretch of blue streaked with the thunderous shapes of military helicopters. Dozens. Flying low, black shadows slicing across the horizon.

Why are they flying in formation over town?

Before I can spiral too far, my phone buzzes. *Dad.*

It's a picture of my mom, Dad, and Felix all crammed into the frame, grinning like idiots in front of a berry bush. Dad's holding the bucket up like a trophy, even though he can't eat a single one without breaking out in hives. I laugh under my breath. Mom's shielding her eyes from the sun, Felix has purple juice smeared all over his mouth like he's been caught red-handed. The field behind them stretches out forever, bright and golden.

Berry picking today his text reads.

I snap a quick picture of Jane curled up on the couch, totally absorbed in her movie, her hair sticking up like a little haystack.

Movie marathon. Wish we were there. I type and hit send.

A few seconds later, his reply pops up.

Bring her next time. The raspberries are practically as tall as she is.

His words feel warm, grounding. But when I glance back at that video…those endless military helicopters, the sky full of rotors.

The military…

Ding Dong!

"The pizza's here," I mutter, shaking off the unease as I get up to grab it.

I set the box on the table, and Jane claps happily as I hand her a slice.

"Um get a plate, I'm sick and tired of always cleaning up after you both."

I roll my eyes. Pizza barely has any crumbs. I grab napkins and a plate for us, Jeremy takes his food without so much as a thanks. We eat in silence. Jane hums along to the movie, her tiny feet kicking against the couch.

Jeremy speaks half-acknowledging me, his gaze still chained to the screen, "You should do something about your hair by the way. You look… rough."

I freeze mid-bite, fingers tightening around my crust.

"I *just* got off a shift," I respond slowly.

He shrugs. "Doesn't mean you have to look like shit."

I press my lips together, swallowing back the lump in my throat.

After the movie ends, I see Jane yawn, her eyes drooping.

Jeremy nudges me. "She's your kid. Put her to bed."

I exhale sharply, and stand up without a word. I scoop Jane into my arms, and carry her to her room. As I tuck her in, she whispers,

"You don't smell Mommy."

My heart drops. He shouldn't be saying shit like that to me at all, but most definitely not in front of Jane. Maybe it is time to think about leaving.

If I can't do it for me, I have to do it for her.

I kiss her forehead, my voice soft, "Thank you baby girl, I love you, sleep well my lovely. Angels on your pillows."

"I love you too Mommy."

I leave her with a kiss on her cheek.

I close Jane's door gently, and let out a slow breath. The second I am alone; I feel the exhaustion settle deep into my bones.

My skin wears the grime from work and the weight of the day clings to me. I need a *long* hot shower.

Steam curls around me as I step under the hot spray and I let the water wash away the filth. I close my eyes, willing myself to relax, to push aside the unease that being at home inspires. The bathroom door creaks open. I stiffen.

Jeremy.

I don't turn around or acknowledge him. I hope maybe, *just maybe*, he will take the hint. I feel his presence before I feel his touch, the heat of his body pressing too close. His hands slide around my waist, his breath warm against my ear.

"Been thinking about you all day," he murmurs, voice low and too sure.

His fingers trace my skin, a touch that should be intimate but instead makes every single nerve in my body jump at once.

I swallow hard.

"Jeremy, I'm tired."

He chuckles, nipping at my neck. "So? You just lay there anyway."

I pull away, reaching for my shampoo. "I said I'm tired."

His grip tightens for a split second before he lets go and steps back with an irritated huff. "Of course, you are."

I keep my back to him, hoping that he will leave. Instead, he mutters, "You're lucky I even *want* you looking like that."

I clench my jaw, forcing myself to stay silent. Arguing will only add fuel to the fire. The door slams behind him. Not a care in the world that our daughter is trying to sleep.

I throw both my middle fingers hard at the door and mouth out the words *'I hate you'*.

I stand there for what feels like forever, letting the water run over me, washing away the ghost of his touch. When I finally turn the faucet off and step out, the house is eerily silent. I dry off, pull on the first oversized shirt I can see and walk into the bedroom. Jeremy is already in bed, his back away, blankets yanked over his shoulders. I slip in beside him, staring at the ceiling. My body is heavy, but my mind won't stop spinning. Tomorrow has to be better. Deep down, I know it won’t be.

The alarm blares at 6:30 AM, cutting through the silence of the room. I quickly shut it off, careful not to wake Jeremy. He is sprawled out on his side, still dead to the world and snoring softly.

Good.

I slip out of bed quietly, throwing my uniform on in the dim light by memory. The house is deadly still, the kind of peacefulness that only exists before the day truly begins. I pad down the hall and I ease Jane’s door open and step inside. My sweet girl is curled up under her blankets, her tiny form rising and falling with steady breath. I hate waking her but I know she will have a better day at daycare than stuck at home with Jeremy. I kneel beside her bed, and brush a stray curl from her face.

“Good morning, my beautiful girl,” I whisper.

She groans sleepily, rolling over.

I smile, as I gently shake her shoulder. “Come on, sweetheart. Time to get up.”

She mumbles something incoherent before finally cracking her eyes open. I help her sit up, as she rubs the sleep from her face. Together, we go through our morning routine, brushing our teeth, smoothing our hair down, and picking her outfit out.

As I slip on my shoes, I give a quick glance toward the bedroom. Jeremy still hasn’t stirred.

Typical. No ‘Good Morning’. No ‘Have a Good Day’.

Just silence. I lift Jane into my arms, balancing her on my hip.

"Say bye to dad," I murmur flatly
"Bye daddy"
If he is awake, he doesn't even move.

Figures.

I don't waste another second. The crisp morning air greets us as I carry Jane to the car, and buckle her into her car seat. She giggles when I kiss her forehead, her smile warming something frigid in my chest. At least she is happy. At least today she is somewhere safe. I climb into the driver's seat and start the car, beelining it straight for my favorite coffee drive-thru. The familiar hum of the engine and the soft tunes from her favorite show, make the morning feel a little lighter.

"One apple juice for my sweet girl," I sing, passing the drink to Jane as she beams in the backseat.

I take a sip of my coffee, already feeling more human. A second cup of coffee sits in the cupholder beside me. Kate's usual order. As I pull up to the daycare, the tension in my shoulder's melts. She will play, laugh, and be around people who actually care.

I just wish I could say the same for myself.

Upon arriving, I park in Kate's driveway and unbuckle Jane from her car seat and with Kate's coffee in hand, I carry Jane to the front door. I prompt her to ring the doorbell and within seconds Kate appears, rushing to greet us. I am always the first to arrive.

"Hey Violet, and helllloooo Janey-poo!" Kate greets us warmly, clutching Jane close into a hug, "Come on in."

I assist Jane in removing her shoes and take off my own before climbing over the baby gate and arriving at the familiar kitchen table.

"I got you a coffee," I say to Kate, a smile instantly spreading across her face.

"I wish I could stay longer and chat, but I'll be late if I linger too much," I lament.

"It's okay, Vi. I'll see you in a couple of hours!" She reassures me.

We exchange a hug, and then I turn to Jane, kneeling down to meet her at eye level.

"Have a good day today, baby girl. Be nice for Kate, and Mommy loves you and will see you soon," I said, planting a kiss on her forehead, wrapping her in a tight hug.

"I love you too mommy," she whispers in my ear.

"Bye, guys," I say as I shut the front door.

I hop into my car, turn the key and feel the engine rumble to life beneath my palms. I flip through my radio presets until I find the perfect song to set the mood. Something upbeat, something that makes me feel *alive*. 'Praise Jah in The Moonlight' by YG Marley comes across the shuffle and I leave it there. I roll down the window a crack, letting the cool morning air wake me up as I back out of the driveway. I might go buy a joint on my way home today. A little something to unwind. I don't drink or smoke cigarettes unlike most of the moms I know. Before I got pregnant, I would smoke weed almost every day. A sweet release. Jeremy had always complained of the smell and convinced me to quit in the first place.

What if he smells it on me and freaks out? Then I just leave right?

I'm sure my mom and Dad would let me stay with them. I drum my fingers rhythmically on the steering wheel, lip-synching to the song and attempting to forget all the hardship at home. Just as I was getting lost in the music, the radio cuts in with a news alert.

"…the man was seen *eating*…yes, *eating*…the victim before authorities intervened. Officials are urging people to stay indoors as they investigate…"

I wrinkle my nose, immediately reaching for the dial.

Nope. Not today.

I switch it to my playlist flooding the car with the sweet escape of rock music. I wasn't about to start my day with *that* kind of energy. Just as I started to relax again, my phone buzzes in the cup holder.

"Jeremy." I sigh begrudgingly, already dreading whatever nonsense he had to say.

No Jane on my day off? Too sweet.

I roll my eyes.

Too sweet?

What the hell did that even mean? Before I could type out a response, another text pops up.

Maybe I'll actually get some peace and quiet without you two annoying me. Anyway, hopefully no kids die on your watch today. :)

A familiar heat rises in my chest but I refuse to let it ruin my morning. Was that supposed to be nice?

Screw him.

I toss my phone back down and turn the volume up using Sleep Token to drown out the frustration bubbling inside me. Pulling into the ambulance station, I park and step out shaking off the lingering irritation.

Focus.

I'm not about to let him poison my entire day. I head inside, clock in and slip into work mode.

People to help. Lives to save.

At least here, I *matter.*

"Hey, Violet!" greets Phil.

Phil is my partner for this month and we've been responding to calls together for the past four months. As a father of three daughters and now two granddaughters, he has always understood and supported me, he is also one hell of a paramedic. The work day starts immediately as the alarm blares obnoxiously.

"Ready to go?" Phil asks, his excitement contagious.

"Hell yeah," I respond with even more enthusiasm.

Ronda, our extra medic today, joins us and we all settle into our positions, ready to hit the road.

"Dispatch, what's the address?" Ronda asks over the radio.

An older lady responds.

"1240 Range Road 22. It's an acreage about an hour away, so you better get going."

Her voice carries a firmness that heightens our urgency.

"On it. Tell us what we're dealing with," Ronda requests.

The dispatcher relays the information, informing us that we're responding to a twenty-five-year-old male with a possible heart attack. His girlfriend is unaware of what happened and he's barely breathing.

"The girlfriend is currently on a 911 call."

In a sudden realization, I recognized the address as Grace's residence, where she lives with her boyfriend. Worry creeps in and as if Ronda senses it too, I feel the acceleration as she presses down on the gas pedal with more urgency.

An hour later, we finally roll in, the wait stretching longer than it should have. My heart sinks as we pull in; confirming it as Grace's house. Ronda skillfully parks the ambulance, and we rush inside to assess the situation. As we enter, we see Grace's boyfriend Jeff, lying on the ground, still as a board, and Grace checking his pulse.

"They just got here. Thank you for your help. Bye."

Grace hangs up the phone.

"Thank God you guys are here..." She pauses, locking eyes with me, "Violet!" she yells My grip on the moment softens.

I give her a tight hug and ask her what happened.

"Well, we were just about to make some soup because Jeff said he wasn't feeling very well. Then he said he was having chest pain and just collapsed. He's really pale, and I don't think he's breathing. Oh, Violet, please help him," Grace pleads.

"I can't promise anything, but we will take a look."

While I am talking to Grace, Phil and Ronda are checking Jeff's vitals and decide it is best to transport him. I tell Grace to stay where she is and inform my coworkers that I will retrieve the stretcher.

I grab the gurney from the back of the ambulance, and return to my team. We all coordinate a lift to ensure Jeff is safe and secure. Ronda and Phil quickly wheel him out.

"Grace!" I yell for her attention and she looks up at me from the couch. "You can follow us to the hospital to watch over Jeff or come with us now in the ambulance. The choice is yours."

"Thanks Vi, I'll drive so we can come home tonight."

I signal my agreement and we leave the premises simultaneously. I take the driver's seat now, and Ronda joins Phil in the back assessing Jeff to ensure he stays alive. I knock twice on the driver's wall to signal that I am ready to go. I flick the sirens on and we go speeding down the back roads. The urgency of the situation presses against me like a horse is sitting on my chest. Suddenly, a loud knock jolts me from my focus, echoing through the ambulance.

"Are you guys alright?" I shout, but there is no response, "I'm pulling over!"

Veering to the side of the road, I leap out of the ambulance, a new notion of seriousness propelling me towards the doors. Grace pulls up alongside me and calls out from her window her voice laced with concern.

"Stay there!" I command, my voice frayed with panic. I fling open the back door, and my heart stops at the sight that greets me. Jeff is hunched over Ronda's body, his hands clutching what appears to be her intestines, feasting upon them. His once-familiar features are twisted into a grotesque visage, his skin pale, blood dripping from his mouth, his eyes ablaze with madness. Ronda and Phil lay motionless on the ground.

"RONDA! PHIL!" I scream, my voice cracking with panic, but Jeff's slow advance silences my cries.

"GRACE, STAY IN THE CAR!" I shout, my words, a desperate plea to keep her safe. I run towards the ambulance.

"Jeff, are you okay?"

Jeff answers with a moan, his jaw dislodging and mouth dripping with blood. With trembling hands, I pull Jeff out and slam him to the ground. Checking on Phil, my worst fears are confirmed. There is a gaping wound on his neck and his pulse is crawling. Tears cloud my vision as I struggle to comprehend the horror unfolding before me. Then a guttural sound pierces the air, and I turn to see Ronda, pale and barely conscious, her lower body gruesomely severed. As I move towards her, Phil begins to stir, his movements erratic and menacing. With a strangled cry, I stumble out of the ambulance.

What the fuck?

I run my hands through my hair, frantically scanning the scene for Grace, I hear her scream pierce the air. Jeff has attacked her, his savage hunger attempting to consume her arm.

"GRACE!" I shout, my heart pounding with terror as I rush towards her, determined to protect her at all costs.

"Get the fuck away from her!" I yell, pushing Jeff to the ground with all my strength.

"Move over," I instruct Grace, my mind racing with the need to escape the nightmare unfolding around us.

I swing open the driver's door and slam it into drive.

"Put this on your arm to stop the bleeding," I say, pressing a few napkins from the center console against Grace's wound. My breath is ragged, my pulse a wild drumbeat in my ears. Jeff is gone. Like no heartbeat–dead. Whatever is left of him isn't him anymore.

How was he able to move again? Why was he eating human flesh?

Grace clutches the napkins to her arm. Her wide and terrified eyes locked onto mine. The coppery scent of blood mixes with the acrid stench of whatever the hell that thing Jeff has become. I swallow hard.

"I'm taking you to the hospital Grace, everything's going to be okay," I lie out of instinct.

CHAPTER 2

VIOLET

"Grace, talk to me. Are you alright?" I ask frantically.

Shock is etched across her face, her eyes wide and unseeing, trying to process the horrors that I too was struggling to make sense of.

"My arm hurts…" she squeaks out, managing a weak smile that evolves into a small giggle of relief between us.

"What happened? Do you know why Jeff did that?" she stammers, her voice hollow with disbelief.

"I... I don't know exactly, but he attacked Ronda and Phil. He was... I'm sorry Grace…he was eating them." I replied, my voice trembling with disbelief.

A heavy silence fell over us as we absorbed the grim reality; they were *dead*. I reach out and clasp Grace's hand, giving it a reassuring squeeze.

"I'm getting you help, it's just a bite you'll be okay… promise." I declare, determination setting in.

I press the gas pedal harder. My mind keeps looping back to it all, back to Jeff. One minute, he is Grace's boyfriend. The next, he is lunging at her like some rabid animal. I steal a glance at the passenger seat, her hands are trembling as she presses the napkins to her arm. She is breathing too fast and her entire body is shaking. I want to say more to calm her, but how can I when my own thoughts are spiraling. That wasn't Jeff, not the way I knew him. I swallow hard, forcing myself to bring my focus back to the road. The highway stretches ahead, empty except for us. I press harder on the gas, needing to put as much distance between us and whatever the fuck happened to Jeff as possible.

Was Jeff sick? Was it some kind of infection? No…no. People don't act like that. There's no virus like that. People don't just…

I exhale sharply and grip the wheel tighter. I can't let my mind go there. After what feels like an eternity the town's familiar skyline rises in the distance.

The gas station.

The old diner.

It all looks the same, untouched and *normal.* Relief floods me, but then quickly vanishes.

If everything is fine here, then what the hell just happened back there?

I floor it, racing toward the hospital. I rush Grace inside when we arrive. My uniform is still splattered with blood. The triage nurse quickly ushers her away for immediate care. I manage to slip a 'I'll see you soon' in there before she disappears behind the emergency doors. Great, now I was left to explain the nightmarish events.

"Tell us what happened," prompted a nurse.

Gathering my thoughts, I begin, "My team and I responded to a call about a twenty-five-year-old male with a suspected heart attack. We assisted him at his residence and were on route to the hospital when I had to pull over because..." I paused, taking a deep breath to steady myself, "he was... attacking my crew.... eating them. I tried to check on them, but they became something else. Then he ran after Grace and bit off part of her arm."

The words feel surreal as I recount the incident, each one proof of the horror we had just escaped.

The nurse's gaze bores into me as he poses his next question. "Ma'am, have you consumed any drugs or alcohol today?"

Shock surges through me, followed by a wave of anger.

"My best friend just got attacked, two highly capable paramedics on my team were too, and there's a man out there who's sick and eating people!" I exclaim, my voice rising involuntarily towards the end, drawing the attention of the waiting patients nearby.

"Ma'am please lower your voice. We will dispatch officers to the scene and ensure everyone's safety," he assures me calmly amidst the tension.

"May I go check on my friend now, please?" My voice is tight with frustration. The nurse gives me a curt nod and without wasting another second, I follow the directions to Grace's room. My hands tremble as I push open the door. There she is, arm bandaged, ghostly pale, connected to a heart monitor that fills the silence with soft, rhythmic beeps.

She's okay.

"Grace?" I whisper, stepping closer.

Her eyes flutter open, dull and unfocused. She turns her head toward me, and I put my hand over my mouth, the breath catching in my throat. Dark veins snake up her neck and across her face, spreading like the cracks of shattered glass. Her skin, once so full of life, is a sickly gray.

"My god… your face…your neck…" My voice wavers, fear clawing at my chest.

She exhales a shaky breath, her lips parting as if to speak, but no words come out. Only a small, broken sound; a whimper. Of pain or fright, I can't tell. Then, the monitor's steady beeping stutters. My eyes widen.

"Grace?"

The beeps quicken, erratic, wild then flatlining before I can even comprehend what's happening. A single, piercing note fills the room.

"No. No, no, NO!" I lunge forward, pressing my hands to her chest. "Stay with me!"

I start compressions, my arms shaking as I count under my breath. This isn't happening. This can't be happening. I've saved people before. I've done CPR a hundred times but this was *Grace.*

"Come on, damn it!" My voice cracks as I keep pushing, desperate and frantic.

The intercom crackles to life, a frantic announcement cutting through my panic but I barely hear it. All I can hear is the flatline. All I can see is my best friend slipping away. I persist in my attempts to revive her with CPR, even as the nurses flood into the room, their hands grasping at me, attempting to pull me away.

"GRACE!" I yell, my voice raw with desperation.

"Wait here!" The nurse orders sternly, slamming the door shut behind her.

Outside the room, I sit with my back against the cold wall, my head bowed, hands gripping my knees so tight my knuckles ache. My mind becomes a warzone of memories. Grace laughing in the halls of our high school, late-night talks about our futures, the way she always knew exactly what to say when I needed her. Now she is gone. Tears stream down my face, hot and relentless but I barely notice.

Is she really gone?

The thought claws at my chest, a desperate whisper of denial. I have known death for many years but this feels impossible to grip.

What if she wasn't really dead? What if I had just walked out too soon? I should go back. I should check again.

My body tenses, ready to push off the floor, to run back into that room and make them do something. I remember the veins. The way they crawled across her skin like something out of a nightmare. The way Jeff had lunged at Grace, hungry and inhuman.

Didn't Jeff have the same looking black veins? No…

Something heavy sinks in my gut. If she wasn't dead, if she came back, she wouldn't be Grace anymore. The air around me feels too thick, like it's pressing in and suffocating me. A scream tears through the halls. High-pitched, sharp and raw with terror. My head snaps up. Down the hallway, a nurse stumbles backward, clutching her neck, blood seeping through her fingers. A man stands in front of her, his stance eerily familiar. My breath hitches.

Just like Jeff.

I think I'm starting to panic again. I spin on my heels sprinting back into Grace's room just as the nurses are making their final notes.

"Time of death, 12:45 PM."

I grip the doorframe, my nails digging into the wood. I want to scream, fight, to do something, but I can't, I just stand there, staring at my best friend's lifeless body. I feel completely and utterly powerless. I can't help but hope and beg the powers that be that she will just wake up. Any second now, she will blink those brown eyes and groan about how awful the hospital lights are. As if by command Grace's eyes do exactly that, although she doesn't complain about the lights, a guttural, unnatural growl rattles from her throat instead, low and raw.

"Grace!" I rush toward her, desperate, clinging to the last shred of hope that I have. "We've got to go, there's another man in the hall…he's like Jeff! He's dead and eating people…we need to leave…"

Wait, why is the heart monitor beside her still flatlining? Oh, God.

Bloodshot eyes lock onto mine, unblinking and empty of recognition. Her skin is pale and waxy, veins darkening beneath the surface like black ink spreading through water. She lunges at me. A garbled snarl tearing from her throat, her mouth opening wide and dripping with thick and grayish bloody sludge. Pure terror floods my veins. I stumble back, instinct taking over, my body screaming at me to run. My mind refusing to believe this is *my* Grace. My friend and sister in every way except blood. But this…thing in front of me…this wasn't her anymore. I shove her with everything I have, which sends her crashing to the floor.

"Don't let her get close to you!" I scream at the nurses, my voice frantic. "I've seen this before! She's not…she's not human anymore!"

They are frozen, confusion and horror showing on their faces. A pit forms in my stomach. It is a deep and gnawing dread.

What is happening right now?

I turn and run, my heart hammering and my breath coming in sharp, panicked gasps. Behind me, a wet, sickening growl echoes through the halls, followed by the sharp, terrified screams of the nurses.

I don't look back…I can't

As I pivot to flee, my eyes widen in horror at the scene unfolding before me. Two more *things*, their bodies twitching unnaturally and their faces twisted with mindless hunger, descend upon a nurse. She thrashes beneath them, her screams muffled by the sickening squelch of teeth tearing into flesh. Blood splatters against the sterile white walls, painting a grotesque mural of death. They devour her like ravenous animals, stuffing chunks of her into their mouths as if they hadn't been fed a day in their lives. A sharp cry tears through the hall. I snap my head back toward Grace's room. More screams, raw with agony and terror. They'd been bitten too and they're turning.

Get out Violet. Before you end up just like them.

I turn and sprint, my feet barely touching the linoleum. The sound of flesh tearing and bones snapping mixes with the wet, guttural growls of the things behind me.

Move. Move. MOVE!

I skid around the corner, nearly colliding with a gurney. A doctor stumbles into view, his coat soaked in blood and his hands trembling. His mouth opens to ask something, but before he can, a figure launches at him from behind. I scream and push him out of the way.

I've got to get out of here.

I sprint toward the nearest stairwell, shoving through the door so hard it slams against the wall with a deafening bang. My heart pounds and my vision tunnels. From somewhere behind me, a chorus of snarls and wet hacking breaths follow. Those dead things are coming. A deafening siren rips through the hospital's intercom system. Its shrill, looping wail clawing at my eardrums.

CODE BLACK. CODE BLACK.

My lungs freeze…a bomb threat? Dread grips my chest like a stain. I push forward, the alarm drilling into my skull, each step down the stairwell fueled by sheer panic. My legs burn, but stopping isn't an option. Violent explosions tear through the building. The walls tremble, dust and debris rains from above as the stairwell groans under the impact. The shockwave hits me like a sledgehammer to the chest, nearly knocking me off my feet. Somewhere above, the shriek of twisting metal and shattering glass fills the air. I grip the railing, my fingers aching from the sheer force of my grip.

Were those missiles?

My mind reels, panic clawing at my throat. Fire alarms shriek in response to the threat, blending into the chaos.

Smoke.

Screams.

The coppery scent of blood.

A symphony of anarchy. I have to keep moving. My only thought… *Jane.* I have to get to her. Peering cautiously through the small window of the waiting room doors, I spot military officers moving through the chaos, their gazes sharp, scanning every person like they are hunting something.

Why is the military at the hospital?

The thought barely has time to settle before the first gunshots ring out. A woman with a hospital gown shrieks. A man with an oxygen tank stumbles backward, clutching his chest as blood blooms across his hospital gown. A nurse raises her hands, pleading.

Pop. Pop. Pop.

My back hits the wall, breath hitching as my mind struggles to process what I am witnessing.

Why did they just kill those innocent people? They weren't sick.

A deafening ringing fills my ears, drowning out the chaos beyond the door. My heartbeat pounds in my skull, my hands shaking violently as I force myself to breathe.

"Hey you!"

I turn to see guns pointed at me. Time to go. I duck as they start shooting at me.

I have good reflexes, assholes, and I'm not sick.

I bolt for the stairwell, every muscle in my body screaming to move faster. My hands fumble with the door handle before I wrench it open, slipping inside just as another round of gunfire erupts behind me. There is only one way out now and it is through the morgue. The overhead lights flicker erratically, casting eerie shadows across the cold, sterilized walls. The metallic scent of antiseptic barely masking the stench of putrid rot. I swallow hard, forcing my trembling legs forward.

"Hello?" My voice was barely a whisper, cracking with unease.

The sound echoes back at me, swallowed by the oppressive silence.

THUD

A guttural moan follows, low and inhuman from behind one of the morgue's steel doors. I turn just in time to see a hand slam against the glass of one of the storage drawers. The body inside writhing violently, its fingers clawing at the small window, aware and very much alive.

Another thud.

Then another.

One by one, the locked drawers tremble, the bodies inside convulsing. My stomach lurches as I take a shaky step backward. A wet gag claws up my throat, bile burning my tongue. I double over heaving my guts, my hands bracing against my knees as my body rejects the horror in front of me.

No, no, no, this isn't real. This can't be real.

A metal door bursts open and a figure tumbles out. A young man, his body stiff and eyes sunken, a twisted thing where life had once been. His mouth stretches unnaturally wide, a ragged, gurgling moan escaping his throat. He has a tag on his toe, so how is he moving if he's clinically dead? Then he jumps in my direction. Pure terror jolts through me, snapping me out of my nauseating thoughts. I stumble backward, my feet slipping on the cold floor, and turn to run. I have to get to Jane and make sure everyone is safe.

I slam through the stairwell doors, my pulse hammering as I scramble up the steps two at a time. The scene outside is one of utter pandemonium, with helicopters circling overhead and armed personnel swarming the area. Another explosion rocks the hospital, this time visible from my vantage point. My body starts to tremble with fear and doubt. I locate Grace's car and waste no time in starting it, my hands shaking as I peel out of the parking lot. The city is falling apart. It's like a meteor shower of missiles. My only thought.

Jane. Jane. Jane.

The roads, once familiar, are now a war zone. Cars sit abandoned, doors flung open, belongings are scattered across the pavement. Smoke makes it hard to see the people running around. Some screaming, others limping, and some… not people anymore at all.

A man sprints into the street, waving his arms frantically.

"Help me! Please!"

I barely have time to react before a blur of movement tackles him from behind. A woman? Or what used to be one, latches onto his throat, tearing into him with frenzied hunger. His screams turn into a gurgle as I swerve past, my insides twist into a knot. I scream and press harder on the gas. I can't stop. I have to get to Jane.

A sharp boom echoes through the air. A bright spot arching downward before erupting into a vast explosion, flames licking up from its landing point. Air tangles in my throat as I realize the horrifying pattern. They are aimed.

The daycare…

A strangled 'no' rips from my lips as I attempt to make the car go faster, my tires squealing in protest. A sickening crack rattles the hood as a body tumbles over the windshield, its face twisted in a grotesque snarl before rolling off onto the street. I don't stop. The closer I get to Jane, the worse it becomes. People claw at my windows, desperate, their eyes wide with terror.

"Please! Take my son!"

A woman clutches a crying toddler, pounding on my passenger-side window.

"I'll do anything! Please! I don't want to die!"

I choke back a sob, my hands trembling on the wheel. I can't stop. If I do…if I let myself hesitate. I'll never get to Jane. The daycare comes into view, or what's left of it…a wall of flames devours the building, black smoke swallowing the sky. The playground is a twisted, burning husk, the swings still swaying eerily as if untouched by the chaos. I slam on the brakes, my chest heaving.

Jane.

Panic seizes me as I veer towards the engulfed area, my pulse pounding in my ears. I park the car haphazardly, and sprint towards the burning house, my throat constricting with each labored breath. Flames lick at the structure, casting an eerie glow on the devastation before me. Tears blur my vision as I scan the wreckage, searching desperately for any sign of life amid the charred remains.

"JANE!" I sob, my voice hoarse with grief.

"KATE!" I scream into the inferno, the sound of my anguish met only by the crackle of flames, broken only by the distant moans of the undead.

No familiar voices to comfort me in this moment of despair. A different kind of tear stings my eyes, ones filled with panic, mixed with the smoke. I grapple with the devastating reality before me. I know with crushing certainty that I have lost not only my beloved daughter but also some of my dearest friends. The weight of grief bares down on me like a leaden shroud, leaving me to face the unimaginable truth.

Was this the apocalypse?

CHAPTER 3

VIOLET

I stumble back to the car, and collapse into the driver's seat, my body wracked with sobs, and my muscles aching with the weight of my grief. Clutching the steering wheel, I check my phone for any sign of service, desperate to call someone…anyone, but the screen mockingly displays:

NO SERVICE.

In a fit of anger, I hurl the phone against the dash and slam the door shut. The anger quickly gives way to a chilling realization. Jeremy will be at home. I have to be the one to tell him that Jane, Kate, and Grace are gone. Wiping my tears, I speed off towards our house.

Navigating the streets is a nightmare; the undead are everywhere, turning every corner into a labyrinth of horror. The thuds of bodies hitting the car become a haunting rhythm, that I ignore and find myself disassociating from just to cope. As I approach my street, I notice fewer undead, offering a small albeit fragile sense of hope. I park haphazardly on the sidewalk and run inside, bursting through the front door.

"Jeremy!" I shout, my voice echoing through the empty house. A faint grunting noise coming in response from upstairs.

I find him lying against the wall, blood splattered on every surface, a gruesome bite mark on his neck…and our neighbor face down, his head pierced with the railing from our stairs. I run towards Jeremy. Panic surges through me as I try to staunch the bleeding with parts of my over-shirt. He turns slowly towards me, a fleeting look of recognition in his eyes mixes with a sorrowful acceptance.

"Violet," he rasps, his voice so thin I almost think I imagine it. "I'm…sorry."

Sorry? That word from him almost made me laugh. If it weren't for the way his skin had already gone pale under the sweat, I would have.

"Sorry for what?" My voice cracks, part disbelief, part exhaustion. "For all the ways you made my life hell? Or for dying on me now?"

I move closer anyway, pressing a hand to his shoulder to steady him as his breathing comes in shallow pulls.

"Jane… didn't… make it." I confess, my throat tight. The truth lands between us like a stone. His eyes flicker, but I can't tell if it is pain, or if he cares that our daughter is gone. He lifts a shaking hand, and brushes my hair from my face. An oddly gentle gesture from a man who'd once known every way to hurt me without leaving a mark.

"I… need to… tell you something," he wheezes.

"Okay?" I say, trying to keep my voice steady.

"… Kept… them… from you… in the drawer… letters…" His breath stutters, his gaze glassy. "I… love…" Then his head drops forward, the rest stolen from me forever.

"Jeremy! No, no, no!" I grip his shirt, and shake him as if I can rattle his soul back into him. My hands go to his neck on instinct.

No pulse.

Not even the faintest beat.

I sit there, holding the dead weight of him, tears hot on my face. Some are born of grief. Some…are not. Of all the things he could have said in his last breath, he chose to disclose letters. Letters he'd kept from me. I lay his body on the ground gently and kiss his forehead one last time. With a heavy heart, I drift in sorrow to our bedroom. I rifle through the top three drawers, finding nothing but shirts and underwear. Desperation growing, I open the bottom drawer and move the socks aside, revealing a box I have never seen before hidden at the back. I carefully pull the box out and sit on the ottoman, my hands shaking as I open it. Inside are letters, neatly folded. I unfold the top one, my eyes quickly scanning the first line:

Dear Ocean Eyes,

My breath catches in my throat. Only one person has ever called me that. I skim to the bottom, my heart pounding. The letter is signed, *'With love, Ryder.'* With trembling hands, I begin to read:

Dear Ocean Eyes,

Every day out here feels like an eternity without you. The nights are the hardest. The silence amplifies my longing to be near you. I think of your smile, the way your eyes light up when you're happy, and it gives me the strength to keep going...

Tears well up in my eyes, blurring the words on the page. Ryder's handwriting, so familiar and comforting, brings a wave of bittersweet memories rushing back. I read on, losing myself in his words, each sentence a testament to his love and the sacrifices he was making.

...I dream of the day I can feel your face again, to feel your heartbeat against mine. Until then, know that my love for you is unwavering. With every beat of my heart, I am yours.

With love, Ryder.

I clutch the letter to my chest, feeling a deep ache in my heart. The silence of the room envelopes me, a stark contrast to the turmoil inside.

I thought Ryder died?

I reach for another letter, eager to immerse myself in Ryder's words, when suddenly, a noise shatters the stillness. A faint, shuffling sound echoes from the hallway. I freeze, my breath hitching. The sound grows louder, a slow, dragging movement. I place the letter back in the box and rise from the ottoman, my heart pounding in my ears. As I step cautiously into the hallway, the sight before me makes my blood run cold. My boyfriend, a previously lifeless body, is now standing, swaying unsteadily. His eyes are vacant and hollow. He lets out a guttural moan, as his head jerks toward me.

"Stay back," I yell, my voice wobbling.

I take a step back, my mind frantically searching for an explanation, a solution. His steps quicken, his arms outstretched and reaching for me. I stumble back into the bedroom, my eyes darting around for something, *anything*, to defend myself. As he draws closer trying to bite me, I grab the nearby lamp and hold it up defensively.

"Please," I beg, my voice cracking. "This isn't you."

I may as well have been speaking another language, as he runs at me again. With a desperate cry, I swing the lamp, striking him across the head. He staggers, but it isn't enough to stop him. I swing again, tears streaming down my face, each blow a mix of horror and sorrow. Finally, he collapses to the floor, motionless. I drop the lamp, my hands shaking. Sinking to my knees beside him, the weight of the moment crashing down on me. The aftermath of what I have done is everywhere. In the silence that follows, I realize that nothing will ever be the same. Life as I have known it, has been snuffed out. I sit on the floor, staring at Jeremy's lifeless body. My mind is a fog of shock and disbelief but a primal instinct for survival begins to push through the haze.

I have to move.

I have to survive.

Taking a deep breath, I force myself to my feet. My movements are mechanical as I grab a backpack from the closet and begin filling it with essentials. Canned food, a flashlight, batteries, a small first aid kit, two water bottles, a knife. Things that will keep me alive.

My eyes fall on the box of letters from Ryder, and I take one last look at Jeremy and the home we once shared. I carefully grab the letters and place them in the bag. They were a connection to a love that felt more distant with each passing second.

"I'm sorry," I whisper, my voice breaking.

I turn away and head for the door, my thoughts turning to my family. I need to know if my parents and brother are safe. I run towards the car and waste no time shifting into drive.

The drive feels unreal, the world outside has morphed into a nightmare. Shadows move at the edges of my vision and the silence is eerie, broken only by distant screams and the occasional shuffling of feet. I turn the corner and my heart sinks. A horde of dead blocks the road, their bloody eyes turning toward the car. There are helicopters flying past every few minutes, with the occasional bomb ricochet. One bomb drops a little too close, causing me to lose control and crash into a bush. Panicking, I reverse, but more dead have shuffled in behind me blocking my path. Trapped and realizing the car is no longer an option. Going on foot would give me a heightened awareness of my surroundings and I could move quieter.

I grab my backpack and take a deep breath, opening the door. The moment I step out, the undead's moans grow louder, and they lurch towards me. I have learned that they stop moving if I bash them in the head but that's messy and it takes too long. If one gets close to me, I'll use my knife or dressing cutters to make sure they can't bite me. I run and my heart pounds in my chest. My footsteps echo off the buildings, and the undead's moans grow fainter as I put distance between us.

I sprint down an alley, hoping it will lead me closer to my parents' house. Every shadow seems to hide a threat, every noise a potential danger. I keep moving, my breath coming in ragged gasps. Finally, I reach the familiar street where my parents live.

My legs ache, and my lungs burn, but I can't stop now. As I approach the house, I see that the front door is ajar. Fear and hope battle within me as I cautiously creep inside.

"Mom? Dad? Felix?" I call, my voice trembling. Only silence greets me. I steal along through the house, checking each room. In the living room, I find signs of a struggle. Overturned furniture, and broken glass. My heart pounds with fear as I edge down the hall to my parents' bedroom. There, I find my father, crouched in a corner, clutching a baseball bat, his eyes wide with fear and grief.

"Dad!" I cry, rushing to his side.

"Violet, thank God," he whispers, pulling me into a tight embrace. "Your mother and Felix...they didn't make it. They turned."

A sob catches in my throat.

"Jeremy and Jane didn't make it either." I pause to think. "Where are they now?"

"I'm so sorry sweetheart ... they are in there. I couldn't... I couldn't do it."

He points to my brother's bedroom across the hall.

Pulling air into my lungs, I stand. "Stay here Dad, I'll take care of it."

I ease myself to the bedroom door and open it slowly. Inside, my mother and brother, now undead, turn their heads toward me, their eyes bloody and hungry. The motherly love that once wrapped around me like a warm blanket now only exists in memory. Her eyes, once soft blue pools that crinkled with every smile are now clouded and sunken, ringed with bruised purple. The gentle curves of her face have hollowed into sharp edges, her lips pulling back to reveal teeth clotted with blackened blood.

My brother... God, my brother. The boy who used to smirk at me across the dinner table, flick peas at my head, and laugh until he cried; he was unrecognizable. His skin, an ashy grey, was split like old paper. His once-bright eyes have gone milky and vacant. Where his grin used to be, there is only a twisted snarl, jaw hanging at an unnatural angle.

They weren't mine anymore. Just the husks of the people I loved, forever trapped in this nightmare of the undead. I bolt out of the room, screaming and sobbing uncontrollably. As I slam the door behind me, I collapse to the floor, my chest heaving with broken cries. I feel my father kneel beside me, wrapping his arms around me in a desperate attempt to offer comfort.

"We can't leave them like this," I finally manage to choke out, wiping away my tears. "We need to let them rest."

"I couldn't do it," Dad said, eyes fixed on the floor. "They've turned. They don't look like Noelle and Felix anymore."

He runs a hand over his face, like wiping away the memory would make it hurt less.

"It started with a cough. Just a little one. Your mom kept saying it was nothing. Just the air, just the stress. Then Felix got it too. Fever hit them both the same night, burning hot, like their skin was cooking from the inside."

His voice cracks, but he keeps talking.

"By morning, their eyes were bloodshot. They weren't talking right. Words came out all jumbled, like their brains couldn't keep up. And then the bleeding started, first from their gums, then their noses. Felix's little hands left red smears on the walls."

I can feel bile rising in my throat.

"By the second night, they weren't them anymore. His gaze drops to the ground, shoulders shaking. "Your mom's skin…it went grey so fast. Her eyes clouded over, and she just…stopped blinking. Then she started making this sound…low, like she was choking...but it wasn't her voice anymore, and Felix…"

He swallows hard, shaking his head.

"His mouth was dripping blood, Violet. Not his own. His little hands…."

His voice breaks.

"They were clawing at me like I was a stranger, like I was food."

I could see it in his face. How the people we loved had been stripped away in minutes, replaced by something hungry and wrong.

"They look like monsters now," he says, quieter.

I nod in agreement, the weight of his words sinking in. They weren't themselves anymore, and the house, once brimming with cherished memories, now felt like a hollow shell, nothing more than a mausoleum of the life before it. Suddenly, a deafening boom echo from outside. We rush out and see small missiles streaking through the sky, raining down on different parts of town. I spin towards my father, our eyes locked in a moment of shared understanding.

"I think we should burn the house. Then they will be at rest here."

"Good idea," he replies. "I'll grab some gas from the garage."

I sprint to my old room, frantically searching for any photos I can find to preserve any small part of our lives before this. I tear through my vault of childhood memories, the urgency of the situation adding a frantic edge to my movements. The once-cozy space now feels alien and foreign, but I force myself to focus. I pull open drawers and rummage through piles of clothes, finally uncovering a stack of old family photos. There is a photo of my mother, her warm smile captured perfectly, and one of Felix, his eyes sparkling with mischief. Tears blur my vision as I gently place them in my backpack. Just as I am about to leave, my hand brushes against a small, dusty photo album. I open it and gasp. Staring back at me is the last photo of Ryder and I, taken right before he was deployed five and a half years ago. His arm is around my shoulders, and we are both smiling, oblivious to the heartache that lay ahead. The sight of his face, full of life and hope elicits a fresh wave of tears to flow. Another missile strikes, shaking the entire house. Before I can fully process the emotions surging through me, my father's voice cuts through the haze.

" It's time to go" he says at my door, haste lacing his words.

I quickly wipe my tears, gently closing the album and placing our photo with the other photos in my backpack. I take a lasting look around my room and memories flood my mind. I hurry downstairs, ready to face whatever comes next.

As we exit the house, all I see is my childhood home. I stand frozen in place, the flames devouring the house with an intensity that seems unnatural. Thick, black smoke billows into the sky, twisting and curling like something alive, while the fire roars, crackling as it burns through wood and glass with ruthless precision.

I can feel the heat on my skin, oppressive and suffocating, while the pungent smell of burning wood and fabric claws at my throat. The home I had known, filled with memories, warmth, and life, is collapsing into a smoldering heap, consumed by a force I can do nothing to stop. Every snap and hiss seem to mark the end of another irreplaceable moment lost forever to the blaze. The noise of the house burning is silenced by the groaning of the dead.

The air thickens with the weight of fear, pressing down on my chest like a warning. The world around me no longer feels safe. Every familiar sound is replaced by the frantic rhythm of danger. My instincts, sharp and undeniable, stir inside me, telling me there is no more room for doubt, no more time to wait. It is in the tremor of my hands, the quickening of my breath, and the way my mind suddenly clears, focusing intently. I need to move, to escape, and to stay alive.

"We need to find a radio and somewhere we will be safe."

I give a small motion of agreement. Then a realization knocks softly. A quiet certainty that settles deep within me and pushes me forward. It whispers that survival isn't an option anymore, it is a command that I have no choice but to follow.

CHAPTER 4

RYDER

1 Day Earlier

I guess you could say the trip back home was…well, it wasn't exactly homey. No one ever tells you how fucking strange it is to walk back into a place after years of being away. This town hasn't changed much though. Same old cracked sidewalks, same greasy diner where everyone knows your name. My only issue is that my grief has swollen into a shadow I can't outrun.

"Well, look who the cat dragged in boys, Ryder *fucking* Kent!" My old buddy Pete says with a wry grin, shaking me out of my sprawling thoughts. He's standing at the bar, nursing a beer.

"The infamous war hero, back in town. What's it like out there? I'm surprised you didn't lieutenant Dan on us!"

I snort and wave at the bartender.

"Mobile order for Kent."

He turns to walk toward the kitchen.

"Nope, didn't Lieutenant Dan on you, but it does look like your mom gave you too many boxes of chocolates."

The guys laugh.

"Any cool war stories for us Kent? You've been gone for like six years or something."

"The only stories I've got involve a lot of sand, MREs, and dudes who think they can handle whiskey better than they can handle their own egos."

I take the seat next to him, grimacing at the stale air and the stench of fried food. I wasn't really back for a hero's welcome. I'd been around too long to care about that kind of thing.

"But yeah, I've got a few stories. You want the one where I almost got shot by a guy who couldn't tell I was on his side?"

Pete raises his eyebrows. "You've got to be fucking kidding' me, right? That one's got to be good."

"About as good as almost being shot in the head is." I say, grabbing a glass of water from the bartender and jerking my chin upward. I don't drink, never really have. Well, I had more than a few when my parents died back before high school but I realized pretty quickly that drinking doesn't solve any of your problems so I quit as fast as I had begun.

"When you're out there long enough, you start questioning whether anyone really knows what side they're on anymore and trust me Pete, I'm not the poster boy for the whole 'loyalty' thing, but after a few years, you start feeling like a stranger to the world you once knew."

I don't expect Pete to understand. Hell, he is barely coherent enough to remember I was here tonight, let alone comprehend what the inside of a war zone feels like. There was something cathartic about unloading to someone who didn't actually care too much. The air feels thick with unsaid things. An undercurrent of tension I can't quite put a finger on. I have felt it building up ever since I left the desert.

"Your tattoos look sick," the bartender says, handing me my takeout order and relieving the tension.

I mumble my thanks as I glance down at my arms, tracing the lines with my eyes. Both sleeves are colored trad style. Bold outlines, deep reds, yellows, and blues, each piece telling a story. The left arm is a storm of skulls, daggers, and serpents, all classic motifs screaming danger and defiance. The right bursts with roses, dragons, and flames, a testament to passion, loyalty, and survival. Together, they don't just cover my skin but they mark every choice, every fight, every scar I've carried. I glance at my watch.

"I should probably hit the sack, Pete. Big day tomorrow."

He chuckles and nudges me with his elbow. "Big day? What's so big about a day in this hellhole?"

"I'm not sure yet," I say with a grin. "But whatever it is, I doubt it's going to be pretty. You know how these things go."

"Nothing is ever *pretty* with the military in town." The bartender adds.

I raise my water as an acknowledgment of the truth. Everything about the actual job sucked but it was the satisfaction of knowing I was doing *some* good that did it for me. That's why I wanted to join in the first place, so I could help the people who need it. I chug my water, hand the bartender a fifty-dollar bill and tell everyone to have a good night. I find my rental truck in the parking lot and lean on the bumper, sparking up a joint.

"Oooooh how I've missed you…" I whisper to myself taking a long, slow drag.

The familiar burn settles in my chest, grounding me in a way nothing else does. My phone buzzes in my pocket, pulling me from the moment. Ryan's name flashes on the screen, his text as predictable as ever.

You should get back to base now

I exhale, watching the smoke fade into the night typing quickly.

Whatever you say Calloway.

After pressing send I lift my gaze letting it drift to the sky, to the quiet endless stretch of stars. Just like that, she's there in my thoughts. *Ocean eyes.* Here, in this same town. After all these years, I wonder if she ever thinks of me, if she ever looks up at the stars and wonders the same. No, I don't want to know, because if she doesn't, if I'm nothing more than a ghost of a memory to her, I'm not sure I can survive the emptiness that would swallow me whole. Maybe she's a star now. A bright point I'll never reach, and maybe she's gone, truly gone, leaving only the endless night between us. I close my eyes for a second, just feeling the night around me before slipping my phone back into my pocket. I actually should hit the dispensary before it closes. God knows when I'll have time to restock.

The streets are quiet, just the hum of a flickering streetlight and the distant rumble of someone's shitty muffler echoing off the brick. I keep my hood up and my head low, boots heavy on the sidewalk as I ghost forward to Budzilla. The green neon sign buzzes weakly against the window. Inside, it smells like cedar chips, air freshener, and twenty different strains of peace. I lean against the counter.

"Just an ounce of something strong," I say. "And a few packs of papers."

He slides a jar across the glass. Indica-heavy, pungent dark green buds with names like "Deadweight" or "Violator Kush." I don't care. I just need it to burn slowly and hit hard. I need something that can drown out the noise, or at least soften the edges. The guy rings me through and bags it all up in brown paper. I pay in cash, always cash.

"Enjoy," he mutters with a bored smile.

"I plan to."

The weight of the ounce presses against my thigh in the pocket of my jacket. Comforting in its own fucked-up way. When everything else feels unpredictable, at least this…this I can roll, light, inhale, and maybe forget even if it's just for a little while.

I find my room, dropping my bag by the door with a heavy sigh. Tossing my phone onto the bed I flop down next to it, scrolling absently through my photos. Our photo still pops up in my gallery. Her smile, one I could never forget. I didn't even know if she was alive. I hadn't heard a word from her. No letters, no messages, fuck all. The silence cut deeper than I wanted to admit. Maybe she has moved on, or maybe she's dead.

Get over it, Ryder

I drag my thumb across the screen as if it can erase the hollow ache in my chest. She's probably better off without me anyway… but that thought did nothing to ease the emptiness; it just made it heavier. I linger on the photo a few seconds longer, wishing it could tell me anything that would ease the sore spot that grew around the love I had for her. With a heavy sigh, I shove the phone back into my pocket. No point picking at a wound that won't heal tonight.

I jump in the shower. A quick rinse, enough to wash the day off my skin, not nearly hot or long enough to drown the thoughts. I brush my teeth as if it makes a difference. I towel dry my hair, pull on a clean shirt, and drop down onto the bed with that familiar weight still riding me.

Won't sleep so why even bother.

Instead, I reach into my coat pocket and pull out the brown paper bag from the dispensary. I set it down in ritual, peeling back the fold to reveal a dense, crystal-dusted ounce of the good stuff. Earthy, potent, and almost sticky under my fingers. I crack open my tin. The old red velvet cigarette container I'd carried around since forever. Scuffed and dented, but reliable. Inside is my favorite lighter, a couple crumpled roaches, and space for exactly five big joints if I packed 'em right. My own emergency kit. Sanity in a pocket-sized box. I start grinding the bud down, slow and steady, the smell thick and comforting. I roll the first one fat. Then another, and another. I keep going until I have five neat and solid soldiers stacked beside me on the desk like a row of middle fingers to the universe.

One for bad nights.

One for worse ones.

A couple for the silence.

One just in case I feel like remembering her.

I slip them into the tin, thumb brushing the edge of the lighter, then click the lid shut with a soft metallic snap. I put my little Cheech and Chong set up and the remaining bud in my duffle bag. Either way, it helps. Then and only then, did I crawl back into bed. Not to sleep, just to wait for the next storm to weather.

The next morning, the familiar hum of military bureaucracy settles over me like an itchy blanket. The briefings, the uniforms, the cold coffee that you pretend isn't as terrible as it is. Everything feels like it is just another Thursday. I sit down at the long conference table, the guys filling in, some of them still half-asleep, others trying to look important in their uniforms. I glance around the room, my eyes finding the orphan crew, the only faces I care about recognizing.

Ryan Calloway sits across from me, expression unreadable and his arms crossed. He keeps me in check like an older brother. When I first joined, he had my back, and he still does. No questions, no conditions, just solid loyalty. A few seats down, Jake Foster leans back in his chair, smirking at something someone has said. A mean bastard, always looking for an opportunity to put someone down. He never misses a chance to taunt me, and I never give him the satisfaction of reacting. He is Major Tompkins' lapdog, the type to kiss ass to climb the ranks. I don't like him, and he sure as hell doesn't like me.

Joe Hawthorne gives me a small nod from his spot near the end of the table. He stands six feet tall, solid and stocky, a bit on the chubby side, but every ounce of him radiates the kind of quiet power you learn to respect fast. Short, tousled brown hair frames a face that somehow carries equal parts mischief and calculation, and his deep brown eyes are sharp, constantly scanning and always measuring. Pale-skinned soldier, through and through, dripping sarcasm like it was oxygen, the kind of guy who'd flirt with anything that moved and handle his guns with the care of a father cradling a newborn. A war buddy. One of the few I'd trust with my life. We'd been through hell together, and that kind of bond doesn't break, not even in a room like this.

Beside him, Andrew Sinclair sits with an easy, relaxed posture, offering a quick grin when our eyes meet. He stands about 5'9", lean but solid, with jet-black hair that never stays in place for long. His skin is a warm, deep caramel. A tattoo of Jesus curls along his forearm, and instead of the dog tag most of us wear, he favors a simple cross around his neck, a quiet marker of faith amid chaos. On the battlefield, he relies on his logic and precision, analyzing every angle and risk. Underneath it all, he has that sense of humor you need in the military to survive, the kind that makes the darkness bearable, if only just for a moment. We'd all been in Afghanistan together, shared the same hell and the same scars, seen and unseen. I'd been in the military longer than them both, but in the warzone, rank doesn't matter much, only skill, trust, and nerves do. The tension in the room is heavy, a storm brewing just beyond the horizon. I lean back, rolling my shoulders. Whatever is coming, it isn't going to be good.

"Alright, listen up," Major Tompkins says, standing at the head of the room.

Broad-shouldered and towering just enough to dominate any space he enters, carrying himself with a rigid, square-backed military posture that demands attention. His jaw is sharp and jutting, his cheekbones high, with a sweep of sandy-blond hair that stubbornly refuses to stay flat no matter how much he tries. The smile is all dog and pony show, sharp and mocking, never softening the steely, unreadable gaze of a man who doesn't give a damn if we like him. Results are all that matter, and he got them. Strategy by force, or by the silent promise that he won't hesitate to kill if necessary. That kind of certainty is what has kept us alive these past few years.

"We've got a situation."

Of course, there's always a situation, right? However, when Tompkins says it like that, with a tightness around his eyes and that strange edge in his voice, I can tell this isn't our standard run-of-the-mill mission.

"Intel's coming in from all over," he continues, clicking through slides on the projector.

The boardroom feels like the wrong kind of place for this meeting. Like we've been shuffled into some corporate office and handed a case file, expected to play detectives instead of soldiers. The first slide is a grainy satellite image of a military camp, maybe fifty kilometers from here. It doesn't look like much, just some tents and a few trucks scattered around. It is the next slide that made everything in me go still.

"This is a contamination zone," Tompkins says, his voice sharp. "There's an outbreak and people in the camp are showing signs of infection. These people are eating other people, folks."

I lean back in my chair attempting to process.

A virus? Is this some kind of joke? I turn to look at Ryan, who's eyes greet me with the same 'what the fuck' expression.

"Hold on," I say, raising my hand. "Eating other people? You're telling me this is...Like, what? People are…"

"Cannibalizing each other?" Tompkins cut me off. "Yes. That's exactly what I'm telling you."

He whirls back to the screen, showing us a few blurry videos of men and women stumbling around, their faces contorted in what can only be described as a grotesque mix of rage and hunger. It looks like a scene from one of those B-rated horror films. Seeing it here on a government intel screen, with red markers around the infected individuals, makes my stomach churn. I can't bring myself to watch as they tear into the living. I have to turn my eyes, swallow hard, and pretend I am not losing my breakfast over it.

"How bad is it?" Foster asks.

"Worse than you think," Tompkins says. "We've had confirmation from three different sources that these people are becoming something not entirely human and they're spreading it…fast."

I feel the weight of those words sink in.

"So, what's the plan?" Hawthorne inquires.

Tompkins spins around, his face grim. "Our orders are to move in. We're going to a makeshift quarantine camp to secure it, neutralize the infected, and bring any survivors from town back for quarantine. This is a containment mission. I need everyone to be sharp. No mistakes."

I raise my eyebrows, "You're seriously telling us that we're going in to neutralize the infected?"

Tompkins shoots me a look. "Yes, Kent. That's exactly what I'm telling you. Get it together. We don't have time for jokes."

Great. Another day, another war waiting to happen. Only this time, the enemy was eating people. I glance around the room, seeing the same doubt I am feeling mirrored in everyone else's eyes., but Tompkins has a point. There isn't time to question what is happening. We have a mission. Whatever this virus is, it is spreading faster than anyone anticipated. Tompkins steps up again, flipping on every light in the room. The sudden brightness is like a slap, searing against my retinas. The weight of what we are about to face presses down harder.

"Alright," he barks, snapping my attention back to him. "You're going to need to be quick and precise. The only way to stop them is a headshot. You all know what that means. Aim for the head. No exceptions."

He looks around the room, catching each of our eyes before continuing. "And for Christ's sake, don't hesitate. If you hesitate, you'll be one of them. Do you understand?"

A chorus of grumbled *'Yes, Sir'* responses fill the room. I feel a knot in my stomach, but I don't let it show.

"Good. Now, Corporal Kent…" Tompkins pauses as if he is weighing something in his mind, "You're on temperature duty. There are a few others I have from other bases coming to help out. So, get your ass in gear and take temperatures of anyone we bring in. We can't afford to have infected slip through the cracks, so no one's getting in without being checked. Understand?"

"Temperature duty?" I ask, trying to keep the disbelief out of my voice. "You're giving me that job? When we're about to face a goddamn horde of potential sick people?"

"Consider yourself lucky," Tompkins said, eyes narrowing. "Your job is to keep us from getting sick, and if you screw that up, it's your ass. Now that's an order soldier."

Great. As if the situation isn't bad enough, going in hot to deal with something no one can explain, now I have to take temperatures like I am working a fucking flu clinic but what choice do I have? Tompkins isn't exactly giving me room to argue.

"Calloway and Hawthorne…" Tompkins continues, turning his gaze toward my friends, "You'll be going out to sweep the town," he says. "Round up any survivors you find, but don't get too close unless you're certain they're clean. We can't risk exposure. Teams are sent in to assist with the buses. Get as many survivors as possible, but stay sharp. Understand?"

Ryan's face doesn't change, but I can see the unease on his face. He isn't too thrilled about the idea of wandering around, looking for sick people and I don't blame him.

Tompkins looks over at Foster and Sinclair.

"Foster, you're with Sinclair. You're holding the perimeter. Make sure no survivors try to slip past, keep everyone in line, and don't let any of the sick wander. Stay ready, and don't let a single thing catch you off guard."

Foster smirks, folding his arms. "Sounds like a Sunday stroll."

I shoot him a look. "Maybe try not sounding like you want to get yourself killed."

Foster leans against the wall. "Temperature duty, huh? You're really climbing the ladder, Kent."

I fix him with a look. "Better than treating danger like a game and hoping luck forgives your stupidity."

He laughs, eyes glinting. "And maybe you should try not acting like you're the only one who has a brain in this room."

I inch forward, words like a blade. "Try me again, and I'll make sure you're the next meal for the sick."

"Wow, real scary, Kent." He sneers.

Sinclair steps between us, his expression dead serious.

"Enough. Both of you. We've got a job to do, no time for playground arguments. We're on the same team…remember?"

I force a breath past my teeth, every muscle in me still strung tight like a wire, but I ease back a step. Foster flashes me that smug little curve of his mouth. Not quite a smile, more like he's savoring the fact I didn't break his jaw. His eyes flick toward Tompkins, who's already sliding to the side of the room, acting like he owns every square inch of it.

Bootlicking bastard.

A few of the guys begin talking and gathering their gear, but I am too busy with my own thoughts. I push off the wall, moving for the door, but freeze as something sharp pricks my ear.

"Tompkins knows more than he's letting on, he's been on the phone all morning talking to officials." Someone whispers from behind me.

I freeze, but don't turn around.

"Yeah, I heard the plan is to kill the survivors," a voice replies in a hushed tone, "You think he's hiding something? About the virus?"

"I don't know, man but I've got a bad feeling about this. I don't trust him."

The conversation is cut off as I hear Tompkins' voice call for us to start moving out. *Shit.* My mind is racing, but there is no time to speculate. Not now, not when we were heading straight into the unknown. I glance over at Calloway, his expression matches mine, confused and uncertain, but ready to do our damn jobs.

We step off the military bus and the brisk air slams into me, biting through my jacket.

"Stay alert," Tompkins orders as he leads the way, "And remember, once the survivors arrive, if you hesitate, you die. Simple as that."

"Guess we're camping out in the middle of nowhere now," Hawthorne mutters as he tosses his duffel bag to the side, "Although it could be worse. At least no one's trying to eat me yet."

"That you know of," I shoot back, giving him a quick grin.

A few of the guys laugh, but there is no real humor in it. Everyone is on edge. This is like some twisted game of survival, and no one has a fucking clue how it's going to end. Pretty normal day for us actually, except everything we've faced so far, we've been trained for, and nobody trained us for this. The sound of helicopters and jets roaring overhead cut through the conversation. I watch as a group of military jets soar above the building, heading in the direction of the nearest city.

"Why the fuck do they need the missile team?" I mutter under my breath.

Calloway frowns, looking through the same window. "They're not going to nuke them, are they? I mean, shit, that's one way to make sure they're contained."

"Why the fuck would they do that?" I ask, more to myself than anyone else. "If they want people to survive, why bring the bomb squad? For sick civilians? It makes no sense."

"We're just the grunts," Sinclair says with a shrug. "Maybe it's on a need-to-know basis, and we…don't need to know."

That didn't sit right with me. The idea that they'd wipe out an entire area to stop a virus didn't make sense, not when there were still people left to save. If this was some kind of full-scale military operation, why the hell were they wasting resources on missiles and jets?

"Yeah, well, I don't trust it," I muse. "Something's off."

Tompkins is busy barking orders, setting up more defensive positions and making sure we all stay busy. He hasn't divulged anything about the airstrikes or missiles. Hours drag, but eventually everything is set. The field around us has transformed into something out of a deployment. Rows of chain-link fences slice up the open ground, hemming us in. White canvas tents sag under the weight of the damp air, each one marked for temp checks, gear stashes, or sleeping quarters. It smells like sweat, steel, and mud. No different than Afghanistan. Except there's no sand choking the air, and good thing too because I do not miss that.

At the far edge of the field, two hulking makeshift structures loom. They aren't really new, just an old industrial building someone gutted and patched up with fresh plywood and corrugated tin. I remember driving past it back in high school on my way to some party an hour from here, never thinking I'd see the inside. Now it's been reborn into something between a bunker and a grave.

Two more hours pass and the buses start to roll into camp. They aren't like the kind you'd see picking up school kids; these buses are military-grade, heavily armored and painted in drab green. They stop at the entrance of the camp, the tires squealing as they come to a halt. The doors open wide, and I see them and their tired, scared faces. Some of them look healthy, others… not so healthy. You can tell by the way they walk and the blank stares in their eyes. A few are even dragging their feet. I do a brief count.

"Shit," one of my fellow temp takers' mutters, voice barely above a whisper. "Is that it? Is this all that's left?

"This can't be it," I say, voice steady. "There's more. There has to be."

"Everyone in line!" Foster barks, and everyone but me jumps. I don't flinch. My eyes are still scanning. Right on cue, six more buses roll up, tires kicking up dust. Packed full of people.

Oh fuck….

CHAPTER 5

VIOLET

Flashes of rotting faces fill my mind, their lifeless eyes fixed on me. I stab their decaying heads. The crunch of bone echoes in my ears, blood splattering against my arms, and the stench of decay clings to the air around me. One after another, they fall. Limbs twisting unnaturally as they hit the ground, my breath coming in ragged bursts. The weight of survival presses down hard as a distant missile strike wobbles my knees and a rough grip yanks me back to reality. My heart is still racing as I trip into the narrow doorway of a dimly lit convenience store.

"Focus," he whispers, his eyes scanning the darkened aisles. The distant moans of the sick fade as we look inside, my hands still trembling as the rush of adrenaline slowly ebbs.

As my eyes adjust, I notice the faint rustle of movement in the shadows. My dad's grip loosens, and I turn my head slowly, instinctively reaching for my knife. I see three people huddled behind an overturned shelf, eyes wide and faces pale with exhaustion. A survivor, barely breathing, stares back at us sheltering two little girls in her arms. Their expressions, a fragile mix of fear and relief. I freeze when I recognize the woman.

"Mrs. Finley?" I ask softly.

Her hollow eyes look up, relief washing over her features.

"Violet?" Her voice wavers as she stands, the tension in her body easing.

She motions toward the two girls.

"These are my grand-daughters. We've been hiding here since the first missile hit. My husband…" She pauses, glancing at a door on the far side of the room, her voice barely above a whisper. "He's feeling a little…under the weather."

My dad's eyes follow her gesture, his face grim. Twisting his mouth and speaking so low only I can hear.

"He's still moving in there."

I glance at the door, a hollow ache gnawing at me.

Stay calm Violet

"I'm sorry to hear that." I say, my voice steady even though it feels like I'm barely containing the chaos inside.

"It's just me and my dad, Arthur." I gesture to my father, not stating the obvious that *no one else I knew had made it.*

Finley nods slowly, her eyes full of sorrow and something else. Perhaps the same determination I feel at the edge of my own fear. She swallows hard before speaking.

"Do you have any idea why the military is starting to bomb us?"

I glance at my dad, the question heavy between us. His face is set in stone, but I can see the same thought playing in his mind.

"No," I say, my voice low but firm.

"We came here to get a radio. Hopefully, that will give us some answers."

My eyes flicker toward her two grandkids, their wide, innocent eyes staring back at me, clueless to the world outside.

"There are people sick... and hurt...like your husband…" I stop short, not wanting to go into detail, not in front of the kids. "It's dangerous out there. You need to find somewhere safer."

Finley looks away, her hands trembling.

"Good luck out there. But we will wait for help here," she whispers, her voice so soft I almost miss it.

She sinks back down, pulling her grandkids close, as if her arms alone could shield them from the world waiting outside.

"We are going to grab what we need and leave. We will come back for you if we can," my dad's voice is steady despite the chaos I can hear building in his chest.

I force a smile, though my heart aches when I lean down to speak in her ear, "The only way to stop the dead is through the head. Get yourself a weapon."

I liked the sound of that Dead…head.

"Look what I found," My dad holds up a battered walkie talkie type radio, its antenna bent but intact.

I turn sharply towards him, as he kneels in front of an old wooden cabinet at the far end of the store. He pulls the doors open slowly, revealing a pile of old radios stacked inside. A small selection, dusty and forgotten, but something about it feels significant. I stand off to the side, watching as he sorts through them with care, his fingers brushing over each one.

"That one should do," he mutters, lifting an old-fashioned radio from the back of the shelf.

It is bulky, with a worn leather case and brass knobs, the kind you see in black-and-white photos of the early years. He cradles it in his hands, inspecting it with a kind of reverence, and I realize in that moment just how much he is depending on this. Just as much as he depended on food, finding shelter, and supplies. The radio wasn't just a relic, it was our new lifeline.

"Let's hope it still works," his voice low, almost talking to himself.

He sets the radio on the counter, carefully turning the dial. I watch him for a moment more before something catches my attention. A soft noise from behind the office door and I know exactly what it is. The old man. My pre apocalyptic therapist's husband. The scrape turns to a dull thud, like something shifting in the dark and I freeze.

"Dad…" I whisper, my voice tight.

He doesn't hear me at first, he's too focused on the radio static. His fingers twisting the dial slowly, the static increasing in volume. Then he stops, also noticing the sound. The radio hisses louder and a low moan vibrates through the store. The soft shuffle of feet scraping against the floor, slow but deliberate, fills the space between the static.

"Dad." I repeat, louder this time, as a chill creeps up my spine. "We need to go. *Now.*"

His eyes narrow as they snap up at me. He turns toward the office door, the color draining from his face as the noise grows louder. The dead man in there is stirring and growing increasingly restless.

"That damn thing can hear us." My dad hypothesizes, already opening the back door, a flash of panic in his eyes now. "We need to move."

I take one last look at Finley and grab the radio from his hands without thinking, clutching it to my chest as we rush into the alley behind the store. The noise behind us escalates into more banging, more rakes against the wood. The radio in my hands spits static, crackling in my ears. Behind us, the groans of the undead rise, rattling the walls of the street. I tighten my grip, heart hammering. There is no time to chase voices through the fuzz. The world we knew had to wait. The Deadheads were close, closing in with every staggering step. I slam the radio off, silencing its hiss.

The sky bruises darker by the minute, smoke coiling thick and stubborn in the air, burning the back of my throat. Above it, the steady thrum of helicopters cuts through the chaos, each blade-beat rattling in my chest. Dad pushes ahead, glancing back just once, his stride fierce and unrelenting. I follow close, every step quick and controlled, the rubber of my boots whispering against the pavement. The highway stretches before us like a lifeline, the only one I know that won't be barricaded.

First come the panicked voices, splintered and frantic. Then the gunfire before the steady rattle of machine guns drowns everything else. It's this sound that drags me out of my daze. We crouch low behind a rundown house, the wood siding flaking beneath my palms, splinters biting my skin. Dad presses a finger to his lips, and I force myself to stay still, to listen. The steady drone of boots on asphalt grows louder, too measured, too exact to be anything but military. I steal a glance around the corner. A bus hulks in the middle of the street, its paint chipped, windows black with grime. Soldiers move like machines rounding people up, shoving them toward the open doors. They don't speak, don't explain, just shove. Pleas and screams fill the air, raw voices breaking against the wall of rifles and uniforms. A woman claws at the doorframe, begging, her words drowned out by the bark of orders. A man lunges, trying to pull her free, but a rifle butt slams into his ribs, dropping him like nothing. They herd them inside like cattle. I duck back fast, spine pressing hard into the peeling siding. My lungs ache from holding my breath, the stench of smoke and sweat mixing in the air. Dad's jaw is tight, his eyes locked on the ground like he already knows what comes next.

"Should we follow that bus?"

My dad's jaw clenches, his expression carved from stone.

"I don't trust them," he mutters, his voice edged with anger.

Under normal circumstances, I would've rolled my eyes, dismissed it as another one of his conspiracy theories but this time… my gut agreed with him. Something about this didn't feel like a rescue. It felt like a trap just like at the hospital.

"Okay, let's go around…"

Before we can move, a soldier spots us.

"Hey! You two…over here!"

We freeze. Within seconds, they were on us rifles raised. I quickly put the radio in my backpack and put my hands up.

"We're not going!" My dad resists, trying to pull me away, but the soldiers grab him.

"You don't have a choice," one of them barks, shoving us toward the bus.

Another soldier grabs my arm, and yanks us forward.

Great. There is no escape.

A line of soldiers blocks every path, their faces cold and unreadable. One by one, they rip off our backpacks, tossing them aside as they rummage through our belongings. Their hands move with a practiced, methodical precision, searching us for weapons. They carefully pat us down, checking every inch, sparing no part of us. With a harsh grunt, the men toss our backpacks back at us. I quickly glance inside, my eyes scanning for anything that might be missing, but everything is there, even the radio.

My dad and I had hidden our knives on us with careful consideration and of course, we didn't carry guns.

"Move!" the soldier shouts, shoving us toward the waiting bus.

We stumble forward under their unrelenting grip. Another soldier forces me down hard onto the cold, worn leather. The door slams shut behind us. There is no point in resisting now. We sit on the bus, packed shoulder-to-shoulder with other townsfolk, all of them looking scared and filthy. The air is soured by bodies, ash, and the metallic edge of panic. People whisper in hushed tones, their eyes darting around as if searching for a way out. A soldier stands at the front, scanning the bus with cold, assessing eyes before speaking into his radio.

"Bus 13 is full."

"Take them to the screening." The order crackles from the soldier's radio, flat and cold.

The engine growls awake beneath us, vibrating through the metal floor. The bus jerks forward, a shudder that rattles the loose windows in their frames. I steal a glance at my dad. His jaw is clenched so tight the muscle in his cheek jumps, his eyes fixed straight ahead, as if he could will himself into stone. Whatever he's thinking, he's locked it away where I can't reach

"They didn't take the radio," Dad mutters, tapping the dented metal casing like it's some kind of secret weapon. "Probably didn't even recognize what it was. It's too old and useless to them."

A smile tugs at my lips, but it vanishes as the bus jolts over a pothole, rattling my teeth.

His voice lowers, heavy and certain. "When we get to this screening… we need a plan. A way out. We can't stay there."

I agree and continue to look out the window for any signs as to where we might be going. I know this town like the back of my hand. The only thing is, now it's getting dark.

CHAPTER 6
VIOLET

I swear I've been here before. We arrive at a fenced-in camp, the high walls are lined with barbed wire and armed guards patrol them in full gear. The air is thick with tension as the bus screeches to a halt, and the soldiers waste no time yanking people from their seats and forcing them into a rigid line. As we trudge forward, I try to steady my voice, desperately hoping to reason with them.

"I'm a paramedic!" I call out, my eyes darting between the soldiers. "I can help. If anyone's injured, I can assist."

For a brief moment, I think I see hesitation flicker across one soldier's face, but it is gone in an instant and the others ignore me entirely, their focus unyielding as they continue to bark orders, forcing us toward the front of the line. One soldier, towering over me, shoots me a glance.

"Keep moving," he snaps, his tone leaving no room for compromise.

The entire field is filled with everyone from around town. Ahead of us, soldiers are taking temperatures and checking people's eyes, undoubtedly looking for the signs of infection. The crowd stretches back, their faces fading into shadows, impossible to see clearly. The line stretches out like a slow-moving snake, and each step brings us closer to whatever fate awaits us. I turn to my dad as the panic gnaws at me.

"We can't get separated," I whisper desperately, scanning the field for any chance to escape.

His eyes hold that familiar fire, but there is nothing we can do, not in this patrolled line We slog closer, the sounds of crying children and frantic whispers filling the air. Suddenly, shouts erupt. A family is being separated. A mother, father, and two kids. The father fights hard, swinging his fists wildly at the soldiers as they try to drag him away.

"No! Don't take them! They're not sick!" His voice breaks with desperation.

A gunshot rings out. The father crumples to the ground, blood pooling beneath him, and the soldiers haul the mother away as the kids wail helplessly. I did notice that they had shot the man in the head. Do they know? They drag the body away, his family crying out in the distance. As we edge forward, I keep glancing around, desperate to spot any gap in the fence, any small hope of escape. There had to be a way out of here. *There's always a way.* My fingers dig into my palms as we creep closer to the soldiers, desperate for a shred of luck.

Then I see him. ***Ryder.***

He is standing there in uniform, a temperature scanner in his hand. I hold my breath in my throat. I haven't seen him for years, I thought he was dead, and then the letters; now here he is. A soldier on the other side. The same side that was tearing families apart. My Dads eyes widen as he too notices him. Ryder hasn't noticed me yet, his attention locked on the task at hand. One by one, survivors are yanked forward. His eyes flick over each person like a predator circling prey, lingering just long enough to measure them, but giving nothing away. Then, with a flick of his hand, he sends them shuffling to their designated lines, their footsteps hesitant, carrying the weight of the unknown. After what feels like centuries, He looks up, and our eyes finally meet. For a second, time simply stops. His face changes. First, his eyes widen with shock, disbelief, and something else flickers there. Fear? Relief? I can't tell. I don't know him anymore. For that split second all of the chaos around us disappears. My mind races, trying to make sense of what is happening. Ryder is alive, right here in front of me.

"Step forward." His voice is tight and controlled, but his eyes say something entirely different.

"Ryder?" I whisper, barely able to speak.

I feel frozen, torn between wanting to run and wanting to reach out my hand to touch him. He isn't just another soldier. He is Ryder, my Ryder, the person I thought I'd lost. The person whose letters are in my backpack. I wanted to scream, jump, and pull him into my arms. I am so unbelievably happy to see him…but was he happy to see me? He probably thought I ignored him all these years.

No. I didn't get the letters until now.

I'm trying to communicate this to him with my eyes when the scanner beeps. His gaze locks onto mine, and for that solitary moment, the world fades out once more. I can see the same emotions swirling in him that I feel in myself. Perhaps a distant part of me did know him. He inclines his head subtly toward the soldier beside him, prompting the soldier to shove me forward into the *not sick* line, snapping me out of the moment.

"Watch it!" Ryder's voice cracks like a whip. He steps toward the soldier, his glare sharp enough to cut. "Touch her like that again and I'll break your goddamn arm."

The soldier rolls his eyes. I can't stop looking, even as the soldier shoves me again. Ryder is still watching, his expression conflicted. Torn between duty and something else, something I can't quite name. Then it was my dad's turn and I glance back ignoring the soldiers' tugs on my arm.

"Normal," Ryder reports.

The older soldier beside him shoves my dad toward me. Dad's hand grips mine firmly, his touch rough and pleading as he rips me toward the group of people. Faces glisten with sweat, pale and drawn, eyes darting, hands clutching at arms and coats like fragile lifelines. My feet stumble over the uneven ground, but my dad's grip keeps me moving, his pace relentless.

A single shot cracks through the air. Gunfire erupts from every direction, echoing off the walls as the sick drop one by one. At first, I convince myself it is some sort of safety measure, but panic quickly takes over. I glance back to see Ryder still standing there, frozen. His eyes remain locked on mine, full of disbelief, as though he can't quite process that I am really there. It feels like I'm tearing a piece of myself away and when I finally turn my head, severing that unspoken connection, I know it is a bond I can no longer hold onto in this world.

My dad and I are herded inside the camp, soldiers flanking us on all sides, rifles at the ready. I can feel the weight of the survivors' stares from inside, watching the fresh meat from a distance like ghosts trapped in the in between. The groans of the dead that line the fence, attracted to what I assume is the sound of bullets and screams of panic. A soldier yells orders, his voice sharp and cold.

"Inside! All of you, move!"

My dad squeezes my hand, urging me forward as we are forced through the door. The interior is dimly lit, the air stale and suffocating. Bunk beds, dozens of them, are crammed into every corner, lined up in long rows. The mattresses are paper thin, barely more than scraps of fabric stretched over metal frames. This looks more like a prison than a survivor's camp. The soldier at the door points to the bunks with his rifle.

"Pick a bed and stay there. You're not allowed to leave unless we say so. We will have a food station setup just outside this room for one hour. Anyone caught outside this room after that hour will be shot."

The walls seem to close in right then and there as the faint sounds of sobbing from the far end of the building mingle with the metallic squeaks of the bunk frames. We find two empty beds in the corner and sit down, the metal groaning beneath our weight. Staring at the floor, the reality of the situation sinks in like ice in my veins. This camp definitely wasn't a refuge. After I'm not sure how long, the door swings open, and we are ushered out into the common area. My dad stays close as we join the line for food. I am hoping maybe Ryder will be the one assigned to serve us the food or at the very least be a part of the watch crew. Military men stand nearby, eyes trained on every movement, ensuring no one strays too far or makes any sudden moves. My hopes are shattered when I don't see him. The food is laid out on a long table. Something that might have been soup is sitting in the middle with some stale croutons and water bottles. It wasn't great, but it would keep us alive.

We grab our bowls and find a quiet corner to sit. The food is bland, but my stomach has been growling for hours, so I eat. My dad does the same, though he barely looks at me. His mind seems far away, his thoughts just as heavy as mine. Through a small window on the side of the room, I see Ryder standing by the entrance, talking to two soldiers. His posture is stiff and his movements deliberate. He gestures toward the far side of the camp, and one of the guard's nods and walks off in the direction Ryder has indicated.

Ryder stays behind for a short time, his gaze sweeping over the compound. For a moment, I think he sees me. There is something about the way he carries himself, like he belongs here, like he has some sort of authority. He eventually walks away. I glance over at my dad. He hasn't noticed, his attention still on his food. I bite my lip and decide not to mention it…for now. What if telling him makes everything worse? What if Ryder's on the wrong side of this, and I'm just some stupid girl who never answered his love notes, standing in the crossfire of a war I don't even understand. When we are done, we walk back to our room, the guards watching us every step of the way. Once back inside, I feel the weight of the past few days crash down. The room feels even smaller now, even more suffocating in its stillness. My dad stretches out on his bunk, his eyes closing, and I do the same. Eventually, exhaustion takes over, and I drift off. Hoping that when I wake up, there will be some answers waiting or at least a plan to get us out of this place.

I'm running, but the ground keeps slipping beneath my feet. Jane's screaming…no, she's crying. I can't stop the lampshade from shaking in my hands. The flash of fire lights up her face, and for a second, I think I've done it. I scream, a sound that tears through me, but the echo is drowned out by another. Grace. Felix. Mom. She's lying there, her chest a dark, spreading stain, and no matter how fast I run, I can't reach her. The day home explodes around me. Kate's thrown into the air, a twisted blur of color and chaos. Jeremy. He's moving, alive, eyes wild and furious, and he's screaming at me. "This is your fault! Everyone's dead because of you!"

I wake with a start, my chest heaving, sweat soaking my hair, my hands trembling. I don't even have time to catch my breath. I blink, disoriented, and find Ryder crouched beside me, his face etched with worry, a finger pressed to his lips.

"Shh," he whispers, eyes darting around. "I can get you out of here, but we have to go now."

The panic from my nightmare hasn't fully left me and for a moment, it is hard to tell what is real. My pulse races as I look over at my dad, who is now the one being startled awake. His eyes flicker with confusion, quickly replaced by the same tension Ryder carries. Ryder grips my arm, pulling me out of my haze. I grab my backpack and follow him. He moves swiftly, guiding us through the dimly lit hallways, his presence like a shield, steady and sure. I forgot how tall he was. My dad follows closely behind. We pass the rooms quietly, careful not to wake anyone. In one of the rooms, a family lays sleeping, their bodies huddled together for warmth. One of them, an older woman, stirs slightly, her eyes catching mine in the dark. Her gaze is filled with terror. A silent plea echoing through the air. I put my fingers to my lips, a soft *shh* slipping from my mouth, my heart breaking for her. She doesn't respond, but I see the fear in her eyes as we disappear into the shadows. I close the door on our exit, sealing the older lady inside her fate. The hallway feels colder now, empty. We can't afford to hesitate. Ryder leads us toward a door with a neon exit sign above it. Before we fully reach it, he slows. The distant sound of soldiers laughing and the clatter of plastic bowls being cleared fills the air. It is a reminder of what we are up against and how easily everything could fall apart. Ryder meets my gaze; his bright hazel eyes soften.

"Once you're out of here, there's no coming back. You need to understand that."

I swallow hard. "Why are we leaving? Isn't this a survivors camp?"

He pauses to look around and his voice comes out in hushed tones, "The military plans to kill everyone here, they think everyone's infected."

"What do you mean? They're going to… No, they can't…"

His stare turns stoic and distant, "I think they're terrified. They're trying to quarantine the city, but they can't. There's already whispers that it has spread." Ryder shifts in place nervously. "The people here…they won't comply, so they're going to eliminate them. I've seen the orders. I've heard them talk."

"You're sure?" I whisper, almost afraid to believe it.

"I'm sure." Ryder takes a step closer, his eyes never leaving mine.

Dad opens the door, interrupting us. "We've got to go Violet, there's a jeep here."

My mind spins trying to process what he is saying, "We can't just leave you behind."

For a brief second, his eyes lose their edge, just enough to let me see him. His hand brushes against mine, a fleeting touch that sends a wave of warmth throughout my body.

"I can't leave. Someone has to convince them not to go through with this slaughter. If I leave now, all of this…everything…it falls apart. *I have to stay.*"

My eyes drift to the ground.

"I *will* find you," he says softly, catching my chin tipping it up to look at him. "But I can't come with you now. I've made a promise to others here. I can't just run."

"Promise me you'll find me," I whisper, my voice trembling as our fingers intertwine.

My hand feels too small against his, but the warmth and steady pressure are enough to anchor me. Ryder squeezes my hand once, slow and deliberate, like he's sealing a vow in that simple touch.

"I swear it, Ocean Eyes," he says, his voice low and steady, but every syllable hums with a weight I can feel against my chest.

I press my palm harder into his, feeling the pulse beneath his skin, the steady rhythm that mirrors my own frantic heartbeat. My body aches to stay here forever, to sink into him, but the world has other plans. All I can do is hold on to this, to the promise his fingers carry, and believe that no matter what hell comes next, he will find me.

"Violet… there's someone coming, let's go." My dad cuts in once more.

Tears sting my eyes, but I blink them away, trying to be strong. "Where do we go?"

"Start heading southwest towards Banff," he says, reaching into his jacket.

He pulls out a set of keys and presses them into my palm.

"The Jeep is waiting for you. Extra gas in the back. It'll get you there. Stay away from the main highways. The military's taken them over, take the backroads if you want to avoid their patrols. It's your only chance."

I take a shaky step back, clutching the keys tightly.

"Please be safe," I plead, my voice breaking.

"I will be," he responds, his voice quiet but resolute. "You stay safe too. Go now before they realize the Jeep is missing."

With one last lingering look, I start toward the exit where my dad stands waiting, his face tight with concern. Just before I reach the doorway, I turn on impulse. Ryder doesn't flinch when I come close. He never has. I rise up on my toes, press a kiss to his cheek, and let my lips linger by his ear. "Thank you," I whisper, hushed enough that only he can hear. His jaw tenses, but he says nothing. I pull away fast, before I change my mind and walk toward my dad without looking back. If I do, I'm not sure I'll be able to leave at all. I have to trust him.

He will find me.

CHAPTER 7
RYDER

Watching the taillights of the Jeep disappear into the night feels like someone is twisting a fucking knife in my chest. My pulse hammers like a warning, my blood boiling. She was here and now she's gone, and I couldn't go with her. Ryan walks next to me, matching my pace.

"You good?" he asks, though the answer is pretty goddamn obvious.

I am spiraling.

I scoff, shaking my head. "Good?" I parrot, my voice dripping with sarcasm. "Yeah, just fucking fantastic bud…What the fuck is wrong with me?"

I turn, running my fingers through my hair and staring into the night's void.

I still mean something. Does she know I didn't completely abandon her? Does she know about the letters? I thought she might be dead or that maybe she just hated me. I let her go…again. No, I was helping her. Doing my duty but making sure she wouldn't die here. She is alive. My fucking head hurts. I need a joint.

I manage to get none of this out and Ryan stays quiet as he watches the gears turn.

"Dude, you have nothing to worry about. When we decided the plan, I made sure Tompkins was distracted, everyone else was either drunk or locked in their quarters. I don't know what this girl means to you but she's safe now, Ryder. Stop spiraling," he says, like that somehow makes everything better.

"Safe?" I laugh bitterly, shaking my head again. "In the middle of all this shit?" My fists are clenched and my jaw is tight.

"She has no fucking backup, no one watching her six. I'm the one who's supposed to keep her safe. You call that safe?"

Ryan stays silent for a moment.

"Would you rather she stays here and get shot like the others? You did the right thing. Also, that guy is with her right, he looked more than capable of watching her six. She's alive and on her way to an actual survival camp. That's the goal, right?"

The goal? I'm not worried about the goal anymore. The goal isn't worth shit if she doesn't make it. I should go after her. No, I can't, I have to help everyone here. FUCK!

"Yeah, right," I mumble. "She's out."

But I'm still stuck here, feeling like I've fucked everything up. I should've gone with her. I'll find her. I will.

Before Ryan can respond, I hear footsteps approaching. I don't have to look to know who it is. *Foster.* I can smell his rat stash from a mile away. He is the one person I don't want anywhere near this conversation. He doesn't even bother with a greeting, just smirks.

"So, the great Kent, *the fucking hero*, decided to break some rules?" He sneers. "Leaving the rest of us to clean up your mess. Real noble of you."

I whip around to face him, my fists clenched even harder.

"Fuck off, Foster," I bite out, taking a step toward him. "You saw nothing."

Foster's stupid grin only widens. "You're breaking protocol, Kent. You're just a fucking coward, hiding your secrets, while the rest of us have to deal with the fallout."

My hands are shaking now, but it isn't from fear. It's from pure, unfiltered rage.

"I'm not hiding anything, you incoherent fuck," I snap. "I'm doing what I have to do. You don't even know what's going on, because bitch boy privates don't get inside intel."

I take a step closer, "You're just pissed because I snuck someone out while you were busy sitting around with Tompkins' dick in your hand."

Foster steps forward, but I don't back down.

"You think I give a shit about your little girlfriend, Kent?" His voice is mocking, full of that cocky arrogance that makes my blood boil. "You think I'm just going to let you take off and leave the rest of us behind while you play hero? Nah, man. I'm going to Tompkins. I'm going to make sure the people who don't fall in line get what they deserve. What did she take again? Jeep number fifty-nine?"

That was it. That was the last straw.

He has to die now.

I grab him by the front of his shirt, yanking him close enough that our faces are mere inches apart.

"I always knew you were a fucking rat," I seethe my grip tightening. "Listen to me, Jake Foster. If you try to pull anything that messes with her or her safety. I'll fucking kill you."

Foster doesn't even flex a muscle, his smug grin is still there, but there is something different in his eyes now. Maybe it's the fact that he's realized I'm not fucking joking.

"Fuck you Kent," he says but this time, there is less confidence behind it.

Calloway puts his arm out to stop me from punching him.

"He's not worth it Kent."

"I'll make sure you never see daylight again. I don't care if I have to feed you to one of the sick." I hiss as he cowers off.

I turn to Calloway.

"We need to figure out what the hell Tompkins is planning next. Kill every fucking survivor but then what?"

"Yeah, I agree but first don't you think we should get our rest? It's been a long day and we will need our wits about us tomorrow." He responds with his annoying logic.

"I agree. Thanks for helping me get her out." My mind is screaming, my body is on edge, and I am stressed as hell. Rest is probably far from any realm of possibility.

"No problem, man. I know you'd do the same for me"

I make the trek to my bunk anyways, but sleep is a joke this evening. Instead, I drop to the floor and start doing push-ups, trying to burn off the stress that has continued to build up since I first laid eyes on her again. I can't do shit about being so fucking helpless. She was there…right in front of me…but I couldn't be with her. What makes everything worse is that she looked so goddamn good, even covered in different stages of decaying blood splatter.

She was wearing a paramedic's uniform, so she must've finished school. It was her eyes that made my heart ache. *Fuck*. Her beautiful sapphire eyes were swollen like she'd been crying. I understand better than anyone the horrors of what this world is. Shit, I'll probably never be able to shake off the residual grime.

In the line when we were taking temperatures the tension was so thick you could cut it with a knife. Armstrong, one of the other guys, had missed his head shot on some dude who looked sick as hell and didn't pass the temp check. The guy came back a few minutes later like he'd been pulled straight out of a fucking horror movie. His skin was decaying, eyes bloodshot as fuck, black veins running through his face. He looked like a walking demon. A *Dybbuk*. I put a fucking stop to it. Right between the eyes. That is the first time I've seen someone with the virus come back after being shot. Honestly, it is so fucking disturbing. I don't know if it's a blessing or a curse, but when shit hits the fan, something in me just flips. My emotions shut down and my body starts to move on instinct. I do what needs to be done. Maybe that's what makes me a good soldier but watching someone turn into that? It rattled me completely. I've seen death and lived through hell, but nothing…and I mean nothing…prepared me for that. The way the body convulsed, the sound of bones snapping like dry twigs, the look in their eyes… the part that's human just... disappears. What happens to them isn't death. Death is a kind stillness and whatever is happening to the sick is by far worse.

"Forty-eight... forty-nine... fifty."

Sweat drips as I halt my stress relieving activity. I sit up and wipe the perspiration from my face when my duffle bag triggers thoughts to flood my mind. I have to go after her. If this is the apocalypse, if everything's falling apart, I want to at least be with her.

Am I going to risk it all on the look in her eyes?

I pack my bag, grabbing whatever I can find, which is easy because I don't ever really unpack.

"Fuck," I breath, rubbing my face.

This isn't easy for me. I'm not one for disobeying orders but I'd do anything to be with her again and this might very well be the apocalypse and my very last shot at a second chance with the girl I never stopped loving. I unlock my door, and push the thoughts aside for now. I need to act; not dwell on shit I can't control. I skulk to the kitchen where there are protein bars and water bottles to add to my bag. I know exactly where they keep the good snacks, high on the top shelf, hidden from the other survivors.

The Survivors.

Right. They're all going to fucking die. What the hell can I even do? Let them free? Where would they even go? My body goes deathly still as the hallway light flickers to life, casting a harsh glow through the dark. I curse under my breath and quickly duck into the pantry, trying to hide my 6'7" frame behind the shelves. I am not exactly built for stealth, but I'll be damned if I'm not going to try. The footsteps get closer and Tompkins comes into view talking to someone on his phone.

Wait, the cell towers are down. So how the hell does he have service?

I make the choice to follow him, because I'm the type who has to know everything. Especially if it can clarify some secrets that I might be being kept from. The more fucked-up a situation, the more I need to understand what is really going on. I press my back against a door, trying to stay as quiet as possible, and listen.

"The horde is set free."

Horde of what?

"How long until you get here? There isn't much time"

How long until what gets here?

"Just me. Yes confirmed. Roger that. I will be outside west of the camp."

I keep my back against the wall as he rushes off to prepare for his secret rendezvous party of one.

I have to leave. Right fucking now.

I grab my bag and sprint towards Calloway's room. My heart thrums with a mix of fear and adrenaline. When I get there, his door is wide open. I walk in, unprepared for the goddam nightmare before my eyes. A fucking Dybbuk is kneeling over him, devouring his neck like a rabid animal. I turn around and clock another coming right at me. The creature pushes me into the wall and the knife I reach for clatters to the ground. *Dick.* I push its head away from me, its teeth snap unnervingly. I am *for sure* not letting this thing anywhere near me. I struggle against the unnatural strength of my assailant.

The only way to kill them is through the head.

I desperately look to my left for some kind of weapon, and luckily find the fire extinguisher. I repeatedly bash the dead person's head against the fire extinguisher and the sound of its skull cracking and splintering echoes through the room until it falls to the ground, bits of brain left between my fingers. I grab my knife and rush to the other Dybbuk. I stab the head, feeling a sense of satisfaction as the blade sinks into the soft part, and with one fluid motion I push it off my colleague. I look him over and check the side of his neck, the part that hasn't been bitten, to see if he is still alive. I press my fingers to his neck, hoping…*praying*…for a flutter, a beat, the faintest of pulses. My hand drops. The edges of the world smear and tilt, like I'm staring through a cracked lens. The weight of it lands on me, hard and sharp, like a fist smashing into my chest. Ryan Calloway is gone. Dead. My knees feel hollow. I let my head drop, jaw aching, letting the grief and rage flood me. My throat burns as my fists curl at my sides. I want to yell, to punch something, to drag time backward with my bare hands. Instead, I stand, swallow the lump in my throat, and raise my hand in a slow, steady salute. The motion feels heavier than it ever has before. My eyes sting, but I don't wipe them. I let the tears rise, and honor him the only way I know how, with a soldier's farewell. I crouch beside him again and reach for his sidearm. I pry it loose gently, as if he might still feel it.

"I'm not letting you come back like one of them," I whisper to his ghost.

I check the chamber for a round and stare at his face one last time. Eyes half-open, mouth slack. My finger hovers on the trigger.

"I'm sorry, brother," I say, voice barely holding steady.

Then I aim between his eyes and pull the trigger. The shot cracks through the silence. Blood blooms against the concrete like a dark flower. The only thing left to do is grab a nearby blanket and pull it over his body covering him completely, like he deserves. After a long pause, I stand up swallowing the grief deep down where it cannot slow me. There's no time to fall apart.

Back to work.

I rush forward in haste towards the survivors' bunker, Ryan's pistol at the ready, but as I approach, I am met with a blood-curdling scream that tunes every one of my nerves to survival. I sprint toward the scream, round the doorway and freeze. Blood spatters the walls, tables overturned, bodies jerking in unnatural rhythm. The dead are everywhere, tearing into what's left of the living. One man's hand claws weakly at the floor before teeth drag him back into the mess. A woman's cry is cut short, swallowed by a wet, tearing sound. My grip tightens. There's no thinking, only moving. I shoot some down to try to save as many survivors as I can, but there are at least twenty Dybbuks, and I am starting to get overwhelmed. Every few minutes they double, and next thing I know there are fifty of them closing in on the remaining living. Their eyes fixed on me like predators, and I know I can't take them all down alone. The military personnel who are with us start shooting the sick, the sound of gunfire rings through the room, but they too are quickly overtaken and attacked, their bodies falling to the ground. Their shrieks are cut short, gurgling through the thick metallic blood filling their mouths.

I manage to grab a few survivors and lead them outside, driving them back as we advance, my gun discharging in desperate bursts. I hear a commotion coming from the other side of the compound. A helicopter descends from the sky, its rotors whipping up a frenzy of dust as it lands with a deafening thud. My eyes widen in outrage as I watch Tompkins, that treacherous son of a bitch, sprint towards the chopper with a look of utter disdain on his face. I feel a surge of rage course through my veins. He *is* abandoning us, leaving us to face the hordes of undead alone.

I yell out to him, my voice hoarse, "You're just going to leave us here to die? You are a fucking coward!"

My words are laced with venom, and I can feel my heart seething with hatred. Tompkins turns to face me, a sneer twisting his lips. His eyes seem to bore into my soul, filled with a deep-seated hatred and a sense of superiority.

He spits out his words, each one a dagger, "You're all on your own, Kent. You're not worth saving, you're just a fucking nobody."

His words are a slap in the face, a brutal reminder that I am nothing more than a disposable pawn to him.

"Fuck you" I snap.

Tompkins laughs and retreats into the helicopter. The helicopter lifts off, its rotors churning up a maelstrom of debris. I am consumed by a wrath so intense; it threatens to engulf me whole. I feel like I have been punched in the gut, and my lungs seize leaving me gasping. I watch in impotent fury as the helicopter disappears into the distance, making me question my whole life in service. I am left standing here, feeling like I've been left to die, like I am nothing more than a sacrifice to Tompkins' ambition. The lividity and hurt boil over inside me, threatening to spill out in a torrent of violence and blood. I order the survivors to get on the nearest bus, and then I hustle back into the compound to see if I can save anyone else and to alleviate the uncomfortable feelings brewing inside me on these biting fuckers. I edge down the hall, blood slick on my hands. Every door

I push open breathes rot. A Dybbuk lunges from the shadows. I drive my knife up under its jaw, twist, and let it drop. The next room echoes with another snarl, another bullet. I keep moving. Someone in here has to still be alive. I detect the sound of footsteps behind me. Spinning around I find myself practically nose to nose with Jake Foster who is standing in the doorway, a sly grin spreading across his face.

"Kent." His voice is low and menacing.

I raise my gun, my finger tightening on the trigger. "Foster, what the fuck are you doing?"

Foster just laughs. "You'll never shoot me, Kent. You're too much of a *pussy*."

I take a step back, my eyes scanning the room for any other signs of danger. Then I see a lighter in Foster's hand. He flicks it open, and a flame erupts from the top.

"You're going to burn with this mess that *you* caused." His eyes gleam with madness.

I watch in horror as he tosses the lighter onto the nearby curtains.

"I didn't cause this you dumb fuck, did you not just see Tompkins abandon us all? He left you here too you fucking jarhead."

The flames lick the room, spreading quickly. I turn to run, but Foster is too quick. He tackles me to the ground, his fists flying. I try defending myself, but he is too strong. He pins me down, his hands wrapping around my throat.

"You deserve this and I can't wait to watch your life leave your eyes."

I struggle and kick, but Foster is too powerful. I am starting to lose consciousness, and the flames are getting closer and closer.

"Guess what Kent. I know that girl you snuck out is going to the Banff survivor camp, I'll be sure to comfort her with my cock when she finds out you're dead."

Something inside me roars, a violent thunder that shakes through my chest. Her face burns in my mind. *Those eyes*. She deserves more than this hell, more than being left to fight it alone. She deserves to know exactly how much I love her, how far I'd go, how much blood I'd spill just to keep her breathing. I promised her I would find her. I wasn't about to break that promise. Not for Foster…not for anyone. I wrench free of his grip, fury boiling through me, and drive my fist into his face. The crack of bone is sharp and satisfying, a vicious punctuation to the unspoken warning; Her name is Violet and Violet is *mine.*

Foster stumbles back, wiping his nose and giving me just enough time to get to my feet under me. I lunge at him, wrath driving me forward. My fist connects with his jaw, snapping his head back as we crash to the ground in a tangle of limbs. We roll, grappling, fists flying, each punch fueled by furor.

"You are a fucking idiot," he spits, malice twisting his words. "You really think she gives a fuck about you?"

The flames creep closer, heat searing the edge of my vision, but I don't care. I slam him down, my hands closing around *his* throat now, feeling his pulse hammering beneath my grip.

"You'll never find someone like her," I snarl, my voice low and shaking with frenzied energy. "Not in this life…and not in the next."

He tries to defend himself, but I'm too forceful now. Blinded by my anger, unable to see or think clearly. All I can do is feel, and what I feel is a deep-seated desire to kill. I'm interrupted by the sound of groaning and shuffling footsteps reverberating through the air, growing louder with each passing moment. It's safe to say they are attracted to noise and this fight is not exactly quiet. I tear my hands from Fosters' throat only to drive my boot into his knee with every ounce of weight I have. The snap is sharp and wet, his scream ripping through the night. He tries dragging himself away from me, but I stomp the other leg until it crunches, leaving him twisted and disfigured. I don't bother hiding my grin as I crouch over him, my breath coming hard.

"You don't get a clean death, Foster," my voice is low and full of venom. "You get to feel it coming for you."

I leave him there and bolt. When I glance back, the first of the horde is stumbling toward him.

"You're too much of a pussy to finish me, huh?" He screams after me, voice cracking with panic as the groans grow louder. "Got to let them do your dirty work?"

I watch, numb and detached as they descend upon him, their teeth and claws shredding into his flesh.

"Ryder!" he pleads, clawing at the ground, trying to drag himself away as the sick swarm him. Hands grasp every part of him, pulling and tearing like starved animals. "Help me! *Please*!"

I just stand there. Watching. I should feel something but bad people don't deserve sympathy. He wouldn't have saved me. Hell, he would have laughed if it had been me in his place. Still, as his screams turn to gurgling gasps, the hairs on my neck stand up. Not because he is dying but because I realize what I have just done. I left him to die, just like Tompkins left all of us. I clench my fists, jaw tight, forcing the thought down. No. Tompkins did it out of cruelty. He did it because he saw us as pawns, as disposable tools. I did it because Jake Foster isn't worth saving. At least, that's what I tell myself as I grab my bag and turn from the gruesome scene. I stumble out, gasping for air and I look back, watching as the camp burns to the ground.

Fucking Christ.

I run outside to meet what's left of the living. I sling my bag over my shoulder, breath ragged, sweat stinging my eyes. My pulse pounds like war drums in my ears. Every shadow and every noise could mean death and I'm on high alert. I round the corner to see Hawthorne and Sinclair…alive. I sigh with relief.

"No time to celebrate," Hawthorne rasps, bracing his rifle against his shoulder.

The night quivers with movement. The dead pour from the tree line, drawn by the scent of gunpowder and sweat. Their moans bleed together into something low and primal, their throats bubbling out wet, animalistic groans that vibrate through the ribs. I surge forward through the grass, the moonlight glinting across the blade in my hand. One clean thrust through an eye socket with a sharp twist. Hawthorne's rifle barks behind me, the muzzle flare carving harsh light through the dark. Each shot finds a skull, jerking heads back in sprays of red and bone. Sinclair's shovel whistles past my ear, connecting with a skull that splits like overripe fruit.

"Keep moving!" I shout, kicking a dead man off my boots.

The bus is in sight. The survivors we have collected scramble up the steps, screaming and shoving one another in panic. The sick relentlessly try to press in. Hawthorne grabs a woman, hauling her up as I turn, slashing another Dybbuk down. Sinclair slams the bus door shut just as a rotten hand claws at the frame.

CHAPTER 8

RYDER

I slump into a seat as the bus rumbles forward, the weight of exhaustion pressing down on me. Blood drips from my knife onto the metal floor, but I barely notice. My heart is still racing, my ears still ringing from the chaos outside. We made it. Some of us had at least. Sinclair drifts between the rows, lips moving as his gaze flicks from face to face. His fingers tap each seatback in rhythm. *One, two, three*, counting under his breath, eyes narrowing whenever a space sits empty too long. The inside of the bus feels suffocating, frantic whispers and quiet sobs closing in on me.

"Ten." Sinclair reports.

Hawthorne swears under his breath, gripping the steering wheel in front of him. A woman clutches a little boy to her chest, her face streaked with dirt and tears. An older man sits in silence, staring at the blood on his hands. A teenager, maybe fifteen, is crying and rocking slightly, whispering someone's name over and over. A younger guy, maybe early twenties, finally speaks up, his voice shaky.

"Where's Carter? Did anyone see him?"

No one answers.

A woman near the back chokes on a sob murmuring to herself

"He…. he was right behind me…"

Another survivor, a man with a deep gash on his arm, slams his fist against the window. "This is fucked. We should've waited longer!"

Sinclair shoots him a hard look. "Waiting would've gotten us all killed."

I barely hear them as I stare at the empty seat across from me.

"Is this all who's left?" Hawthorne asks, his voice quieter now.

Sinclair exhales, then turns toward me. "Where's Foster? Armstrong and Calloway?"

I swallow against the ache, my grip tightening around my knife.

"They didn't make it."

The bus ambles along in silence. The woman with the little boy wipes at her tears. The guy who asked about Carter just stares at the floor. No one has time to grieve, not now. I'm not thinking about Jake or Ryan and the atrocities that were committed like I should be. I am thinking about her; Violet. She is somewhere out there, in this nightmare. Is she safe? Is she even alive? I want to believe she is. I need to, but doubt gnaws at the edges of my mind.

Sinclair exhales, shaking his head, turning back toward the front of the bus, "Doesn't matter now," he says, forcing his voice steady. "We need to figure out our next move."

"Nearest towns about fifty kilometers out. We head there, get supplies, and then go to the Banff survivors camp." I suggest.

Hawthorne gives a slow dip of his head, "Yeah. Good idea Kent."

I force myself to focus as the bus rolls over at least twenty sick, creating a limb soup underneath the bus. I look out the window and whisper to the stars.

Ocean eyes, please stay safe. I'm coming.

A violent jolt rocks me awake as the bus hits something. A pothole? An animal? A Dybbuk? My head snaps up, and I see Hawthorne gripping the wheel, his eyes fixed on the road as we enter what is left of town.

"I passed out?" I ask groggily, my voice thick with exhaustion.

Hawthorne lets out a sharp chuckle.

"Oh look, Sleeping Beauty is awake. Hope you didn't think this was all just a bad dream, cause it's not."

He shoots me a glare through the rearview mirror. Sinclair, sitting near the front, rotates to scan the bus.

"We need to figure out exactly who's with us. No one's said a damn word since we left." He pauses, eyes sweeping over the handful of survivors. "Ten of us left… out of what, two hundred?"

A deafening quiet hang in the air.

Hawthorne sighs, "And we were waiting for you to wake up, so you could tell us what the fuck Tompkins said before he bailed. I still can't believe that bastard left us."

"I knew he was fucking up to something," Sinclair mutters, shaking his head. "I saw it at the debriefing. Something was off."

I swallow, my throat dry, "He said we were nothing but pawns in a bigger game he was part of. Then he got on a helicopter and fucked off."

Hawthorne scoffs "Fucking coward."

I turn my gaze to the windshield, and my eyes widen. Streetlights lean like drunks over shattered pavement, windows gape hollow and black, and what's left of Main Street smolders under a haze of ash. Buildings reduced to rubble, streets littered with debris, fires raging in every direction.

"Where the hell are all the dead fuckers?" Hawthorne mutters, bringing the bus to a stop.

"That's a damn good question," I reply, scanning the destruction outside.

I get up and address the group.

"Alright, listen up. We all know those things out there are dangerous, but we need to stick together if we're going to survive. My name's Corporal Ryder Kent. This is Private Joe Hawthorne and Private Andrew Sinclair."

A young guy in his early twenties is the first to speak.

"I'm Theo. Theo Sparks."

One by one, the others introduce themselves.

"This is my son, Dion," adds a woman, wrapping a protective arm around a small boy. "I'm Teresa."

"Jalen." The teenage boy chokes out.

Another young woman chimes in, "Emily Scott."

"Wilson Norton. Ex-military," an older man says with a sharp nod before saluting us.

I return the gesture. "Pleasure, sir."

Before anyone else can speak, Wilson's expression darkens. "You boys might want to take a look at this guy's arm."

My heart skips a beat and I rush to the back of the bus where a man sits hunched over, gripping his arm, seeping through his fingers and dripping to the floor.

"What's your name?" I ask, my voice tense.

"Kian," he whispers.

I jerk my chin toward his arm, the question clear without a word. His jaw tightens before he peels his hand back, revealing the wound. Blood slicks his skin, dark and steady, but the edges are clean. No torn flesh, no ragged teeth marks. Just a straight, ugly slice, the kind a blade would make, not a mouth. The tension in my chest eases, my breath slipping out slow. It is a gash. Not a bite.

"Does this bus have a first aid kit?" Wilson asks, scanning the overhead compartments.

Sinclair searches through the storage bins before slamming one shut in frustration.

"Not anymore."

I wipe a hand down my face.

"Theo, keep pressure on that wound. We need to stop the bleeding until we can find a pharmacy for bandages and antibiotics. We have no idea how this virus spreads."

Turning to Sinclair and Hawthorne, I point toward the door. "There's one nearby. Let's move out."

I pull a rifle out and waver a moment before handing it to Wilson.

"Nobody leaves this bus. Do not open the doors for anyone but us. We'll be right back."

The bus falls quiet, but their eyes tell me they understand. I step outside into the ruins of the world we once knew. I grip my knife tightly, and secure my pistol, scanning the street before us. The pharmacy stands just ahead, its glass doors shattered, shelves barely visible through the overturned aisles and scattered debris.

"Alright, boys, let's keep this like a regular mission," my voice subdued. "In and out. No unnecessary noise. Sound draws them out, so no guns. Knives only."

"They go down with a stab to the head, right?" Sinclair asks, gripping his combat knife.

"That or the base of the skull. Just don't fuck it up."

Hawthorne takes point, moving in a low, controlled stance toward the entrance. As we step inside, the smell is the first thing to hit us. Stale, moldy, and thick with something rotten. The whispered scrape of movement resounds from deep within the store. Hawthorne raises a fist, signaling for us to freeze. There are two distinct sounds. One near the back, but another coming from an aisle to the right. I motion toward Sinclair, pointing to the right aisle, then gesture to Hawthorne to watch the back entrance. He nods, gripping his knife as he moves into position. Sinclair and I advance toward the first Dybbuk, a former store employee in a ripped blue vest. It looms hunched over a toppled shelf swaying slightly, its head twitching at random intervals. Sinclair advances first, his footsteps soundless. With a swift sweep of his hand, he plunges his knife into the base of its skull. The thing stiffens, letting out a soft groan, then crumpling to the ground.

One down.

My gaze snaps to the second one. Its foot is dragging along the cracked tile behind the pharmacy counter. It had perhaps once been a customer, an old man, judging by the thinning gray hair and wrinkled skin now slack with decay. I approach from behind, steadying my grip. My knife sinks into the back of its skull, cutting off whatever unholy energy had been keeping it upright.

I exhale slowly, signaling to Hawthorne. "Clear."

He steps further into the pharmacy and Sinclair joins us, already scanning the pill bottles.

"Alright, antibiotics. Let's not waste time," I grit out, sweeping my flashlight over the shelves.

"Cipro, amoxicillin, doxycycline…" Sinclair reads off labels, shoving bottles into his pack. "These should cover most infections."

I keep watch as they load up, my mind running through the risks of staying too long.

"Yo," Hawthorne suddenly whispers from the other end of the counter, holding something up between his fingers. "Check it out."

I squint. Small foil packets glint under the beam of his flashlight. *Condoms.*

"Well, guess I won't be needing these anymore. Not like I was getting laid before, but now? Pretty sure my chances are dead. No pun intended," Hawthorne adds with a wink and a smirk.

Without missing a beat, I grab a bottle of lube from the shelf beside me and chuck it straight at his chest. He catches it with a grunt.

"What the hell?"

"You're going to need that more than the condoms," I mutter, turning away. "Might help you jerk off a little quieter while we try to survive out here."

Sinclair snorts behind me. Hawthorne just grins and holds the bottle up like a trophy.

"Apocalypse essentials, baby."

"Yeah, for the world's loneliest toolkit." I say dryly.

Sinclair leans on the counter with a smirk. "Please, like *you* get any action Ryder. I've never even seen you with a girl like ever. You practically sleep with your rifle."

I go still for a second, the shelves around me blurring out. Her breathless voice still haunts me. Her phantom nails carve fire down my back, her body arches into me like she is trying to burn herself into my skin. No one's ever felt like her. No one's ever *been* like her. The heat, the tremor, the way her pulse matched mine. It wasn't just want, it was recognition. Like she was made from every piece of me I thought I'd buried. *Fuck…* nothing before or after ever came close.

"Kent?" Hawthorne pry's, tossing a bottle of Advil at my face. "You good?"

I shake my head a little too quickly. "Yeah. Just...thinking."

Sinclair rolls his eyes. "Is Kent thinking about women? *Must* be the end of the world."

"Yeah...guess it is." I shake my head with a low laugh trying to push the memories back down and the mission back into focus. Now wasn't the time but goddamn I wanted it to be.

"Let's go," I bark, throwing one last glance at the darkened store around us. "Before we have more company."

Sinclair ghosts along my left, rifle steady, boots whispering against the tile. Hawthorne mirrors him on the right, his breath slow and controlled. The air is thick with that sterile, medicinal sting, but underneath it lingers the sour rot of decay. Shelves cast long, broken shadows across the aisles, to the left a bottle roll, clinking once before settling. It sounds like it came from behind the office door. I signal for them to hold position as I step forward, my grip tightening around the hilt of my blade. I soundlessly count to three then push the door open, ready to drive steel through whatever happens to be lurking inside.

"Please don't kill me!"

The voice is raw and panicked. Not the growl of the dead, but a desperate *human* plea. My eyes lock onto a wide-eyed, dirt-streaked red-haired woman crouching between overturned boxes and a bunch of open bottles of pills.

I hesitate, the name tumbling into my mind a second too late.

"Kate?"

She moves her head up and down frantically, chest rising and falling with ragged breaths.

I lower my blade an inch, still trying to process. I hadn't seen her in years. High school was maybe the last time. She had been one of Violet's best friends.

"Holy shit," I breathe out. "You, okay? Why are you in a pharmacy office?"

Kate blinks against the low light, squinting at me like I am a ghost pulled from her past.

"Wait… do I know you?" she asks, voice hoarse and trembling.

I step closer, lowering my weapon.

"It's me. Ryder Kent. We went to high school together; I graduated a year before you. Norbrook Secondary. Friends with Violet."

She stares harder, her brows furrowing.

"Ryder? No fucking way." Her voice cracks with disbelief. "Jesus, you look like you crawled out of a war-zone."

"You're not far off."

Her expression shifts.

"Have you seen her?" Her voice rises with sudden desperation, "Violet. Have you seen Violet?"

I stiffen, the mention of her name slamming into me like a freight train.

"Yeah," I say softly. "I snuck her out of our military camp before it got overrun."

Kate's lip's part and I hear her breath catch in her throat. "You saw her? I…I watched her get shoved into a military bus with her dad, Arthur. I don't know if they made it out. I thought she was…" She trailed off, emotion choking her words.

"She made it," I reply firmly. "I told her and her dad to head toward the survival camp in Banff."

Hawthorne and Sinclair pivot sharply toward me.

"Wait, what?" Hawthorne says, eyes narrowing. "You never told us any of that."

Sinclair crosses his arms, looking between us. "Damn, didn't realize you were running solo missions before we were blessed with your presence. When were you planning on telling us?"

I rub the back of my neck, avoiding their stares.

"It's complicated," I grumble.

"Everything's complicated now." Sinclair snaps.

"It was the best shot she had. You guys knew the plan was to kill all survivors. I couldn't let that happen to her."

Kate lets out a shaky breath finally sitting up from against the wall, eyes shining.

"At least she's alive," she whispers. "That's more than I could've hoped for."

Then looks up at me, her eyes narrowing slightly. "You were always kind of a mystery back then Ryder. Guess some things don't change."

I half-smile.

"Yeah, well. The world flipped on its head. Guess I just kept my footing."

Sinclair raises an eyebrow. "Seriously dude? You couldn't have mentioned the part where you pulled off a rescue op like some post-apocalyptic James Bond?"

Kate gives a short, humorless laugh. "Guess he's always been a sucker for Violet."

I meet her gaze but say nothing.

What the hell does she mean by that? Violet and I had always kept our 'hangouts' private with no labels, no drama. How would Kate know anything about it? Did Violet talk about me? About us?

That old ache stirs in my chest. Half guilt, half longing. Part of me wants to press her, find out what she knows, more specifically what Violet had told her. Now wasn't the time so instead I make a mental note to inquire about Violet later.

“Let's go, we have a bus full of survivors, we will take you there.”

We carry on, our weapons drawn again. Behind me, I hear one of them shift their grip on their blade, clearly stewing on the same things I was avoiding.

“You know,” Hawthorn mutters, “You’re a damn mystery, Ryder. You’re out here saving women, pulling secrets out of thin air. Anything else you want to drop on us?”

Before I can answer, Sinclair jumps in, tone dry.

“Seriously though, who is Violet? Some lost girlfriend? Secret wife? Government experiment you fell in love with?”

I glance over my shoulder trying to hide the flicker that hits me at the mention of a lost girlfriend.

“Enough,” my voice rings out with an edge too sharp. “We’ve got more pressing shit to deal with than my love life.”

Inside I am already slipping. Five and a half years. And it still feels like yesterday. Her breath on my neck. That damn look in her eyes right before she walked away from camp.

Hawthorne grumbles under his breath in response “Figures. Another damn mystery.”

Before anyone can add any more fuel to the fire, the air shifts and a low, guttural moan breaks our conversation. Then the slow, unmistakable scrape of feet against linoleum jars us back to reality. The humor drained from the air.

“Company,” Sinclair whispers, raising his knife.

We shift into position. The first one goes down easy, my knife sinking into the soft tissue beneath its jaw. Sinclair takes out the second, slamming it against the shelving before delivering the kill shot. Kate lets out a yelp as the third lurches for her, but Hawthorne gets there first, driving his blade through its skull in one clean motion. The last one comes at me faster than I expect. I barely have time to react before its rotten fingers graze my arm. I twist, shoving it hard against the wall before sinking my knife straight through its eye socket. The store falls silent once more, the scent of death thick in the air.

"Let's move," I demand, adjusting my pack. "We need to get Kian patched up before he bleeds out."

We quickly run back to the bus, and show Kate to one of the open seats before rushing to Kian, who is pale and clammy. His wound isn't life-threatening. Yet.

"Got antibiotics," I say, handing Sinclair the bottles we'd managed to grab. "Let's hope they work."

Kian winces as we clean his wound, but he looks on in gratitude. While we are tending to Kian, Kate introduces herself and even recognizes Teresa, someone she used to work with a few years back. I smile. It is nice to see people who knew each other reuniting…and there it was again, the ever-returning tinge of sadness in my heart reminding me that I am painfully missing someone I saw less than 24 hours ago. I hand our patient one of the water bottles and give him two pills to get ahead of the infection.

He squeaks out a small "Thank you."

"You're welcome," I say handing him a protein bar and moving to the next person. It's not long before another voice pipes up.

"I'm starving," one of them groans.

"I'm so thirsty," another chimes, their voice weak.

I sigh internally fighting the growing knot in my stomach. I walk back to the front of the bus and pull the last of the protein bars from the case, passing them out, along with water. Good thing we always kept a stash of these on each bus. The sound of gratitude mixed with the frantic rustling of packaging fills the cramped space as people devour their small rations.

How the hell am I supposed to do this?

We only have twenty-four protein bars and forty-eight water bottles. That's it. A handful of people on a bus and none of us know how long we will be stuck here or how long it will take to get to safety. I rub my hands over my face, trying to push the panic and anxiety down. My thoughts race faster than I can keep up with.

No manual for this one, Ryder. But you've handled chaos before. You'll handle this too.

I finish my bar and take a deep swig of water, swallowing against the tightness in my throat. The responsibility is overwhelming. There is *no one* else to take charge, *no one* else to lead these people. It's all on me.

"Any idea what time it is?" Wilson asks, breaking my thoughts.

Sinclair is the one to reply. "There hasn't been any service or internet since yesterday afternoon. So, we all ditched our phones."

"My watch says ten AM."

"Thanks Ryder," Wilson replies satisfied.

"Maybe we should take this time to rest," I offer to everyone. "I haven't heard any bombs or missiles since yesterday so we should be safe here."

The exhaustion on the bus is palpable. Everyone, myself included, is running on fumes. One by one, they lay down, finding what little comfort they can in the cramped vehicle.

"I'll take the first watch." Hawthorne's voice punctuates the air.

I go through the motions to agree but I am interrupted.

"Um… sorry to bother you, but my son needs to go to the washroom."

If you told me two days ago, I'd be peeing outside of the military bus, in the street, in broad daylight, I would've asked for whatever you were smoking. It's like Dion's bladder sent a signal for everyone's bladder to go off. I'm just thankful it wasn't a number two…yet…we would probably have to go and loot some toilet paper from somewhere. After everyone was done with their business, Sinclair gave each of us a squirt of sanitizer as we return to the bus and before you know it everyone was off to dreamland.

Sleep takes me before I even realize it, and when my eyes blink open again, the world is swallowed in darkness. The bus hums softly around me, shapes lost in shadow, the air heavy with warmth and the low, rhythmic sound of quiet snores drifting through the stillness. I pat Hawthorne on the back then climb onto the roof of the military bus, knife still in hand, scanning the ruined townscape as the others drift back into a restless slumber. The night is thick with stillness broken only by the low, haunting moans of the dead and the fragile chirping of crickets as if nature hadn't gotten the apocalypse memo. My gaze lifts to the stars, their cold light scattered across the sky like tiny fragments of something we've lost. Maybe this was supposed to happen, maybe we've been pushing Mother Nature too hard, taking too much, and now the world was resetting itself in the most brutalist way possible. Even if that were true, there is one thing I know for certain. I can't wait to see Violet again.

There have been other women over the years, I wasn't a nun contrary to my team's belief. Any woman afterwards was nothing but a fleeting pin point that never lingered. Nothing ever felt the same as her, no touch ever burned like hers. She had always been different and she had always meant more. I let out a slow breath, reaching into my bag, my fingers finding my red metal tin. I flip it open, pulling out one of my tightly rolled joints and a half-used lighter. A ghost of a smirk tugs at my lips as I spark the flame, shielding it from the wind as I light up. The first inhale hits smooth, a welcome warmth against the cold night air. Memories flitter in the haze. It always comes back to that first night after I moved away. She'd driven hours just to see me.

No plan.

No pressure.

Just Violet showing up in ripped jeans, her hair wild from the wind and her smile even wilder. We spent that night watching movies we didn't finish, passing a bong back and forth on my bed, talking shit and laughing until it turned into something more. God knows how many times we went at it…It got so raw at one point, we had to stop and raid the kitchen for coconut oil. She made some joke about it being 'organic and ethically sourced,' and we both lost it. Even in the morning she couldn't keep still. Sliding her ass against me, subtle but not subtle at all, signaling she was ready for another round. I was too, hell I always was when it came to her.

Then there was that time she gave me road head. We were supposed to be heading to a lookout, but five minutes later I'd pulled off onto some back trail because I couldn't think straight. Bent her over the side of my truck right there under the moon. We were still laughing when I realized I'd accidentally finished all over the running board trying not to come inside her. After the fire and lust and the goddamn poetry of remembering her, comes the part I always hate remembering. That last night. I told her I'd write her cute letters if I didn't have service and I did. Every damn month. Letters she's probably never read or maybe she has read them and just never gave a fuck. Words I poured out like they'd fix something, like they could close the distance between us. She never answered them. She smiled that day and even kissed me like it wasn't really goodbye when she walked away and I let her. Our final farewell.

Why the fuck didn't I fight harder? Why didn't I drive back, show up at her door, tell her everything I felt? What the hell was I so afraid of? Rejection?

I exhale slowly, watching the smoke disappear into the night sky. Soon, if the gods were willing, I'd see her again. I always knew we'd find our way back to each other. I just didn't think it would take the goddamn apocalypse to make it happen. Maybe fate had a sick sense of humor or maybe Violet and I were just too damn stubborn to stay apart. Either way, here we were dodging bullets, stabbing Dybbuks, and trying not to die before we got the chance to say everything we never did. I take another slow drag, the burn settling deep in my lungs. Of all the ways I pictured seeing her again, covered in someone else's blood with a knife in her hand wasn't exactly at the top of the list but hell, if anyone could make survival look sexy it was her. I let my head fall back against the cool metal of the bus roof, eyes tracing the constellations above. The stars are the same as they've always been. Steady, constant, and untouched by the chaos down here. Just like her. Even after all these years, even after all the shit we'd both been through, Violet had to feel something. I saw it in her eyes. No apocalypse, no army, no undead nightmare is going to change that. I smirk, exhaling a slow trail of smoke.

Soon Ocean Eyes, soon.

CHAPTER 9
VIOLET

I can't believe that I just saw Ryder. *Ryder fucking Kent.*

"Dad, can you believe that was Ryder?" I say looking back hoping to catch another glimpse.

"I thought he was dead."

He was dead.

I swallow down the lump in my throat and reached for the map in the glove box, my fingers flexing around the edges.

"I did too," I murmur, but the words feel hollow and listless in my mouth.

I squint into the darkness wondering where the hell we are, searching for road signs, but there is *nothing*. Just the endless stretch of empty highway and the faint outline of trees pressing in on both sides. The only light of the evening comes from the moon, and the bright white headlights.

"I know where we're going," my dad says, his voice steady. "I used to drive these back roads as a kid."

I glance at him surprised.

"Of course, you did."

He had spent his whole life here, crisscrossing the province, taking the roads less traveled. First on his motorbike, then in whatever old truck he was fixing up at the time. I had spent countless summers riding shotgun, watching the landscape blur past. That felt like another life compared to where we were now in the timeline. My fingers linger on the map before folding it up and tucking it into my backpack. If he was sure, then that was good enough for me.

"Why don't you figure the radio out?" His voice is rough from exhaustion.

I grab the knob and start tuning through the channels, each turn met with bursts of static. White noise fills the car, an empty reminder that the world had gone quiet.

Shhhhhhkkk—*nothing.*

Shhhhhhkkk—*still nothing.*

Then, for a brief second, a voice crackles through.

"…safe zone…north of…"

The signal fades before I can make sense of it. I twist the dial frantically, trying to bring it back, but only a static answers. A few channels later, another voice emerges.

"This is the Canadian Emergency Response Network. If you can hear this, proceed to the nearest safe zone. Be advised: major cities are overrun. Travel with caution. Do not attempt to engage the infected. May God be with you all."

Silence follows, and then the message begins to loop. I exhale slowly, my fingers falling from the dial. The radio is useless. Just more proof that no one is coming to save us. We drive in silence. I let out a long yawn, and he instinctively follows suit, stretching in his seat. The dim glow of the dash reads **3:00** a.m.

"I think we should pull over, regroup and sleep."

Whatever food we had eaten back at the camp wasn't sitting right. Dad hesitates, gripping the wheel like he wants the opposite. I understand why he is hesitant. Stopping means we are vulnerable but we have no choice; we have to call it a night. I scan the area, searching for any nearby houses. A small acreage sits in the distance, its windows dark, the surrounding land eerily quiet. It looks long abandoned and maybe it was. I point toward it, and my dad gives a silent nod before steering the car off the road. We pull up beside the house, parking out of sight in case of the unlikely passerby. The place is old, its wooden siding weathered and peeling, but it still had a certain sturdiness to it. Dad reaches into his bag and pulls out two flashlights handing me one. I smile.

Knock. Knock. Knock.

"Anyone there?" I call out.

Silence.

No movement.

No response.

Dad reaches for the door handle, testing it. It turns easily in his grip. *Unlocked.*

"Stay close," he whispers, his voice barely more than a breath.

The moment we step inside, the air feels wrong. It's heavy, stale, and carrying the faint sting of metal beneath layers of dust and mildew. The kitchen looks like it's been torn apart. Cupboards hang open, their contents scattered across the counters. Dried blood streaks the wall, smeared in uneven lines, like someone tried to crawl away or fight back. We move slowly through the room, eyes sweeping every corner, every shadow.

No movement.

No sound.

Dad lifts his hand and gives a short, sharp whistle. The sound bounces off the walls, travels up the staircase, then fades. Nothing answers.

"Clear enough," he says finally, tipping his head toward the second floor, though his gaze lingers, like he doesn't quite believe it.

We climb the stairs, our steps careful, but the upper level is untouched. Almost pristine, even. Sheets still tucked into beds. Clothes folded on dressers. Like the family that lived here had just *vanished.* At least I'd get some actual sleep tonight.

"Okay," Dad exhales. "Let's see what we can loot in the kitchen."

Loot. Just a word, but it felt so wrong. Like we weren't people anymore, just scavengers picking apart the remains of someone else's life. I glance around the house. There are still pictures on the walls, smiling faces frozen in time. A little girl with missing front teeth, a couple in their wedding attire, an old dog curled up on a couch. These weren't just empty buildings. People had lived here. They had laughed, argued, and celebrated birthdays. Once upon a time, a family sat at this very table for dinner, talking about their day, completely unaware that their world as they knew it would be ripped away. Now I'm here, taking what they left behind. This isn't how life is supposed to be. I should be at home, worrying about work or what movie Jane wants to watch on a Friday night. Not breaking into houses and rummaging through cabinets hoping to find an expired can of soup or a half-empty water bottle. I shouldn't be walking into rooms wondering how many bodies I'd find. Shouldn't be slowly learning to kill without remorse. I clench my fists, forcing myself to move forward because this *is* life now. Whether I like it or not. We reach the basement door. Dad goes in first, his flashlight cutting through the darkness as we descend the creaking wooden steps.

I think I hear groaning.

Three Deadheads are chained to the exposed wooden beams, their arms stretched, fingers clawing at the air. Their throats rattle with wet, hungry growls. Slumped in the corner against the concrete wall is a man. A shotgun resting loosely in his limp hands, his head tilted unnaturally to the side, a dried gunshot wound at his temple. A single bite mark mars his forearm.

"Poor guy lost his family too," I release it like a sigh, glancing at the three girls chained up.

Their sunken eyes lock onto me, as they snap their teeth, straining against the restraints that hold them. I know what has to be done. Without hesitation, I step forward, dissociating as I plunge my knife into their skulls. Dad helps me and one by one they stop moving. My mind numbs, shutting off every emotion and any attachment to what they might have been before. By the time I step back, my hands are steady. My dad crouches beside the dead man and checks the shotgun.

"Fully loaded," he exhales, weighing it in his hands.

He pauses while he checks the chamber. "Except for one."

I glance around the basement. In the opposite back corner, past a toppled shelving unit, I spot something. I nudge my dad and point. Carefully, we step over the debris, and my heart leaps when I see water bottles. A whole case, still sealed.

Jackpot.

I grab the case and head upstairs, dad illuminating my steps for me. My stomach clenches and for once it isn't from stress. I need to eat something. Placing the water bottles on the table I start rummaging through the kitchen pantry again. I push aside dust-covered jars and empty boxes, hoping for something. Literally anything.

" Yes!"

I find six cans of ravioli, two cans of tuna, and two cans of corn. It might as well be a feast. I let out a sharp whistle, and my dad appears in the doorway. His eyes land on the small pile of cans, and his exhale sounds like relief.

"I'll take both cans of tuna," he says, already reaching for them.

He knows I hate canned fish. I hate seafood in general actually. I grin.

"Fine by me but I'm claiming the corn and we can share the ravioli."

He raises an eyebrow. "Obviously."

I roll my eyes as he checks the rest of the cabinets, but nothing else useful turns up. We make do with what we have, heating up the ravioli on the small camping stove my dad luckily always carries in his pack. It isn't much, but the warmth of the food, the taste of something other than whatever the hell they served us at the camp, feels like a strange kind of luxury. We sit in silence while we eat, the dim light of the flashlight casting long shadows across the walls.

After we finish, we turn our attention to securing a place to sleep. The master bedroom looks like the safest option so we drag the mattress from the other room onto the floor, then push the heavy dresser against the door, forming a decent barricade. Just in case anything or anyone came wandering by in the night. A low, rhythmic thump interrupts the stillness. Something in the distance.

"Do you hear that?" I whisper, holding my breath. We both freeze, listening. The sound grows louder, unmistakable now. The steady **whup-whup-whup** of helicopter blades slice through the sky. We run to the window and peer out through the slats of the blinds. There, in the distance, a dark helicopter hovers low, sweeping slowly over the treetops before banking and disappearing into the horizon.

Dad squints after it.

"It's probably heading toward one of the survival camps."

CHAPTER 10
VIOLET

A sudden bang jolts me awake, my heart immediately pounds like a drum in my chest. Another crash, louder this time. I bolt upright on the mattress.

"Dad!" I hiss, reaching out and shaking him hard. "Dad, wake up!"

He groans, groggy and disoriented, rubbing his face as he sits up. "What the hell…"

Thud… thud…thud…

Something was definitely on the other side of the door. The dresser we'd pushed in front of it rattled slightly. I rush toward my bag, grabbing my blade. My dad grabs the shotgun we'd found, then chugs the last bit of water from a bottle as if it was coffee and he was late for work. He pumps the shotgun with a heavy click-clack.

I shoot him a look. "Seriously? That's loud as hell!"

He shrugs, whispering back with a smirk, "What? Maybe they just heard me snoring."

I glare at him. "They probably did."

He gives me a guilty smile before hustling toward the barricaded door. "Let's do this quietly. If we're lucky, it's just a few."

The dresser clatters to the floor. The door creaks open an inch and that's when the first one shoves its way in. My dad kicks it back, sending it stumbling.

"Guess we're not lucky."

I lunge, blade out, jamming it into the side of its skull. It drops like a sack of rocks. One by one, they continue pushing through the door, arms flailing, teeth snapping. Eight of them. I counted fast. My dad blows one away with the shotgun, the blast deafening in the tight space.

"*Sound*, Dad." I snap through clenched teeth, swinging my blade into the next one's neck.

"Sorry!" He shouts.

I duck as another one reaches for me. I shove it hard against the wall and stab it clean through the eye. Blood splatters my jacket. Great another blood stain. Dad grabs one by the collar and shoves the barrel under its chin before pulling the trigger. A wet spray hits the ceiling. The last Deadhead charges at my dad, snarling and twitching. He steps aside at the last second, and I finish it with a sharp thrust of my knife. Silence returns, dense and suffocating.

Dad wipes his forehead with his sleeve, panting. "I did not think I snored that loud."

I let out a breathless, nervous laugh. "Next time, sleep quieter."

Breakfast is the two cans of tuna and a can of ravioli from last night's loot. Dad opens them with his pocket knife while I wipe my blade clean. The tuna smells so sharp and salty, I almost gag while I eat my Chef Boyardee. We sit at the kitchen table like it is a normal morning. As if our fallen family members would pad down the hallway at any moment and join us. Afterward, I slip into the bathroom and close the door. I stand in front of the bathroom mirror, slowly weaving my fingers through my black hair as I proceed to braid it. The motion comes to me automatically, something I used to do before everything went to hell. Loop, pull, loop. I find a few pony tails in the drawer, use one for the braid and put the rest in my pocket. My eyes meet my reflection, what is left of it anyways. Hollow cheeks, dirt smudged across my skin, dried blood along my jaw. I barely recognize myself, or maybe I do, maybe that's what scares me, that this is just who I am now. It hits me all over again. This *is* life now. Not high school. Not college. Not sneaking texts to Ryder when I shouldn't. There is no more hanging out with Kate, and

Grace. No more coworkers. No more hearing Jane's cute little giggle. They were gone. *Everything* was gone. Now all we've become is blood, running, hiding, killing, looting and surviving. I blink hard, trying to shove the thoughts down, and look away from the mirror.

I grab one of the half-full water bottles from the counter, twist the cap off and pour a bit into my hands. The water is ice cold. I suck in a sharp breath as I splash it over my face, scrubbing at the grime and sweat and blood that clings to me like it now belongs there. I am shaking, but I have no clue if it's from the cold or everything that has been lost.

I pivot towards the toilet and lift the lid off the tank, dipping a clean rag into the water. It isn't exactly a luxury spa, but it is something. I wipe down my arms, neck, even my jacket. Every stroke makes me feel a little less like a walking corpse. Then I use the toilet, and just stand there for a second, leaning on the sink, breathing and trying my best to wash my hands with no running water. We still don't know how this infection is spread.

My braid rests over one shoulder, still damp on the ends. I stare at the mirror again. I don't know who I am becoming. I know I have to keep going. Even if all I can do right now is braid my hair and pretend that act has some kind of profound meaning. As I step back into the hallway, I see my dad emerging from the other bathroom, a few rolls tucked under his arm and his sleeves wet. We meet in the kitchen, and he holds up the toilet paper like a prize.

"I remember a few years ago, people fought over this stuff in grocery stores. Now it's just free for the taking."

I snort. "We're basically royalty now."

He grins and tosses his haul into his backpack. I carry the remaining water bottles from the basement to the Jeep, lining them along the back seat and floor. Then I pull the map from my backpack and set off in the direction I last saw my dad.

He is in the living room, digging through drawers and cabinets. I spread the map across the dusty coffee table and flatten the creases with my palms.

"We need to figure out the route to Banff," I say.

He looks up from a drawer filled with loose bullets and screws, "You sure about Banff?"

"Yes," I answer without hesitating. "If Ryder told us to go there, then I think we should. That helicopter last night was heading west. That has to mean something."

My dad leans over the map, scanning the back roads and highways. "We could follow the 1A west. It'll be slower, but less likely to be blocked by the military or the sick."

I nod, tracing the path with my finger. "That works. I just… I need to find him, Dad."

He's quiet for a moment, a slight twitch in his jaw. "What if he's not the same person anymore?"

"I'm not the same either," I said softly. "None of us are."

He sighs through his nose, "Alright. We'll go."

I carry the extra gas from Ryder, pouring it carefully into the tank. My dad keeps watch while I hold the funnel steady. Once that is done, we find a few abandoned cars scattered near what is left of their respective driveways. Using the siphoning tube, he'd salvaged earlier; we drain what we can. As he works on the last car, a low groan rang out from the trees. A Deadhead wanders out alone, slow, dragging a bullet wounded leg behind it. My dad pulls his hunting knife from his belt and waits, letting it come close before driving the blade up under its chin with precision. The body drops silently onto the grass. He wipes the knife clean on his jeans and looks at me.

"We've got enough gas now," I say, my voice steady. "Let's go before we lose daylight."

He tilts his head in agreement, putting the extra gas in the back. I stand outside, the morning air sharp in my lungs, and take one last look at the house. From a distance, it almost appears untouched, just a quiet, weathered home tucked away from the world. The chipped paint and sagging porch don't tell the full story. I let my eyes linger a moment longer, trying to process the weight of what we have witnessed. The grief hovers just out of reach, something I don't have time to feel. With a steady breath, I walk toward the Jeep, leaving behind the ruin, the silence, and whatever pieces of the past were still clinging to the shadows. Then I climb in beside him, pull the door shut, and unfold the map once more as we drive off.

A few hours pass. The wheels hum steadily beneath us as we roll down the cracked backroads, the military jeep jostling over uneven patches of asphalt. Outside the window, the world looks empty—abandoned cars line the ditches like forgotten skeletons, their doors left ajar or windows shattered. Figures stumble aimlessly in the fields beyond, slow and broken, their movements barely human.

No birds.

No distant engines.

Only wind and the occasional shadow of something moving in the trees. My dad adjusts his grip on the wheel.

"Do you think the military pulled everyone out of the town? From the farms, the cities too?"

I look at the lifeless scenery, scanning for any flicker of normalcy. "Maybe. Or they didn't get the chance."

His eyes narrow as he keeps them on the road. "Feels like everyone's already dead. That's why the bombs and missiles stopped. Nothing left to kill."

I don't respond. A weight settles over my chest like a heavy blanket. He might be right. I just don't want to believe it. *Everyone is dead.* Ryder isn't though and that gives me some semblance of hope.

A few minutes pass in a lull until my dad reaches toward the center console.

"Huh. There's something in here."

He pulls out a dusty CD and squints at the label.

"Military issue. Looks like some kind of classic rock mix."

He slides the disc into the player. Static crackles for a second, then a heavy guitar riff explodes through the speakers, dark, gritty, and familiar. I sit up straighter, my heart doing this weird skip.

"Wait…" The words quivering out, recognizing it instantly. "No way."

Dead I am the one, exterminating son… the voice growls through the jeep, loud and unapologetic.

"Dragula," I whisper to myself, a surprised smile tugging at the corners of my mouth.

Ryder had made me listen to this song years ago. Back when things were still okay, before deployment, before everything fell apart. I remember him grinning behind the wheel of his rusted-out Chevy,

"It's not about monsters. It's about driving. Slamming into the back of your Dragula. The gearshift is the Dragula. Down-shifting. Getting power. Going fast as hell."

He always had a way of finding poetry in mayhem. I lean back, letting the beat hit my chest. For a second, the world outside doesn't exist. No ash, no ruins, no undead. Just the roar of Rob Zombie and Ryder's voice echoing in my head like a ghost wrapped in sound. My fingers tap harder against the door as I mouth the lyrics, half-laughing to myself.

My dad glances at me sideways, raising an eyebrow. "I didn't know you knew this song."

I smirk. "Yeah…someone made sure I'd never forget it."

His expression softens just a little before his eyes drift back to the road. The music surges as the chorus kicks in, the jeep rumbling beneath us like it is feeding off the song's energy. I let myself fall into it, feeling something close to alive. Ryder had once said this song made him feel untouchable. For a second, it almost made me feel that way too. My dad turns down the volume suddenly.

"Look," he says, pointing to the right side of the road.

A sun-faded sign leans at an angle.

Survival Camp. Banff Directional Post 2km.

The arrow underneath points straight ahead.

"Do you think it's still there?" I ask, sitting up straighter.

"Only one way to find out."

We barely travel another hundred meters before having to slam on the brakes. A massive pileup blocks the road Cars are crumpled together like toys in a toddler's tantrum. Some are scorched, others flipped completely. Doors are flung open. There are busted tires and shards of glass coating the pavement. Some still have the undead trapped within them. Their hands grasping at the windows as we drive by.

"Jesus." My dad mutters, pulling the Jeep to a halt.

I look to the left. The road beyond the divider is mostly clear.

"We could try the other side," I say.

A quiet agreement ripples through the angle of his chin, reversing a little before carefully turning into the opposite lane. The pavement is cracked and overgrown, barely wide enough to navigate. The drive is bumpy, our tires bouncing hard against broken asphalt and potholes. My teeth click together with each jolt. One particularly sharp turn throws me against the door.

"Okay! Slow down," I snap, gripping the handlebar above the window.

"I am slowing down!" he replies, swerving gently.

After twenty minutes of dodging debris, we crest a hill and the view steals the very breath from our lungs. Canmore lay ahead, or what was left of it.

Buildings collapsed in on themselves, their skeletal remains reaching toward the sky like begging hands. Smoke still curled from blackened rooftops. Craters mark the earth. Scorches on the earth from the missile strikes, at least a dozen litter the town. Cars are flipped, smashed into storefronts or stacked like barricades that had failed. The road itself is torn up, massive chunks lifted and twisted, making it completely impassable for the jeep.

"Holy hell." My dad whispers.

I stare, unable to look away, "It's like the ground exploded."

"We can't drive through that," he says, shaking his head. "No way."

"Then we walk."

He turns to me, mouth drawn in a tight line, "You really want to head toward that?"

"We don't have another option. If Banff is still there, we need to get to it. Ryder could be waiting there."

The words hang between us like a challenge. He looks away for a moment, jaw clenched.

"You really think he's still alive out there?"

"I have to."

My dad lets out a slow breath. "Alright. We pull the jeep into the tree line, keep it covered in case we need it again."

We find a small break in the brush and park it deep behind a thicket, tossing a tarp of tree debris over it and laying branches across the top. Once we are sure it is hidden, we strap on our packs and trek toward the edges of Canmore. As the ruins loom closer, my dad breaks the silence.

"We could scavenge a little, see if anything's left."

"I don't know." I say adjusting the strap on my backpack. "We could lose daylight. We're already on foot."

"Supplies might be running thin. Even one can of food could help."

He isn't wrong. I just don't want to step any deeper into a graveyard than we already have.

"We'll check a few places," I say, glancing toward the jagged remains of what used to be a Tim Hortons. "Quickly. Then we keep moving. Banff's not going to wait for us."

We weave between the ruins, bending around abandoned carts and glinting shards as we approach what is left of a Save-On-Foods. The windows have been shattered, and the entrance hangs crooked on its hinges, creaking slightly in the breeze. I can see faint streaks of dried blood on the automatic door sensors.

"Are we clear?"

I step ahead, knife drawn, scanning each aisle from behind shelves, "Looks like it."

The place has been picked through, but not stripped completely. We find a few dented cans. Black beans, chicken soup, peaches, plus a case of bottled water shoved behind a collapsed cereal display. I stuff what I can into my pack, wiping dust off a can of tomato sauce with my sleeve. It's weird, the things that feel valuable now. Not phones or clothes. Just food and supplies.

We don't linger.

Not a sound stirs.

Even the air feels frozen, thick with waiting.

We leave even faster than we arrived and make our way toward the Shoppers across the lot, half its sign missing. Just **SHO** remains, hanging crooked as if the building itself is as exhausted as we are. With my knife ready, we move forward, the air thick with ash and stillness.

Inside the Shoppers is worse than the grocery store. It is darker, more shelves have been overturned, and the floor is littered with packaging and broken tiles. The smell is heavy. Mildew, rot, and something sour underneath. As we venture deeper, I catch movement near the pharmacy wall. Two former employees teeter out from behind a collapsed aisle, red vests still half-hanging from their shoulders, name tags smeared with blood. Their limbs twitch and their jaws snap at the air as they come toward us, moaning through ruined throats. I don't hesitate. My knife slides clean through the temple of the first as it attacks me. It collapses against a shelf that gives way under the weight, scattering cough syrup and gauze. My dad handles the second with his hunting knife, driving it up through the underside of the chin before kicking the body off. We breathe heavily, listening intently but nothing else stirs.

"We're good," I say, wiping the blade on my jeans. I crouch behind the customer service desk and pull the map from my pack, flattening it against the scratched-up counter. Dad leans over my shoulder, eyes narrowing.

"We're here…" I trace the faded line with my finger. "If we take the lower pass, we might make it close to Banff by nightfall. Maybe, if we move fast."

"Do you think the survival camps are still there?" He asks, not looking at me.

"I don't know," I admit. "But we need to find out."

He sighs, rubbing a hand down his face. "Then let's stop wasting time."

We leave the store with heavier packs and tighter grips on our weapons. The silence returns the second the doors swing shut behind us. Still, something in me has shifted, the adrenaline and momentum finally kicking in.

After about four and a half hours of walking, my legs start aching in that deep, burning way that never fully goes away anymore. My boots are starting to rub raw against my heels, and every step feels heavier than the last. We stop at the edge of a narrow clearing, crouching beneath the shade of a leaning pine tree. My dad pulls off his pack and tosses me a bottle of water. I catch it with ever stiffening fingers. Dust floats in unmoving shafts of light, as we chew through a couple of granola bars from the Shoppers stash. They taste like cardboard, but at least they fill the hollow in my stomach.

"You remember that time we got lost hiking when I was ten?" I ask between bites of what was left of a granola bar.

My dad lets out a short laugh through his nose. "Yeah. You refused to turn around, and said the map was wrong."

"It was wrong," I say, a small grin tugging at my lips. "You trusted that dumb tourist trail app."

He smirks, shaking his head. "We ended up following a deer trail for two hours before realizing we were walking in a circle. Your mom was ready to strangle me."

I smile, even though the memory stings a little. "She made us hot chocolate when we got home. Like we were brave survivors or something."

"She always made things feel okay," he bows his head slightly, a ghost of a smile tugging at the corners of his lips.

My chin lowers, a soft surrender. "Felix fell asleep in the car, remember? His head kept knocking against the window."

Dad chuckles under his breath. "He had that tiny backpack he insisted on carrying. It had one juice box and a toy dinosaur in it."

"The triceratops," I reminisce, laughing softly. "He thought it would protect us from bears."

A heaviness settles between us, unspoken but there. Felix's absence sat in my chest like a stone. I didn't have to ask if Dad was thinking about him too. It was all over his face.

"He was so little," I whisper. "Too little."

Dad doesn't say anything, just looks out over the broken hills and beautiful mountains. I watch his throat tighten as he gulps, then looks away.

I breathe in deep, trying to push down the ache in my chest. "I wish I could go back to that hike. Even if we were lost. Just to hear him laughing again."

His voice comes quiet. "Me too, kiddo."

The quiet between us is heavier after that. It isn't uncomfortable, just full of things we don't say anymore. We continue walking, the terrain slowly turning rugged as we advance deeper into the mountains. Trees close in on both sides like sentries. The wind whispers through the branches above, and every now and then, I think I hear something or someone moving just out of sight.

About twenty minutes pass, we turn a bend in the trail and only to meet a jagged old sign half-buried in the dirt. Most of the paint is peeled off, and the metal is twisted like it had been torn by something massive. I step closer, brushing off moss and dirt until I can read what is left.

"Survivor Camp. Banff Outpost," I read aloud, my throat going dry. The arrow beneath it points uphill, barely hanging on.

My pulse quickens. "It's real. Ryder wasn't lying...this place exists!"

We follow the trail up, hearts thudding louder than our footsteps. As the hill crests, I stop so abruptly my dad nearly runs into me. Before us is devastation. The remains of the outpost are nothing but jagged, burnt rubble. Buildings are flattened, hotels torn down, scorch marks everywhere like the place had been struck dumb by the blasts. Smoke still clinging to the air, sour and sharp. Something metallic twists in the wind with a slow, eerie screech. Then I see the sea of bodies. Moving, groaning, shambling in a tangled mess at the bottom of the hill just beyond the wreckage. There has to be hundreds. Maybe more. Their moans reverberating up through the mountains like a death rattle.

"Oh my god…" I breathe.

My dad steps in front of me, hand reaching back instinctively like he used to when I was little, keeping me behind him. They are all at the bottom of the slope. Clumped together in a twisted, seething mass. Some crawling over others. A few are impaled on jagged rebar or twisted steel, limbs twitching uselessly. One has its leg completely crushed under a collapsed wall, still trying to claw its way out with what is left of its fingers. It looked like they had fallen, or had been driven there.

"Jesus, that's the most I've ever seen in one place, they must've swarmed the camp… then got pulled in by the sound, maybe explosions… or gunfire?"

Dad scans the wreckage slowly, jaw clenched. "Could've been the final stand. Someone tried to hold the line… and the noise drew them like flies."

A few of the infected are staring up toward us now, sniffing the air or sensing the shift in the wind. One lets out a low, rasping growl, and the others twitch in response which makes my stomach drop.

"We should move. They're going to notice us."

Dad steps back a few feet, hand tightening on the shotgun slung over his shoulder. "We can't go down there, not without getting torn apart. We need height and most importantly…distance."

I pull the map from my pack and spread it out on a relatively flat patch of rock. My hands shake slightly as I trace the path with my finger.

"If we cut east… through this ridgeline," I say, pointing, "We might be able to loop around the horde and get into another part of Banff from the north. There's still a trail system here, if it's not completely destroyed."

Dad crouches beside me, studying it. "We'll burn daylight getting around that way."

"Do we have another choice?"

He hesitates then signals his agreement with a quick motion. "Alright. But if the path is blocked, we fall back. We're not dying up here for ghosts."

My chest tightens. Ryder could've been down there. Could've been in that camp. His last words still echo in my mind.

I'll find you.

I swallow the lump in my throat. "We have to try."

Dad stands up, offering me his hand and I take it. "Then let's get moving. Quietly."

We back away from the ridge, the sound of the horde growing fainter as we scramble uphill again, heading deeper into the wild. The trees swallow us whole and behind us, the dead keep reaching. Ahead of us, I can only hope something worth finding still remains.

CHAPTER 11

VIOLET

Banff's northern side peaks over the horizon like a wound in the forest, smoke curling in the distance and the faint scent of ash hanging in the air. I have to see if anyone made it. Maybe I'm looking for Ryder. Maybe I'm just looking for anyone.

The trees grow dense, branches claw at our jackets as we keep low, slipping between shadows. The trail under our feet had once been a hiking path, probably popular back when people cared about trails. Every so often, we can hear the horde behind us. Groaning, stumbling, scraping through what is left of the town. We weren't far enough.

I feel it before I hear it. A vibration that moves through my boots and into my chest. A deep, guttural growl, like the earth itself is warning us.

I freeze. "What was that?"

My dad's face goes pale. He doesn't speak. He doesn't have to. A massive grizzly bear emerges through the underbrush, its fur caked with dirt and streaked red with blood. Perhaps its own but unlikely. It lumbers forward on thick paws, sniffing the air, head swaying, a growl rumbling low and long. I stare. I don't know what to do. I was not fucking trained to handle this type of situation. My dad slowly pumps the shotgun, the click loud in the still air. He looks at me, lips forming the words, '*Stay calm*'. Pointing at me, then two fingers to his eyes. '*Watch me*'. We back away, inching downhill, trying not to startle it.

No eye contact.

No sudden moves.

"Hey bear," my dad calls, voice calm but loud enough to carry. "We're not prey."

The grizzly grunts, tilting its massive head as if it understood him but didn't care. It doesn't move, it just stands there, huffing, pacing, and watching. We keep backing up until we hit a slope and then my foot catches on a rock. I tumble backward, hitting the ground hard and letting out a grunt that echoes off the trees. The bear rears up with a thunderous roar. My dad fires once, not to hit but to scare. He tumbles down the hill after me, then hauls me up by my jacket, his eyes scanning my face.

"You, okay?"

I nod, even though my knees scream and my elbow throbs.

"Good, let's go!"

We don't wait another second. We just start running. The forest lights up with sound. Not just the bear but now there's moaning, groaning, cracking twigs; the unmistakable sound of the undead heading our way. I look left. Distant shadows sway. Faces, bodies, all rotting and hungry. We had arrived back at the horde. Another roar from the bear splits the air.

Great...of course it's following us.

" I have an idea."

I look at the forest and then to the growing horde. Then I scream. Like I was a leading *'final girl'* from one of my favorite horror movies. It is deafening. Tearing through the trees like a razor, sharp enough to slice the silence clean in half. My breath catches in my throat, heart lurching. The dead jerk their heads in unison, their twisted faces snapping toward the noise like puppets on strings. Their steps are synchronized, shuffling and stumbling along. I was right, they *are* drawn to sound, like moths hurling themselves into open flame. My dad catches on instantly, a half-smile crossing his face. Joining me in the cathartic release while simultaneously slamming a rock against a tree, drawing even more attention. The grizzly barrels after us, just a few hundred feet behind.

Then, like we'd scripted it, the bear lets out another thunderous roar that echoes through the trees. The bear is huge, its' roar is deep, primal, and earth-shaking. In the next breath, it bolts straight into the sea of the dead. The force of the bear's charge sends Deadheads flying like broken mannequins. Bones cracking and rotting limbs torn from cadavers. The grizzly swipes with massive blood-caked paws, splitting skulls like melons, its jaws clamping down on whatever it can catch. Snarls and groans tangle together into a horrific symphony.

For a moment, it looks like the bear might win. It rips one undead in half, sends another sailing into a tree, crushes three beneath its sheer weight. But the horde keeps coming. They swarm its legs, crawl up its back, latching onto anything they can bite. Blood sprays. The bear roars again but this time in agony. It thrashes wildly, shaking off a few, but more climb on. Their numbers are relentless. Dozens overwhelm it, dragging the beast down beneath a tide of clawing, snapping bodies. That's when I notice some of the ones who haven't reached the bear. Their heads turn, noses twitching, blackened teeth bared. Eyes like hollow pits locked onto us. Hungry.

"They see us," I breathe, already taking a step back.

The last thing I see before we bolt is the bear's massive form buried under a writhing mass of the dead, still fighting, still roaring. Without hesitation we run. Not a thought, not a breath, just instinct. My boots pound the earth, lungs burning as twigs snap beneath our feet and branches claw at my jacket. We don't dare look back. The snarls behind us are too close. We don't stop running until the snarls behind us have faded into the forest, swallowed by the frenzy we left behind. Either the bear distracted them long enough or we have finally outrun them. I double over, hands on my knees, gasping. Dad drops beside a tree, chest heaving. For a long moment, neither of us speak. Just the wind and the sound of blood thundering in my ears.

"We lost them," I manage between gulps of air.

He wipes sweat from his brow with the back of his hand. "For now."

I don't respond. Instead, I drop to my knees and started searching the ground, my fingers closing around the first flat stone I can find. Then another. I don't know why I am doing it at first, only that I have to. My dad watches for a beat, then joins me without a word. He doesn't ask what I am doing. He just understands. We work quietly, side by side, choosing rocks with weight and shape, stones that will hold steady against the wind. Each piece feels deliberate, like we are building a headstone for a town that had been alive just a few days ago and now… was gone. One by one, we lay them out, shaping the letters with rough edges and trembling hands. Dust clings to our skin, our nails blackened, knees pressed into gravel as the words take form:

BANFF GONE

I sit back on my heels, staring at it.
"Someone needs to know," I exhale.

He needs to know I was here.

" Someone will. Thanks to you. Good job kiddo." he says, patting my shoulder. "Now let's get back to the jeep."

We don't linger. There is nothing left to search, no more survivors to call out for. Just the departed behind us and a long road ahead. We turn our backs to the smoking wreckage that used to be Banff and start the five-hour trek back to Canmore. The mountains loom larger now, their edges jagged against the gray sky. The trees lean in close, casting shadows that dance like whispers. Every branch snap makes my pulse jump. Although my legs burn and my shoulders ache from my pack, we just keep moving. Eventually, we reach the jeep. Still hidden, untouched. A small, improbable victory.

I open the passenger door and pull out the folded provincial map. I lay it across the hood like it holds the answer to something cosmic. My eyes scan the creases, my breath coming out in a sharp huff. I scratch my head, frustration boiling up.

"So… where the fuck do we go now?"

My dad doesn't look up from the map. "Watch your language."

I scoff. "I'm out of places to go, Dad. We've crossed off every option. Do you think we have enough gas to make it back through Jasper and into BC? I know it's a long haul, but once summer ends, I don't want to be stuck in Alberta. Not when winter hits."

He runs a hand through his hair, eyes tracing the map. "That's not a bad idea. Jasper was mostly torched after last summer's wildfire, which means fewer people. The military might've skipped it."

He nudges me aside to get a closer look, his finger trailing along the winding roads. "We could backtrack a bit…take the old route up and cut west. If we leave early, we might get halfway there by tomorrow night."

"Except there's a goddamn horde down the street," I say, folding my arms. "Sleeping anywhere near here is asking for death."

He looks at me, pauses, then sighs. "Yeah… you're right."

I try not to grin, but a small flicker of satisfaction sparks in my chest. Until reality settles back in.

"Okay," he continues, hunched over the map. "We've got food, water, one blanket, a full tank, and some extra gas cans. Let's hit this town here, it's a small town about three hours out. That should put us far from the horde. Then we can solidify a proper plan."

He folds the map, and tucks it away.

"Okay, let's gear up to leave." I say, giving Canmore one last look over my shoulder.

I honestly can't believe it's gone. As we start to drive, I reflect on the moments when we were here as a family and how I wished I had gotten the chance to take Jane. She would have loved the trees and mountains, if only I hadn't worked so much. I wipe a tear away and start to think of all the people who lived there who had no idea, and how we didn't see any survivors, not even *one*. All those people. All those lives. Just...erased. Like they'd never existed. The trees would grow back and forget us, too.

I had seen distinct military uniforms in the mess of corpses, but that didn't mean anything. Most faces were torn beyond recognition. Just masses of blood and ruined flesh. I kept telling myself I would've felt something if he was gone. I would've *known,* but what if I didn't? I hadn't even known he was alive all this time.

I will find him. I have to believe he is still out there. Still breathing. Still waiting, because if he isn't….

I don't let myself finish that thought. I close my eyes instead. At least in dreamland *everyone* is alive.

CHAPTER 12

RYDER

"It says Banff gone, you dumbass," I say low, smacking the back of Sinclair's head with just enough force to make my point.

"Ow…yeah, no shit," he grumbles, rubbing the spot. "I was just trying to lighten the mood, man."

"Does that mean we have nowhere to go now?" Teresa asks quietly, her arms wrapped protectively around her son.

Her voice cracks a little, and that did more damage than any announcement ever could. I look around, taking in what is left of the place. Flattened buildings, scorched ground, shattered glass. I'd only been here a few times before I got deployed. Now it looks like a postcard from hell.

"Let's regroup," I say, forcing some kind of authority into my voice. "Figure out our next move."

I walk a few steps away and sit down hard on a chunk of concrete, pressing my hands into my hair like I can squeeze the answers out of my skull.

Was that a message from Violet? Was she trying to warn me? Had she even made it to Banff at all? Maybe the sign had always been there, maybe she saw it and turned around. Maybe she never even went.

My thoughts spiral faster than I can catch them.

"Hey," Hawthorne says gently, sinking down next to me. "You're spiraling, bro."

"No shit."

"We could stay here tonight, regroup in the morning, or we go back the way we came. Either way…"

"Either way, I still don't know what the fuck I'm doing," I snap, then sigh. "I just want to find her. That's all I've wanted since day one. But now there's people…like, *actual people*. Counting on us. *On me.* And I'm out here falling apart like it's my first day on the job."

Hawthorne's expression softens, "If you're worried about Violet… don't be. She's strong. If she saw what we saw, she probably bounced."

I look up toward the sun, squinting. Then Kate steps into the light, arms crossed, the wind catching the edge of her jacket.

"I might have an idea."

Hawthorne raises an eyebrow. "Please tell me it doesn't involve prayer or cannibalism."

Kate ignores him. "Do you guys have a provincial map or something? I know my way around here. If Banff is gone, there might be better odds heading west towards B.C. They might have something left, or even smaller outposts."

I glance at Hawthorne. He glances at me.

In unison we speak, "There's a map on the bus."

The bus's door creaks open, and we file in one by one, the stale air thick with sweat and exhaustion. Kate unfurls the crumpled provincial map across the dash of the bus. The thing looked like it had seen two wars already but it would do.

"Alright," Kate says, tracing her finger along the faded roads. "We're here. Just outside of Banff. If we head west, we can take the Trans-Canada Highway through Golden and maybe even toward Revelstoke if the roads aren't completely fucked. B.C's got more forest cover, smaller towns…better odds of not running into the dead. Plus, we don't want to be here when the -40 winter starts in a few months."

Sinclair leans over, brow furrowed. "You think we'll find anything in those towns?"

"Maybe not people, but supplies, maybe fuel…gear. Most people fled the cities, but small-town grocery stores and gas stations might still have stuff. We'd have to sweep fast."

"Canmore first then," I say. "We stock up. Food, meds, fuel. Anything that'll keep us moving. If Banff is torched, chances are a lot of people skipped this place. We might get lucky."

"Big if," Hawthorne says, pulling out a protein bar and taking a slow bite. "But hell, why not. We're due for a win."

The rations are running low. Like, dangerously low. I lean in closer, eyeing the terrain between us and Golden. A couple narrow passes, steep in some places. Rockfalls, blocked roads, hell, even a downed bridge could screw us, but it was a path, and we need one of those right now.

"We'll head to B.C at first light," I say, fingers tapping the map. "One more night here. We sweep Canmore in teams tonight. Grab what we can. Then west. No detours."

"And the people?" Sinclair asks, jerking a thumb toward the back of the bus, where the rest of the survivors are huddled in the dim light.

"They stay on the bus," I say. "We can't drag civilians through every dark alley in town. We scout, clear, and bring supplies back."

Kate taps her finger on a cluster of storefronts on the north end. "Small shops, maybe a pharmacy. Could be meds still tucked away in the back rooms. I can sweep there by myself."

I shake my head, stepping in. "Nah, we'll check it together. I want eyes on anything medical, and you know this town better than I do."

She looks up at me, surprised. "Alright. You and me then."

"I'll hit the grocery with Sinclair, maybe fill up a few shopping carts" Hawthorne says, cracking his neck like he is about to lift a truck. "Food first. Always food."

I point toward the west end of town. "There's an outdoor gear shop there. If it hasn't been blown up, we might find camping stoves, blankets, fuel. Stuff we can't live without once we're out of this bus."

Sinclair leans in. "You sure about pairing off? What if we run into something we can't handle?"

"We split up, but we don't disappear," I say, looking at each of them. "If anything goes sideways, *one gunshot.* Just one. We hear it, we drop what we're doing and regroup here. No questions."

We all look at each other for a moment. Silent but united.

No more waiting.

No more reacting.
Time to move with purpose.

Hold on, darlin. I'm coming.

I look around at the remaining bus occupants a last time. They all look back at me worried.

"We'll be back before the sun's fully up." I glance at Wilson once more, his steady gaze meeting mine. "Be careful, old man. And keep them safe. Remember one gunshot."

"I've got this," Wilson says, his voice as rough as the world around us.

We step off the bus and I clap Hawthorne on his shoulder. "Let's move out. Me and Kate pharmacy and camping store. You and Sinclair grocery store. Keep it tight, keep it quiet."

Hawthorne stretches his neck while cracking his knuckles. "Food, gear, and maybe some meds. Whatever we can get. You ready for this mission Sinclair?"

"Hell yeah!"

"Hey, while you're getting food, grab some rice or cereal. Easy snacks. If we find a camping stove, we can make tons of rice for everyone." Kate adds.

"Fuck, rice sounds good," Sinclair says, simply craving anything that isn't a damn protein bar.

"Good idea, Kate. Oh, and no condoms or lube this time, boys."

Kate gives me a confused look, clearly not in on the joke, but laughs anyway. Hawthorne throws me a middle finger in response, but I just chuckle. It is always fun messing with him. Kate and I watch the boys head off before I turn to face her. She checks her weapon one more time, eyes steady and calm.

"Ready when you are."
I grin. "Let's go."

CHAPTER 13

RYDER

The front door hangs open, swinging like a broken jaw. The inside is a mess. Overturned shelves, ceiling panels on the floor, and half the place looks like it has been shelled. I press my back to the wall beside the door and knock gently.

A single Dybbuk stirs, stumbling near the back, dragging a busted leg behind it.

That's weird, why aren't there more of them?

I put the thing down fast and beeline for the rear where they keep all the important bottles. Kate grabs a basket lying on its side, dirtied with dust and God-knows-what. I hold my flashlight and start looking. I end up just sweeping everything into it. Antibiotics, painkillers, gauze rolls, antiseptics, bandages, burn cream, cough meds, syringes, anything that isn't expired or open.

"We had to do basic medic training when I was with the boys, but after we got attacked in Afghan...I had to do more than most. Is there another basket?"

She hands me a second one without a word. I keep loading.

"Why were you in that storage closet, Kate?"

She freezes, staring at me. "Why would you ask that?"

"Figured since we knew each other, you might feel safer talking to me. I saw the pills all over the ground."

She doesn't answer right away. Then, without looking at me, she snaps, "How long were you in town?"

"The night before it all went to hell. I even went to Lou's Diner."

She huffs. "This is going to be a long conversation, Ryder. Are you sure you're ready for it?"

"We literally have nothing but time."

Kate exhales shakily. I keep digging through drawers with the flashlight in my mouth as she speaks.

"I was at work. I went out to set up outside playtime, and then...My house got bombed."

"Outside playtime?" I peek over the counter.

She half-smiles, sad and hollow. "I run a daycare…*ran.* In-home daycare. All the kids…" Her voice breaks, and she drops to her knees holding her face. "They died."

I kneel beside her instantly. "Kate, hey. I'm sorry. That's not your fault"

"Why did I live? Why me? They were just kids... they deserved more than that."

I stand, trying to keep my own emotions in check. "This world isn't for kids anymore. If they'd made it, who knows what horrors they'd have seen. Hell, even Lil' Dion has seen shit that no kid should ever experience."

She stands too, face darkening with something dangerous.

"Violet's daughter was in my house when it got hit. So that's why I hid and tried to take all those pills. Luckily, I didn't, but I couldn't face the truth of what had happened…"

I can only blink as it feels like the floor is falling out from under me.

"She had a *daughter*?" I turn away, gripping my hair, and slamming my fist into a nearby shelf. "How old?"

"Three."

Three. Jesus. Well, that answered my question. *It wasn't mine.*

"She never heard from you. She said you were going to send her letters. You didn't. Then six months later you died."

I turn, fists clenched, fury radiating. "I fucking did. I wrote Violet every goddamn month while I was deployed. I called when I could and it always went to fucking voicemail. I poured everything into those letters. I did everything I could from a fucking war zone."

My knees give. I sink to the floor, hands on the back of my neck, breath shaking.

Kate crouches next to me. "She never got them. Not a single one. She was heartbroken, but then Jeremy came along and at first, he was sweet, but after she got pregnant…"

I don't even look up at my hands resting on my knees. "Go on…"

She clears her throat, swallowing back her own pain. "He *changed*. Started calling her names. Told her she was lazy, ugly. I saw bruises sometimes when we met for coffee. She always made excuses…but I knew."

My heart is a stone in my chest and my ears ring. Violet had been hurt. Betrayed, alone, and I hadn't been there to stop it. For the first time since making my decision to join the military I am filled with regret. My vision blurs at the edges. Like my brain can't handle everything hitting me all at once. My knuckles hit the tile harder than I mean them to, the basket I've been filling tips and spills across the dusty floor. Pill bottles clattering, bandages unrolling like ribbons.

"She was alone. She needed me."

Kate doesn't say anything. Just stands a few feet away, giving me space, like she knows I am unraveling, and I suppose that's because I am. Full-on crashing out actually. My chest feels like it is caving in.

"How long," I croak, barely recognizing my own voice. "How long after I left did she get with him?"

Kate hesitates. "About…one year. Maybe less."

A laugh tears out of me but it isn't humor. It is bitter and broken.

"One year. Fuck." I wipe at my face even though there aren't tears yet, just sweat, dirt and shame. "Was she just…trying to forget me? Did she think I ghosted her? That I didn't care?"

"You died." Kate says, and I can hear the strain in her voice.

"No," I shook my head, gripping the back of my neck hard enough to hurt. "No, I wrote. I even sent her a stupid postcard from the base in case she thought the others were fake…."

"Where did you send them?".

"To her house," I say without thinking. Then I freeze.

Arthur

I look up slowly, like it takes a whole minute for the thought to fully land in my skull.

"Her dad was the one checking the mail. He always was a wannabe soldier, control freak, always had to be the one calling the shots."

"Her dad showed her a letter saying you died and your body could not be returned to Canada." Kate's eyes widen like she realizes it too, "You think… he kept the letters from her and lied that you were dead?"

"**FUCKKKK**" I slam my fist into the side of the metal shelving, the sound echoing through the pharmacy. A few boxes topple off the top row, but I don't care.

"That fucking bastard told her I was dead. He's sick." He always hated me; thought I was a burnout. I bet he thought he was protecting her." I stand up fast, my breath hitching. "He let her *believe* I abandoned her."

Kate steps forward, her hand on my arm. "You need to keep it down Ryder. You didn't and deep down I think she knew, but when you're hurting that bad, you cling to whatever's in front of you."

"And that was Jeremy."

Kate nods slowly.

I swear, if I ever see Jeremy or that lying fuck Arthur … I don't even know what I'll do. Part of me wants to kill Jeremy. Part of me just wants to ask Arthur why."

"Was Jeremy with her when you saw her?" Kate asks.

"No, it was just her and her dad"

"In all honesty that might mean Jeremy is already dead."

"Well, if he is, I hope he fucking suffered, Ocean eyes didn't deserve to be treated like that, especially after she carried his…"

Bile rises up in my throat.

"I'm sorry."

I can't answer. I just stand there in the ruins of the pharmacy, surrounded by broken shelves and busted boxes and a hundred pills I can't even name. I think about ending it all here and now, she can find me in the afterlife instead and we can finally be together. My mind flashes back to when I was writing to her, pouring my feelings onto pages. Hoping she would be kicking her feet happy to read our inside jokes and me finally showering her with the love she always deserved. Only to have the reality sink in that she didn't even get *one.*

Fuck, I want to shoot everyone I see, I want to burn what's left of this pharmacy down. Fuck! I should have been there. I should have just come back. I'm going to kill him.

He carved betrayal into her soul. So no, I won't kill him. That'd be too clean. I'll peel away every lie he ever told until he drowns in the truth. I'll drag him to the edge and make sure he understands, every tear she shed, every night she thought I was dead, *is on him.* The only reason his heart will keep beating is because she'd hate me if I stopped it.

"She's out there Ryder, and we need to find her. *You* need to find her. So, let's just get these baskets back to the bus and then go to the outdoor store."

Oh…. I'll find her and when I do, I'll tell her own father lied to her.

CHAPTER 14

RYDER

Kate pulls a couple of compact stoves from under a collapsed shelf, metal clanking as she tosses them to me. I throw them into one of the four hiking backpacks we've managed to snag.

"Grab the mini propane tanks, and anything that doesn't scream *instant death.*"

We pack fast; blankets, tarps, ten compact sleeping bags, water filtration straws, a set of multitools, lighters, a flare gun with a few rounds, eight tents and a couple of heavy-duty utility knives.

Kate grins as she holds up a fire starter kit and shoves it into her pack. "Almost makes me miss summer camp."

We are zipping up the last of the bags when the sound cracks through the air.

One gunshot.

We both halt.

"Did that come from the bus?" Kate says, voice tight.

"*Shit.*" I sling two packs over my shoulders, and grab half the tents. Kate takes the last backpack, and the other four tents then we haul ass out the back door, not bothering to look back. As we round the corner near the pharmacy, we spot Sinclair and Hawthorne pushing two rusted shopping carts overflowing with supplies.

"Yo!" I shout. "Was that you guys?"

Sinclair is wide-eyed and panting. "No, we thought it was you!"

"What the hell happened?" Hawthorne stutters.

"Don't know yet. Let's move. What the hell is all that?"

"Survivor's starter pack," Sinclair replies, chin lifted, as he slaps a box of Frosted Flakes. "Cereal, rice, water, Gatorade, and some blessed beer."

"And toilet paper!" Hawthorne adds, holding a 12-pack like it's sacred scripture. "Apocalypse or not, still got to wipe."

I raise an eyebrow. "You planning on starting a toilet paper shrine?"

"Not just toilet paper," he says, rummaging through the pile. "Wipes too. Can't have just paper. Got to be thorough."

He holds up a three pack of flushable wipes.

I stifle a laugh. "Of course, it is, Captain Hygiene."

Hawthorne beams, chest puffed. "Thank you. One day the world will thank me for this."

I shake my head. "Okay let's get a move on you goons."

Our feet move before our minds catch up, running as one. Wilson is on top of the bus, rifle braced, eyes locked down the main road.

"Report!" I bark, rushing up.

He doesn't take his eyes off the distance. "East road. Horde incoming. Maybe a few minutes out."

I climb up next to him and get a glimpse. A mass of them all slow, groaning, and swaying in sync. My eyes widen.

Holy shit.

"Alright!" I shout, dropping down and turning to the group. "Let's move! Teresa, Jalen, Theo, Emily, Kian. Grab the food and supplies. Get it on the bus *now*!"

Teresa scoops up Dion rushing to grab the nearest bag. Jalen and Theo run for the carts, grabbing boxes. Emily is already throwing packs up the steps. Kian winces as he lifts a case of water with his bandaged-up arm, but doesn't stop.

"Let's go! We only have a few minutes!"

Kate is already inside, organizing supplies and making space.

"Wilson! Come on old man!" I shout scrambling up the side ladder and grabbing Wilson by the arm, and yanking him down from the roof.

The moment we are all inside, I slam the door shut and twist the lock. Everyone stares at me, eyes wide. I raise a finger to my lips, while moving my hand down.

"Shhh. Get down"

I climb into the front seat, pop the roof hatch, and slide my upper body through the opening. The wind cuts cold against my face. I raise the flare gun, aiming past the ruined barrier to the crumpled sedan half-tipped in the ditch, and fire.

FWOOSH. POP.

The flare streaks across the sky, glowing red like the settled sun before bouncing off the car's hood. A second later, the alarm shrieks to life, blaring loud and broken.

Horn.

Siren.

Horn.

Siren.

I duck back inside and pull the hatch shut. The only sound is the rasp of our collective breathing, then right on cue, the groans of the dead. Low at first. Moaning, guttural sounds that send goosebumps straight up my spine. A shuffle. A snarl. Then dozens. No, *hundreds.* The bus begins to tremble, a deep vibration through the floor like we are sitting inside a giant's heartbeat. I crouch beside the others, pressed against the cool metal wall, pistol across my lap. Feet scuff against the gravel outside. Limbs scrape along the metal siding. A hand slaps the window beside us, smearing it with dirt and blood. I can hear them breathing. Wet, labored and hungry. One slams its face into the glass with a moan so deep it sounds almost human.

We don't move.

We stay silent.

We don't even dare to breathe.

Dion, crouching beside his mom, trembles so hard his teeth chatter. Then I hear the faint hiss of liquid hitting the bus floor.

My eyes flick right and catch the dark stain spreading on his pants. The poor kid has pissed himself, and God help me, it breaks something in me. He is just a kid. He should've been learning to ride a bike, not hiding from monsters in a military bus. He clutches his mom tighter, burying his face in her chest.

She holds him close, whispering "you're okay, you're safe," and we all pretend not to hear.

I want to tell him everything is going to be okay. That I'll keep him safe. That the world hasn't ended yet, but my mouth won't open. I just sit there, fists clenched around the gun, feeling helpless. It takes twenty… maybe thirty minutes for the horde to pass. When the last scrape fades into the distance, we stay frozen another five just to be sure.

We just survived a huge ass horde.

Sinclair stands quietly for a moment, then gives a small sigh and digs into one of the bags we'd stuffed under a seat. He pulls out a roll of toilet paper, one of the sacred treasures of the post-apocalypse and gently tears off a thick handful. He walks over to Dion and crouches beside him. Hawthorne follows suit with his wipes.

"Hey, little man," Sinclair says softly.

"It's okay. Happens to the best of us." Hawthorne adds.

Dion looks up, red-faced and tear-streaked, but he doesn't cry again. Sinclair gives Teresa a glance, in which she returns a head tilt of approval. Sinclair and Hawthorne then help clean up the mess, careful not to make Dion feel any worse than he already does. Hawthorne throws the spoiled wipes out the window, followed by using sanitizer. Then reaches into his backpack, and pulls out a rolled-up pair of gym shorts, bright blue with an old band logo faded on one side.

"Here," he says, handing them over with a small smile. "Bit big, but they're comfy. Got a drawstring, too…fancy, right?"

Dion gives the tiniest laugh, and that alone feels like a goddamn miracle.

"Thanks," Teresa whispers to Sinclair as he stands up.

He just shrugs, brushing his hands on his pants. "Figured the kid deserves a win today."

I watch it all from across the bus, my heart caught somewhere between breaking and mending. This moment, small, quiet but mighty meant everything. We may be beaten to hell, terrified, running on fumes but were still…trying. Still *human.* Somehow, that had to count for something. One by one, people curled up on the seats or floor. Theo and Emily pass out near the front. Kian cradles his bandaged arm and leans back, eyes already shut. Teresa wraps Dion in one of the fleece blankets. Even Kate, tough as nails, finally lets her shoulders drop.

Wilson stays up. He sits near the front, rifle across his knees, eyes scanning the road like he is back on watch in some goddamn desert.

At some point, sleep takes me.

The smell of instant coffee drifts through the bus like an ancient offering. It is bitter, hot, and made from freeze-dried grounds we found in the camping store but hell, it was coffee.

"Where'd we get cups?" I ask, eyeing the strange assortment.

"Scavenged while you sleepy heads were busy in la la land." Kate said, holding up a kid's plastic Paw Patrol mug.

"Chase was a brave little bastard," Hawthorne adds with a fake wipe of a tear. Half the group chuckles.

"The rest of us got stuck with Solo cups?" I eye my flimsy red goblet like it might dissolve in my hand. "Guess class is dead too."

Wilson raises his cup with a grumble. "Cheers to plastic dignity."

Everyone clinks their solos cups together like it is the last frat party of the year. Once everyone on the bus has a cup of coffee in hand the five of us gather together at the front by the map.

"Banff's a crater," I say, tapping the blacked-out mark where our hopes used to be. "So, we go around. We take the backroads, north, up through the valleys, follow the service roads and cut west toward Jasper."

"We'll avoid the main highways that way," Kate adds. "Fewer people. Fewer… problems."

"You mean corpses," Hawthorne says, already chewing on a protein bar. "Say it with your chest."

Kate rolls her eyes.

"Alright," Wilson rumbles, arms folded across his chest like some hardened old war statue. "We stick to back roads, only stop when we have to and keep our eyes sharp. Hordes move fast."

"Yes, good idea. We should leave now." I conclude.

Then, in perfect unspoken sync, they all look at each other.

"Bathroom break?"

"God, yes, Thanks Kate." Sinclair groans.

The overgrown service station beside us has barely-functioning plumbing. That doesn't stop the eleven of us from claiming it like kings. A brief truce with comfort. Even if it smells like something crawled in there to die months ago.

Outside, as we load up our gear and check over supplies one last time, I catch Hawthorne sidling up beside Kate.

"So, uh, just putting it out there...end of the world and all...if you ever feel like experimenting…"

Kate gives him a look so deadpan it might bury him. "I'm into girls, Hawthorne."

He blinks. "Oh."

Then she claps him on the shoulder. "A for effort bud."

I nearly spit out my water, laughing. Even Wilson cracks the corner of a smile.

"Jesus Christ," Sinclair mutters, wheezing. "You crashed and burned harder than the cities."

Hawthorne holds his hands up, grinning like a dumbass. "Hey, worth a shot. We're all going to die anyway."

"Not if I can help it," I retort, "Alright, let's move out. Jasper's not going to find itself. Stay sharp. Stay quiet. And no flirting."

"I wasn't flirting!" Hawthorne shoots back.

"Sure," Kate smirks. "Let's go, Romeo."

With everyone back from their respective bathroom breaks, we climb onto the bus, the door groaning closed behind us. Eleven souls, stitched together by loss and survival, settling into our worn seats as the engine rattles to life.

CHAPTER 15

VIOLET

By late afternoon, we finally roll into what is left of Rocky Mountain House. The streets are mostly quiet, just the whisper of wind through broken windows and the occasional groan of a loose sign swinging in the breeze. My legs feel stiff from the drive, and the moment we park, I step out and stretch until my spine cracks.

"Looks quiet," I report, scanning the remains of a nearby grocery store. A deer bolts out the shattered front window as if in agreement. We both jump in unison and then watch as three dead follow it.

Dad sighs one hand resting on the Jeep's hood. "Quiet doesn't mean safe. Let's eat, then scout."

We find a rooftop spot above a convenience store, overlooking the ruined main street. I crack open a dented can of chili while Dad chews through three coffee crips. The silence between us isn't heavy; it is the kind born of survival, the kind you learn to respect when every sound might mean something's coming. That's when we hear footsteps. Two figures approach cautiously from the west, hands raised. A man and woman, maybe mid-thirties, wearing patched-up outdoor gear and bright orange armbands.

Not military.

Not raiders either.

The woman smiles like we are old friends. Dad cocks his shotgun.

"Hey!" She calls out, "Didn't mean to startle you. We saw your Jeep. You from the military?"

Dad stands slowly. "Just passing through."

The man steps forward. "We're at a camp. About twenty minutes north, near an old resort. Safe, good people, food, protection, everything a survivor needs."

I squint. "Are you recruiting?"

"We're extending a hand," the woman replies. "Most people don't last long alone. You'd be welcome."

Dad looks at me. I already know what he's thinking. We've been through too much to just trust strangers with open arms and utopia promises. I don't like it either, but I can see the storm clouds in the distance, and we haven't found a place to sleep yet.

"Maybe next time." Dad says flatly.

The man introduces himself as Jared, like he'd heard Dad's excuse a hundred times. His partner, a woman named Celeste, stands quietly beside him, eyes bright and a little too calm.

Jared nods. "We'll wait an hour. Then we will head back. After that, the doors close."

The way he says it makes the hair on the back of my neck twitch.

"We don't lock them," Celeste adds with a strange softness, the walking spirits do. Once night falls, you're either part of the circle, or you're not."

They turn and walk off down the street, disappearing around the bend like ghosts.

"We *could* use a safe place for the night," I say, quietly. "Just one night. Then we move on."

He lets out a sharp breath, not even looking at me.

"No. No way."

"It's a safe place," I press, "It's food. You want to keep sleeping in a busted-down house every night?"

"I'd rather sleep in the Jeep than shack up with people who talk about the dead like they're prophets," he snaps "Did you hear them? Spirits? Circles? They're nuts Violet!"

I take a step toward him. "So, what's the plan, then? Keep driving until we hit another dead-end? Until we run out of fuel or get overrun again?"

"Don't twist this," he growls, pointing a finger. "This isn't survival, it's suicide. You saw the way their eyes lit up talking about them—*the dead*. Like they're sacred."

I pause, trying to find logic behind the rising panic. "Then we go in with our eyes open. One night. We keep to ourselves. We leave at sunrise."

He shakes his head, but the fight in him is wearing thin. I can see it in his shoulders. The exhaustion. The fear.

"They're crazy."

"We've met worse."

He glares, then looks away. "One night. The second anything feels off. We're gone."

An hour later, we find Jared and Celeste waiting beneath the broken gas station sign.

"We'll go," Dad says gruffly. "But we leave if we want. No questions, no sermons."

Jared smiles like he'd been expecting this. "Of course. No one is forced to stay. If your path leads elsewhere, that's the will of the Blessed."

Celeste tilts her head, her voice dreamy. "They'll know your heart. The dead...they see us better than the living ever did."

Dad and I exchange a look. A silent *what the hell* that neither of us dare speak out loud. Still, we follow them, every step feeling more like we are walking into the jaws of something we couldn't yet name.

"We walk there, no cars," Jared says, pointing at the Jeep.

"It's a Jeep not a car, and fine," Dad gruffs.

We follow them north into the tree line. Just as the sky turns burnt orange, and the forest grows thick. We walk until we reach what looks like an old mountain retreat. After ten minutes, wooden lodges appear. Nestled in a clearing, string lights glow gently overhead. People wander barefoot through grass, humming and smiling as if there weren't people rising from the dead all around us. The air smells of incense and rot. A large hand-painted sign reads:

THE AWAKENING: PEACE THROUGH DEATH, LIFE THROUGH UNITY."

What the fuck

They welcome us with food. Soup, flatbread, some kind of dried fruit. Everything tastes weirdly sweet. My skin itches under the stares of people swaying in circles, chanting low under their breath. Like everyone is riding the peak their high about to go to a rave.

"Can you make out what they're saying? My mouth, full of bread.

"I heard the chosen one like five times, but I can't hear anything else. They are fucking weird Violet."

"Maybe they are just super religious, nothing wrong with a bunch of people who believe in being a good person, like look at this food, it's the best thing I…*we* have had in days" I say taking another huge bite of bread.

"What are those crosses over there?" he says, squinting.

We step forward, bread still in my hand, closing the distance. *Then I see it.* Behind the main lodge, inside a makeshift fence. Deadheads, four of them. Their arms outstretched on crucifixes, while a few Deadheads roam around them. People kneel before them, sobbing, offering flowers, and whispering prayers.

Dad tenses beside me. "We're leaving. *Now.*"

Before we can think about an escape route, two robed figures approach.

"Just one night," one says, voice syrupy smooth. "Let your energy align."

The door of our prison cell slams shut behind us with a cold, metallic click. I spin around and grab the handle, twisting hard.

Locked.

"No," I hiss, yanking it again. "No, no…. come on."

Dad skirts to the window, rattling the bars with a growl. "Steel. Reinforced. They locked us in."

I turn back, chest heaving. "Our guns are gone."

He curses under his breath, checking our bags on the floor. "They left our packs. Food, water…but no weapons."

"They let us keep just enough to think we're okay," I snap. "They want us compliant, not dead."

"This was a mistake, I should've said no. What the hell was I thinking?" Dad exclaims.

"You weren't! Neither of us were! We walked right into it."

He turns on me, eyes blazing. "We were desperate, Violet. You wanted to believe them too."

I bite the inside of my cheek enough to taste my own blood

"I didn't think we were signing up for some backwoods death cult, Dad! I thought maybe…just maybe...we'd found a place that wasn't a nightmare."

His shoulders drop, breath heavy. The anger melts into something heavier. *Guilt.*

"They took everything that could help us fight. We're sitting ducks in here."

"We still have our bags, food. First aid. My flashlight. We're not screwed. Just cornered."

I still have my letters

"We need to get out *now.*"

"I'm not sleeping in this room," I say, arms crossed. "We find a way out or we make one. Before they come back for whatever they think is next."

Outside, drums start to pound a steady beat, like a heartbeat coming through the floor. I don't want to imagine what they are preparing outside. No one has returned to check on us, and the room grows colder with the dark. Still, we are locked in.

What the hell have I done?

I sink to the floor, elbows on my knees, fingers tangled in my hair. A silent sob rattles through my chest before I can stop it. My throat tightens, my body trembling from more than fear.

"I'm sorry, Dad, this is all my fault."

There is a pause, then I feel his hand on my shoulder.

"Hey," he says softly. "It's okay. We're okay."

I look up at him through tears. His face is drawn and tired, but his eyes hold that same stubborn calm I remember from when I was a kid and thunder shook the windows.

"We've gotten through worse, and I'm not letting anything happen to you. Not now. Not ever."

The drums outside slow to a dull, rhythmic thud, like a warning wrapped in a ritual they've practiced. Dad shifts against the wall and motions for me to sit beside him. I curl up next to him, backpack clutched to my chest as if it might shield me from the nightmare outside.

"We'll sleep in turns. Just for a few hours. Get some of our strength back."

I close my eyes and try to quiet my thoughts. It isn't easy with the sound of the drums still beating through the floor. Each one feels like a countdown and I have no clue when it will end.

The soft click of a lock comes in loud and clear, waking me with high alert. The door creaks open, and light spills in. Dim and yellow tinged, for a moment it reminds me of a campfire light. A tall man stands in the doorway, his bare chest smeared with something dark and flaking. Red paint, or perhaps not paint at all. His eyes lock on me.

"You," he says, voice like gravel. "The girl comes first."

My stomach drops. "What the fuck are you talking about?"

Dad steps in front of me so fast I barely register the motion. "You're not taking her anywhere."

Three more figures appear behind the first. One holds a crude wooden staff; the other a curved blade that looks more ceremonial than functional but sharp all the same. The third is the source of the flickering light appearing with a torch in hand behind the other two men.

"You said we were free to leave," my voice shakes.

The tall man doesn't even blink. "The spirits changed their will. Tonight, is the offering. They chose *her*."

Dad shoves one of the men, trying to block the doorway with his body. "You'll have to go through me."

The first man swings with brutal precision. His fist cracking into Dad's jaw with a sickening thud. Dad staggers back, a little dazed, blood already trickling from his mouth.

"No don't hurt him" I lunge toward him, but the two others grab me.

Their rough hands are on my arms, dragging me from the room as I scream and kick. I use everything in my body to escape these men but then *wanna-be Carrie* slaps me.

"They must feast, the gods are hungry tonight."

"Fuck your gods" I spit, my saliva connecting with his eye.

Another slap. I look back just as the door slams shut behind me, sealing my father inside.

CHAPTER 16

RYDER

"This town actually looks a little less nuked than Banff."

"Eyes on the goddamn road, Sinclair" I bark, leaning forward in my seat.

Like the smartass he is, catches my eyes in the rear-view mirror and raises his eyebrows about to say something clever. Before he can, I feel a tap on my shoulder. Emily.

"Uh, hey," she says awkwardly. "I think I'm going to need..."

She glances around, spots Kate, and bolts toward her like I am some sort of bomb. She whispers something in Kate's ear, and I watch Kate's face shift like someone has just slapped her with a wet fish. Kate turns to us, already walking over.

"We need feminine products," she says, deadpan.

Hawthorne chokes on his instant coffee and sprays a mouthful across the floor like a busted fire hydrant.

"These two jackasses didn't grab anything for the girls," Kate says, glaring daggers at him while swallowing her disgust. "Neither did we."

Hawthorne raises a hand in mock defense. "Yeah, probably because I don't have a puss—"

"Ah, ah!" I cut him off with a sharp point of my finger. "Don't even finish that sentence."

I sigh and stand up, stretching my back with a few satisfying cracks.

"Alright. We'll stop in this town. Try a few houses, maybe a corner store. Rest up for the night. Sinclair—you hear that?"

"Already on it, boss," he says with a salute.

"I'm not your boss."

"Oh, right. Uh, sorry. Buddy? Brother?"

"Kent. Or Ryder. *'Buddy'* makes me want to hit you," I say with a glare that could crack concrete.

Kate is already halfway down the aisle, explaining the plan to Emily, who in turn passes it along to the others. They relay the message like a little game of apocalypse telephone, nodding and adjusting gear, the energy shifting into something a little more focused. We slow as we reach the edge of the neighborhood. The first house comes into view.

I exhale through my nose and reach for my knife

"Alright, let's see what this towns got."

The bus hisses to a stop at the curb of a half-collapsed bungalow. It looks like it once hosted Sunday barbecues and Christmas mornings. Now it's nothing but peeled paint, shattered windows, shrouded by an eerie silence that feels heavier than the sky. Kate was already at the door, rifle slung over her shoulder.

"Let's do this quick. Hawthorne and I will clear the main floor. Sinclair, take the back."

We fan out like we'd done this a hundred times. Hell, we had. The front steps groan under our weight. I raise my blade as we reach the open door. Inside, old photographs still hang crooked in the hallway. A birthday balloon sags deflated in the corner like it had given up.

"Clear left," I call as I push into the living room, eyes scanning every corner.

No movement.

No groans.

Just the ticking of a broken clock on the wall.

Hawthorne peels off into the kitchen. "Someone left a half-eaten can of ravioli. Gross."

"If it's not moving or moaning, bag it," I say. "We're not picky anymore."

Kate and Emily disappear down the hallway toward the bathroom and bedrooms. I check the hall closet. Coats, boots, a dented umbrella. I kick the door shut just as Sinclair's voice comes through the back screen door.

"All clear back here."

"Same here," I reply.

A moment later, Kate calls from the bathroom, "Got some pads and tampons under the sink. Not a ton, but enough to buy us some time."

Emily adds, "And toothpaste! Yay!"

I love the small victories. I step into the kitchen where Hawthorne has opened a cupboard while talking quietly to himself.

"Tomato paste, green beans, and expired condensed milk. It's like someone raided this place but left the weird shit."

"We take everything." I say grabbing a plastic bin from the pantry and dumping whatever isn't moldy into it.

We meet in the living room and regroup. Kate has a plastic grocery bag full of random supplies, and Emily clutches a box of tampons like a damn gold bar.

Sinclair reappears from the back door with a smug grin. "Guess who found more toilet paper in the garage?"

"Not a competition, Sinclair, but congrats on your paper throne."

As we turn to leave, a thud echoes upstairs. Everyone freezes looking up towards the sound at the same time.

Hawthorne whispers, "Nope. Fuck that. Not dealing with attic gremlins today."

Kate raises her rifle slightly. "Could be a raccoon."

"Or it could be one of those twitchy bastards," Sinclair adds, hand drifting toward his hatchet.

I weigh the risk for half a second before shaking my head. "Not worth it. We've got what we need. Let's move."

Back outside, the sky is dimming. The sun starts to bleed behind the mountains. We load the supplies onto the bus quickly, eyes flicking constantly toward the horizon. Everyone is quiet, the adrenaline still pulsing, tension clinging to us like sweat. Kate climbed aboard last, clutching the bag of essentials. She hands it to Teresa, who smiles softly and mouths her thanks. Dion peeks from behind her legs and gives me a little thumbs up.

"See?" I tell Sinclair, "We're saving the world, one tampon at a time."

He rolls his eyes and climbs back into the driver's seat. "Let's hit the next spot before the sun bails on us."

The bus rumbles back to life. I drop into one of the seats by the window, my gaze drifting back to the house we'd just cleared. The windows are shattered and sun-bleached, blankly staring out like hollow, watching eyes. Just another empty shell in a world full of them. Then something catches the edge of my vision. Half-hidden by the tree line, tucked between tall grass and shadow. The shape is unmistakable. My heart stops. It was a Jeep, *her* jeep

"Stop the *fucking* bus!" I bark, surging to my feet.

The brakes screech as Sinclair reacts. The moment the doors open, I shove past Hawthorne who's standing in the aisle hard enough that he stumbles into a seat, then I leap down the steps and into the open.

"Ryder!" Kate shouts behind me, but I don't stop. I can't.

My boots hit the pavement and keep moving, gravel crunching beneath them, breath burning in my lungs as I sprint toward the edge of the woods. Branches claw at my arms, but I don't feel them.

There it is.

The Jeep sits like a ghost. Partially hidden and dust-coated, but not abandoned. Not really. I reach out, hands trembling as I touch the hood.

Still warm.

I back up, eyes scanning everything. The doors are shut. No blood. No shattered glass. No signs of a fight. The keys are gone. The packs in the backseat are missing, but she isn't there. Just… gone. I grip the edge of the door and lean my head against it, letting out a sound somewhere between a breath and a cry. I can still smell the faint trace of her, and something I can't name but know like I know my own heartbeat. She'd been here recently, and she was close. So, fucking close. I have missed her by minutes, if that. The air suddenly feels too thick to breathe. My fingers curl into fists. I want to scream. Tear into the trees. Call her name until my voice breaks. Instead, I just stand there. Frozen. I don't know which way she went. Or who she might've been with. Or if she was running toward something… or away. Foot steps crunch behind me. Kate's voice, soft and hesitant, breaks the silence.

"Ryder… it's hers, isn't it?"

I clench my jaw so tight it hurts.

"She's alive. She's out there."

Kate doesn't say anything. Just stands beside me, her hand resting lightly on my shoulder. For a few more seconds, I let myself believe that maybe…just maybe. Hope isn't a weakness after all.

Sinclair crouches beside the tire tracks. "Doesn't look like a rush job. They left on foot."

"Which direction?" I ask, already moving to the edge of the brush.

He points north, into the tree line. "Tracks lead into the trees…human. At least four sets."

Kate rushes up behind me, brow furrowed. "You think they ran into trouble?"

I don't answer.

I already know they had.

I drop to a crouch, fingers grazing the dirt as if it is sacred. The print is faint, almost gone but I'd know that tread anywhere. The way the heel dragged slightly. The angle of her step. It was hers. I didn't need to measure it or second guess. I'd walked beside her long enough to know every quirk in her gait, every scuff in her boots. You don't forget the footsteps of someone who once walked through your heart.

"They didn't leave because they wanted to," I say quietly.

Hawthorne spits into the dirt. "So, we follow."

"And fast," I say. My fists clenched so tight my nails bite into my palms.

If they touched her…if they so much as looked at her wrong… I'll turn that whole fucking forest into ash. We sprint back to the bus, my breath clouding in the cool evening air. My pulse drums against my skull, every step echoing Violet's name. I slam the door open.

"Wilson," I bark, "You're in charge again. Lock the doors. Don't open them for anything but our voices."

He rises from his seat, already reaching for the rifle we'd given him earlier. "Copy that. You bring her back."

Kate starts gathering gear with practiced hands. Her rifle, a hunting knife, a flashlight, and one of the heavy-duty packs. Hawthorne grabs extra ammo and his hatchet, slinging a crowbar over his shoulder like an afterthought. Sinclair silently hands out water, energy bars, and a med kit, his face set in stone.

"Where are you going?" Teresa asks, eyes wide with worry, her arms around Dion.

"To get Violet," I say, zipping up my jacket and checking the knife at my belt. "We won't be long."

Theo looks as though he wants to argue, but Wilson claps a hand on his shoulder. "They know what they're doing. Let 'em go."

Kate gives Emily a quick reassuring hug, then follows me out the door.

The woods are dense, shadows coiling through the underbrush like living things. Moonlight starts filtering through the pines in thin, silver streaks, catching on leaves and glinting off our weapons. Every sound feels louder in the quiet. Our footsteps, the rustle of branches, the distant call of some wild thing we don't want to meet. So, we climb the trail that is extremely narrow and steep, winding up through jagged rock and moss-slicked logs. Sweat clings to my skin despite the cold.

We stop dead in our tracks because just below us, tucked into the clearing like a secret is a camp. Golden lights are strung between trees. Wooden lodges circle the courtyard. A firepit flickers at the center, thin ribbons of smoke curl towards the sky. People wander barefoot in the grass, their hands raised and heads tipped back like they are praying or praising something I don't see. The chants are a low, eerie hum, and the chanters move in slow, swirling patterns like they are performing some fucked-up dance. It doesn't feel real. It feels like a hallucination. A fever dream pretending to be a utopia.

Hawthorne crouches beside me, eyes narrowed. "What the fuck is this?"

Kate unslings her rifle slowly. "A cult," she whispers. "It has to be."

"Then we burn their dream to the ground," I say, my voice barely more than a growl.

I scan the crowd, heart pounding so hard it makes my vision blur.

Hold on, Ocean Eyes. I'm close now.

I observe for another few minutes, memorizing patrols, the way the robed figures move, where they enter, how the buildings align. The place is built like a maze, meant to lull, confuse, control.

"We're not going in loud," I say, eyes never leaving the center lodge. "We pick them off quietly. Find her. Then we scorch the place."

The others agree, but I am already gone. I weave between the trees, letting the shadows eat me whole. As I creep forward, the world narrows. My heart thuds, not from fear but from something deeper. Darker. A storm inside me cracks wide. Every memory of Violet. Her voice, her laugh, the way she used to roll her eyes when I said something smart-assed. It all comes flooding back in a sudden, blinding wave. Then the images twist. Her in that Jeep. Scared. Her being taken by these fucks, tied down, controlled, and hurt.

I become something else.

Not a soldier.
Not a man.
A weapon.

Fueled by everything they took from her and anything they might've done to her, I shed the last pieces of hesitation and let the fire in me *burn*. The first robed man I find stands near the edge of camp, fumbling with a stick of incense and humming a creepy little chant. I am on him before he can blink. One hand over his mouth, the other driving my knife up into his kidney, slow and deliberate. He gurgles into my palm, twitching like a dying fish. I twist the blade, letting him feel every second of it.

No scream. Just a wet whimper. Then, nothing.

I drag his body behind a lodge, wiping my blade clean on his robe. My breathing is too calm, like I'd done this a thousand times. I would do it a thousand more if it meant getting her back. I look toward the center lodge again. Warm yellow light spills through the cracks in the wood. Somewhere inside that glow, I knew she was there.

My Violet.

They didn't know it yet, but I was death coming for them and I wasn't leaving without her. Someone spots me near the main path, but I am faster. I slam her against the wood, hand over her mouth, and shove the knife up under her ribs.

Warm.

Wet.

Done.

When I regroup with the others, Kate's eyes widen with shock.

"Jesus, Ryder. You're like… covered in blood."

"They don't get to live," I say, wiping my blade on my pants.

"Okay, Kent, let's get this shit done," Hawthorne says grinning as he pulls out a massive hunting knife. "I've been itching to use this."

Sinclair raises an eyebrow, patting Hawthorne on the back. "So, everyone dies? We're not helping anyone?"

"Who the fuck is there to help other than Violet, Sinclair?" I snap, loading rounds into my pistol. "These people are nuts. We are doing what's left of the world a favor."

"They are sick, but still humans" Sinclair stutters, shaking his head but falling into line.

My heart doesn't beat anymore, it *burns.*

"I won't stop until I have her. Anyone between me and Violet is already dead. Yeah, they're human on the surface, but their loyalty lies with this cult. Keep up, or don't."

I snap my pistol shut.

CHAPTER 17

RYDER

We advance together while the beats of the drum rise in tempo. We pass more followers, some dancing, some whispering prayers to the Dybbuks, others arranging flowers in strange spirals on the ground. No one notices us. The drumming is loudest near the largest lodge. Like a ritual heartbeat. That must be where she is.

"We need a distraction," Hawthorne says.

I scan the camp and freeze. A line of corpses nailed to towering crucifixes, limbs twisted, heads slumped. What the fuck was this place? Some sacrilegious nightmare, masquerading as salvation? They almost looked human still. Like the crosses hadn't just held their corpses but stolen the last of their humanity

"I've got one," I point toward the grotesque display.

I circle back while the others watch my six. Then with a chin flick to Sinclair, I slip through the brush behind the wooden shrines. The stench is unbearable. The air is thick with flies and decay. The dead sway in their bindings, jaws gnawing at the wind. I sneak around them slowly watching and counting. Ten Dybbuks circling around the four corpse nailed crosses. I crouch beside the makeshift gate holding them in and climb up to reach the back of the crosses. It's times like this I realize, being tall has its perks. I don't have to dangle like a moron just to cut the bindings.

Lucky me.

The follower fuckers in this camp are too busy chasing their own delusions to notice me, but I start working on my distraction with haste. The first corpse's arms are tied tight with rotted rope, half-sunken into the dude's arm. It looks like someone tried to make a scarecrow out of rotting meat and lost interest halfway through. I slice the restraints. The thing drops like a sack of brittle bones, twitches like a seizure victim, straightens, and stands. His joints crack like old wood.

One down.

I execute the rest of the plan quickly. Cut. Drop. Rise. Repeat. The Dybbuks shudder awake one by one, eyes black and hollow. This is a slow-building symphony of death, and I am the conductor. Once they are all loose. I stand behind the fence. Watching them groan and pace. I scan the camp again. People are milling about, barefoot and dazed, ignoring the low, rhythmic drum beats like they are nothing but a soundtrack to their enlightenment, instead of a horror show cacophony.

Fucking weridos.

I shift my head as I hear a girl scream. Then I see some shirtless asshole, smeared in dried blood like war paint, leading the others. *Great.* Another tall guy. Love that for me. Pretty sure he thinks he's the messiah. I can take him.

Following him…*fuck*…three men clocked in righteousness and dragging a woman like an unwilling offering. A woman about to burn for all their sins.

Violet.

I see her even through the haze and distance. Half a football field away, blurred by firelight and smoke, but I'd know the shape of her in my goddamn sleep. The curve of her jaw, the way her shoulders tense when she fights like her bones still remember defiance. Her limbs are flailing, her throat raw from screaming, and still, she doesn't give in. That's *my* girl. My body wants to attack instinctively and without second thought. Like it doesn't give a shit about strategy or timing or staying alive. Every cell in me begs to run, to tear through these lunatics, to kill every single one with my bare hands and rip her free but I don't.

Couldn't. Not yet at least. Instead, I crouch there in the dirt, behind rotting wood and rusted nails, teeth grinding until the ache in my jaw blinds my vision. Smoke curls from the fire pits ahead. I can see the others through the undergrowth. Hawthorne, Sinclair, Kate, eyes wide, waiting for me to make the call. I catch their gaze one by one. Sinclair's jaw is clenched, hand already ghosting over his rifle. Hawthorne looks like he wants blood. Kate's eyes are all worry, flicking between me and the lodge where Violet is being dragged. I shake my head once. Then lift two fingers–*stay* and press them to my lips–*silent.* Hawthorne and Sinclair do not move at all, but I can feel the tension coil tighter in their frame. Kate's hands tremble around the hilt of her knife, but she drops lower into the brush. I hate myself for staying still. I hate that I have to play it quiet when every part of me wants to rush in guns blazing. Violet is in there, *screaming.* I am here, buried in shadows, a monster holding the leash on worse monsters. This isn't about me; this is about her. Soon I will let the leash go. Let the dead walk. Let the cult burn. Let the night remember what it means to cross me. The Dybbuks notice her too. Heads lifted in eerie unison, snapping toward the sound of her cries like marionettes pulled by a shared string. Their nostrils flare, mouths slightly open, tasting the scent of her fear on the wind. I tell myself to wait. I can't enact this plan until I know she's safe inside, safe from them, or trapped like bait in a cage, whichever way you want to look at it.

She screams out again. High, hoarse, furious. It tears through me, sharp as a blade. A sound I'll never forget. It is the sound of the woman I love being dragged to her death. It kills something in me. I am simmering. *No* boiling. No *burning.* I will carve through this whole fucked-up camp if I have to. I will make them regret ever laying a single hand on her. I want them to scream louder than she has. I want their blood on my hands, sticky and hot, proof that I've unmade them. She kicks again and they curse at her, like she is the problem. Like they aren't monsters. Then the main lodge swallows her whole. The doors shut, her screams are silenced, and that's my cue.

I rise slowly, one hand already on my pistol, the other on the rope holding the Dybbuks in place. My breath is shallow. She's mine, and they touched her. They don't get to walk away from that. They don't get to fucking breathe. Not after tonight. Let the dead have them. Let the forest remember their screams. I unlatch the rope gate and slip behind the fence just as the Dybbuks begin to scatter. First with that drunken, jerky stagger, then something animalistic shifts within them. Like the scent of blood lit a fire in their rotting veins. They drag forward and hell comes with them. I run the opposite way, heart thundering. Keeping to the shadows, I find a rack of wind chimes hanging beside a stone altar littered with flowers and rotting fruit. With one savage swing of my elbow, I shatter them. Then I vanish into the tree line, and just as I hoped, the dead answer. I need them to take care of the people in the camp so I can go save my girl. They arrive from the dark, groaning. Their movements aren't random. No, it's like watching death itself choose who to take. They barrel through the camp, jaws snapping, eyes wild, my instruments of unholy retribution. They hit the camp like a plague. Screams erupt from everywhere.

Some run barefoot, some still holding flowers and feathers, with faces painted like dreamers who had just been woken from their reverie to find themselves knee deep in a nightmare. They collide with one another, fall over fire pits, and trample each other in blind. The chanting dies in a single, strangled sob. Hellglow twists in the smoke as chaos blooms like blood in water. I smile watching the Dybbuks tear through these peace-wrapped psychopaths, and I feel something break free inside me. One remaining restraint snaps, the last piece of my civility. The world makes more sense like this. The dead birthing death, fulfilling their only purpose. It is both grim and poetic and *I love it.* I run back toward the others, crouching in the dark behind the treeline. Hawthorne meets my eyes first.

"Start the fire. Kill anything that moves. I'll get Violet."

No one answers. They don't have to. Their silence isn't fear. It is readiness. The kind of silence that arrives right before a storm tears down a fucking mountain. As quick as I appeared I am gone again, slipping once more through the darkness.

A woman stands at the edge of the torchlight, still humming, like she hasn't heard the carnage behind her or has gone numb to it, accepting the will of the dead. She wears white robes streaked with mud, a crown of dried flowers on her head like a deranged forest bride. I cover her mouth with one hand from behind and drag her into the trees. She doesn't scream. Doesn't fight. She just looks up at me, wide-eyed and still. Like she is grateful. I break her neck easily enough and I don't let go until she is a limp body on the moss, her crown crooked and bloody. What the hell had Violet walked into?

I stalk toward the main lodge, now that the grass is cultist and Dybbuk free. The drums have died but not in me. Their ghost still throbs in my head, a savage rhythm, war-born and blood-hungry. Maybe it is memory. Maybe it is my pulse trying to tear its way out. They call this place a sanctuary and I get to turn it into a fucking slaughterhouse. The structure stands in the dark, patched with rotting wood and prayer cloths stained by time and God knows what else. Through a narrow slit in the boarded window, movement stirs. Figures shift in the flickering glow. Hooded, quiet, waiting like animals circling prey.

Violet

They drag her, rough and unkind, her arms bound by thick rope, wrists raw and trembling. She stumbles, her knees nearly giving out, but refuses to fall. Even like this–dirty, bruised, barely standing; she is the most arresting thing I have ever seen. There is something violently beautiful about it. The way the rope clings to her skin. The furious twist of her body with every step. Not submissive but still restrained, still burning beneath it all. It makes my pulse spike for the wrong reasons. Or maybe the right ones. I don't know anymore. My breath catches as I watch her struggle. The wildness in her eyes. The flushed skin. Her chest rising and falling in broken rhythm. It isn't right to think about it. It sure as hell isn't noble but God, she looked good like that. Both dangerous and deliciously divine.

"Get the fuck away from me," she snaps, her voice cracking as she says it, cutting through the night like glass.

That sound hits something deep in me.

Not pity.

Not sorrow.

Hunger.

A vicious need to take her back, piece by piece, from anyone who's touched her. Then one of them raises his hand and strikes her across the face.

She reels from the blow, hair whipping forward, her body curling instinctively as pain registers. Everything in me goes quiet.

Not calm.

Not rational.

Just still, like the pause before a bomb goes off.

My fingers curl against the window frame, white-knuckled. That man has no idea what he's just done but *I do.* He's made himself the first one to die.

My boots hit the stairs of the lodge without hesitation.

I don't sneak.

I don't creep.

I claim the ground I walk on like it owes me. Every scream that has torn from Violet's throat pulls me forward. Every sob she's swallowed. Every bruise they've left. She believed she was alone in hell, but I'm the devil at the gate, and I am not leaving until every last one of them bleed. I slam my boot into the wooden door.

Once.

Twice.

It buckles with a thunderous crack, exploding off its hinges in a rain of splinters. I step into the glow, slow and deliberate.

"Touch her again, and I'll baptize this room in your blood."

Four hooded heads turn. The tall bastard I assume is their leader, clutches a hammer like a sacred artifact, as if he were about to sanctify her pain in blood and nails, tilting his head when he sees me. The smile he wears isn't surprising. It is reverence like the image of me was anticipated. Just another part of their ritual. I return his grin with a bullet to his skull. It hits the center mass, just above the brow, splitting his face in half and painting the back wall in gray and red. He drops. The second one; the one that hit her, blinks too long in hesitation. His blade slips from his hand, clattering on the wood. His cowardice slows him. I put a round through his spine. He crumples like wet paper, dragging himself an inch at a time, fingers bloody, legs twitching like a dying spider. My boot slams down on his fingers.

"You dared touch her," I growl, voice low and jagged. "You think I'd let that slide?"

I grab his wrist, feeling the tremor of fear running through him, and make the decision that has been simmering in my veins since I saw the first cowardly strike. The hands that touched my Violet will pay dearly. The knife comes down with precise fury, severing them at the wrists. His screams claw at the walls, wet and ragged. He tries to crawl, tries to plead, but his body has betrayed him too much. Blood pools beneath him, dark and sticky, and I watch every shallow breath shake his chest. I feel Violet in mine, her presence fueling every ounce of rage and obsessive protection I carry.

The third screams a prayer, something broken and inhuman. He lunges towards me and I meet him halfway and drive my boot into his gut, folding him in half. My knife is in my hand before he hits his knees. I carve it upward under his ribs. The sound he makes is wet, and desperate. It is the closest thing to mercy I give them. The fourth doesn't run. He stands still, gripping his cross like it gives him divine purpose, his lips muttering a fevered prayer to whatever false god has promised him salvation. His hands shake, but his eyes never leave mine. He thinks faith will protect him. That his blind belief makes him untouchable. I walk toward him slowly. He doesn't move. Maybe he thinks I'll offer him mercy. Perhaps he thinks I want him to beg. I snatch the cross from his trembling grip and bury it in his thigh.

He howls, crumpling forward, and I catch him by the throat, dragging him up until we are face to face. His hood falls back. He is younger than I expected, pale as death and eyes wide and brimmed with fear.

"You pray for a god," I say, tightening my grip, "but I'm the one who showed up."

Then I slam his head against the wall.

Once.

Twice.

A third time.

Blood paints the boards in thick, ugly streaks. He sags in my grip, body twitching, the light in his eyes guttering like a candle snuffed out in a storm.

She was bound at the center of their circle, a crown of thorns on her fucking head, their twisted sacrifice. I see only red.

"Violet," I breathe, falling to my knees beside her. My hands shake as I reach to untie her wrists. All the blood and the bruises I notice makes my heart hurt.

Her eyes flutter, glazed with confusion at first, then focus. She looks like a ghost of herself, pale and broken, a hollowed-out version of the woman I knew. Still, she is the most alive thing in this whole damned place.

"Ryder?" Her voice is a whisper. "I knew you'd come…"

I cradle her against me.

"I've got you Ocean eyes" I whisper back, voice shaking with unrelenting hunger. "No one's ever going to hurt you again. I'll kill everyone here before that happens."

Her body shakes like a leaf caught in a storm. Her breath is ragged, and I can feel the weight of her sobs vibrating through me, like it is the first time she's been able to really cry. I pull her tighter, instinctively, like I can hold her together with my own strength.

The sound of Hawthorne's boots crunching through the wreckage interrupts the moment.

"We got to go, Kent!" His voice is tight and urgent.

I can't move yet not with her so fragile, her tears soaking into my shirt. I grip her tighter, ready to pull her with me, but she stops me, weakly pulling me down.

"My Dad's still locked in a room...we have to go help him."

Fucking Arthur. I honestly forgot about him. Can we just leave him here? My anger flares at the thought of him but I hold my tongue, forcing my emotions back down.

"Okay. Let's get him and get the hell out of here." I barely trust my own words.

Kate appears behind Sinclair. Her voice cracks when she sees Violet, her face shifting between relief and pain.

"Vi?"

Violet's eyes lock onto her, she rises and stumbles into Kate's arms, the two of them holding each other in a desperate, tearful embrace. As they pull away, Kate's eyes zero in on the blood seeping from Violet's head and the angry red streaks on her cheeks.

"Are you okay?" Kate asks, her voice trembling. Violet blinks up at her, still weak but trying to pull herself together.

"Yeah. I'm okay. We just... we have to find my dad."

Kate turns to me, and I can see the understanding flicker in her eyes. She knows why I can't stand Arthur, why every breath I take feels like I'm choking on the bile of everything he's done.

"Where is he?" Kate asks quietly, glancing at Violet.

Violet wipes her tears and stands a little straighter, though she still sways on her feet

"He's in a smaller building on the east side of the camp. Follow me."

Just like that, we are traveling through the camp again, but this time I feel the weight of it all. Not just the camp, not just the danger, but the burden of what had been done to her and the hope that against all odds; that I can fix it.

CHAPTER 18
ARTHUR

It's hard to say what is worse, the silence or the sound of her screams. The moment they dragged Violet out, my chest cracked open. I clawed at the door until my fingers went raw, kicked until my knees throbbed, but it never moved. The room is cold and damp. The kind of place where people don't walk out the same. The bastards had ropes, cloaks, some ritual shit I didn't understand. They called her '*the offering*.' What the hell does that even mean? She's not a goddamn sacrifice. She's, my daughter. Even though the walls are thick, the drums echo from the far side of the camp. It's low and steady, like the pulse of death inching closer. I can only hope she isn't already gone. That they hadn't killed her before I even had the chance to try and stop it. She was crying when they took her, cursing them to high heavens. They hit her when she resisted. I felt it in my bones every time they did. I didn't even realize I was rubbing my jaw until the ache bloomed. One of them caught me when I tried to fight. Fist like a sledgehammer. My jaw clicks every time I move it now. Just another reminder of how useless I was in those moments…how powerless I am in this new world.

I slide down the wall, knees buckling beneath the weight of everything I can't fix. My hands shake as I bury my face in them, my palms slick with sweat and blood. Some of the blood is mine, but some of it isn't. That's a small consolation prize. The floor reeks of mildew, piss, and old sweat, but I don't care. I don't move. I just sit there, listening…waiting. I was supposed to protect her. That's what I told Noelle that I'd do if anything ever happened to her. That I'd keep our babies safe. Now 0ur baby was out there, surrounded by maniacs and drums and fire, and I was trapped behind a fucking door like a useless coward. Tears stain my face and drip to the floor before I have the realization that I'm crying. I don't sob, I just break quietly, and completely.

I press the heel of my hand against my eyes, and will myself to stop, like that would somehow make me less of a failure. My daughter is being dragged off to die and I am curled up in a corner like a scared animal. The drums keep beating like a cruel lullaby. I want to scream. I want to punch through the walls. I want to be anywhere but in this goddamn room.

The drums cut out mid-beat, like someone pulled the plug on whatever twisted ceremony they were playing at. I hold my breath. Then the screaming crescendos, not hers, but *theirs*.

Gurgling.

Ripping.

Bones snapping like dry twigs.

Something slams into the wall with such force it makes me jump, my heart lurching into my throat. I can't see them, but I can imagine the way the dead are tearing through the cult, how they must feed like they are born to it. I don't mean to but I start to laugh. It comes out sharp and manic. A laugh that mirrors the breaking of everything around me.

I scream through the door, "Let me out, goddammit! Let me out!"

I pound my fists until the wood bruises my knuckles but nothing happens.

The ghosts come back like they always do when I'm alone too long. My beautiful Noelle's smile. So soft and tired, always worried for me more than herself. She turned first. I still remember the way her eyes clouded over like frost on glass. I begged her to come back. She didn't.

Felix was only eleven. His mother attacked him. He didn't even cry.

He just said, "It's okay, Dad," before he turned. His skin gray, jaw trembling, eyes empty. I locked them in the bedroom. I stayed outside the door with the bat, sobbing, until Violet found me later. I told her not to look. She looked anyway. I wanted to die that day, perhaps now I'll get my wish.

I can't get the look on Violet's face when she first saw Ryder at the military camp out of my mind. Her eyes lit up; her whole face brightened like the sun had broken through months of gray clouds. God, I don't think she'll ever forgive me when she finds out it was me who hid the letters and that I made up the one saying he was dead. I took her phone and blocked his number. When we went to check her phone because Noelle was worried it wasn't getting texts, I convinced her to change her number. He would never reach her, not if I could help it. I couldn't have my daughter waiting around for a man who might never come home, or worse, a man who didn't have the capacity to be what she needed him to be. He never asked my permission to date her, never truly spoke to me on the few occasions we met. Maybe, in some twisted way, she'll eventually see that her life was better without him. She had Jane and Jeremy. She had her career. She had everything she could have asked for. She deserved all the good things the world had to offer and now it's my fault she was in danger. She didn't deserve this new hellscape.

I press my forehead to the door.

"If I die, at least I'll see them again," I whisper.

Footsteps.

Muffled voices.

Shouting.

Someone kicks the door from the outside and the lock snaps.

"Dad"! She drops to her knees and throws her arms around my neck. I hold her so tight it hurts.

"I'm so sorry," I whisper, my voice cracked and raw. "God, Violet…I thought you…I thought they…"

She doesn't answer right away. A tremor ripples through her shoulders as I pull her close, and that's when I discover the blood matted in her hair, crusted along her scalp, where something must've sat deep and tight. I can see where it tore into her skin and my stomach drops.

"They did hurt you," I say, barely breathing. My hands hovering uselessly, afraid to hurt her more. "Jesus, did they hurt…"

She nods, voice breaking. "They wanted a sacrifice. Said it had to be me. But we made it out."

I look at her again and see the bruises, the split lip, the cracked skin on her wrists from whatever they'd tied her with. I have failed my little girl. That kind of failure carves its name into your soul. My eyes flick up to the door frame.

Ryder, that son of a bitch.

He stands in the doorway, covered in blood and grime, breathing like he'd sprinted through hell. Behind Ryder stands two others. Soldiers who look ready for whatever comes next. It is a relief to see one of Violet's good friends Kate still standing behind them. I always figured it would be Grace who'd survive all this chaos, not her. I didn't know the names of the others, but it doesn't matter. They are Ryder's crew. I let go of Violet and push myself up, every joint screaming like rusted hinges. My eyes lock on Ryder's, burning with something darker than anger. Without thinking, I charge, fists swinging wild.

"Did you do this?" I snarl, aiming for his jaw.

He catches my fist mid-air, twisting it as he beams at me with that infuriating grin.

"Wow, I didn't know you had it in you old man. Slow down there before you throw out your back. Are you seriously asking me that? You think I'd be the one to hurt her? Are you fucking insane?" He retorts, shaking his head with mock sympathy.

"Enough!" Kate steps between us, eyes blazing. "Man up, both of you. You want to throw punches? Fine, but *after* we get out of this nightmare alive. Right now, we have a fire breathing down our necks and a growing horde that isn't done with us yet."

Violet stands sheltered just behind Kate, watching us both with wide, confused eyes. I see the hurt flicker in her, like she doesn't know who to believe anymore. I clench my jaw.

"Let's move," the shorter soldier tosses out under his breath, already scanning the hallway.

We slip out, quiet as shadows, the smoke from the fire curling low through the blood-streaked halls. The heat licks at the back of my neck, the air thick with ash and the acrid stench of burning flesh. Every step is a gamble. Boots crunch over shattered glass, as we skirt around torn open bodies twitching with what is left of their nerves. Gunshots ring out behind us. Short, brutal bursts. Kate and one of Ryder's men hold the rear, knives flashing when the ammo runs dry. Violet stays close, her breath ragged and her body ravaged. A shriek cuts through the smoke. One of the infected staggers from the shadows, jaw slack and smeared with blood, arms reaching out in that awful, dragging way like death itself is pulling the strings. I drive my knife up under its chin, the blade punches through the soft flesh and shattering bone until the body goes limp in my hands. It crumples at my feet as another one pounces on Ryder. He drops it with two clean shots and doesn't stop moving.

I notice a little light from the corner of the camp. Is it a camera? Another shot rings out and we run.

Not a jog.

Not a retreat.

A full-on sprint through hell.

Our lungs burning, hearts pounding, fire licking at our heels. My legs scream in protest of every step, muscles shredded by adrenaline and fear. The forest looms ahead. Our last line of escape somewhere just beyond the tree line. Gunfire cracks like thunder behind us, echoing too loud, too long. We all know what it means. More would come, drawn to the noise and the impossible amount of blood. Chaos follows us like a second shadow, screams, snarls, and the crackling roar of flames devouring what is left of this cursed place.

The Jeep finally comes into view, hidden in the clearing like a promise I wasn't sure I deserved. A military bus pulls up. An old man yanks the door open.

"Let's go! Move your asses onto this bus!"

We stumble in, one after another, slick with sweat and streaked with God only knows who's blood. I don't look back. I don't need to. Some things don't deserve a second glance.

"We've got to move," Ryder barks at the bigger soldier already behind the wheel. "Those shots, *fuck*, every corpse within five miles heard them."

He was right. We'd made it out, but we were far from safe, because the dead are always listening.

CHAPTER 19

VIOLET

If someone had told me four days ago that I'd be on a military bus, wedged between my dad and the guy I haven't stopped thinking about after escaping a Deadhead-worshipping cult, I probably would've called the psych ward to come pick them up.

"Here, have some food and water, guys," one of the soldiers says kindly, handing some supplies to me and Dad.

There are quite a few survivors on this bus. I wonder if this is what is left of the military camp.

"I'm Violet, by the way, and this is my dad, Arthur," I say, gesturing to my dad.

He doesn't say much. Just gives a curt aknowledgment while borderline growling at Ryder. Pretty sure they are having a silent alpha stare-down. Still no clue what that's about.

"The one driving is Private Joe Hawthorne," the soldier continues, "I'm Private Andrew Sinclair."

I shake his hand like we are in some weird post-apocalyptic business meeting.

"You probably don't need an introduction to him," Sinclair adds, "but that's Corporal Ryder Kent."

My eyes flick to Ryder, and my cheeks instantly betray me by heating up. He gives me this lazy, knowing smile, steps closer, and kisses my hand.

"Pleasure to meet you, Violet Hayes," he says, driving a nail into my already-fragile composure. He remembered my last name. *Cute.*

"Ryder, I swear to God, I'll kill you right here if you pull that shit in front of me again," my dad voices out rough, venom tucked beneath the syllables.

Ryder smirks. "Then next time, I'll make sure you're not around."

With a wink, he turns and saunters toward the front of the bus stirring up every old feeling I'd been trying to bury.

"Dad, you seriously need to relax. Ryder's a good guy."

Dad makes a disgruntled *psst* sound and stalks off with Sinclair, who clearly takes the hint and guides him to the back of the bus to meet the others. Kate appears then, giving me another tight hug.

"Can we talk for a minute?" She asks me gently.

I shake my head yes, and she glances toward the front. Ryder is watching us. His expression is unreadable. Something in Kate's face shifts, her usual spark dimming. My stomach knots and I wonder what bad news she has to tell me, my heart tightening at the thought.

"Violet...I'm so sorry about the daycare," Kate's voice cracks as she says it. "I'm assuming you saw it?"

Tears prick the corners of my eyes as the image of the scorched wreckage flashes through my mind. The swing set half-melted, the walls charred black, the smell of ash and something far worse still clinging to my memory. The fire had swallowed everything.

"I was outside, setting up for outdoor playtime," Kate explains, voice quivering with emotion, "Then all of a sudden… the sky just—" She breaks off, her hands shaking despite her efforts to stop the tremors.

"It was bombed. One second I was laying out toy trucks and chalk, the next…" Her eyes lose focus. "Everything exploded. I passed out. And when I came to, I was under some wood and the daycare was gone, engulfed in flames, and… those things were everywhere. So, I just ran and found somewhere to hide so those things couldn't get me. Then Ryder, Hawthorne and Sinclair found me." Her face crumples. "I'm so sorry I couldn't save her, Violet. I'm so fucking sorry. All those kids…they deserved to live. I should've died instead."

She collapses into me, sobbing from her confession. Gut-wrenching, breath-stealing sobs. I wrap my arms around her and hold her tight, pressing my cheek to hers. I can feel the guilt pouring out of her like a poison she can't seem to purge.

My voice breaks, but I make myself speak. "Kate…I forgive you."

She stiffens in my arms, in disbelief.

"I'll mourn Jane for the rest of my life. But this world…it's no place for children. Not anymore. They deserve playgrounds, laughter, story time. They deserve birthday candles and bedtime kisses, not running for their lives."

My voice shakes as I force the words out, my heart clenching. "As much as it kills me to say goodbye, at least she doesn't have to be afraid. At least she doesn't have to wonder where her next meal is coming from…or worry if her mom's going to come back with dead eyes and blood dripping from her teeth."

Kate pulls away, eyes glassy. "Your words… they're almost exactly what Ryder said you would say."

I blink. "You told him? About all of this?"

She sheepishly agrees. "I also told him…about Jeremy." She hesitates, watching my expression carefully.

My stomach drops. "What? Jeremy? Oh god. Well, he doesn't need to worry about him. He died and then I killed him."

I don't know whether to cry or laugh. Kate gives a bitter chuckle.

"Good. He's one of the few people who actually deserved all this."

A jolt of memory flashes through me.

The letters.

The drawer.

"I—I found something," I said, unzipping my backpack. I show her the worn bundle of envelopes. "While he was dying, he said something about a secret…about being sorry. I found these. In the bottom drawer of his dresser."

Kate reaches for them, but I close the flap before she can touch them.

"Not here," I whisper. "I don't want anyone to know I have them. Not yet. Not until I've talked to Ryder."

She understands slowly, "He told me he wrote to you. That you never answered. Said it broke him."

A twinge of guilt curls through my chest. God, I wish I could just walk over to him, grab him by the collar, and kiss him. No words. Just…make him feel what I never got to say. I glance toward the front of the bus. Ryder is deep in conversation with Hawthorne, head turned, his jaw set in that familiar, unreadable way. Before I can act on my impulses a soft voice cuts through the noise.

"Hi," says a woman, stepping into the aisle with a small boy holding her hand. "I'm Teresa, and this is Dion."

I turn to face them. Despite everything, I offer a smile. This world isn't made for kids but I still have a soft spot for them. Especially the ones who are still lucky enough to hold a hand that isn't cold.

"I'm Violet Hayes," I say gently, offering a small smile. "And that's Arthur Hayes, my dad."

The woman's eyes widen slightly with recognition. "I remember you… from the military camp. You're the one he snuck out, right? Before everything went to hell?"

Oh god they know that?

"Yeah… I'm sorry to hear what happened there."

"Yeah… me too. It was madness. We barely made it out alive." She glances down at her little boy and presses a kiss to the top of his head. "Thank the Lord we did, though. That's all that matters now."

I don't say anything. Just meet her eyes and hold the silence, knowing there is nothing I can say to make what she saw or what she lost any easier.

Kate breaks the lull, her voice soft but steady. "Why don't we introduce you to everyone, Violet? You've met Sinclair, Hawthorne, Ryder…and now Teresa and Little Dion." She glances around the bus. "Come on. Let's make the rounds."

I follow her as we move toward the back. My dad trails a few feet behind, ever-watchful and still stiff from the earlier tension, especially with Ryder in the mix. Kate gestures toward an older man sitting by the window with a thick knit blanket over his lap. He looks as though he's seen too many winters and not enough peace.

"That's Wilson. He's sort of our unofficial lookout. Keeps watch when we stop, and doesn't take shit from anyone."

Wilson grunts in acknowledgment, his sharp gray eyes meeting mine. "So, you're the one who came out that cult mess. You got guts, girl."

"Or just bad luck," I say, offering a small smile.

He gives a raspy laugh.

Kate moves on, pointing at a kid who couldn't have been older than fifteen, hunched over a dog-eared comic book. "That's Jalen. He's been with us since the military camp too."

Jalen looks up briefly, then returns to his comics without a word. His hands have a slight tremor to them. Next is a short guy about my age, maybe a year or two older, sitting beside a woman who looks like she hasn't slept in days.

"That's Theo," Kate says. "And that's Emily beside him. They were med students before the world flipped. Kind of bonded over trauma."

"Nice to meet you," Theo says, his voice calm but tired. Emily gives a slight wave, her fingers fidgeting with the sleeve of her jacket.

Finally, Kate gestures to a lanky guy near the back whose left arm is wrapped in a makeshift bandage, darkened by old blood. "That's Kian. He got clipped by a broken fence trying to escape the camp, we got him some antibodies a few days ago."

I stop in front of him, eyeing the bandage. The red seeping through was not a good sign. "Has anyone looked at that?"

Kian shrugs. "Emily cleaned it, but we ran out of proper gauze."

"I'm…well, I was…a paramedic," I say, kneeling beside him before the words have fully left my mouth. "Mind if I take a look?"

A flash of panic registers across his face but he holds his arm out. "Yeah, sure. I mean, if you don't mind."

"Not at all."

Kate hands me a small kit they had stashed nearby. I peel the edge of the bandage back carefully, biting the inside of my cheek. The cut is deep—jagged, swollen, and definitely infected.

"This needs to be cleaned again. Properly. You're lucky it's not worse.

My hands move on instinct, the muscle memory of training and years on the job taking over. Behind me, I hear my dad finally talking with Sinclair, asking about the plan. It feels like we are beginning to find our place here—at least for now. Even though deep down I know peace doesn't last in this world. When I glance back, Ryder is leaning against the emergency door owning the air around him. Arms crossed, jaw set, those hazel eyes locked on me, slow and deliberate, like I am something he hasn't decided whether to devour or protect. It's electric and familiar in a way I'd almost forgotten. The kind of feeling that makes you lean into the flame instead of running from it.

He doesn't move.

Doesn't blink.

Just let's that crooked smile curl the edge of his mouth.

"So, you really did become a paramedic then, darlin'."

CHAPTER 20

RYDER

Fuck, I need a shower. I am trying to win over Violet while wearing a full coat of cultist blood and brain matter. Some real Romeo shit.

"Well, I'm proud of you, Ocean Eyes," I say, giving her the kind of smile that usually came with bad decisions and broken headboards.

I feel those eyes on me, burning holes through the side of my skull. I turn, slow and deliberate, and there he is. The world's largest cock block *Arthur.* Clocking me like a bug under his magnifying glass. That smug, holier-than-thou expression glued to his face like he thinks he has some moral high ground. I stare right back and let my scowl do the talking. The kind that dares, *try me, old man*. Then I pivot back to Violet, because honestly, he doesn't exist when she is in front of me. She's blushing again. That soft flush climbing her cheeks like wildfire. I can't look away. The way her eyes catch the last of the dying light, the way her lips curve when she says my name…God, I am practically drooling.

"Thanks, Ryder. I'm proud of you too," she says, voice warm and honest. "Corporal Kent."

My chest squeezes tight, like she's reaching inside and jumpstarting something that long ago forgot how to feel. The title never meant much before, just brass and blood but hearing it from her? *It hits different.*

"Thanks," I stammer, a little huskier than I mean it to be. My gaze lingers too long. I am locked in, *gone*, sinking into the heat between us not caring if it burns the world down. Then Sinclair grabs my arm and gives it a sharp shake.

"Hey, lover boy. Earth to Ryder." I blink and then blink again. His hand is still on me. I stare at it like it is an insect, unsure if I wanted to squash it or rip it off.

"One sec, Darlin. Apparently, I'm needed."

I glance back at her and when she smiles, it hits like a sucker punch. Just for a second, I forget I am coated in blood and Dybbuk guts. The look on her face short-circuits every survival instinct I have.

Yep... there it is.

I am definitely horny. *Fantastic.* Nothing says great timing like a half-chub and the stench of death.

"We've got to find a place to set up camp," Sinclair says, frowning. "You reek, man. Like… corpse-brothel levels."

"Sinclair, you're absolutely right we do need to find somewhere, but say I stink one more time and I'll throw you off this bus and let the Dybbuks braid your intestines."

He laughs. I don't. I move toward Hawthorne, bumping Arthur's shoulder hard as I pass. He looks surprised, like he thought we were pals now.

Not even close, buddy. I know what you did.

"Hey, Hawthorne. What's our location?"

"Two hours out from Jasper. Maybe less," he says, checking the map.

"Cool. Let's find somewhere to crash. We could use a night where we are not running for our lives."

Arthur leans between us as if I invited him into the briefing. "There's a campground I used to take my family to. It's about twenty minutes from here. No reason the dead would be there. We could have a fire, rest, and regroup. You guys got tents?"

I stare at him hard. "Why the fuck would I trust you?"

"Kent," Kate chimes in, "Stop acting like a pissed-off teenager. It's a solid plan."

Violet agrees behind her.

Kate continues "We stocked up at the camping store. We've got a few compact stoves, propane, blankets, tarps, ten sleeping bags, eight tents, fire starter kits. The works."

Arthur smiles like we're headed on a sleepover and not a pit stop between trauma and survival.

"Nice work," Arthur says, as if he had helped. "I've fished that river plenty of times. I can get us dinner."

I shoot him a look that says '*if you breathe wrong, I might bury you*'. Unfortunately, he is right. Clean water… Hot food…Safe-ish shelter. It sounds too good to be true.

"Alright," I sigh, dragging a hand through my blood-stiff hair. "Here's the plan."

Arthur climbs into the passenger seat next to Hawthorne while I hang back with the others. I don't love giving the guy any more input than necessary, but I also don't know where the hell this campground is. If he tries anything, well...I haven't unloaded my pistol yet. I climb into a seat in the back, slouched low, but my eyes keep drifting. Every few minutes, I glance over my shoulder to look at her. I can't help myself. Violet sits near the window, hands folded in her lap, eyes tracing the trees like she is anywhere but here. When she finally catches me looking, I give her a slow wink. A soft smile playing at the corners of her lips. That one smile did more to me than a warm meal or a full magazine ever could. We drive in silence except for the occasional thump in the distance and Sinclair humming what I think is Highway to Hell. Very on brand.

When we pull into the site, I squint through the windshield. It looks… not terrible. A few leaning picnic tables, a creepy-ass trail sign that probably once said Welcome, and porta potties that I imagine smell like a chemical war crime but there are no fresh corpses, no rot in the air… I've seen worse. Everyone piles out, groaning and stretching like we have rolled up for summer camp and hadn't just survived another brush with hell. I step onto the gravel, stretch, and let my spine crack like popcorn in hot oil relieving the stiffness in my back. The air here is thick with pine, damp moss, and dirt… but at least it wasn't blood for once.

Hawthorne catches my eye across the lot. I jerk my head toward a pair of busted-up RVs parked crooked near the tree line. They are weather-beaten, one with moss growing over the windows like green veins, the other missing a door completely.

"Let's clear those first," I say, already walking swiftly towards the closest one. "You check the far one."

Hawthorne grunts an affirmative and splits off. I swing the door of the first RV open, pistol drawn. The stink hits me first: stale rot, piss, old food, death. The couch is torn, cupboards ransacked, but no movement. I creep in but it's empty. Only the soft creak or rope from somewhere within. I pivot slowly, my flashlight beam catching the hanging figure in the bathroom. At first, it looks as though he is just plain dead. His neck is tilted at a grotesque angle, eyes bulging. A low, wet groan escapes him, his body twitching in lazy, slow motion. Hanging hadn't kept him dead. I step back, bile rising in my throat.

"You've got to be kidding me," One clean shot and the body drops like a sack of meat, swaying against the wall with a sickening thud. Violet is at the door when I step out. Her eyes dart to the newest blood spatter on my sleeve, then to the gun.

"What happened?"

"Guy hung himself. Guess it didn't stick."

Her face falls. "So… even if you kill yourself…"

"You still come back…" The muscle in my jaw ticks while I continue, "Unless the brain's toast, yeah."

She looks haunted. "Grace… at the hospital. She flatlined. I…I held her hand until she was gone but then she woke up."

"I get it." My voice comes out rougher than I intend. "Same thing with my friend Ryan. He was the one who helped me get you out. A Dybbuk got him. I thought it was over. Then he started groaning and I knew what had to be done."

Her throat bobs as she forces the lump down. "So, we're all ticking time bombs."

I take a really hard look at her and I see the sheer gravity of it all pressing into her spine. The grief, the fear, the knowledge that any one of us could go at any moment and come back wrong. I reach out and brush a strand of hair behind her ear.

"Not today," I say, putting my hand on her cheek. "We're still breathing. That has to count for something."

She leans into my hand then nods but her eyes stay locked on the trees, distant and dark.

"Come on," I say, tossing a glance toward the second RV. "Let's go check on Hawthorne."

"I'll take this one…with my daughter," Arthur snaps, already stomping past me like I'd insulted his parenting skills.

I arch my brow. "Go ahead, champ. Just don't cry when she starts listening to me instead."

He shot me a look over his shoulder, but I just smirk. I could say more. I could say *'just don't cry when she starts calling me Daddy instead.'* Hell, I want to but if I open that door, it won't be words we trade. If I'm being honest, I'd probably kill him. Not exactly great for group morale. So instead, I turn on my heel and find Hawthorne leaning against the post near the bus.

He gives me a disapproving look. "Nothing but cut up cushions and empty shelves in that RV. The stores probably already picked clean too."

"Yeah," I say, cracking my knuckles. "I'm praying to whatever apocalyptic god still listens that there's soap left. I'm trying to impress my girl here and I smell like something that crawled out of a Dybbuk's ass."

He snorts. "River's right there."

"Which is exactly why we're going to the store first," I say, gesturing toward the faded wooden shack up the path. "If I'm bathing in river water, I'm doing it with shampoo and not fish piss."

He gives me a dry look. "Alright let's go check it out."

We peel off from the group, heading for what probably used to be the camp store. I glance back at Violet before we leave. She is talking to Kate, but she catches me looking.

The store has been looted once, maybe twice, but we were better scavengers. I yank open drawers and pop open cabinets. Hawthorne tosses me a pack of instant ramen with a *'cat ate the canary'* grin. I hit the jackpot in the hygiene section or what is left of it. A cracked plastic bin holds tiny travel-sized bottles just waiting for me. Shampoo, conditioner, even some sad little hotel soaps wrapped in wax paper. I hold them up like holy relics.

"Oh baby," I whisper, "Come to Daddy."

Hawthorne tosses me a lifted eyebrow look from across the room. "If you start making out with the soap, I'm leaving you here."

Then he pulls out a roll of fishing line and some half-busted rods. "Think we can rig something?"

"Hell yeah. Go get those fish, old-school style."

We make it back to the others just as everyone is collapsing onto the damp picnic benches, looking like the end of a bad horror road trip. Violet sits on the edge, eyes scanning the trees not quite ready to relax.

"Alright, hygiene hour with your favorite apocalypse heartthrob," I say, tossing the tiny bottles onto the table. "Congratulations! You're all getting soap. It's Christmas."

Kate catches one mid-air. "What, no body lotion?"

"Beggars can't be choosers," I say, handing Violet one and letting my fingers brush hers for a little too long. She doesn't pull away. *Win.*

I gesture toward the lake behind us. "River's not warm, but it beats smelling like hot guts. Strip, wash, rinse your clothes. Then hang 'em to dry on a tree or on the ground. Does everyone have a change of clothes?"

Kian groans. "We're doing laundry now? What are we, settlers?"

"Settlers who don't want to die from a staph infection," I say. "You want your crotch to rot off?"

"Fair point," Hawthorne adds, already tugging off his jacket.

Everyone starts rummaging through their packs. Emily pulls out a bundled flannel. Theo has a spare T-shirt stuffed in his waistband. Even Kate, queen of sarcasm, produces a Ziplock bag of clean underwear flexing on the rest of us.

Arthur and Violet just stand there. She doesn't say anything, just gives a small shake of her head. Her shoulders pull in not wanting to be noticed, preferring to melt into the dirt. Of course, she doesn't have extra clothes. The cult barely let her live and we didn't bring the jeep. Without thinking, I step forward, pulling open my own bag and tugging out a folded black shirt and a pair of drawstring sweats.

"Here," I say, holding them out to her. "Not exactly haute couture, but it's clean and smells like me, so… win-win."

She looks at the bundle, then up at me. Her lower lip quivers. "You sure?"

"I've seen you covered in blood and you still look better than half of us," I say, my voice lowering now. "Plus, I kind of like seeing you in my clothes."

A beat passes, my eyes not leaving hers. She takes the clothes wordlessly, and I swear my hand burns for a second where our fingers touch. I turn away before I do something stupid, like make out with her in front of her deranged father. Next to us, Arthur clears his throat awkwardly. Hawthorne notices and pulls a worn hoodie and some cargo pants from his pack.

"I've got spares. Nothing fancy, but they'll fit," he says, tossing them over.

Arthur gives a brief tilt of his head, a rough *thanks* slipping out. I catch Violet still holding my clothes to her chest as if they meant more than they should, and I hoped they did.

Sinclair, Arthur, Wilson, Hawthorne, Jalen, Teresa and Little Dion grab the makeshift rods that Hawthorne has rigged and start lumbering down to the river bend, talking quietly among themselves. Arthur lingers a second, helping Dion with his gear.

"Y'know… I always wanted to take my son fishing one more time," his voice soft. "Never thought I'd get to teach someone else's."

No one says anything. I don't trust the guy, but I'm not heartless.

"All right, filthy animals," I say, clapping my hands. "Go wash up. River's that way. If you see anything dead, kill it. Then rinse off after."

Kian, Theo, Emily, Kate and Violet, all follow me. Kate rolls her eyes, talking under her breath about spa days being better with wine. I just wink at Violet as I start down the path toward the water, peeling my shirt off as I walk.

Once we arrive at the river and everyone branches off. Through my peripherals I see her pulling her shirt over her head, the curve of her back catching the dying sun like a struck match. Water glints behind her like liquid fire, and I have to turn away before whatever scrap of control I have left snaps clean in half. My brain knows better, but my dick sure as hell doesn't. I find a quiet bend further down the shoreline, tucked behind a curtain of evergreens. Finally, alone I strip down to nothing, and step into the cold water. I hiss through my teeth. It isn't comfort, but it is survival. It feels like peeling off armor made of blood, sweat, and weeks of unspoken rage. Soap hits skin for the first time in what feels like forever. *Real* soap. The type that doesn't smell like antiseptic or gasoline. I drag it across my chest, over inked muscle and dried blood, watching the grime swirl off into the current. My skin, already tanned from too much sun and too few shirts, glows beneath the grit. Tattooed sleeves in vibrant ink wrap around my arms like wild stories written in color. I scrub to reveal the art; flowers, skulls, bones, and a shark each one earned, each one remembered. I tilt my head back, fingers raking through wet strands of dirty blonde hair and my scalp sings. My shoulders, broad and tight with weeks of tension, finally let go. I scour harder, trying to erase the scent of death clinging to me like a second skin. Then I get to work on my clothes. I rinse them then slap them over a low-hanging branch to dry.

I slip into my clean-ish clothes smelling like soap and not rotting flesh. It is the closest I've felt to a human being in a few days. I circle back around the bend, damp hair clinging to my neck, skin scrubbed raw and stinging from cold river water and overuse of soap. Violet is sitting by the fire pit with Kate who is poking through twigs and dried branches, trying to build a fire. I join them, tossing in a decent log I found on my way back. Kian and Emily are dragging over a tarp to make a wind block when Kate suddenly goes still. Her shoulders tense, head cocking. The groan gets my attention and my eyes shift in the direction of the sound.

From the brush, one of the dead stumbles out. Gaunt, gray skinned, wearing a faded red vest with a cracked name tag still pinned to the front 'RANDY.' A gas station attendant. Probably wandered out here from whatever shell of a town was nearby. Maybe he'd been looking for help or maybe just ran in any direction not wanting to die behind the counter of a Chevron. None of that mattered now. It leaps, jaws snapping with the wet, hollow, bone-sick sound that has been echoing in my skull for days. Kate doesn't even blink. One clean swing of the hatchet and the head goes flying, hitting the ground like a kicked melon. Blood fans out over the pine needles, still glistening under the last stretch of sunlight. She wipes the blade on her pant leg and goes right back to stacking kindling like it is just another Tuesday.

"Thanks for the assist, Randy," I cheer, nudging the Dybbuk with my boot.

Violet laughs softly but genuine. I'll take that over gold.

"Don't encourage him," Kate remarks.

"I don't need encouragement. I run on spite, soap, and the sound of this beauty's laugh."

She blushes again. God, I missed that soft flush that creeps up her neck. Right now, it looks as if I still have some kind of pull on her. Our team works in sync, side by side, piecing together this mess of a camp for a stronghold. For a glint of a second, it all feels strangely normal. A parody of the world we lost. It's almost human.

Almost.

CHAPTER 21

VIOLET

Dad used to bring Mom, Felix, and I here almost every year when we were younger. It had been a tradition, one of the few constants in our lives right up until the last four years, when life got too busy, too messy, too full of everything but time. I remember telling myself I'd bring Ryder here one day, that we'd sit by the river and skip rocks like we didn't have a care in the world. Funny how things work out.

Now here I am, watching my dad and a few of the others trek back from the lake with a string of fresh-caught fish slung over their shoulders. It looks like salmon, though I can't be sure. Either way, food is food, and while I've never really liked fish before, the end of the world has a way of shifting your palate. Survival doesn't care about preference.

"Dinner is served," Hawthorne calls out with a grin, slapping the fish down across the weathered picnic table, a feast fit for royalty as far as we were all concerned.

"Good job, guys," Ryder adds, his voice steady and just loud enough to command attention. "Now go wash up before we lose sunlight and stay alert. One of the dead tried to sneak up on Kate earlier." He tilts his head toward the Deadhead sprawled beside the benches, its skull caved in like a cracked melon.

Everyone snaps to it without hesitation, even my dad. That alone catches me off guard. Watching him follow Ryder's lead feels…strange. Dad wasn't one to take orders and for some reason, ever since Ryder showed up again, there'd been this tension between them. Something tight and unspoken, a string pulled taut. It doesn't make sense. Ryder had saved me. Literally dragged me out of hell. Dad had always liked him back in high school…or at least, I thought he did. My thoughts are violently interrupted by Kate, suddenly channeling her inner Gordon Ramsay like she is filming an episode of Kitchen Nightmares: Apocalypse Edition. She barks orders at Kian, Theo, Emily,

Ryder, and me with such authority that we all jump into action without hesitation.

"Someone get some pine needles or bark, anything to add flavor!" she shouts. "Theo, start deboning the fish! Ryder, make sure that fire's big enough to actually cook on! Emily, help Violet with side dishes. We are feasting tonight!"

It is chaos, but organized chaos. I scramble to think of a side dish and land on something surprisingly decent, a salad of dandelion greens and rice. Not exactly gourmet but it's better than canned tuna and granola bars. We have a jug of water to go with it, and I find a few beers tucked away in one of the packs that I'm sure the guys will make short work of. I grab two camping stoves and start the rice. Then I set out plastic plates, forks, and cups on the picnic table so everyone can eat together, like an actual group, not just survivors. For a moment, it feels like a normal camping trip. People laughing, moving around with purpose, doing something simple like making dinner. I even show them the old well pump I know about, just past the tree line. With a little effort, it gives us fresh drinking water. Pretty close to unlimited.

While me and Em pick the greens, I can't help but glance over at Ryder who is chopping up small trees for firewood with the hatchet, the same one Kate used to take out a Deadhead earlier. Every swing of his arm sends a jolt down my spine. The way his shirt clings to his back, the muscles working beneath it, the calm intensity on his face. He makes it look easy and I can feel my internal temperature rising.

Fuck. Violet get ahold of yourself.

He knows I'm watching. There is this sexy smirk at the corner of his mouth that gives him away. I've always been so attracted to Ryder, but this version of him? I might need to take a walk back down to the river just to cool off. Once everyone is back from their respective jobs, we set up the tents while Kate and her cooking minions finish up dinner.

"What's the sleeping arrangement, Kent?" Sinclair eyebrows.

Shit. I didn't even think of that. Maybe Kate will let me bunk with her?

"We have eight tents, so only a few have to bunk together." Ryder says, winking at me.

"Absolutely not," my dad says, throwing a pointer finger in Ryder's face.

"I think that's up to Violet, old man Art…" Ryder chirps back.

"Actually, I'll bunk with Kate, Dad."

They both raise an eyebrow. I shoot Kate a *'shut up, it's been decided'* look, and she just laughs at me.

"I want a tent alone," Wilson chimes in.

"I'll bunk with Jalen! I want to see what comics he is reading anyway." Kian says.

That leaves Teresa with Dion, Theo and Emily together. My dad alone. Dumb and dumber together and Ryder by himself which is perfect for me. Once I hear my dad's obnoxious snoring, I'll be sneaking out to see if Ryder and I can talk privately.

"Dinner is ready" Kate yells out and I've never been so happy to hear those words.

We all gather around the picnic table, plates in hand. The dandelion salad isn't exactly restaurant quality, but paired with hot fish, rice and cold well water, it tastes like heaven. Dinner is quiet at first. Just the sound of chewing and the occasional soft murmur. Then slowly, the laughter returns. Even Dad cracks a smile after Jalen nearly chokes trying to eat too fast. Afterward, we set to work securing the camp. Hawthorne and Sinclair walk the perimeter, placing makeshift noise traps with empty cans, glass shards, even string tied to branches. Dad double-checks the bus with Wilson. Kate helps Emily hang laundry while the rest of us clean up dinner.

It is honestly peaceful.

I continue stealing glances at Ryder. He hasn't said much, just keeps pacing near the tree line, his mind miles away. I really want to talk to him. Ask him about the letters and of course thank him for saving me, *twice* now. Dad grabs one of the single tents and mumbles something about needing space to stretch out his back. Wilson claims his own with a grumble about '*old man bones* and Kian practically drags Jalen into theirs, already talking about some vintage comic he'd found. Teresa curls up with Dion in one of the smaller tents, while Emily and Theo zip into theirs without saying much.

"Goodnight dad, I love you" I say, squeezing him extra hard.

"Good night. I love you too." he says, ending the hug and slipping into his tent but not before giving Ryder the '*I'm watching you*' sign, and I giggle when Ryder rolls his eyes. Kate and I share a tent, like we said we would and she teases me the moment we get inside just like I knew she would.

"Girl… Ryder has basically fucked you with his eyes all night."

"Keep it down, I don't think my dad's asleep yet" I say, zipping up the tent. "Also, *yes,* I know he was eye fucking me, I was also eye fucking him…Kate he looks amazing and I know how he feels about me thanks to the letters. Maybe it's our chance to finally be together. Also, can I just say dinner tonight was so well executed. Good job."

Kate laughs at my ramblings "Go and talk to him later tonight. Just be safe, the last thing we need is apocalypse babies." She laughs, finding herself hilarious. "I'm happy everyone enjoyed it and got a nice warm meal. Now I'm going to try and actually get a good night's sleep tonight. I love you Vi."

She rolls over leaving me to myself.

"Love you too Kate."

I lay down and look up at the ceiling of the tent waiting for my moment. Eventually, after one last chorus of grunted goodnights and the occasional shuffle of boots, the camp goes still.

Except for the sound of my dad's signature chainsaw snore slicing through the night air like it always had. That was my cue.

I ease out of the tent, careful not to rustle the zipper too loud. Kate is already asleep, or pretending to be. Either way, she doesn't stop me. I keep low as I sneak past the fire pit, now mostly glowing coals. Everyone seems to be out cold. Hawthorne and Sinclair are sprawled outside their tent, lightly snoring in sync. Perfect.

"Just grabbing some snacks from the store," I whisper, just in case anyone is still awake.

The camp store sits just past the tree line, its wooden sign hanging by one rusted chain like it has given up. The roof slouches inward, windows shattered and sharp, catching the moonlight like broken mirrors. I pause at the edge of the clearing, heart thudding. Ryder is already there, as if he had been waiting in the shadows for me. Leaning against the side of the store, arms crossed, a joint glowing between his fingers. The smell invades my nostrils before I see the smoke curl around his face. Fuck, I've missed that scent. I creep up behind him, quiet as I can, snatch the joint from his hand, and bring it to my lips. The plant hit my lungs hard, sharp, and familiar. Ryder doesn't flinch, just lets his eyes drag over me slowly, memorizing every inch, that lazy, dangerous grin curved his mouth.

"Are you always this direct when you sneak out for a midnight smoke?"

I take a drag, letting the smoke settle deep before blowing it out between my lips. "Only when the company's worth it."

His gaze drops to my mouth, then back to my eyes. "Careful, Hayes. Keep looking at me like that, and I might start thinking you missed me."

I lean in just enough to hand the joint back, my fingers brushing his. "Say I did, what are you going to do about it?"

His grin turns sharp, taking my bait between his teeth. "Depends. Are you looking for trouble…or asking for it?" His voice is low and threaded with something heavier than smoke.

I don't just smile this time. I step closer. My skin buzzes as I hold his stare and the heat crawls up my neck, blooming across my chest.

"I'm asking," I say, my voice quieter now. Not timid. Just honest.

Ryder lets out a low chuckle, shaking his head and I can tell he likes me dangerous. "You always did know how to get under my skin."

"And you never left mine," I say before I can stop myself.

That wipes the grin off his face but only for a second. His gaze shifts quickly, betraying a thought…recognition maybe, or regret. Whatever it is, it changes the air between us. He steps closer, and I don't shy away.

"I thought you were dead before the military camp" I say, my voice cracking at the edge. "Back in Banff… the cult… I didn't know if I'd ever see you again."

He reaches up and brushes a strand of hair from my face, fingers lingering just a second too long.

"You really think I'd let this world take me before I saw you again?" he whispers. "Not a fucking chance."

The joint burns low in his fingers, forgotten.

"I found the letters," The words tumble out before I can reel them back. "While Jeremy died…he said something about letters, and they were at the bottom of his dresser. Every one of them."

Ryder goes still and his eyes harden like ice cracking under pressure.

"I never sent them to him," he said slowly. "I sent them to your house. Your actual home address."

My heart drops into my stomach. "What?"

"Figured your dad might at least hand them over. Guess I was wrong about that."

I take a step back, pulse pounding. "He knew? My dad knew and didn't say a fucking word?"

I turn toward camp, blood surging in my ears, ready to march back and scream the truth in Arthur Hayes' face. Right as

I am about to turn, Ryder's hand shoots out and grabs my arm, pulling me back to him in one quick, firm motion. I gasp. His body is so close I can feel the heat pouring off him, his grip anything but gentle.

"Not tonight," he says, voice low, and possessive. "You'll wake the whole damn camp."

I swallow hard, breath catching as he leans in, his lips brushing my ear.

"You can scream at your dad tomorrow," he whispers, "but tonight… let me show you what those letters never could."

CHAPTER 22

RYDER

The joint hisses out beneath my boot, its ember crushed into the dirt like every half-assed attempt I'd made to forget her. Five and a half fucking years of wondering if I was the only one who felt like something vital had been ripped out and never stitched back in.

I stare at her, like really stare. Her eyes haven't changed. Still a storm I can never outrun. Blue like fresh water, so blue you're willing to drown on purpose. They pull me in, same as they always have. All it takes is a glance and I am nineteen again, reckless and already ruined for anyone else.

"I didn't miss you, Violet." I pull her closer, gaze locked. "I ached for you. Every hour. Every breath. Like something vital was gone and I couldn't survive without it."

She doesn't look away. Her lip's part like she wants to speak, but can't. The weight of everything between us is finally catching up.

"You were the ghost I *never* wanted to stop seeing, and now you're *right here.*"

The air between us feels electric. Heavy with everything unspoken and everything we still wanted. Still *needed.*

"Say something," I rasp.

She shakes her head, but her eyes are all heat. "If I say anything, I'm going to do something reckless."

My mouth twitches. "Then let's be reckless."

I grab her by the back of her neck and pull her in our lips, almost touching.

"You're mine," I breathe, my lips brushing hers. "And I'm done pretending otherwise."

I catch her mouth with mine in a way that feels more like a claim than a question. She gasps but then melts into me with that same fire I remember from the nights long buried. *Fuck,* I've dreamed of this moment. Her hands tangle in my shirt. Mine slide over her curves, soft and familiar. I kiss her like I'm starving, like I've been walking through hell with her name carved into my spine, and this was the only thing that could bring me back.

She bites my lip causing a groan to escape my lips and lands against her mouth, the sound rough and desperate. God, I'd missed this, missed her, missed the way her body fits against mine, like it was made to. The way she tastes like a memory I am not supposed to have survived. When we finally break apart, it is only because we are both breathless. Our chests rise and fall in sync, and I can still feel her heartbeat pounding against mine.

I press my forehead to hers. "Follow me."

She doesn't hesitate. Just laces her fingers through mine as if not a single second had been lost between us. I need to find a place I can bend this beautiful woman over and claim what's mine. *Fuck*, I feel a primal urge to be deep inside her take over me.

Light bulb. The camp store.

I unlock the door and shut it behind us, the click of the lock sealing us into something inevitable. She stands there, barely a foot away, bathed in silver light. Her lips are still parted from our last kiss, chest rising as she tries to catch her breath. I can still feel the dull burn in my shoulders from splitting fire wood, but none of that matters now. The river has cleaned the blood off my skin, but not the hunger that makes my teeth ache. Her eyes drag over me, like she can read every mark inked on my skin, every sharp edge I'd grown in the years without her.

"Ryder. What are we doing?"

"Making up for lost time," I huff, before claiming her mouth again in a kiss that steals the very breath from her lungs.

My hands slide down her waist, tugging at the bottom hem of her shirt. She lifts her arms, allowing me to strip the fabric away. I toss it aside, my gaze drinking in the sight of her soft stomach and the swell of her breasts straining against her bra.

She is exquisite, a living masterpiece carved from the finest curves. Her waist dips in just enough to pull your eyes in, hips flaring out with a bold, seductive grace that speaks of feminine strength and softness all at once. Every line of her body is a promise, from the gentle, voluptuous curve of her form to the smooth, tempting fullness of her thighs. Like an artist painted desire itself in flesh and bone.

I trail my lips along her jaw, down the column of her throat, pausing to nip at the sensitive skin just above her collarbone. She arches into me, a soft moan falling from her lips.

"*Fuck, Ryder,*" she breathes, "I've missed you so much."

Her confession only spurs me on, my hands move to unclasp her bra. The straps slip down her shoulders, baring her breasts to my hungry gaze. I palm the soft mounds, thumbs grazing over her pebbled nipples. She whimpers, pressing into my touch.

"Tell me you want this," I growl, my voice thick with lust. "Tell me you need me as much as I need you."

"Yes," she pants, her nails digging into my shoulders. "Please, Ryder. I need you more than I should, more than I can stand. Every part of me wants this."

Those were the magic words. I capture her mouth in a bruising kiss as my hands work to rid her of the rest of her clothing and shoes. I hoist her up, wrapping her legs around my waist as I carry her to the checkout counter. She gasps as I set her down on the cold surface, her back arching off the smooth wood. I take a moment to appreciate the sight of her, laid out like a feast for me to devour. My mouth starts to water.

"Violet. I craved you. Every fucking day. Your voice, your skin. I thought about us until it drove me half insane." I confess, trailing a hand up her inner thigh. "Now having you spread out before me, here for my touch…"

I sink to my knees, dragging her hips to the edge of the counter. I push her thighs apart, revealing her glistening petals. Violet's chest heaves with anticipation, her thighs trembling slightly.

"I'm going to devour you until you're screaming my name." My eyes darken with possessiveness as I gaze at her.

Violet lets out a shaky breath, a flush spreading across her chest.

"Then what are you waiting for?" She purrs, a wicked glint in her eye. "Show me how much you missed me."

My response is a low, animalistic growl. I lean in, my tongue parting her in one long, languid stroke. She gasps, her fingers tangling in my hair as I delve deeper, savoring her sweet taste. I take my time exploring her, committing every inch of her form to memory. I trace her, swirling my tongue around her sensitive clit until she is writhing beneath me. My hands grip her thighs, holding her open for my relentless assault.

"*Fuck, Ryder,*" she exhales, "This feels incredible "

Emboldened by her response, I slide two fingers into her tight heat, curling them just right. Violet lets out a keening moan, her hips undulating against my face. I pick up the pace, fingers pumping in and out as my tongue continues on her clit. I can feel her walls starting to flutter, signaling her impending release.

"Eyes on me, baby," I coax, my voice muffled against her.

"Come for me," I command, "I want to watch your face twist in pure fucking bliss."

I suck while pumping my two fingers faster. "I'm going to make you come so hard, you are going to see stars."

My words push her over the edge. Violet's body tenses, her back arching off the counter as she cries out in ecstasy. Her inner muscles clench around my fingers as she rides out her orgasm, wave after wave of pleasure crashing over her.

"Such a good girl, for me." I whisper.

I continue my ministrations until she is boneless, collapsing back onto the counter with a satisfied sigh. Once she is spent, I rise to my feet, with a satisfied smirk on my face. Violet looks up at me, her chest still heaving with exertion. She jumps off the counter and pushes me towards it. I lean back against the cold, sucking my fingers, savoring the trace of Violet on my lips.

"You taste *so* fucking delicious."

She locks eyes on me, a satisfied smirk playing at the corners of her mouth.

"Your turn," she breathes, moving down to her knees. "My mouth has missed that big hard cock of yours."

My cock twitches in anticipation. Violet crawls towards me, her movements are sensual and predatory as she settles between my thighs.

"You look so damn sexy on your knees for me, begging to suck me off." I say leaning up, running my hand down her soft face.

"Holy shit," her eyes widen, taking in the sight of the bulge in my pants. "Mmm, let me taste it."

I let out a low chuckle, tangling my fingers in her hair. "You can have every inch of it, baby. Now put that pretty mouth to work."

Violet smiles at me, batting her eyelashes coquettishly before taking off my pants. She leans in to run her tongue along the underside of my shaft from base to tip.

"Fuck, just like that," I groan, my grip tightening in her hair as she continues to lick at my cock like a lollipop.

"I want to hear you moan as you take me," I command, pumping her head. Violet obliges eagerly, sinking down on my length until I hit the back of her throat. She holds herself there, savoring the weight of me on her tongue.

"Mmmmm. That's it, baby." I praise, pumping her head faster. Violet hums in pleasure around my cock, the vibrations of which nearly make me bust, my cock throbbing in her throat. She hollows her cheeks and sucks hard, determined to bring me to the edge.

"Fuck, you are such a good girl for me." I watch as my length disappears between her lips. I let out a guttural moan, releasing her hair, letting my head fall back against the counter. Violet is relentless, her tongue swirling around my head as she sucks me with gusto. I can feel my release building, my balls tightening with the impending explosion but I am not ready for this to end just yet. With a whine of regret, I pull Violet off my cock, my hands gripping her hair.

"Bend over" I growl, my voice thick with desire. "*Now.*"

Violet nods, a mischievous glint in her eye.

"Fuck me like you missed it, Ryder." she rasps, turning around and bracing herself against the counter.

I'm going to *fuck her* like I missed it alright. She isn't going to be able to walk tomorrow.

"Fuck, your ass is perfect," I seethe through my teeth, hands kneading the supple flesh.

"I just want to sink my teeth into these thick cheeks."

Just like old times.

I know she likes it when I leave a mark. Holding the base, I slowly drag my cock up and down her soaked pussy.

"Ah, fuck" I say, thrusting into her in one smooth motion. Her velvet walls envelope me, and it's like my body remembered hers before my mind ever did. I pause for a moment, savoring the feel of her.

"Violet," I pant, my fingers digging into her hips as I began to move. "You feel *incredible*."

Violet moans in response, pushing back against me as I piston in and out of her. The sound of our skin slapping together fills the air, a testament of our primal passion. I lean over her, my chest pressed against her back as I continue my tenacious thrusts. My lips find the spot just below her ear, nipping and sucking at the delicate skin.

"Fuck, Ryder. Your cock is so big." Violet gasps, her nails scraping against the countertop. "Harder."

I bite my lip as my hips inch forward with renewed vigor. She pulses and quivers, a telltale sign of her approaching orgasm.

"God, I've missed this," I grunt, changing the angle of my hips in order to go deeper inside her. "I missed feeling you like this."

"So have I," she whimpers, nails raking down the counter. "No one else has ever fucked me as well as you."

Her words send a surge of possession through me.

"No one will ever get the chance again. This is *my* pussy."

I double my efforts, pounding into her with wild abandon. Violet meets me thrust for thrust, our bodies moving in perfect synchronicity. The pressure builds at the base of my shaft, a sign I am close, but I hold back, determined to make her come again.

Reaching between us, I find her clit, and start rubbing firm circles around it. Violet lets out a choked cry, her body bowing harder against me.

"Oh my god, "She moans, her eyes starting to roll back. "Don't stop!"

I continue my massage on her clit while picking up the pace of my thrusts, driving into her harder and faster than before. The new angle must hit all the right spots because she comes with a scream of my name, her walls clamping down around me.

"That's it, baby," I pant, my breath hot against her neck. "Come for me. Let me feel *my* pussy grip my fucking cock."

The feeling of Violet clenching around me, milking my cock for every last drop, is pure ecstasy. I thrust into her one last time, burying myself to the hilt as I spill inside her.

"Fuck, Violet," I groan, my hips stuttering as I pump. "Take it all, baby. I'm going to fill you up."

Her body trembles beneath me, aftershocks of pleasure wracking her frame. I collapse on top of her, pressing tender kisses along the back of her neck and shoulder.

"I missed being inside you." I say nuzzling into the crook of her neck.

"I missed it too," Violet turns around. "I never want to let you go."

I roll us onto our sides, still nestled deep within her. My hands roam her curves, caressing every inch of exposed skin.

"I'm never letting you go again," I vow.

Violet smiles, leaning in to press a soft kiss to my lips. "Good. Because I don't think I can handle being apart from you anymore."

We lay there for a while, basking in the afterglow of our love-making. I can feel my cum starting to leak out around where we are still joined, and it sends a thrill through me.

"Look at you, all filled up with my cum," I purr, reaching down to push the slickness back inside her. "So, fucking sexy."

Violet bites her lip, grinding her hips against my fingers. "Mmm, I love it when you fill me up."

"Fuck yes," I growl, capturing her lips in a searing kiss. "I want my cum dripping out of your pussy. A reminder that you belong to me."

She moans into the kiss, her walls fluttering around my softening cock.

"I'm yours," she promises breathlessly. "Always have been"

She cradles my face in her hands, steady and soft, her touch turned sacred. Our foreheads meet, breath shared in the narrow space between.

"I got an IUD after Jane. I didn't want any more kids."

"Does that mean no babies? Just us? How long does it last? What happens when it's time to remove it?"

"No babies. Two years left. When it's done, someone just has to pull the string to remove it. I'm not sure how I'll know it's been two years, all things considered."

A low growl hums in my throat. A need, not aggression. Just the weight of every night I'd imagined touching her again without restraint.

"Two years," I repeat, giving it more meaning than time, cradling us in permission for reckless abandon. My dick gets excited at the thought.

"That means I can come in you every time. No pulling out."

I kiss her, slow and demanding. "No second-guessing."

Another kiss, deeper this time. "No fear of putting a baby in you. When all I want is to bury myself inside you, completely, no limits." I breathe against her mouth. "We're doing that again. And again. Until you forget what life felt like without me."

CHAPTER 23

VIOLET

I'll never forget this moment. Ryder's arms are wrapped around me. All warm and rippled muscle, like the world outside has paused just for us. For once, I don't feel like I am barely surviving. I lean into his breath, his hands, and his mouth. Maybe this hellscape hasn't taken everything after all.

"I'm sore," I say while stretching my limbs gingerly after our first reunion.

"Good," Ryder replies with a wicked grin. "It means I did my job right."

Smiling, I climb onto his lap, straddling his hips. I lean in, capturing his lips in a searing kiss. As I feel his cock beginning to stir once more, I grind my hips against his. Teasing him with deliberate friction.

"Fuck," Ryder groans, his hands gripping my ass and giving it a firm smack. The sharp sting only seems to spur me on further. He knows I love it when he does that.

"Round two?" I purr, breaking the kiss to trail my lips along his jawline.

"I'd fuck you all night long" Ryder tilts his head back letting out a huff, his fingers digging into my hips, helping me grind deeper.

"Is that a promise?" I grin, leaning in to capture his lips once more.

This time, I make sure to nip at his bottom lip as I pull away, leaving him breathless and wanting.

The peace shatters in an instant. A scream cuts through the dark, like a blade slicing clean through silk. I bolt upright.

"Did that come from camp?" I ask, breath catching in my throat.

Ryder is already moving me off of him. We go from whatever fragile, dangerous thing this is to survival mode without a word. I scramble for my clothes, fingers fumbling in the dark.

Ryder is already at the door, shirt barely pulled on as I yank mine over my head and shove my boots on. The second we hit the clearing, the cold bites at my skin.

Another scream. This one is sharper, and terrified.

We sprint, our feet pounding the earth, breath fogging in the chill as we tear through the trees. The woods are nothing but shadows and panic now, the quiet shattered. We tear through the underbrush, branches whipping at our arms, and stumble into camp straight into turmoil. Tents are unzipping as we arrive. Shapes stumbling into the open, half-dressed, confused.

"What the hell was that?"

"Who screamed?"

"Someone get a light!"

People stand in clusters, weapons half-raised, eyes darting every which way. My gaze snaps to the center and everything in me stops. Jalen is on the ground, his boot pressed against Kian's chest but…Kian isn't Kian anymore. His eyes are empty, clouded, milky-white. Blood glistening across his jaw and smeared down his shirt like a child had finger-painted rage across him. His mouth twists into something feral, snarling and snapping at his ruined arm. Oh God, his arm. The wound I thought we'd cleaned? It had betrayed us.

"Get back!" Jalen shouts.

My knife is out, hand already lifting when one clean shot cracks through the panic. His head whips back, and the rest of him collapses, all tension gone in an instant. Gasps ripple through the circle of people. My breath hitches. I whip around and see Hawthorne standing near the fire, pistol still raised, smoke curling from the barrel.

"Got him," he says, voice hollow.

Jalen shoves the body off him, panting, his face streaked with tears and dirt.

"Fuck… fuck… he tried to bite me…did he bite me? He was growling… like a rabid dog or something."

"That's what happens when you die now." Everyone turns to me. "The cut on his arm probably got too infected and he passed in his sleep. I first saw someone turn when I responded to a call and then one of those things bit my best friend, Grace. She died from that bite and then came back as a Deadhead."

Kate and I lock eyes as we share the grief of our friend being gone. Holding a first aid kit in her hands she drops to her knees, snapping on gloves.

"Hold still. Let me see. Arms. Neck. Anywhere he could've gotten you."

"I didn't—" Jalen starts, but then freezes. She pulls his shirt where there is a blood stain and then Kate's flashlight illuminates the situation. *A bite.* On his shoulder. Deep and still bleeding.

Her whole face drains of color. "Oh shit."

I can't breathe. Around us, the circle has closed. Faces pale, eyes wide. It was happening. Jalen was going to *die.*

My hand finds Ryder's instinctively. He doesn't look at me, but he grips back tight.

His fingers are warm.

Mine are ice

The silence thickens.

My dad shoots a look at me and him but I just shrug him off. I'll deal with him later. I'm trying to remember how long it took Grace to die from it. A couple hours maybe? Interrupting my math, Emily asks the question we are all afraid to ask.

"Didn't you *just* say your friend died from a bite?"

Everyone looks at me and I can't form words. Jalen's breathing grows erratic, as the reality sinks in and the adrenaline fades. *He was bitten* and there is no cure that we know of. There is only time and not much of it. Ryder's hand slips away from mine. I watch him step forward, toward Jalen.

"How long do I have?" His voice cracks as he pleads, barely more than a whisper.

His face is pale, lips dry, trembling with the weight of what he already knew. Ryder crouches beside him, his features tight with something between fury and sorrow. Jalen's eyes look at Ryder then meet mine.

"A couple hours, *maybe*, I don't really remember how long it took."

Jalen blinks slowly, his chest rising and falling in short, shallow bursts. He is lying on the ground, propped up by a blanket someone has pulled from a tent. The bite on his shoulder is angry and red, the skin already turning black at the edges.

"Guess that's it then."

He doesn't cry. I don't know why I expected him to, maybe because he is only around fifteen. *Still a kid.* Should have been worrying about algebra or getting caught sneaking into movies, not how long he had until he turned into something that craved human flesh. I kneel on Kian's other side and take his hand, surprised when he squeezes mine back. His fingers are freezing.

"Hey," I say softly. "What do you want us to remember you by? For your headstone. We'll make one. Something real."

He doesn't answer right away. Just stares at the trees above us, memorizing them.

"My full name is Jalen Conwell," he finally says, voice barely audible. "Put that. No fancy stuff. Just…my name." He pauses, then adds, "And bury me with my Nightshade comics, okay?"

I smile through the sting behind my eyes. "Yeah. We can do that."

Ryder nods once, jaw clenched so tight I think it might shatter. He stands again, walking a few paces away like he can't bear to be too close.

Jalen turns his head toward me again. "Do you think it'll hurt? The changing?"

"I don't know," I admit. "But we're not going to let it happen while you're still in there, Jalen. You won't feel it. I promise."

He agrees, eyes glassy now.

We stay with him. All of us. No one left.

It isn't until the sun begins to rise, casting soft golden light through the pines that his breathing slows. He stops talking about his Nightshade comics and starts mumbling names. His mom. A dog, maybe. Someone named Benny. His words run together like a fever dream of a half-asleep child. He talks about how he ended up at the military camp. Then, suddenly, he stills.

"Jalen?" I shake him lightly.

"He's gone," Kate says while pressing two fingers on his neck.

Emily and Teresa start crying and I let a tear run down my cheek. How could the world feel so alive and yet so dead? One minute it's pure bliss and the other I'm holding a dead teenager in my arms.

The twitching begins along with the low, guttural sounds the dead make.

Ryder steps forward without a word.

I look away.

The shot echoes once through the trees.

We bury Jalen on a hill just off the trail. We dig the grave, moving the dirt with our hands and sticks. We cover Jalen in a blanket of leaves, tuck his comics inside like a final comfort, and place the handmade wooden marker in the soil

Jalen Conwell. 15.

We do the same for Kian. No one could remember his last name. We weren't even sure how old he was. Maybe thirty. We carve "Kian" into the second marker and place it beside his grave.

Two mounds.

Two lives.

Gone in the span of a night.

We stand together. No speeches. There weren't words good enough for this. When we finally walk away, the weight in my chest doesn't lift. Not even a little. It just settles deeper. We somberly walk back to camp, but the silence doesn't last.

"I told you we should've done something sooner," Emily snaps. "I knew that the cut wasn't just going to go away. We all knew it."

Everyone stops.

Theo turns to her. "What were we supposed to do, Emily? Shoot him just in case?"

Her eyes well up, fists clenched at her sides. "I'm not saying that. I'm saying we should've watched him. We should've kept him isolated. Something! Instead, we let him sleep next to a little kid like everything was fine."

"It was fine," Teresa said quietly, holding Dion a little closer.

"No," Emily spat. "It wasn't. And now they are dead."

Ryder steps in, his voice firm. "That's enough. No one knew he was going to die."

"No," she said, blinking hard. "It's not. We keep acting like surviving is enough. But it's not. We need rules. We need a plan. Or someone else is going to end up buried next."

Everyone goes quiet again. I feel the tremble in my own limbs. Not just from grief but from the fear that she is right, because if we don't get better at this, if we don't learn how to live in this world instead of just surviving it…we will end up dead.

Gone.

Forgotten.

A name on a stick in the dirt if we are lucky.

Ryder runs a hand down his face. "We'll talk tonight. Figure out next steps. But yelling at us won't change what happened."

Emily doesn't respond. She just turns away, wiping her face with the sleeve of her jacket and walks off toward the trees.

We gather around what is left of the fire pit, the sky above us glowing with the early morning gold.

Wilson clears his throat. "I say we stick to the plan. No good will come from lingering here."

Dad crosses his arms stiffly. "We head west. Up through Jasper. Into BC before the snow sets in and look for signs of a survivor camp." He looks over the map, then taps it. "This route here. Violet and I know it. It's quiet. Mostly old logging roads. If the bridges are still up, we can make decent time."

Ryder gives a small grunt of approval. "We're running low on fuel. In Jasper, we need to stop and scavenge whatever gas we can find."

Kate stands beside me, arms wrapped tight around herself.

"Fine. But we don't linger. We get what we need and keep moving. No more makeshift camps like this one. No more waiting to see if someone turns." Sinclair adds.

Ryder rises lingering near the edge of the group, hands shoved in his pockets, watching me with that maddeningly unreadable look. I'm curious about what's on his mind so I join him.

"Holding up okay, darlin?"

I give him a flat look.

"I'll be okay, it's just sad he was so young. I shouldn't stress about it. I might need to have one of your joints to relax a bit."

A smirk tugs at the corner of his mouth. "You looked a lot more relaxed last night, pressed up against the counter."

My face goes hot. "You're seriously bringing that up now?"

He steps closer, his voice dropping to a soft, teasing rumble. "Just saying… I can take the stress away."

I tip my head, meeting his gaze with a flicker of a smile. "Does that come with options? Because you can also just… hold me through it."

His lips brush the top of my head, lingering there, not wanting to pull away.

"I can definitely do that too. *Anything* to see you smile." He pulls my chin towards his lips.

"Ryder!" My Dad snaps, voice cutting through the air like a blade.

I whip around, the heat rising fast. "Seriously? You're going to bark at him like that in front of everyone?"

He takes a step forward, fists clenched. "This isn't the time, Violet."

I feel the dam crack.

"Then when is it the right time, Dad? When are we going to talk about the fact that you…"? I stop myself, biting my tongue so hard it aches.

Not here.

Not with everyone watching.

He doesn't say anything, just stares, chest heaving. That same look in his eyes but this time I wonder if it is anger or guilt.

I drag in a breath through my nose, then look away, grounding myself. "We will talk later."

Kate arches her brow, whispering under her breath, "God, I miss reality tv."

Sinclair glances between all of us, brow furrowed like he is trying to piece something together. "Right… okay. Everyone, pack up the tents and grab whatever supplies are left."

A few heads turn, unsure.

"We leave as soon as it's done," Ryder says, his tone firmer this time.

"I'll check the campers again. Emily, Theo, you two want to help?" Kate asks.

They both acknowledge silently.

"Teresa, Dion, and I will pack up the tents," Sinclair offers.

"I'll give you a hand with that," Wilson adds.

"Hawthorne and I will go over the bus, make sure there are no leaks or fluid issues," Ryder says.

"My dad and I will check the camp store," I add.

No one pushes back. We all knew what needed to be done and I had a father to confront.

CHAPTER 24
VIOLET

Seeing the camp store again twists something deep in my heart. The memories from last night hit me, but I shove them down because I am here with my dad and this is *not* the time.

Gross. Get it together, Violet. You're angry. Be angry.

I yank open a busted cabinet and grab a stack of garbage bags, my movements sharp and fast. "Let's just throw everything in here. We'll sort it out when we get back to the bus."

His boots scrape across the floor behind me.

"Sounds good."

The words burn at the back of my throat. I don't even try to cool them down.

"Why didn't you tell me, Dad?"

He blinks, confused. "Tell you what?"

I drop the bag and turn to look at him.

"Why *did* you tell me Ryder was *dead* and why *didn't* you tell me Ryder sent me letters?"

His face shifts like he has been struck and doesn't know where the punch came from. His mouth opens and shuts like a guppy. He stammers incoherently, no doubt looking for some excuse, some version of the truth that might soften the blow. I step closer.

"Did you know Jeremy hurt me? That he emotionally wrecked me and didn't give a shit about Jane? I hated him. I hated my life. The only time I felt normal was when I was watching people die at work, and even that made more sense than going home to him."

"I…I didn't know, Violet. I swear to God, I didn't know."

"No, you didn't want to know." My chest heaves, my pulse hammering in my ears.

"All you cared about was, 'Did you pass your paramedic test'... 'Do you have a good number of savings'... 'When are you and Jeremy getting married'!"

His eyes dart to the broken window. "Stop yelling. You'll attract the dead."

"Oh, you care about the dead!?" My hands balled into fists. "Why did you hide the letters, Dad? Did you and Jeremey have a weird secret pact to keep me depressed or something?"

He winces like the weight of it is crushing him.

"I didn't want you waiting for a ghost. People don't come back from the military, Violet. They die. And when they do come back. They don't come back the same. You're my daughter. My *beautiful* daughter. I wanted more for you. I wanted you to be happy, not sitting around reading letters from a boy who might never come back. I thought they would stop, but they came almost every month, sometimes twice a month. I asked Jeremy to dispose of them. He told me he burned them all last time we talked about it. "

"Did you even read them?" I hiss. "Those letters… they're the kindest, most honest words anyone's ever said about me. He was fighting for me, and I didn't even know. I was fighting just to survive Jeremy. My only reason for living was Jane."

He reaches for my hands, his voice breaking. "Sweetheart, I had no idea. Why didn't you tell me? Why didn't you say something?"

I yank my hands away. "What would I have said? 'Hey Dad, my boyfriend's a controlling asshole, and I think he might hit me next?' What if he had taken Jane? What if he turned violent?"

I can barely breathe now.

"Those letters could've saved me. *I would've waited* for Ryder. I could've had a real life. And now I'm here…trapped in this lifeless world trying to scrape together whatever meaning I can while figuring out how to love someone again."

His jaw slackens, in disbelief of what he was hearing. "You… love him?"

I hold his gaze, biting back the tears I will not let fall.

"Yeah, Dad. I always have. Even when I thought he was dead."

"This is ridiculous."

"No. You know what's ridiculous? The fact that you thought you could mess with my life. *My* life!"

I turn away, the anger still burning in my chest. I don't even want to look at him right now.

"Violet, wait. I'm sorry, okay? I thought I was protecting and doing what was best for you. That's what every father thinks they're doing. If I could take it all back, I would. Please sweetheart… forgive me."

I take a breath, not to calm down but to keep from screaming.

"I'll forgive you if you do three things," I say, turning back to him. "One, stop looking at Ryder like you hate him or worse, like you want to hurt him. Two, stop embarrassing me every time I'm with him. I'm twenty-nine not fourteen and three? Stop trying to push us apart. I'm going to be with him, Dad. Yeah, it took a fucking apocalypse, but having Ryder here makes it all worth it. I finally feel like I have something to live for. More than I did before. So please… respect me and respect my relationship. If you can do that, then yeah. I can forgive you."

He is quiet for a second. Too long of a second.

"Okay," he says at last. "I love you sweetheart and for what it is worth I really am sorry."

I hug him tightly. I have to forgive him for this to work, for us to work. Plus, he's still my dad and there is no point in holding a grudge with the world in that state that it is.

"I love you too."

We clear the store out completely collecting about four garbage bags full of seemingly random crap. Out here, random crap can save lives. A part of me wants to leave something behind for anyone else who might pass through, but survival doesn't work that way anymore. So, we pack it all. By the time we get back to the bus, everyone else is already back.

"Sorry we took so long," I say. "We had to grab everything."

"No worries," Kate replies, gesturing toward the back. "Just toss those on the bus."

I hand my bags off to Dad and let him haul them up while I go find Ryder. He's still under the hood, checking the fluids like the perfectionist he is.

"Hey," I say.

"Oh hey, gorgeous." He glances up, smiling. "How'd the talk with Pops go?" He stands up wiping some oil on his pants.

"About as well as it could've. I yelled at him, he said he was 'trying to protect me,' more yelling… but now we've got an agreement. So, we don't have to worry anymore. We can just… do this."

I lean in and kiss him. He doesn't hesitate and pulls me in tighter, deepens it, like he's still starving for me.

"I could get used to this," speaks sweetly, his forehead resting against mine.

"Ehem." Kate clears her throat behind us.

"We're busy," Ryder says without looking, turning just enough to block her view with his body.

"Well, the bus is packed, everyone's back, and we got to go," she says. "How are the fluids?"

"Damn, Kate," Ryder smirks. "Bit forward, don't you think?"

I laugh, and she rolls her eyes.

"The bus's fluids, you absolute perv."

"Ah. Well, in that case we need oil at the next stop, and we're down to one jerry can of gas."

"Then let's move," she says, already heading for the door.

I turn to follow, behind us, Ryder lowers the hood with a clang. Just before I am out of reach, his hand catches me on the curve of my ass. I freeze, heat shooting up my neck. When I glance back at him, his sly grin is pure trouble, making it hard to remember all the reasons I should keep my guard up. My cheeks burn, and before I can stop myself, I'm grinning, wide and stupid, as if death hasn't confronted me with every step for days.

Dad is kind of right, this is ridiculous. I shouldn't feel this way. I barely escaped a murderous cult. My hands still remember the weight of the rope. This moment. This stupid, reckless moment, where I feel really, really good…It scares me more than facing my own mortality at every turn.

"Hey Ryder?" My dad calls out.

Ryder raises his eyebrows and slowly turns around to face him.

"This probably doesn't mean much coming from me but I want to apologize for my actions in the past. I see you make my daughter very happy and that makes me happy. Can you forgive a stubborn, stupid old man?" he concludes by reaching out his hand in a makeshift truce.

Ryder looks at me and then back at dad and returns the gesture.

"Yes sir, consider yourself forgiven. Thank you."

I feel a warmth rising in my heart where the dread and grief of the morning had settled. If these two could mend the past, maybe every single one of us had a chance at a future.

CHAPTER 25

RYDER

I lean into Violet, as her head rests against my shoulder. Her breath is slow and warm against my neck and my arm wraps around her. Sinclair and Kate call out inventory, going through the bags they hauled from the camp store and RVs. I half-listen while watching the blur of forest roll past the window.

"A couple packs of ramen... canned beans... batteries... matches... duct tape... ten moose keychains...," Sinclair lists off. "A few half-used medical kits, lots of soap, and like twenty small boxes of condoms?"

Kate snorts. "Guess they really did grab everything eh?"

"Can't blame 'em, apocalypse stress relief." He says winking at me.

I smirk but don't comment, too focused on the soft weight of Violet curled against me. Plus, we didn't need condoms. She shifts slightly, uttering something in her sleep. I tighten my grip around her, pressing a kiss to the top of her head. It hits me like ice water how surreal this all is. Holding her here after everything. My woman, in my arms, while death roams outside. I'd lived in a goddamn warzone for years, so I know better than anyone that the world isn't coming back from this. Not tomorrow, not ever. The Dybbuks were out there, the living just as dangerous, and the only constant was the sound of gunfire and the stench of rot. Yet, in spite of it all… here she is in my arms

Breathing.

Warm.

Mine.

The bus bounces over a rut in the road. My mind keeps slipping back to nights I laid awake wondering if she'd forgotten me, if I'd ever see her eyes again. Then back to the smell of burning flesh in the desert after a raid, when I swore, I heard her voice in the carnage, but found only strangers. Back to every time I'd seen a woman with dark hair in the distance, heart hammering until they turned and I realized it wasn't her. I close my eyes again, holding her tighter, committing the weight of her against me to memory. Every part of me screams to stay in this moment, to believe we can keep it. The soldier in me, the part that knows how fragile '*safe*' really is keeps whispering the truth. We are but a heartbeat away from losing it all again. Still… my mouth forms a smile. The biggest one I have had in years, because if the world was ending, I was ending it with *her*.

"Ryder."

Someone shakes my shoulder. I blink awake, instinctively reaching for the knife at my hip until Sinclair's face comes into focus.

"We're here," he reports. "Outskirts of Jasper."

I sit up straighter, gently shifting Violet off my chest without waking her. I move sluggishly to the front of the bus, peering out the wide windshield. The town looks untouched. No signs of fire damage from missiles, just the old wildfire scars. A gas station sits off the side of the highway, with a few blackened storefronts across the street, the windows blown out and signs melted.

"Where is everyone? The whole town looks like worm food," Hawthorne trembles behind the wheel.

"Let's keep it that way," I reply.

Violet is still curled on the seat. I brush a kiss against her forehead, then her cheek, then the corner of her mouth. She stirs with a soft sound, eyes fluttering open, and I smile like some lovesick idiot. Who the hell even was I anymore?

The bus comes to a stop and the others shift awake behind us stretching and groaning as the bus doors creak open.

Hawthorne and I are the first ones out. Sunlight glints off the blackened remains of the storefronts across the street, turning everything into a weird, ashy shimmer. The wind carries that old wildfire scent of burnt pine and melted plastic. Ghosts of a disaster that hit long before the world ended. I tap the butt of my knife against the side of the bus, the sharp clang ringing out across the empty street. We wait. A collective groan answers.

Shadows emerge near the burned-out corner store. Four Dybbuks, staggering slow. The memory of being human still clinging to them. Skin pale but mostly intact, eyes clouded but not sunken, like they'd only just crossed that line between alive and dead. Their mouths hang open, slack with hunger, and every twitch of their limbs is eerie and unnerving. I tilt my head once to Hawthorne and we split.

The second one charges forward towards me. I shove it hard, sending it sprawling onto the ground, body twitching in a sick rhythm. Before it can rise again, I kneel and slam the knife down, burying it in the soft spot just above the jaw.

Across from me, Hawthorne has already dropped his. Efficient, and clean. There is definitely a certain kind of adrenaline that comes with killing Dybbuks. At least for me there is. Did that make me a psychopath or did it mean I was adapting to this new world? We stand in the silence that follows. Only the wind stirs now, carrying the stench of decay and burnt earth.

"Clear," I say finally.

We return to the bus. Everyone is waiting near the open doors, eyes scanning the streets like more might appear any second.

"Alright," I call out. "We're sweeping the gas station first. Grab the last garbage bags and take anything that isn't bolted down like food, meds, batteries, *anything*. Hawthorne and I will check for oil and fuel. Let's move."

We search the gas station like a pack of wolves, grabbing everything useful and tossing it into the garbage bags from the last haul. Chips, water, medicine, oil. Anything worth a damn. Hawthorne and I refill the bus with the last jerry can and change the oil while Kate keeps watch.

I hear another groan echo low across the gravel. Wet and dragging, like someone was gargling tar. I freeze, one hand still on the oil cap under the bus.

Another moan. Closer.

I shimmy out fast, the concrete scraping my back as I roll.

Violet is already on it. The Dybbuk stumbles toward her, half its jaw sideways and hanging, teeth clicking like windchimes in a storm. She doesn't flinch, doesn't even fucking blink. Just grips her blade tight and drives it straight into the side of its skull. Deep, clean, and practiced. The body crumples at her boots, twitching once, then stillness takes over and *fuck me but* I think I groan louder than the Dybbuk. She stands there, panting slightly, the sunlight catching the edge of her blade and the sheen of sweat on her neck. Her chest rises and falls with adrenaline, her fingers still curled tight around the handle not quite ready to stop. Her cheeks are flushed, lips parted, her eyes sharp and wild.

Goddamn.

Every inch of her screams *deadly weapon*, and all I can think about is how badly I want to claim her right here in this moment. Oil-stained hands, blood on her boots and all. There is something unholy about how ravishing she looks with a corpse at her feet, so raw and visceral.

How the hell did I get so fucking lucky?

She catches me staring and I can't help the cocky grin that tugs at my mouth as I give her a wink. Her face pinkens just a shade.

"Nice form," I call out, letting the amusement smolder in my gaze.

She rolls her eyes, but the edges of her mouth tilt in invitation. I duck back under the bus before I do something stupid.

Watching her fight like that? Handle herself like she doesn't need saving? That does things to me. *Dangerous things.*

The sun is crawling down the horizon by the time we climb back on the bus. Sinclair slides into the driver's seat, adjusting the mirrors. Wilson perches next to him, keeping an eye out the window with that old-man military stoicism that makes everyone feel safer. Inside, we set up fast. I turn the row behind the driver's seat into a makeshift pantry. Snacks, bottled water, vitamins. Anything we need easy access to on the road. The seat right behind that becomes the hygiene stash: toothbrushes, soap, menstrual stuff, sanitizer, towel paper. Not glamorous, but holy hell, it made a difference to be somewhat organized.

"Alright, listen up!" I call out as people settle in. "The front seats have food and water. The next row has hygiene. If you're starving, thirsty, or smell like Hawthorne, feel free to help yourself."

People chuckle, but they get the message. Hawthorne is so deep in conversation with Arthur and Theo he doesn't even hear the dis. Kate, Teresa, and Dion are huddled in the back left corner, chatting like old friends. Turns out Kate used to work with Teresa back in the real world. Their laughter gives the space a strange sense of normalcy. Some of the group munches on snacks, sipping water like it is champagne. A few nod off, heads already bobbing gently with the rhythm of the road. I sit at the very back with Violet, the faint purr of the motor blending with the low chatter. Her head rests on my shoulder and her warmth soaks into me like sunlight. I look out at the world rushing past again. Ash trees, blackened branches, the empty ruins of what used to be. Surreal doesn't even cover it. The woman I thought I lost, tucked against my side while the world burns around us against all odds.

She stirs a little.

"I want to show you something," she whispers.

Every nerve in my body lights up. I turn to her, eyebrows raised, "Yeah?"

She reaches into her bag and pulls something out.

Letters? Wait, are those my letters?

"You have them with you?"

"Yeah, I took them once I found them. I read two already and I just want you to know that your words…they are the most *beautiful things* I have ever read. I think maybe in a past life you were a poet, Mr. Kent" she teases, flicking her lashes.

The pull is quiet but fierce, dragging both breath and voice down with it. I cup her cheek, pulling her in for a deep kiss not caring who sees us.

"I'd be your poet" I stammer against her lips. "Because my heart only yearns to speak your language."

She pulls away from the kiss. "Did you mean everything you said?"

"Of course, I did. *I still do.* I genuinely thought you felt the same way. So, when I wrote the letters, and I didn't hear back from you… I was scared something happened. I couldn't do anything. I was in the middle of the desert with maybe four days off the whole time I'd been deployed."

Violet's fingers play with the edge of the paper for a moment, trying to focus.

"I was angry at first, angry that you left. That you didn't fight harder to stay, but when I found your letters and read your words… I don't know, Ryder. It felt like they reached inside me and shook loose everything I buried just to survive."

I lean in, pressing my forehead against hers. "I would've moved heaven and hell if I could. You *have* to know that. Every day out there, I wasn't living. I was just waiting to feel you again."

She smiles heartbreakingly beautiful.

"I grabbed our picture. Me and dad burnt the house down because my mom and brother had turned…. and I didn't want it to burn. You know just in case I'd never see you again," she said, reaching into her bag.

She unfolds it carefully, a sacred relic of the past. It was creased and faded, corners worn down from too much handling, but it was still me and her. Younger…cleaner…grinning like idiots, my arm slung around her waist.

"You kept this?" My voice breaks halfway through the question.

"Even when I wanted to forget. I couldn't."

Something in me splinters, the part that has stayed cold and walled off to survive, cracks wide open under her gaze. She saved a photo from our past. She chose to carry me with her when the world went to hell. *She does love me.* I kiss her again. Slower this time. With the kind of tenderness that doesn't need explanation. When we finally pull apart, she curls into my side, laying her head on my chest.

"So…" she says softly, fingers tracing the dragon tattoo on my arm. "What now, Ryder?"

I look out the window at the dark road ahead. "Now? We take it one day at a time. Every day I get to be near you is one the universe finally got right."

She lets out a quiet breath, a weight she'd carried for years lifting just enough to let her breathe again.

"I missed you," she whispers.

I hold her tighter.

"I missed you too" I say, voice broken. "I also missed me, turns out I left myself here with you."

CHAPTER 26
VIOLET

We sit close but I can't help it. Not when he smells like the woods we used to sneak out to, like long drives with the windows down, like every warm memory I'd buried under the rubble of the last five and a half years. We don't speak like we are trying to catch up. We talk like we never stopped. Like the years hadn't torn us apart. Like the blood, silence and death hadn't carved gaps into who we were.

"Sometimes I wake up, and I think I hear Felix and Jane calling for me."

He doesn't say anything right away. Just tightens his grip on my hand.

"I still see Ryan; he was like a brother to me. The day I lost him… he got attacked and I had to…"

He stops. He doesn't have to finish. We have all done things we aren't allowed to forget. The silence stretches, but it isn't uncomfortable.

"I don't blame you," I whisper, eyes fixed on the seat in front of me. "For whatever you had to do."

"I don't blame you either. We were just surviving."

We stay like that, wrapped in each other's quiet understanding.

"You're safe now," he promises. "*With me.*"

For the first time in a long time, I actually believe I'll be safe.

The sky turns dark and Sinclair pulls the bus over into a hidden parking nook surrounded by trees. The engine clicks off, and one by one, the others settle into sleep. I am about to do the same when Ryder gets up and rustles through his duffel bag and holds something up with a mischievous grin. His red tin container. He pops it open.

"How about a little midnight smoke?" A spark of mischief plays across his face.

Kate perks up from her seat. "If we're lighting one up, count me in."

We pass the joint back and forth under the stars, the smoke curling lazily into the cool night air. It softens the edges of everything.

Kate breaks the quiet, her tone teasing but gentle. "So… are you two, like, a thing now?"

I open my mouth to speak "I…"

Ryder cuts in before I can even figure out what I am trying to say.

"Yes. Definitely a thing. She's off-limits, Kate."

Kate snorts, "Please. I wasn't asking because I want to date my best friend. I was asking because I'm happy for you guys. I remember Violet telling me once she thought you might be her soulma…"

My head whips around so fast I almost get whiplash.

Kate, shut the fuck up! I scream inside my brain, practically willing her to stop with sheer psychic force.

Jesus. Soulmate? We're not even official. I mean… we kind of are. But we haven't had that talk. He hasn't asked me anything. We are just kissing and fucking like the world's ending…. which, it technically has. But still. I can't drop the "you're my soulmate and I'll love you forever "bomb yet. Even though he is perfect and I do feel like he was made for me. That's like… marriage talk. That's forever talk. How could we even have a wedding in this new world? I'd want a nice wedding dress and everything that comes with a reception. Not Deadheads wandering all over the place and half of us covered in blood. I mean we wouldn't have to pay for anything, we would just have to scavenge…. If he asked me right now, I'd say fuck yeah, this man is my husband. I don't give a fuck.

"Earth to Violet?" Kate says, waving her hand in front of my face.

I blink. "Yeah, sorry. This weed is really good."

"It is good. What happens when you run out Ryder?" Kate asks, suddenly sober at the thought.

Ryder shrugs. "We're in B.C. I'm sure we can find a dispensary or two."

"Assuming they're not blown to shit," I challenge.

Ryder's eyes widen like he hadn't even thought of that. The three of us laugh quietly.

We swap a few stories, ones that don't hurt too much to tell and we just exist together in the strange, brief calm. For once, I don't feel like I want to be anywhere else.

Eventually, Kate starts, yawning, "Alright lovebirds, I'm off. Don't do anything I wouldn't do."

"That leaves a lot of room," I smirk.

She laughs and shakes her head then disappears into the bus.

I pivot to Ryder, my hand finding his. "I know where we are. Follow me."

I lead him through the trees, the moonlight guiding us past the brush and broken logs until we reach it. The waterfall, just as I remember it. Cascading into a basin that shimmers like aquamarine glass.

"It's perfect," Ryder breathes, taking in the sight before us. "Just like you."

I smile, tugging him closer by the hem of his shirt. "I wanted to show you my favorite spot."

He leans down, capturing my lips in a slow, sensual kiss. Our tongues dance together, exploring and teasing, as his hands roam my behind.

"I'll show you my favorite spot" he teases, scooping my ass in a tight squeeze. Making me giggle.

"*Fuck me*," I whisper delicately against his mouth.

"Patience is a virtue, Miss Hayes, "he says, biting my lip. His fingers trail along my skin, leaving a trail of goosebumps in their wake. He puts his large hands under my shirt, moving my bra to the side. I moan as his thumb grazes over my nipple, my back arching into his touch. Ryder's other hand slides down my body, dipping beneath the waistband of my sweats.

"Fuck, you're already so wet for me," he groans, slipping a finger inside my opening. "Beg for it."

"Ryder, please? I need you to fill me with your cock and your come."

"Mmm, so greedy," he teases, slipping a second finger inside me. "I love how much you crave me; how desperate you are for my touch."

I gasp as he curls his fingers, hitting that sensitive spot deep within me.

"Your fingers *feel so good."*

Ryder continues his rhythmic movements, adding a third finger and pumping them in and out of my needy pussy. My moans grow louder, my body tensing as I race towards my peak. I see a lightning strike in the distance, but am quickly distracted by my flooding orgasm.

"Come for me, baby," Ryder commands, his thumb finding my clit and rubbing tight circles. "Let me feel this pretty pussy come all over my fingers."

Thunder rumbles, muffling the sounds of pleasure escaping my lips. Which is a good thing because I'm loud enough that any surrounding Deadheads would be drawn right to us. Suddenly, he withdraws, leaving me whimpering in protest. He then takes his fingers and sucks them clean.

"Tastes like mine," he says.

Jesus Christ…this man.

A raw, primal hunger surges through me as I watch him clean the mess I've made. Something ancient and carnal stirs awake inside my bones. Before I can stop myself, I float toward him, driven by instinct, by need, by that goddamn magnetic pull that only Ryder could ever make me feel. I am just about to crash my mouth against his when the sky cracks open above us, a torrential downpour spilling over like the world can no longer suffer the tension between us.

He grabs the back of my neck with that rough tenderness only he knows how to give me, pulling me into him like he is yet again starving for the taste of me. *Fuck*, I'm starving for him too. His mouth meets mine in a kiss that is anything but gentle. It is desperate. Our tongues tangle in that slow, perfect rhythm that belongs only to us. He kisses like he fights the dead, relentless, brutal, like the world might disappear if he doesn't devour every last piece of me. I melt into him, into the storm, into the way his body heat presses through our soaked clothes. It feels like coming home and losing myself all at once. He pulls back, just barely, breathing heavily against my lips stripping off his shirt. Looking like a Greek God carved out of sin. his inked muscles dripping wet, every inch of him gleaming beneath the rain. Then he slides off his pants, exposing his toned Adonis belt. He looks like he belongs to another world, one darker and far more tempting. My eyes travel down Ryder's nude form, landing on his impressive erection standing at full attention.

"Eyes up here, darlin', he teases, stroking himself.

I smile, flushed, lips still tingling. My fingers travel to the hem of my own shirt, my bra and my sweats, exposing myself to him. Making him lick his lips. He turns and jerks his head toward the waterfall. Making his way through the basin, stepping through the mist, a shadow slipping between worlds. I bite my lip, heart pounding as I contemplate following. He stands just beyond, outstretching his arm, the tattoo on his skin to gleaming like it is etched from obsidian.

Beautiful.

Dangerous.

Mine.

I dip into the water and find his hand. Then with one swift pull, he yanks me through. The icy water drenches me in seconds. My back hits the damp rock wall with a soft thud, and his body presses warmly against mine a second later. Our mouths find each other again, this time slower and deeper. Making up for every moment lost, every inch of time we've been apart. His lips bruise mine, and I kiss him harder. I want to live in this kiss, drown in it, let it ruin me completely. Behind the waterfall, the world falls away and only we remain. The roar of water muffles everything beyond the veil, turning the chaos of the world into a distant hum. He grabs my ass and lifts me in one swift motion.

"Look at me" he demands while positioning himself at my entrance, the head of his cock pressing against me.

"Good girl" he whispers, holding my gaze.

His hands grip my hips with a bruising force as he slams into me. His thick cock stretching me to the limit causing me to moan loudly in his ear.

"Take it, baby," he growls, his voice rough with desire. "Take every fucking inch of me."

I cry out in pleasure, my back arching off the rock as he pounds into me mercilessly.

"Yes, Ryder," I pant, my nails digging into his sweat-slicked skin. "Harder. Fuck me harder."

He obliges, his hips snapping against mine with force.

The cold mist kisses our bare skin. I can see the water cascading down just inches away, like a living curtain stitched from silver. Hypnotic in the way it shimmers, how it dances in slow motion around us, sealing us inside this secret place where nothing can reach.

"You're mine. No one else gets to touch you like this. No one else gets to hear you scream their fucking name."

I respond by clenching around his thick cock.

"I'm yours, Ryder."

With a guttural grunt, Ryder picks up the pace, grabbing my tits forcibly swirling his tongue on my nipples. His hips snap forward as he chases his pleasure. I can feel him throbbing inside me, growing harder and thicker with each thrust.

"You feel so good. I'm going to fill you up so fucking deep." His eyes dark with lust as he thrusts into me.

I let out a breathless whimper, my head thrown back in pleasure. His hand cracks across my cheek violently. Skin meeting skin with a snap that echoes louder than it should've. Heat blooms instantly, a sharp sting spreading like lightning across my face. I gasp, my eyes flying open to meet his intense gaze.

"I said, eyes on me."

I didn't think I could get any wetter. Before I can react, he crashes his lips against mine in a hungry kiss, his tongue invading my mouth and claiming me thoroughly. I melt into it, my body responding to his dark possession.

He breaks away, his breath hot against my ear as he whispers, "You like that, don't you? You like it when I take control, and make you my little slut."

His palm meets my ass cheek in one clean, ruthless arc. No warning, just the sudden burn of skin slapping skin. The sting spreads fast, rising under the surface like fire, leaving my pulse pounding in my ears

"Yes," I moan, tilting my hips to take him even deeper. "I love being your little fuck toy."

Every sound is swallowed by the thunder, making every intake of breath, every heartbeat a confession only we can hear. Light fractures through the drops, making the air itself pulsate with our breath. It is euphoric. Like we'd found the eye of the storm, and in it, we were the only two people left alive. A cocoon of water and shadow, where time doesn't matter and nothing else exists. A few more powerful thrusts and then we are coming.

"Fuck yes, take it all!" he roars, spurting thick ropes of semen deep into my welcoming pussy. "Feels...so *fucking* good."

I milk his cock for every last drop, my inner muscles fluttering wildly around his pulsing shaft. "Oh god, I can feel you coming inside me…"

"I'm never leaving this spot," he declares, nuzzling into my neck. "I want to stay buried inside you forever."

I laugh breathlessly, swatting at his chest as his lips trace the curve of my jaw. "As much as I'd love to stay tangled up in you forever, we should probably clean up and get back to the bus before the sun catches us."

He groans, low and reluctant. His hands linger on my hips like he can't let go, and when he finally pulls out, we both inhale sharply. A shared sound of pleasure and protest. The loss of him leaves me aching for more. We step into the cool basin of the falls, the water shocking against our overheated skin. I shiver, not from cold, but from the aftershocks still rippling through me. He swims beside me in the moonlight, the water lapping softly around us. His touch isn't rushed, it is deliberate, each swipe of his hand over my skin means something. His touch follows the line of my thigh in slow worship, lingering, afraid of forgetting my details.

The rain has stopped, but the world hasn't gone still. Not completely. The air is still charged. Steam rising in curling tendrils from the forest floor, the last drops of the storm evaporating into the electric hush that follows. The trees are soaked, dripping rhythmically. A jagged bolt splits the sky, carving light through the dark like a wound. Everything is silver for a heartbeat and the world lights up in pulses. My breath catches every time the sky flares. Ryder's face illuminates in the flashes. Shadowed jawline, wet dark blonde hair slicked back, eyes that gleam like something feral under starlight. No sound but our breathing.

When he finds a streak of blood or dirt, he doesn't just wipe it away. He studies it first, each mark telling a story he desperately needs to understand. He dips his hand beneath the surface, scooping the cool water into his palm, and letting it trickle over my skin with the gentleness of rain, observing the way it runs down my body memorizing every path it takes. His thumb grazes my cheek, and I catch the way he looks at me. His gaze stays fixed on me, unblinking and full of so much unspoken depth my breath hitches. More than love and lust, heavier and tangible, this was something truly divine. He tucks a damp strand of hair behind my ear with the same care he might handle glass, and his lips brush my temple. No words pass between us, but he says everything in the way he touches me. His hand finds mine beneath the surface, our fingers lace creating a silent promise between us.

We walk through the woods slowly, the world around us quiet except for the rhythm of our steps and the occasional rustle of leaves. He leans in now and then, stealing kisses like secrets. Every time his lips touch mine, it feels like a vow neither of us dare to speak out loud. His breath brushes against my ear as his fingers slide along my waist.

"The way you look right now? I'll remember it for the rest of my life." His mouth grazes the curve of my neck, lips ghosting over damp skin. "I swear, you were made just to ruin me."

I laugh softly, but he catches my chin, his gaze suddenly serious.

"I mean it," he says. "You're mine, and I'm yours. Whether we make it out of this world or not."

His words land in me like sparks, each one igniting something within my heart.

"Say it again," I whisper.

He kisses the corner of my mouth, then my jaw, then presses his forehead to mine.

"You are mine and I am yours Ocean Eyes."

CHAPTER 27

RYDER

I would never breathe a word of this to a living soul but honestly, I think I prefer the world like this. No cities screaming with deadlines. No pretending like rent and broken dreams don't crush your chest every morning. No false smiles or empty parties or answering to some rank that thinks they own you. Survival isn't ideal for the living, but perhaps we're living more than we ever have. I know that's messed up. Wanting this hell to keep going. But without it, I wouldn't be here with her and I wouldn't trade this bloodstained, burned-out, batshit apocalypse for anything if it meant having to lose Violet again.

I used to think the military gave me purpose. That I was a part of something bigger than myself. I was always the kid who had to be strong. Since the age of twelve, I've been pulling my own weight, trying to fix a world that never gave a shit. Now I see things so much clearer. The old world was noise. The new one is stripped down, honest, ugly…but real. Real is the only thing I want, especially with her.

She's curled up next to me now, asleep against my side like she belongs there. God, I can almost let myself believe she does. I keep thinking I'll wake up and this will be another cruel dream but then she shifts and talks to me in her sleep, and it hits me all over again. *I love her.* Not in the '*let's date and see where this goes*' way. Not in the '*she's hot and fun and I like kissing her*' way. No, *I love her.* I am going to skip the whole girlfriend thing and put a damn ring on her finger. I catch myself thinking about it too much lately. If there's still a jewelry store standing at the next stop. Hell, even if there's just one display case with a ring that hasn't melted into glass, I'm grabbing it. Doesn't matter if it's gold, silver, or wrapped in duct tape. If it fits her finger, it's good enough. Actually, I'm going to hope it's a silver one. She likes silver.

I know it's crazy. We're literally surrounded by Dybbuks that eat people but none of that matters when she touches me, remembering every inch of my skin from before the world went dark. Making me believe in something outside of myself again. She's been through hell. Lost her mom, her brother, her best friend, her little girl, and still, she gets up and smiles at me like I might be worth something. That strength guts me and I swear I'll protect her until there's nothing left of me to sacrifice.

Even now, as we roll past fields and wreckage and mountains cracked by fire, I can't stop looking at her. The others are laughing up front. Kate's cracking jokes with Teresa. Hawthorne's teaching Dion to whistle. Arthur and Wilson are arguing over something dumb. Emily and Theo reading some books they found. It feels like a weird, broken little *family*. One we built from scraps and survival. I catch myself smiling, of all people. I've had a permanent scowl fixed on my face since I was in my teens. I call my new state of being the Violet effect.

It's been six hours on the road now. The sun dips behind the clouds too tired to keep watch over us. I've seen beauty out there before, Afghanistan sunrises, mountain ranges in Alaska, but this broken stretch of highway lined with pine and ash feels transcendent.

Sinclair's voice cuts through my thoughts, loud from up front, "We're here. Kelowna."

I blink out the window. A city won't be an easy fight but there might be a jewelry store and safety.

"Alright, let's make sure there's not a shit ton of undead," I say, gently stirring Violet awake.

The city—what little remained—smoldered like hell itself had grown weary and struck a match for amusement. Most of downtown Kelowna is ash and steel bones, burnt-out cars line the streets like twisted, open caskets. The storefronts are blown to hell, windows shattered, with only a few buildings still upright. Worse than the wreckage are the wet groans and dragging shuffles of disconnected limbs. The undead are here, swarming, slow and twitchy, sniffing the air like bloodhounds. I count at least thirty in our immediate view, some wandering near a burned restaurant, others aimlessly bumping into walls like broken wind-up toys. Their gross heads turn as the bus drives by.

We took the road up toward West Kelowna. It is steep and winding, with enough brush and elevation to lose most of the infected. Every kilometer makes the air lighter, buildings cleaner. Less rot and fewer bodies. The road widens near a business strip, and we spot a gas station, a still-standing Tim's, and a cannabis shop at the end of the strip with intact windows and an OPEN sign hanging crookedly, like fate herself is inviting me to walk in. We park the bus on a side street, hidden beneath a cluster of pines. I kiss Violet's head, a second attempt to wake her up from her beauty sleep. I ease her head down onto the seat, my fingertips tracing her cheek before slipping away. I clear my throat to wake up everyone.

"Alright, squad," I say, grinning like an idiot. "We are in Kelowna now, there were a few dead at the bottom of the hill so stay alert if you leave the bus, we are here for gas and any other supplies. Use the hiking packs in the back of the bus and grab everything. If you see something move, make it stop. If it smells like shit and moans, it's not a corpse, it's just Hawthorne."

Hawthorne rolls his eyes. "You're so lucky you're freakishly tall or I'd throw hands."

Violet chuckles and bumps her shoulder into mine, whispering in my ear, "Lucky for me, I happen to like skyscrapers."

"You keep whispering in my ear like that, and we won't make it down the strip." I say, letting a knowing look pass between us.

Sinclair, Hawthorne, Kate, my love and I, branch out from the group to look for things down the strip. By this time, we are an oiled machine, our rules and roles well established.

We clear a block and a half, not without sound, but quiet enough to not attract a horde. Just the occasional moan in the distance and the crunch of gravel. This place was definitely on the bomb squads hit list. Hawthorne abruptly looks to his right and it interrupts my thoughts.

A Dybbuk comes limping out from behind a rusted-out civic. Its cheek shredded down to teeth, one eye dangling like a popped grape. It clocks us and picks up speed, dragging a foot that has no toes left. Without a word, Hawthorne and I advance–two shadows in step.

I catch it mid-lunge with a boot to the chest. It thrashes, snarling wet and loud. I pin its neck under my heel and draw my blade, shoving it through the eye socket with a sick crack.

Hawthorne nudges the corpse with the barrel of his rifle. "Ugly son of a bitch."

"Still better lookin' than Sinclair," I joke, yanking my knife free.

Kate lets out a snort, stepping up beside us wielding a cracked aluminum baseball bat she'd looted from a store window like it was Excalibur. Another Dybbuk rounds the corner. Its skin leathery, hands twitching mid-nightmare. Kate lines up like she is at a driving range.

"Fore," she speaks out in a hush, then swings.

The bat connects with a meaty crack. The Dybbuk's head flies sideways like a discarded football, its body crumpling in a twitching heap. Brain matter sprays against the wall behind it, in an abstract mess of gore.

"Gross-ass bitch," she says, shaking blood off the handle like it was nothing new. She should've joined the military; she would have done great.

Two more stumble out from the ruins of a florist's shop. One darts straight for Violet and the second it lunges for her, everything inside me snaps to kill. She spins around, ducking under its grasping hands. Using a broken rebar rod, she'd picked up off the side of the road, she drives it right through the creature's mouth and out the back of its head, a morbid shish kebab. The body twitches and collapses at her feet. Violet easily kicks it off the rod, and keeps moving. Goddamn Angel of Death.

My limbs spring into action before my thoughts catch up. The second one comes up on us fast, teeth bared, arms flailing, eyes white and bulging like a junkie off a bad trip. I don't have time to draw anything. I duck under its half-ass swing and grab it by the collar, using its own weight to throw it into the pavement. I drop down with it, elbow raised high, and smash it twice right in the side of its skull. Bone cracks under my arm, the impact shooting pain up my triceps, but I don't stop. The third hit caves in its temple like a dropped pumpkin. I sit back, chest heaving with blood on my skin that isn't mine.

Great, now I need another shower.

I look up and Violet is watching me with this half proud, half worried expression. Our eyes lock for a second. She smiles at me deviantly and I return the gesture.

So, she likes it when I kill Dybbuks with my bare hands…noted.

The red on her cheeks is an indication that if I took her into the woods, stripped her naked, and took what's mine, I would slip right in.

Sinclair jogs up, winded. "Are you guys good?"

Kate gestures to the gore on her bat. "Fine. Ryder made out with a corpse, though."

"My lips are only for this beauty" I wink, wiping off my elbow. "Plus, the thing came onto me."

Hawthorne cracks a smile.

"Hey look!" Kate says with a raised eyebrow. "I think we've earned ourselves a smoke break."

The cannabis store is heaven. Untouched and smelling like my dreams. Earthy, dank, and a faint citrus note. The buds are still sealed…papers…grinders…*fucking edibles.*

Hawthorne lets out a low whistle. "Sweet mother of ganja."

Violet's eyes light up. "I've never been so turned on by a weed display before."

We make a circle around the counter. I roll a fat joint, light it, and pass it around like holy communion. The first inhale hits a little too hard. We end up collapsed in a pile of beanbags that smell like patchouli, laughing our asses off at a dead guy who is twitching against the store doors and windows trying to get in. The fucker is really going for it. His rotted palms squeak against the glass like his sheer desperation can melt through the reinforced windows. His face is mashed sideways, one cloudy eye staring directly into the void. The Dybbuk starts a slow, jerky grind. Hip-first. Like a half-decayed undead Elvis trying to seduce his way inside. His forehead keeps thumping rhythmically against the window, smearing a trail of gory drool and dried blood, and his knee twitches like it is stuck in a broken loop. The worst part by far is the eye contact.

"Bro…" Sinclair's voice breaks the silence like a bad laugh track. "Is he dry humping the window?"

Kate chokes on her drag. "Oh my god. He is. Full pelvic commitment."

"I've never felt more sexually threatened by the undead," I half-laugh.

Violet peeks up from my chest, stifling a laugh. "Maybe he's lonely."

"Or maybe he thinks the weed smell means we're serving brains on a goddamn charcuterie board."

"Welcome to the end of the world. Population: Us. Vibes? Immaculate." Hawthorne says while taking a long drag.

Kate cracks open a can of THC iced tea. "I still can't believe this place wasn't looted. A whole-ass dispensary untouched. What kind of apocalypse is this?"

"A polite one," I shrug. "The dead are Canadian too."

Outside, the Dybbuk smacks into the glass again with a meaty think.

Sinclair points. "Oh, we haven't forgotten about you."

It continues slowly smacking the window, while groaning and looking super gross. The decay leaking into its fight to keep moving.

"I'll give him points for persistence," I note, watching him slap the glass. "If he humps that door one more time, I'm taking notes for later."

I wink at Violet, causing her to burst out laughing, and it turns into this little snort that makes my chest feel weirdly warm. She grins up at me with red eyes and wind-tangled hair, and goddamn it if I didn't want to kiss her right there.

"Okay but wait," she says between giggles. "Can Deadheads get concussions? Like, is that why he's walking in weird spirals now?"

"He's rebooting," Sinclair says. "Got to update his undead software."

Kate stands up and points at him dramatically. "If he headbutts that door one more time, I'm naming him Chad."

"Chad the Window Humper," Hawthorne says solemnly. "Gone, but never forgotten."

I just lay there, high as hell, Violet cuddles against me and the world feels a little less cruel and a little more like something we can survive. She draws idle circles on my ribs, laughter spilling like light through cracks I thought were sealed. I look down at her. Her lips are pink from the joint, her eyes lazy and amused, cheeks flushed. I could live in this moment. I could die here and call it a win.

"Well," I whisper, "If this is the afterlife, I'm not complaining."

She smirks. "I like stoned Ryder. He's funny."

I lean in, brushing a loose strand of hair from her face, letting my fingers linger a second too long. Her eyes catch mine bright, blue, full of that spark that always undoes me.

"I like you," I murmur, leaning in, brushing my lips over hers. Slow and soft, like we had all the time in the world. Her fingers curl in the fabric of my shirt, lips parting just enough.

Thud.

Violet shakes with laughter against me, her forehead pressed into my shoulder. "God, this is so stupid."

"I know, and I never want it to end." My voice dips close, meant for her alone as I kiss the top of her head.

It is stupid and ridiculous and it probably won't last past the next town, but for now in this tiny dispensary with the curtains drawn and the smell of weed everywhere, it feels like peace and laughter still has a place in the apocalypse. I kiss her again because the world could fall apart all over, and I'd still want this. I'd still want *her*.

Eventually, everyone gathers up their looted gear. The garbage bags have turned out to be an apocalypse essential. Bulging with snacks, batteries, lighters, and whatever else we can grab. The bags are heavy, but Violet's hand in mine makes the weight feel like nothing. We walk side by side, her laugh still echoing in my ears from some dumb joke Sinclair cracked. I catch her in the corner of my eye. She doesn't see what I see—how she outshines the ruin around us. I'm so caught up in her, I almost overlook the caved in window, and the sign barely holding on.

GEMINI FINE JEWELS.

I slow my pace, letting go of her hand. "Hey, darlin, I think I dropped my lighter back by that dumpster. You go ahead, I'll catch up with you guys in a sec."

She raises an eyebrow. "You sure? We have a bunch of lighters."

I nod, trying not to look suspicious as hell. "Yeah, go on. I'll be right behind you."

She narrows her eyes at me. Smart girl. Can always tell when I am up to something, even when I don't say a word. She lets it go with her little half-sigh, and turns away, bags rustling at her sides. She takes a few steps before pausing like she forgot something, then turns back.

"Be safe," her voice low, commanding more than asking.

One hand tugs at my shirt, the other settling against my jaw grounding me to the moment. Without hesitation or fear she presses her lips against mine, claiming me as if I had always been hers. The kiss is quick, but it doesn't feel small. By the time she pulls away, my brain is a static buzz. I open my eyes to find her already walking off after rewiring every circuit in my body, left with the taste of her in my mouth.

She could kiss me like that right before stabbing me and I'd still say thank you.

I duck off the main strip a few blocks and slip through the broken glass into the jewelry store. The inside looks like a raccoon hosted a kegger. The counters are smashed, velvet boxes tossed like confetti. Shards of glass surrender beneath my weight. Every display case has been gutted, and it's hard to tell if it's from looters or the bombs. Dust blankets the room, a decade's worth of silence packed into mere weeks. Still, I search—because hope is a hard thing to kill.

I find a handful of rings scattered near a busted drawer, most of them gaudy as hell. Gold monstrosities with oversized stones, tacky-ass heart shapes, shit that screams Vegas shotgun wedding. None of it feels like her…like *us*. I pick one up and flip it over.

Too big.

Too shiny.

Too…harsh.

A thin rose-gold ring catches my eye, all dainty and harmless. I can almost hear her voice.

Not a chance, Ryder.

Yeah, she'd hate it. I don't even know her ring size. Not really, but I can guess. I know the feel of her fingers in mine. Probably eight. Maybe eight and a half. I'm like some lovesick idiot in a rom-com. All I need is a sad indie song playing in the background while I dig through the blown-up jewelry store looking for the perfect fucking ring.

Nestled in the wreckage waiting just for me, a slim silver band, barely tarnished, with a single blue diamond set right in the middle. Not too big, not flashy. Simple, clean and just right. The stone catches the light through the cracked front window and glimmers like ice, just like her eyes. I hold it between my fingers and just stare. Everything else fades out, the stench of rot down the block, the creak of the wind through broken awnings, the ache in my elbow from today's fight, none of it matters. I can see her wearing this. Can see myself slipping it onto her hand, her looking up at me with that suspicious stare, like she is about to make a joke just to cover how much it means.

What if I had never joined the military? What if instead of sand and gunfire, it had been grocery runs and dog walks? Would I have taken her to some overpriced brunch spot and bitched about parking instead of writing letters? Would I have proposed with this ring over pancakes and too much syrup?

I picture her laughing at me as I drop the damn thing mid-proposal, bending down only to have her yank me up by the collar and kiss me before I can even ask. I take a deep breath in. Christ, I'm a fucking sap. I turn it over in my fingers, then slip it into my front pocket, close to my chest.

"Hey!" a voice growls behind me.

I turn just as a boot slams into my stomach. The air leaves my lungs like a busted tire. I hit the back counter hard, my head left spinning. I blink slowly, as my vision tilts.

Three men.

Ragged clothes.

Greasy hair.

One has a bat, another a knife, and the third has fists and a face that looks like he chews rocks for fun. My fist cracks square against Bat Guy's nose and I feel the cartilage crunch beneath my knuckles. He shrieks like a kicked dog, stumbling back and dropping the bat with a loud clang against the pavement.

Mine now.

I lunge for it but I am too fucking slow. A sharp burn tears through my side as Knife Guy slices me just under the ribs.

"Motherf—" I hiss through clenched teeth, staggering sideways, palm already slick with blood.

Screw the pain. I swing wild with rage and snatch up the bat mid-stagger, whipping it hard into someone's ribs. The crack echoes, followed by a wheeze of breath as the guy folds in half like a busted lawn chair. A boot smashes into my jaw and the world flips. My skull slams onto the floor, lights explode behind my eyes like a busted fireworks show. Everything rings. Concrete scrapes the back of my skull, and for a split second all I can taste is copper and dust.

"Jesus fuck," I stammer, squinting up.

A shadow steps into view.

Polished boots.

Military cut.

Cold dead eyes like winter steel.

Tompkins.

"Well, well, well" he says, voice all calm and casual like we are running into each other at the gym. "Who do we have here?"

I yanked my gun free and fire a single shot into the roof. A desperate cry for help. Before I can lower my arm, the butt of his rifle comes down hard. White-hot pain cracks through my skull.

Then, just black.

CHAPTER 28

VIOLET

"Was that a gunshot?" Kate asks.

Hawthorne's eyes narrow. "I think that came from wherever Ryder went."

My legs spring into action before my brain can catch up, sprinting down the road. I just need to get to him. I need to see if he is okay. Kate, Sinclair, and Hawthorne are right behind me, their footsteps matching mine as we tear down the street. My lungs burn but I don't stop, not until a glint of metal catches my eye through the trees.

I drop low, ducking behind a bush, chest heaving. Just across the clearing, a black SUV sits with a trailer hitched behind it. It looks far too clean and prepared for the state the world is in. A broad-shouldered man leans against the hood, smoking like this is just another Thursday. Three others move around the vehicle carrying someone. My breath catches when I realize it's Ryder they are carrying. His body is limp, arms bound behind his back, blood smeared across his temple like cruel war paint.

"Ry—" I choke out, but a hand slams over my mouth, silencing me.

I whip around, eyes wide, and meet Sinclair's grim expression.

"Shhh. That's Tompkins."

The name means nothing to me but the way Sinclair says it makes me feel uneasy. My thoughts spiral.

Why did he have blood on his temple? Was he shot? Was that his gun or theirs? Why wasn't he moving?

"Is he dead?" I whisper, throat tightening around the words.

Sinclair shakes his head. "No. He wouldn't take him if he was dead."

I stare back at the scene, helplessness clawing at my chest like a trapped animal. "We have to help him. He's being taken…. he's being fucking kidnapped."

"Keep it down. You won't help him by rushing in and getting yourself killed," Hawthorne says, low but firm. "Tompkins will put a bullet in anyone who gets in his way. I've seen it."

"I can't just watch them take him," I break, tears stinging the backs of my eyes as my fists clench. "I can't lose him."

I turn to Kate who is already looking at me. Her eyes are a mix of sadness and seriousness. She doesn't need me to explain. She understands.

"I'll take the bags. Hawthorne and I will run back, get the bus, and tell the others what happened."

"Okay, good idea. Stay safe guys."

They run off as I stay crouched with Sinclair, watching as they force Ryder into the SUV. His head lolls, eyes half-closed. I feel like I am choking on fear and fury. If they hurt him, I swear to God. I'll fucking put them in the ground.

"Who is Tompkins?" I ask, voice barely above a whisper.

Sinclair exhales slowly. "Tompkins was our Major General. Led the whole unit. He's the one who ditched us the night Kent got you out. Tompkins took off without us in a helicopter."

My mind reels as I put the pieces together.

That sound I heard in the sky when me and dad were at that farmhouse. The helicopter. Tompkins.

"That means they're close, right?" I ask. "That means his camp, his base…. whatever the hell it is…. it's nearby."

Sinclair nods. "It has to be. They wouldn't risk long drives. Not with the limited gas supply. Not with how the roads are. The bus won't be quiet when it gets here. So, we stay down. We stay alert and look for anything that can help us with this rescue mission."

I incline my head slightly, though my gaze remains on the SUV. That's when I notice movement from the trailer.. That's when I notice movement from the trailer.

"Hey, check out that huge trailer."

"Holy fuck, are those biters? Those guys are some sick fucks."

For a second, I think my eyes are deceiving me.

Why would they do that? Why would they steal Ryder? Why the hell haven't they moved yet? They've got him. What are they still doing parked here? Are they waiting for something? For orders?

My pulse is a drumbeat in my ears, panic gnawing at me. My jaw tightens, and before I spiral too far, the men by the SUV start arguing, voices sharp, and irritated.

Good. Keep fighting, you bastards. Don't notice us.

"Think Violet," I babble to myself.

I force a breath, grip my knife until my knuckles ache, and look back at Sinclair. His eyes are wide, waiting for me to come up with something.

"Follow my lead…and keep down so they don't see us. "My voice is a whisper, but there's no mistaking the steel in it.

We slip around to the back of the trailer, crouching low, staying on the opposite side of the arguing men. My knees ache in protest, but I don't dare make a sound. We freeze, holding our breath, as they stomp around to the front and climb into the SUV. The click of doors shutting echoes too loud as the engine roars to life. I brace myself steady, ready to bolt, but they don't drive away. The SUV just sits there idling. They're still arguing inside, voices muffled but loud. I grit my teeth. Every second they stay parked is another second Ryder stays just out of reach. Another second I have to sit here, powerless. I force myself to focus, to breathe, to turn the dread and anger into something useful. I crawl closer to the back of the trailer. Every movement feels too noisy, too slow. My pulse is in my throat now, heavy and hot. There's a Deadhead wedged underneath, its ruined hands clawing blindly toward the sound of me and an idea floods my brain.

I crouch, grab its wrist, and with one clean motion, slice its hand off. The severed stump gushes rotten sludge that drips in slow, sticky globs onto the asphalt. This could work.

"Keep cutting off anything you can," I snap to Sinclair, not looking up.

We work in unison, our motions quick and brutal. Our blades flashing like some macabre game of fruit ninja. The trailer rocks as they finally start to pull away.

Fuck, no…don't leave yet.

The Deadheads jolt with the SUV and one falls to the bottom of the trailer. I swing my knife, slicing its stomach open until its guts spill free, slick and glistening in the faint light. The smell nearly knocks me out, but it doesn't matter. This is our breadcrumb trail. We run for cover, darting into the nearby store. I press myself against the glass, breath held, and watch as the trail we created does its job. The air feels heavy, charged with fear and purpose. I stand for a second, breathing hard, blade still slick in my grip. Then something shimmers in my periphery. Glass, shattered and glinting like ice in the weak morning light.

Sinclair and I end up standing in the wreckage of what was once a place filled with promises. Diamonds meant for happily ever after's; gold bands meant to bind. Now it was stripped bare, display cases gutted, velvet stands tossed and torn. Even in the ruin, it still carries a strange tenderness. A ghost of love stories that hadn't made it past the end of the world. I spy a boot print near the glass door, the same size as Ryders. My stomach coils, tight and uneasy.

"He was here," I say, more to myself than Sinclair. "They must've grabbed him outside, there's no other footprints."

Sinclair glances over, brows pinched. "Fuck, he must have recognized him."

"They must've seen him outside, maybe watching the display…"

Maybe he thought about grabbing something for me. Something stupid and romantic, that left him vulnerable and got him kidnapped. If they hurt him, it would break me. Even in a dead world, Ryder still tried. He'd always had that reckless tenderness when it came to me. Small moments, like brushing a leaf out of my hair right after he killed seven Deadheads, or clearing a whole store just to find me my favorite noodles. That's what unnerves people about him. Not just the violence he is capable of, but the fact that he still loves like it means something. Ryder was mine, and now they had taken him from me.

"They saw him and took him because they thought he was alone," I said, voice steel under all the shaking. "He's not alone anymore."

A low rumble in the distance catches my attention. The familiar growl of the bus's engine growing closer. I exhale hard, relief hitting so fast my knees wobble.

"Finally," I mutter, stepping out of the store. "We've got a trail, we've got backup… and I've got a fuck-ton of rage."

The bus squeals to a stop, kicking up a cloud of dust. The doors swing open, and Hawthorne jumps out first, his face laced with annoyance.

"Sorry," Hawthorne says, glaring at Sinclair. "Little Dion had to pee and so did I." Sinclair rolled his eyes.

Dad appears next, his face going pale when he spots me.

"Violet?" he calls out, rushing over. "Are you okay? You've got…Jesus, you've got blood all over you."

"I'm fine," I say, voice tight. "Look."

I point to the road, to the mess of entrails and gore painting a grotesque path toward where they'd taken him.

"That's going to lead us straight to Ryder."

His eyes follow the line, and then he looks back at me. A mix of pride and relief flicker in his expression. He pulls me into a hug.

"Okay," he utters against my hair. "Then let's go get him."

CHAPTER 29
RYDER

My head feels like someone used it for batting practice. I blink hard trying to shake the fog. Everything is too fucking bright. My arms are numb, wrists burning against nylon rope, that is way too tight.

Am I tied to a goddamn chair?

My boots scrape against concrete when I shift my weight. I jerk my head up. A low, wet moan rings out from a Dybbuk, maybe two feet in front of me. It's chained to a pipe in the wall, face sagging, lips torn back in a permanent snarl. Its jaw clicks open and shut like a broken hinge, the chain around its neck tugging tight every time it lunges forward. What a gross motherfucker. I can smell rot and old blood and that sour animal stink the fresh ones have. My heart kicks into high gear but I hold my ground, not giving anyone the satisfaction of seeing my fear. I hear the creak of a door opening behind me. Heavy footsteps follow, slow and too calm for this shitshow I am sitting in. I don't have to look to know who it is.

"Ryder Kent," the voice sounds smooth and cheerful as if this is just a family reunion. "Well, shit. You made it out alive."

I crane my neck and sure enough… Major *fucking* Tompkins.

Still smug.

Still in uniform.

Even has the gall to wear his damn medals, like the world hadn't gone tits up and he hadn't left an entire platoon to die in that overrun camp forsaking everything they stand for.

I laugh. "Can't kill a cockroach, right?"

He smirks like I am the prodigal son returning home. "You always were my best soldier."

I want to spit in his face, but I am too dehydrated.

Instead, I ask, "Where the hell am I?"

Tompkins walks past me, casual as ever, as if we were back at base. He stands next to the corpse, just out of reach, as if he was observing a pet dog.

"This?" he says, gesturing around. "This is home. A little sanctuary carved into the bones of a mountain. A bunker built by the people who knew this was coming. You know the *important* ones."

You mean the politicians…CEOs…celebrities. The ones with enough money to buy their survival.

He looks at me earnestly. "You could live here too. You should, actually. You're exactly the kind of man we need around here."

I don't respond. I just watch him weighing every word and measuring every movement. My brain runs laps while my face stays still. If I want to get out of here…if I want to get back to her, I have to play this smart. I can't lash out, can't snap, I have to act like I am in, like I could be one of them.

"So what?" I say. "You keep me tied up, then offer me a housewarming gift?"

Tompkins chuckles. "Just a precaution. You know how it is. Can't trust just anyone but if you swear the oath…"

He moves closer to my face now, adding some drama into his monologue. "If you can *mean* it…they'll accept you."

"Oath?"

"You'll see," he says, waving his hands dismissively and leaves as if that explained everything.

I sit there for a while, wrists burning, stomach twisting in knots. The chained thing keeps snarling and snapping. I stare back at it, unblinking one thought in my mind.

Violet

Violet

Violet

After some time two ‘guards’ all in black come to retrieve me. One of them crouches, slicing through the ropes at my wrists with a hunting knife. The cord gives way, and a rush of blood burns through my arms like fire ants have taken up residence under my skin.

“Easy,” I growl as the guard yanks me to my feet like I weigh nothing.

My legs wobble, knees locking and unlocking as the circulation returns. I don’t fall but damn, it is close.

“You're lucky I don’t bite,” I mutter, voice low but sharp, hoping it wouldn’t go unnoticed.

They don’t react, they just start walking, herding me through the hallways like a bovine being led to its slaughter. They shove me down a narrow corridor, cold and quiet and it swallows all the sound, nothing but my thoughts echoing back at me. The overhead lights buzz and strobe, casting a sickly yellow halo along the cracked concrete walls.

How do they have…power?

The smell of bleach and rancid meat invades my senses. Clean and rot simultaneously like someone is trying way too hard to hide something in plain sight. My nose wrinkles. I know that smell.

Something died in here. Or is about to…

I take slow steps, dragging one boot slightly just to be a pain in the ass. The guards don’t look back.

I know a fucking death march when I’m in one.

Every instinct I have is screaming, but I keep it buried.
No twitching.
No panic.
Eyes forward.

"Nice place you got here," I say, letting sarcasm drip off every syllable. "Cozy. It's just missing the welcome mat and the fresh cookies."

Still nothing. Real rough crowd. My shoulders ache, but I hold my head high as we pass a thick metal door on the right. Screams leak through the cracks, muffled but unmistakable. Definitely human and they sound panicked. My jaw clenches.

What the fuck is this place really?

Tompkins said '*bunker*', but it feels more like a prison or a slaughterhouse with better interior design. We turn a corner and they bring me to a stone room with a drain in the center. Stained rust-brown and slick-looking, like it's been scrubbed, but not enough. On a metal table: a knife, a live pig, and a basin.

What the fuck…

Tompkins stands across from me, hands behind his back, all official.

"The oath is old. Blood in, blood fed."

One of the guards grabs the pig and holds it over the basin. I am handed the knife. I hesitate. Not because of the pig but because of the pit they roll open. A metal grate slides aside, and the stench hits like a freight train. A dozen Dybbuks packed in tight below us, clawing at the grates with bloody nails, their heads jerking erratically toward all the sound. I look to Tompkins for further instruction.

"Now feed the elders."

This guy is fucking nuts. How did I not see this before?

I slice the pig's throat. Not proud, not ashamed, just another necessity. Its blood fills the basin almost immediately. I lift the pig and trudge towards the metal opening. The carcass is heavy in my hands, still twitching as I walk it to the edge of the pit. My boots stick slightly to the concrete, coated in blood and something else I don't want to identify. I drop it in and it flops low and wet like the death rattle of lungs trying to remember how to breathe. One of the corpses below lets out this guttural choking sound, somewhere between a growl and a sob as the others surge. They fight over the fresh kill like rabid dogs. I watch one rip the pigs face in half with its teeth, skin still on its lips from the last thing it ate. Another slams its skull into the wall in a frenzy trying to grab a chunk.

Jaws snap.

Bones crunch.

The sound of teeth scraping against each other is louder than it has any right to be. Then to my surprise, I am showered beneath the basin of blood.

"He is now cleansed and belongs to the holy family." Tompkins says, his voice smooth and proud, like he'd just knighted me instead of dragging me into some corpse cannibal blood cult hellhole.

I want to break his fucking jaw. Just one good punch to shatter those smug teeth, wipe that bullshit smile off his face. The kind of punch that leaves a man tasting pennies and spitting blood through his gums Instead, I nod and unsuccessfully attempt to clean off some of the blood that now stains me.

Smile Play their game. Live long enough to tear this place down from the inside out.

I can feel his eyes on me. Assessing, measuring, proud in that weird, twisted way cult leaders get when one of their own doesn't flinch at the crazy. I keep my gaze steady, pretending I'm not covered in pig's blood and that I hadn't just watched a pit of moaning corpses rip it apart like a goddamn sacrifice to some made up God of rot and ruin.

"You're going to do great here, Ryder," he adds, clapping a hand on my shoulder.

I almost jerk away. Instead, I smile with just enough teeth to make it almost friendly.

"Looking forward to it, sir."

Every muscle in my face locks down like steel cables are holding it together. I keep my hands at my sides, clenched just enough to feel my nails dig crescents into my palms.

Lie better than they do. That's how you live long enough to find Violet.

A moment later, one of the guards waves me forward, and Tompkins points subtly toward a hallway dressed up to look like a luxury hotel corridor. Carpeted floors, gold trimmed sconces. A manufactured lavender scent pumping through hidden vents to mask the underlying stench of bleach and rot. They push me into a room and when I step inside, I don't know whether to laugh, vomit, or torch the whole fucking place. There is a huge bed with soft looking sheets. A tray waiting for me with steak…. actual steak…and mashed potatoes, gravy still steaming like it had just come from a restaurant kitchen. A glass of red wine sits amongst silver cutlery and a goddamn cloth napkin. To the left a door left open a crack reveals a marble bathroom. It looks like a five-star hotel but all I can hear are the screams behind the steel doors and all I can see is the pit of dead things eating meat. All I can focus on is the oath I just took, and the blood still dripping off me.

I stand under the shower for what feels like an hour, steam rising around me, washing off the filth, the blood, the stink of everything I'd just done. It felt wrong. Like they had tried to erase what I am. I won't be fooled by fancy food or hot water. I already found my forever and she's probably freaking out, wondering what's become of me.

After I dry off and dress in the black clothes they left for me, I wait until the hallway outside is clear. Then I crack the door and slip into the corridor quiet as a ghost. Time to find out what these bastards are really hiding.

For a tall guy, I move like a goddamn mouse. Adrenaline zips through my veins like battery acid and I fucking love it. I trail behind two clueless pricks, slip down a hallway, and duck into the first door I can find. It's a storage room filled with stale industrial air. Shelves of canned food, and oddly enough flowers line the walls. My confusions only grow. I drop low behind the metal counter, heart pounding but steady and controlled. I can hear footsteps and low voices.

"You know what, Jared? I should've let you die that day. You're proving to be really fucking useless."

"I'm sorry, Celeste! They just drove too fast."

"Yeah, well, you might've ruined it for all of us."

I raise an eyebrow.

Okay, drama.

My ears perk when I hear the next sentence.

"Who cares about some bitch anyway? Her and her bus friends can die for all I care."

Bus friends?

"It'll be hard to do that when we can't fucking find them!" she snaps, smacking him upside the head with a satisfying crack.

My hands clench into fists. They were talking about *our* bus. I stand, slow and deliberate. Both of them snap their heads around like someone pressed the panic button.

"This is a private conversation," Celeste snarls, narrowing her eyes.

"Oh shit," I say, all innocent-like. "This isn't the bathroom?"

I fake a confused glance around. "Whoops. Got a little lost."

Jared squints at me, stepping closer. His face twists as recognition sparks.

"I know you..." he mutters. "You're the one who destroyed The Awakening camp." He jabs a finger into my chest, his voice going low and mean. "You ruined our offering. Stole our black-haired whore."

What the fuck did he just say?

I wasn't planning on killing anyone today but the day has already been full of surprises. I crack my neck, glancing for a moment at the ceiling.

"Oh, I think I remember now" I say, stepping in closer. "I did *ruin* your fucked up little cult. Killed everyone there." My voice drops. "Looks like I missed a few."

I drive my fist into his gut with enough force to lift him off his feet. He wheezes, his body folding and I grab his shirt and slam his face into the counter. *Twice.* Blood splatters the cabinets. I throw him backward and he hits the shelf hard, metal rattling, cans clattering to the floor. He comes at me again, swinging wide like an amateur. I duck, step in, and deliver a brutal elbow right to his jaw. His bone cracks beneath the hit, and he drops like a sack of regret.

Celeste turns to run.

Big mistake.

I lunge and grab a fistful of her hair, yanking her back so hard she shrieks. Her heels fly off. She kicks and scratches, but I slam her head against the cold metal counter.

"Tell me what you know about the girl and the bus!"

Her breath comes in ragged bursts, blood trailing from her lips. She glares at me like I'd murdered her puppy.

"Fuck you," she spits.

I yank her head back. "Try again."

"The girl…" she coughs, eyes darting to the crumpled body of the guy I'd already dealt with, still twitching on the floor like a broken wind-up toy. "They're looking for her… Tompkins wants her alive. He said she's…" she hesitates, biting down on whatever words almost slipped.

"She's what?" I bark, tightening my grip until her hair strains under my palm.

"You're too fucking late," she sneers and with zero hesitation, she hawks blood and saliva straight into my face.

My jaw clenches.

Wrong move bitch.

I slam her head again, harder.

Once.

Twice.

Three times.

A wet crunch echoes off the walls as her skull repeatedly meets steel. Her body goes limp in my grip, sliding down the cabinet like a sack of meat. Blood smears the metal like finger paint. I wipe the spit off my cheek with the back of my hand, breathing hard. The rage still sizzles under my skin. They knew Violet. They were planning something and now I was going to find every last one of these fucks and burn this place to the ground.

One body at a time.

CHAPTER 30

TOMPKINS

I've never trusted Ryder Kent, not for a second. I let him think his pitiful sacrifice meant something. Let him bleed and sweat like some noble little martyr, so proud of gutting that pig as if it proved anything. It was funny watching him posture like a good soldier, like he belonged. Eyes wide, hungry for approval. He follows orders like a dog desperate for a leash, never realizing the whole damn game is rigged. The only reason I didn't put a bullet through his skull outside that store is because I want to watch him rot from the inside out, slow and helpless. A walking failure. A breathing monument to everything I lost. Ryder could never be my protege because there was someone before him, someone worthy of my time. *My son.*

He was the prototype. Sharp wits, iron mind, and obedient to the bone. I built him from the ground up, blood of my blood, weaponized and perfect. He bore my name like a badge of honor and never once questioned the mission. Until a simple recon and extraction. We'd done it a hundred times. Then the ambush.

Gunfire.

RPGs.

Heat that peeled the sky back.

His voice crackled in the comms, calling for backup. I told them to hold their position. He obeyed, like he always did and it got him killed.

No body.

Nothing to bury.

Just ash and absence.

My legacy died screaming in the sand and with it, the last things that made sense. My wife couldn't stomach the cost, said it was my fault and she left me. So, I gave her what she deserved. Made her my first test subject in the new world. I watched her turn after I shot her, watched her devour her new husband, dumb fuck that he was, and laughed while she did it. Now she moans in a cage like the rest of them.

A trophy.

Just like Kent will be.

I picked him up when he was young, angry, damaged and stupid. I thought I could salvage the wreckage. Turn it into something useful. Maybe even replicate what I lost but Kent never bent right. He cracked, he questioned and he looked at me like I was the villain in his little origin story and maybe I was, but monsters make weapons. It's martyrs that make corpses.

When the camp fell and the biters came swarming through the fence the evac chopper had one open seat. I left him behind without blinking. Told myself he wasn't worth it. Thought I'd start again with better clay but he lived and that was the truest betrayal. Now he walks around like he matters. Like he's some grim fucking knight on a holy mission. Protecting people, falling in love, playing hero, but I know the truth. He's just a shadow, a second draft, a constant reminder that I couldn't bring my son back. He should've died when I left him in the dirt.

The surveillance office hums, blue light glaring from the monitors. One screen displays the sublevel feed. Storage B. I lean in sneering. Kent has Jared on the ground, punching him over and over, Celeste's screaming like a cornered animal. *Pathetic.* She backed the wrong man. Jared was never going to save anyone and if Kent wasn't beating the memory out of him, I'd have done it myself.

"You think you're something now?" I mutter at the screen. "Think you've won just because you found out we knew? Because you figured out we've been watching since we bagged your girl? Violet, was it?"

I hadn't given her much thought. When she and the old man got snatched by The Awakening, I barely blinked. Just more raw material for our horde but then Kent came storming in with Sinclair, Hawthorne and that red-headed bitch. Guns blazing and blood boiling. All that havoc for one girl and a dying man. It would've been noble if it weren't so fucking stupid. Still…I watched.

Every frame.

Every scream.

Every bullet.

Kent tore through that cult like vengeance was a religion and Violet was the altar. The kind of rage I used to respect. After the survival base fell, I counted them among the dead. Had the footage to prove it. Corpses stacked like sandbags. Jared and Celeste managed one thing right. They tagged the bus. The tracker had fit perfectly under the frame. Kent was still just a trained beast in a soldier's skin but he was *my* beast. I forged him in fire and shame. Everything he is came from me. He's not a savior. He's my failed experiment. I glance to the side, fingers brushing past scattered reports, stopping on a half-empty plastic bottle. I pick it up squinting at the logo. Unassuming, generic and harmless. The kind they hand out in schools, offices, and emergency shelters. I smile.

The irony never gets old. This…this innocent little bottle brought the world to its knees. A miracle. We pumped the virus through the water, and the sheep drank it willingly. Begging for hydration and when they turned? The panic was delicious.

"I'm glad we did it," I whisper, lifting the bottle. "The world needed a mass reset."

I toss it aside and slide the military chip into the reader. The screen lights up with the satellite imagery. A blinking blue dot traces a narrow road not far from here, the bus.

"They're close to us?" I say, voice flat with amusement. "Cockroaches. Resilient little fuckers."

Rocky stands at the door, silent and ready, waiting for my command.

"They've seen too much. They'll talk. Eventually. They always do."

I don't even turn to face him.

"Full kill order. No survivors. Do not shoot them in the head, I want Kent to see them in their biter forms. I want blood, not excuses."

He nods, grabs his radio and vanishes like smoke. Back on the monitor, Kent has stopped hitting Jared. Celeste whimpers as she crawls across the floor. The rage in Kent's face hasn't faded. He thinks this ends with his precious girl alive. Thinks they'll ride off into the sunset like he's the hero of some second-rate novel. Let's see how brave he is when the fire catches everyone he cares about. A few moments later. A knock rattles the door. Too soft, too unsure. It opens before I give permission.

"Sir…uh…we've got a problem," the guard stammers, sweat already gathering at his brow. "One of the rotter's… it got out."

I stare at him for a beat too long. I let the silence sink in, leaving him squirming. I turn off the camera screen and stand, slow and deliberate, swiping the entire stack of folders, schematics, and reports off my desk in one violent sweep. They scatter across the floor like trash.

"Of course, it fucking did," I spit.

He flinches.

"Why am I surrounded by idiots who can't even keep a corpse in a cage?"

He opens his mouth to stammer something else. I raise my gun, "Spare me."

I shove past him, boots heavy on the floor as I storm down the hall.

"You better pray it didn't bite anyone," I threaten. "Or I swear I'll throw you in the fucking cage next."

CHAPTER 31

RYDER

My knuckles are still wet. Celeste's blood clings to my skin, becoming a part of me. My breath comes hard and heavy. Jared is a heap on the ground, his face a pulpy mess, twitching like a squashed bug. They've earned every broken bone. I stand over them, chest rising and falling like a caged animal, vision painted in red. That feral, brutal part of me, the one I usually keep buried, is wide awake now and it liked the way they screamed. A noise outside snaps my head toward the hallway. I creep toward the door, slow and silent, cracking it open just enough to peek through, and there is the source. Tompkins, strutting like the smug bastard he always was, and a wiry guy next to him. The little guy looks like he hasn't eaten in days, maybe weeks. Moving silently, I slip out, letting the sound of their footsteps fade ahead of me. I retrace their steps in the direction they came from, the corridor dim, smelling of stale air and dust. A light flickers above a slightly ajar door. I push it open with my boot and step into what looks like an old surveillance office. Papers litter the cold floor like confetti. Most of it looks like useless bullshit. Memos, faded schematics, old rosters, but then a logo catches my eye. Familiar and military-grade. I crouch down, fingers brushing across corners of crumpled sheets and drop into the chair behind the desk. It creaks under my weight. I lean back, sheets spread across my lap, and started reading. My stomach drops. These are coordinates, names, sectors. Not just notes, these are locations. Underground facilities, all coded in military shorthand, marked up with red pen like someone is planning something big.

"Jesus Christ…" I whisper, eyes scanning faster. These are the secret bases where all the other greedy fucks are hiding out. I fold up as many as I can, my hands moving fast, shoving them into my pockets.

The rest of the papers don't make sense, just time stamps. I start pulling open the drawers. Tompkins was an asshole, yes... but a smart asshole? No. If there is something worth hiding, it would be in plain sight. I check under the water bottle. *Nothing.* Underneath a pile of dog-eared memos and useless clutter, my fingers brush the corner of a thick, black folder. A single word stamped in faded black ink across the front:

Operation Dominion.

I open it quickly and scan the document. My eyes widen. Tompkins isn't just some well-connected opportunist. He's part of a top-secret society that had known this was coming. One hidden base in every province only accessible to those 'worthy' of the invitation, chosen by the elite. My vision floods red.

They planned this

I keep reading. Each base is stocked with military-grade weapons, food printers and power systems running off the earth's natural resources.

Unlimited power.

Unlimited food.

Unlimited control.

That explains why my food looked so fresh on the tray. The most shocking piece of information is that they have been planning this since 1990. Since I was a little swimmer in my dad's balls. Before I'd even existed, they were designing the end. This 'infection' wasn't some fluke...it was engineered. A hybrid strain; rabies spliced with listeria. Effecting the host post mortem. All they needed to do was kill us. It also says they sprayed the berry fields with hay fever and for consumption so if anyone survived, they would be eliminated by sickness. That's why the bomb squad showed up and that's why every town we have been to looks like a graveyard. I turn to the last page.

...contaminate all water, infect the masses. Lakes, rivers, water filtration systems, and water bottles...

My eyes drift to the half-empty water bottle on the desk. *No...* I pick it up and hold it to the blue light on the desk scanner. *It was you.* They put it in in the fucking water. That's why you come back, why everyone came back after they died. They didn't just make monsters; they created an army of undead cannibals so they could rule the ashes and handpick their own kingdoms. Tompkins wasn't just a monster. He was a god in his own head.

The adrenaline hits like caffeine straight to the bloodstream. My fingers tremble. I notice a flash drive on the desk, labeled in thick, block letters:

MILITARY BUS 783.

My heart stops. That's our bus. I scan the desk and see the USB sticking out of the computer hard drive. They'd been tracking us this entire time. I stand so fast the chair screeches across the floor. Rage flares in my chest like a goddamn wildfire. I need to get out of here and find the others and tell them. I don't even get a second to process because I am once again interrupted by voices echoing down the hallway, distant but getting closer. I dive behind a tall cabinet, practically folding myself into it. Not easy for a guy my size, but flexibility isn't just for yoga girls and cultists. I hold my breath. Heart pounding so hard I can hear it in my ears. The footsteps get louder and the voices closer. I squeeze my eyes shut.

Please do not come in here.

CHAPTER 32

VIOLET

Finding Ryder is the kind of miracle you don't waste time questioning. We'd followed the trail of guts up the mountain, each step sinking into churned-up dirt slick with rot. The stench of death clung to the air, marking the way like a grotesque breadcrumb trail. Finally, the compound revealed itself. Hidden in plain sight. At first glance, it looked like nothing more than a jagged cut of mountain rock, collapsed and forgotten but the closer we got, the clearer it became: a dugout carved straight into the earth, its garage entrance disguised with carefully placed stone and debris. A fortress masquerading as ruin. That's when the reckless plan came to life in my head. Hawthorne and Kate would create a distraction to turn the guards' attention away and while they pulled the strings, I'd slip in with Dad, and together we'd get Ryder out. Simple enough.

We wait, crouched in the brush, until an opportunity comes. Two black SUVs roll out through the camouflaged opening, same as the one that had taken Ryder. Only this time they weren't hauling cages full of Deadheads. We seize the moment and slip inside like shadows in their wake. The light all but vanishes when the garage door clangs shut behind us. Darkness swallows everything, broken only by a thin, fractured glow bleeding through a crack high above. My eyes adjust slowly, and the shape of the room bleeds into view.

Rows of SUVs line the cavern floor. Fifteen at least. Glossy black metal hulks that seemed to breathe menace. Three large trailers sit abandoned nearby, but the air around them reeks of decay, the metallic tang of blood clinging to the walls. Death lives here. Two separate doors stand at the far end of the space. Dad meets my eyes, his expression carved in stone, unshakable in the way only he can be.

“We’ll cover more ground if we split up.”

I swallow hard, forcing myself to nod, even as my stomach knots tight. Splitting up never ended well, not for Scooby Doo and not for us. Separate the group, and someone gets lost, trapped… or worse…kidnapped. It was how we ended up here in the first place.

Kate's voice comes out firm, shaking me back to reality, though my hands continue to tremble at my sides. “Hawthorne and I will take the door on the left.”

Dad and I would take the right. We agree to meet back at this garage, once we’ve done what needs to be done. My pulse thunders in my ears as we step toward the door, knowing each choice pushes us deeper into the lion’s den.

The place is a maze, and I swear whoever designed it was either drunk or insane. We get turned around twice, once in a room that turned out to be an indoor pig farm. Reeking, squealing, lit by a single swinging bulb. Again in another room that looked like a café straight out of some dystopian fever dream. Chrome counters, flickering neon signs, that too-perfect artificial coffee smell that makes my skin crawl. We don’t stop. Ryder is all that matters, and I’ll search this whole damn compound to find him.

Then a voice.

His voice.

“VIOLET!”

My legs burn as I push forward. For a heartbeat, the world is empty, silent except for the pounding of my pulse. Then…there he is. Standing in the hallway, chest heaving, eyes locked on me like I am the only thing left worth looking at.

My Ryder.

Alive.

Breathing.

Here.

I almost fall to my knees. The air leaves my lungs in a sob as I stumble toward him, faster, until I am in his arms, clutching him like if I let go, she'd vanish.

"I thought you were dead… I thought I'd never see you again."

Ryder's hands come up to cradle my face, thumbs brushing away tears I didn't even realize were falling. His forehead rests against mine, and for a moment, the world narrows to the warmth between us, the faint tremor of his breath.

"I knew you'd find me," his voice barely steady as his fingers trace along my jaw. His thumb grazes my lips, and it feels like he's memorizing me all over again. "I knew you'd come for me."

Then he's pulling me in, his hand sliding to the back of my neck, fingers curling into my hair and his mouth finds mine. The kiss crashes into me, wild and unrestrained, tasting like fear and survival and everything we almost lost. The next kiss softens, slows into something sacred taking root between us. And the third… the third is pure confession, every word we never said stitched into the space between our lips.

"Okay, kids," Dad's voice cuts through the moment, gruff but relieved. "We've got to move before they notice Big Bird here is missing."

I give a small huff of a laugh, but his arms don't loosen.

"He's right… but you came for me. *Damn.*" His voice softens. "And you found me."

Fuck. I didn't want that kiss to end.

"This way," Dad hisses, grabbing my arm and yanking me forward.

I latch onto Ryder's hand, gripping tight, and the three of us move in sync through the shadows. Footsteps and voices drift closer. Too close. We duck into the nearest room, my heart pounding in my ears. The room is empty. *Lucky us.* We stay still, holding our breath, until the voices pass, then slip back into the winding corridors. One right, two lefts, a short staircase, and finally, the concrete echo of the parking garage. Hawthorne and Kate emerge from the far side stepping out of thin air.

"Great distraction, guys," I breathe

"Hey, Kent," Hawthorne says, then looks at Dad. "Good to see everyone's alright."

"Thanks, man," Dad says.

"We need to move. Tompkins is the devil in human skin, and the longer we're here, the more likely we end up dead." Ryder adds.

No one argues. We fan out, creeping between the rows, searching for keys. Every creak of metal and distant shuffle of movement makes my nerves flare like fire under my skin. I drift toward the light, fingers brushing over dusty dashboards, center consoles, and cold, unyielding cup holders. Then the feeling of metal under my fingertips. *Keys*. My chest swells with a brief, almost foolish relief.

"Yes," I whisper, barely daring to breathe.

A man's voice slithers from the darkness "Who are you?"

I freeze, and look up, catching his shadowed outline… and then I run.

"Hey! Stop there!"

I catch the others' eyes, sharp and urgent, silently begging them to understand. My fingers fumble against the fob, desperate, until the SUV's lights blink in the dim, a small beacon of hope. It sits closer to the exit than the rest. *Perfect*. We travel fast, each step a muted thump against the concrete. Behind me, the man's steps grow louder and heavier. His breath hitches; the click of his radio splits the low hum of the garage, slicing the tension. My eyes burn as every overhead bulb snaps on at once, blinding me, flushing the shadows in harsh, sterile light. My stomach twists into knots, and my chest constricts. Everything I had feared in the silence of the garage has just found me.

"Leaving so soon, Kent?" His voice is smug, like a cat toying with a cornered mouse.

"Yeah, thought I'd see myself out" Ryder snaps, trying to keep his tone steady. "Not really a fan of the whole kidnapping thing. Or the random animal sacrifices. Or, you know… poisoning the water."

That last part hangs in the air like smoke. My head tilts.

"Did you start this?" I question Tompkins, my voice sharper than I intend.

He smirks at me like I'm prey caught in his snare. "I'll get to you in a minute."

With a lazy wave of his hand, he signals someone. Two men step from the shadows, reeking of sweat and oil, their filthy palms clamping over mine and Kate's mouths before we can scream. I thrash, muffled curses spilling uselessly against their hands.

"Hey! Don't fucking touch her!" Ryder's voice cracks like a whip, low and lethal. His eyes burn, a storm barely held back.

"You think you're better than this world? Better than me Kent? I've built something here…order and purpose…while the rest of humanity rots in the streets. Every sacrifice, every choice I've made, has been for the greater good."

He turns to face me. "And you… you waltz in here, breaking what you don't understand."

His words are thick with self-righteous poison, every syllable meant to hammer us down. I barely acknowledge him. I can't hear much over the pounding in my ears. My pulse seems to scream *get out, get out, get out*. Ryder stands like a killer ready to strike, shoulders squared, jaw tight, eyes locked on the General with a heat that if looks could kill, would have burned holes straight through his arrogant smirk. "That's what you consider as honoring your duty? Poisoning the world…kidnapping…playing God while everyone else scrambles to survive? You're pathetic, hiding behind your walls." Ryder spits.

The General turns slowly, like he'd been waiting for this moment. His eyes lock on Ryder, and I feel my chest tighten.

"You… you should understand, don't you?" he says, voice low, dangerous. "You've killed to survive. You've made the hard choices, watched people die. You know what it takes to hold power… to control it. You think you're different?"

Ryder stiffens. I can see the muscles in his hands flexing, ready to strike. Tompkins just smiles, savoring it, letting the weight of his words hang between them like a blade.

"I'm building a new kingdom. And every kingdom needs a strong hand. Without control, humanity destroys itself."

Ryder tilts his head, lips curving into a sneer that is nowhere near a smile. "You mean you destroy it, and call it salvation so you can sleep at night."

Ryder must have struck a nerve because the General's eyes narrow, a flicker of irritation cracking through the mask. He steps closer, the muzzle of his gun lifting toward Ryder's chest. Ryder doesn't so much as blink.

"Go ahead," he goads, the taunt sliding between his teeth like a blade. "Prove to everyone here that you're just another coward with a trigger."

The air thickens. I can see Dad tense in my periphery, I can feel Kate's breath hitch beside me, but all I can focus on is Ryder. Unmoving, unblinking, daring the man to end it. The General chuckles low in his throat, but it doesn't reach his eyes.

"You've got a mouth on you, boy. Shame it's going to get you killed."

"Just let us go, man," Hawthorne suggests, his voice measured, trying to keep the situation from spiraling.

Tompkins's smile sharpens. "Hawthorne. Nice of you to join the party. That's General to you."

He raises a handgun, the metal catching the fluorescent glare as he levels it at Hawthorne's chest.

"Let's just calm down, no one needs to get hurt here. Just let us go," Dad adds, stepping forward playing diplomat in this nightmare.

The guards drag Hawthorne forward, shoving him between Kate and I. Now all three of us are locked in their grip. Helpless, breathing the stink of their clothes, hands still clamped over our mouths. I can feel Kate's arm twitching beside me like she's trying to calculate how many bones she could break if she just had one second free.

"You're the old man from the cult camp, aren't you?" Tompkins' voice slithers through the air, casual and mocking as he toys with the handgun in his grip.

His gaze flicks up suddenly, his eyes landing on me, and before I can react, my captors' hands leave my mouth still pinning my hands behind my back. The General uses his rough fingers to seize my cheeks, forcing my face up to meet his.

"That means you're the girl they kidnapped," he says, the corners of his mouth curling into a sick grin. "Now this is all starting to make sense."

I glare at him and spit in his face. "Fuck you"

His grin falters.

"You're going to regret that," he growls, and spits back, hot and foul against my skin.

Ryder explodes forward with a roar, lunging at Tompkins.

"Hold him!" Tompkins barks and one of his goons grabs Ryder from behind, pinning his arms. Tompkins steps forward and drives a kick into the back of Ryder's knees, forcing him down.

"Get the old man," Tompkins orders.

Another guard seizes my father, wrenching his arms back.

"Dad! No, leave him alone!" I scream.

Tompkins turns to me with the slow, deliberate cruelty of a predator savoring its prey.

"Tell me, *Violet*. Who do you think deserves to live? Ryder… or your dad?"

My heart stops. Dad meets my eyes across the space, and for a moment, the frenzy around us fades to a slow, heavy hum. His lips move, and I read them without sound; *It's okay.*

I shake my head violently, tears blurring my vision.

"No… please. Don't do this, I'll do anything, kill me instead," I choke out, my voice raw and fractured.

Ryder's jaw snaps tight, and he shouts, "Stop this shit, Tompkins! You're not going to…"

Before he can finish, one of Tompkins' men steps forward, slamming a rough hand over Ryder's mouth. His words are cut off, muffled, the desperate fury in his eyes screaming louder than any sound. Ryder struggles, but the grip is iron, and the menace in Tompkins' smirk says everything: *You're not stopping me.* Tompkins leans in slightly, his gaze sharp as broken glass.

"If you don't choose fast, I'll do it for you," he hisses, and I can feel the weight of inevitability pressing down on me. I can't choose between the man I love, or my father. My mind fractures under the weight of it, and suddenly I'm drowning. Pulled under by wave after wave of memories. Dad's laughter when I was small. His arms around me the day the world ended. The moment I found him again, alive, when I'd stopped believing it was possible. The long road to Banff. The smell of dust in the camp store. The cold grip of fear on every adventure. And now… here. *Hell.*

I force my eyes to his, searching for something, some way out, some miracle. But all I get is the faint movement of his lips. *I love you.*

The gunshot is deafening. Dad's body jerks, and then he's falling.

Everything stops. The room, the air, even my heartbeat feels frozen. A scream rips from my throat, raw and shattering, mirrored by Kate, Hawthorne, and even Ryder. One of the men holding his mouth yelps as Ryder sinks his teeth into the hand pressing against him. A punch follows, hard, sharp, fueled by pure rage. The guy crumples back, wheezing.

Ryder shouts, venom dripping from every word, "I'm going to fucking kill you!"

My chest tightens, every nerve screaming as I watch everyone fight for their lives, the raw, unhinged energy pulling me along with them. My hands shake, but I can't tear my eyes away. I want to help, to scream. Tompkins only laughs, backing toward the exit.

"Let them go. They'll die out there anyway."

He and his men finally pull back, wiping the slick, dark blood from their hands and faces with the backs of their sleeves. One of them spits, a sharp, wet arc landing inches from Hawthorne's boots. Another lets out a cruel laugh, spitting straight at Ryder, who snarls in response, eyes blazing with fury. Their laughter echoes through the cold, lit garage as they slam one heavy door shut behind them, the metal rattling with a finality. Then, with deliberate malice, they throw another door open, and the world is suddenly alive with groaning, shuffling bodies.

Deadheads.

The sound of their dragging limbs grows louder, closer, and I feel the icy brush of panic crawl up my spine. Every instinct screams at me to run, to grab Ryder, to save Dad, but the sheer weight of it, the inevitability of what's coming, presses down like a physical force. I try to steady my breathing as Ryder barks orders. I drop to my knees beside Dad. He's still breathing, barely. Tompkins shot him in the chest, buying me just a few fleeting minutes.

His voice is faint, but it finds me. "I'll… tell your mom you love her, and Felix too."

"No, no, no… stay with me," I sob, clutching Dad's body against me, my tears soaking into his shirt. His blood is warm and slick against my fingers, the metallic scent clogging my throat until I can barely breathe.

"We can't leave him here!" I plead, my voice breaking.

Ryder shouts over the bloodshed, jerking his arm toward an SUV parked crookedly in the middle. His eyes lock on mine, sharp and unyielding, before he turns to cut down another Deadhead closing in on him.

I hook my arms under Dad's shoulders, my muscles screaming with the strain. Kate appears at my side, her face pale but determined, and together we drag him across the floor toward the vehicle Ryder pointed out. My feet drag through a haze of fear and memory. Hawthorne's grunts and the sickening crunch of bone echo behind us as he holds the dead at bay. Ryder's already in the driver's seat when we reach it, slamming the key into the ignition. The engine roars to life and we heave Dad inside, collapsing over him just as Hawthorne dives in and slams the door.

"Go!" Kate snarls, her voice sharp with urgency.

I fumble in the center console, fingers brushing against scattered papers, loose change, and dust-covered trinkets.

Click.

My hand closes around a small, cold device. The garage door opener. The SUV lurches forward, tires screaming as Ryder floors it, and we tear out of that nightmare, hurtling straight into another. I clutch Dad's shoulder, feeling the weight of him slipping away as the SUV rattles down the darkened road. His breathing is ragged, shallow, each exhale a sharp stab in my chest.

"Dad… please… hang on," I whisper, voice breaking.

His hand twitches in mine.

"I've got you. Just… stay with me."

Ryder glances back, his jaw set, eyes dark with frustration and helplessness.

Kate stabs me with reality. "He's not going to make it, Vi. We have to move fast."

I shake my head, tears streaming down my face. “No. Don’t… don’t shoot him yet. I… I can’t. Not like this. Not while he’s still… here.”

Hawthorne turns to me, knife in hand. “You can stabilize him. Strap him in, get him back to the bus safely.”

With trembling hands, I use the seatbelt from the SUV, cutting it with Hawthorne’s knife to make a crude harness. I gently secure Dad in the middle seat, careful not to jostle him. Holding my sweater to help stop the bleeding. His face is pale, lips barely moving as if he’s whispering something I can’t hear. My fingers graze his cheek.

“I’m so sorry, Dad,” I choke out. “I can’t… I can’t fix this.”

Ryder grips the wheel, his knuckles white, “We’ll make it. We’ll get him there.”

Deep down, I know it’s too late. By the time we pull into the place we left the bus, something else is wrong. Smoke curls into the dusting sky, flames licking the horizon. Deadheads stagger between smolder, groaning. The bus…the one that was supposed to be our safe haven…is just charred metal now… everyone is gone.

I scream, a raw, ragged sound that tears through the night. “No! No! This… this isn't happening!”

Ryder skids the SUV to a stop, but I can’t move. I’m frozen with grief, staring at the wreckage. Dad’s hand twitches again, and I grab it, holding it to my chest.

“I can’t… I can’t let you go like this,” I whisper, sobbing. “Not yet. Please… just let me hold you.”

I cling to him, rocking slightly, whispering fragments of love and apology until the tears blur everything into darkness.

Ryder clears his throat softly. “Darlin… we have to move. We can’t stay here.”

“I know,” I squeak through ragged breaths, pressing Dad closer. “But… not yet… not until… I’ve said goodbye.”

CHAPTER 33

RYDER

"Sinclair! Wilson!" My voice is hoarse, raw from screaming and from the weight of everything we'd just survived. The world outside is turbulent incarnate. Dybbuks are sprawled across the street, twitching and snapping at the air. The bus looks like it has been blown up. Smoke curls into the sky, black and heavy, mixing with the stench of burnt rubber and blood. A few soldiers from that fucked-up base we'd just left lay scattered on the ground, some still twitching. I'm glad Wilson could get a few of 'em. Tompkins had done this. That motherfucker was going to die. I could feel my hands shaking, not with fear, but with pure rage.

I yank the walkie-talkies and guns from the few bodies that still have them, slinging them over my shoulder. My hands are shaking, adrenaline is still burning, and the stink of blood and smoke is thick in my nostrils. I jog back to the SUV, scanning the street as I climb in.

"We have to find cover," I bark, slamming the door. "This is going to draw more Dybbuks, and I don't want to get stuck out here with the lot of them circling like sharks."

I start the engine, the growl of the motor echoing off the ruined buildings.

"Where to?" Hawthorne asks. My hands tighten on the wheel.

"House. Nearest one that looks intact," I stutter, eyes on the wreckage around us. "We'll hole up for the night, regroup. Get our heads clear."

The SUV rattles down the shattered street, tires crunching over debris. Buildings half-collapsed. We weave around dead bodies and burnt-out cars. I steal glances at Violet in the backseat, curled up against her dad, eyes wide and still catching the shadows that dance in her eyelashes. My chest tightens. She'd seen so much today. I couldn't let another second of this world hurt her.

"Found one!" Kate's voice snaps me out of my thoughts.

A small two-story house, mostly intact, with the door hanging on one hinge.

"Looks like we can get in. Quick!"

I slam the SUV into a stop, swinging the door open.

"Move! Quiet and fast!" I bark, gesturing for everyone to follow.

We hustle toward the house, the crunch of debris under our boots loud in the eerie silence. A low, wet gurgle from the back of the SUV. My stomach sinks. I spin around. It's Arthur.

He is slumped forward, tied in with the seatbelt, but his eyes… his eyes are gone. In their place, a milky, hungry void. His lips curl back, revealing teeth I hadn't wanted to see again. The familiar groan of death still living escapes him, a hollow, rasping sound that claws straight down my spine.

Violet freezes, her hands clutching her jacket like a shield.

"No," she whispers, voice trembling. "He… he's…. Leave him like that. Please."

I want to argue, want to tell her the truth in no uncertain terms, but I catch her gaze. She's in shock and denial refusing to see what is happening. I don't have it in me to force it. Not now.

"Okay," I speak, kneeling slightly to meet her eyes. "We leave him… like that. But we stay alert. Got it?"

She nods quickly, not taking her eyes off her father. I can feel her shaking, I can feel the pain in every tense line of her body.

"Everyone, inside. Move!" I shout, breaking the spell. Hawthorne, Kate, and Violet obey, moving fast into the house. I cast one last glance at Arthur. My new friend, her father, now something else entirely.

Four walls, a roof that wasn't caving in, and a door that at least still had hinges. That was more than most places had these days.

"I'm staying down here," Violet says immediately, her voice soft but firm, arms wrapped tight around herself as she stares out the front window.

The SUV sits in the driveway, the outline of her restrained father still visible. My chest crumbles just seeing her look at him like that. Kate's boots thud against the floor as she gives the upstairs a quick once-over.

"Two bedrooms. Both are clear. I'll take one. Hawthorne, you get the other. Don't snore too loud or I'll kick you." Kate huffs.

Hawthorne lets out a low chuckle, already fishing the extra walkie from my pack. "I'll keep the comms. If anything pings, I'll hear it first. Don't worry. I've been told my snoring sounds like a chainsaw, but at least it scares the dead off."

Kate rolls her eyes. "Yeah, well, I want some damn sleep tonight. Don't wake me up unless you want to join them."

"Copy that," he says, raising two fingers in mock salute.

I shake my head, "Feels like I'm running a bad summer camp. The only difference is half the campers are dead already."

"Camp Apocalypse," Kate snorts. "All the s'mores you can choke down, provided you can kill the squirrels first."

"Don't tempt me," Hawthorne says. "I miss roasted marshmallows more than I miss my ex."

"Exhumer humor," I mutter under my breath, earning a short laugh from Kate before she disappears upstairs.

I do a sweep of the first floor, making sure none of the doors creak open to reveal surprises. I shut doors, shove chairs under handles, stack whatever I can find against them. Nothing fancy, just enough to make noise if something tried pushing through. I leave the front door alone until I am ready for sleep. When I return, Violet is on the couch which she's pulled to the window. Her hands are pressed to the glass like she can reach him through it somehow. My ribs feel too tight for my heart.

"You don't have to stay there all night," I say quietly.

She shakes her head without looking at me. "I need to. Just… let me."

I want to argue, to tell her she needs rest more than staring at a ghost tied in a seat belt but the words stick in my throat. So, I just stand beside her, close enough that my arm brushes hers, and stay there with her in the dim glow of the dying day. I crouch next to her on the couch.

"We're safe for now," I murmur, brushing a strand of hair from her face. "Tonight, we rest. Tomorrow… we plan."

She leans against me, letting out a shaky breath. I kiss her temple, letting the weight of the day melt for just a second. Outside, the apocalypse waited, but inside, we carved out a tiny pocket of calm and I wasn't letting anyone touch it. I slowly join her on the couch, fitting almost perfectly behind her. Violet takes a slow, shaky breath and after a while leans back against me on the couch. I drape a blanket over her shoulders, then rest my chin on the top of her head, savoring the small, fleeting sense of safety. She falls asleep in my arms, and my grip tightens, a fragile ache threaded with relief. I slip my hand into my pocket and pull out the map of Tompkins' Mountain compound. It is detailed, meticulous, every hidden base marked, every entry point noted. Next to it, the typed letter I'd found. The only proof and confession of their plan, the blueprint of all the horror they'd unleashed. I trace the lines with my finger, my mind already racing.

I kiss Violet's head softly, careful not to wake her, and then nudge her to curl deeper into the blanket. My hands linger over her shoulders before I sneak out of the room. Outside, I sit against the house, joint in hand, the night air tasting like ash and pine. I light it, inhaling, letting the smoke calm the fire in my chest for a moment. I study the map again, eyes scanning every detail, every weak point.

"I'll kill you Tompkins" I whisper to myself.

The walkie buzzes suddenly. Some Dybbuks that have gathered nearby, alerted by our earlier movements, raise their heads. I crush the joint between my fingers, letting the ember die. I don't want them near the house. I grab my knife, slipping into the shadows. The first one lunges from behind a broken fence.

I spin, catching it with my elbow and slam it into the dirt, driving the knife through its skull as it twitches. Another rushes at me. I use the momentum, slamming it against a wall before finishing it with a clean, sharp stab. When the last one drops, silence settles over the street. Broken only by my ragged breathing. My chest heaves, arms slick with gore. I feel… lighter. I look around at the mess of broken bodies, the blood soaking into cracked pavement, and a low manic laugh tears from my throat. I think I've found a new way to let off steam. If I'd done this in Afghanistan, I would've been court-martialed. A mess. Here, they are already dead. If anything, I am just speeding them along, letting their rotting souls finally reach the stars, giving them a fucked-up kind of mercy.

"Hey, buddy, you alright?"

The voice cuts through the night and instinct takes over. I spin and press the edge of my knife against Hawthorne's throat.

"I told you not to call me that," I growl, my voice sharp and dangerous.

His hands lift, palms out.

"Fuck, man. Easy. I heard the walkie go off in the house and noticed you weren't inside. Just wanted to see if you were okay."

His voice cracked. "I can't sleep either… not with Tompkins killing Sinclair, Emily, Theo, Wilson, Arthur, little Dion…everyone…everyone's fucking dead."

His words falter. Then he breaks, shoulders shaking, tears slipping down his dirt-streaked face. My eyes widen. *Damn it.* I don't have the energy for this. His grief, his breakdown. I don't have room for anyone's feelings but my own and Violets. Still… I wasn't heartless. A sliver of sympathy cuts through the cold steel inside me.

I lower the knife, rest a hand on Hawthorne's shoulder, and let out a long, tired sigh. Sinclair had been my friend. A good man, with a family waiting for him back in India. A man who'd deserved better than this rotten world. Wilson, always ready, always steady. Theo and his dumb jokes that actually made me laugh when I didn't think I could with Emily always keeping us grounded. Even Dion, young as he was, had carried his weight without complaint. They were all ghosts now.

"I have a plan," I say at last, my voice low but steady, like gravel grinding in my throat. "Tompkins will pay in blood for what he did to our friends."

CHAPTER 34
VIOLET

My Father's face is twisted into something inhuman, eyes glazed, mouth slack, the sounds he makes ring in my ears. My hands shook uncontrollably when I raised the gun, but I pulled the trigger anyway. The sound still rang in my ears as I dug his grave, louder than any thunder, sharper than any scream.

The dirt dug under my nails and my arms burned as I dragged his body into the hollow in the earth I carved out with broken sticks and raw hands. Kate had been there, I didn't see her but I knew she was making sure I was alright, her jaw set as if holding back words that would have broken me if she spoke them. She stayed making sure no Deadheads came at me until the last clump of dirt hit his chest, until the ground was smoothed enough to pretend it was just another scar in the world. Ryder had tried to stay with me to help. Of course, he had. He offered to take some of the weight, to spare me from the blood on my hands and the ache in my bones but I couldn't let him. I was adamant that this was mine to carry.

My father.

My burden.

My goodbye.

If I let anyone else touch that moment, it wouldn't feel real. It wouldn't feel final.

Later, Kate left with Hawthorne to hunt for weapons. Guns, knives, anything sharp enough or heavy enough to give us a fighting chance against Tompkins and his men. I stayed behind, numb, staring at the patch of earth that now owned my father. Every time I close my eyes, I see it all over again.

The shot.

The fall.

The grave.

My father's death doesn't just haunt me, it lives inside me. Groggy, I drag my hands down my face, my skin sticky with sleep. When I finally force myself upright, the first thing I see through the window is the SUV parked outside. My chest cracks open, grief bleeding fresh all over again. For a moment I just sit there, staring, the ache pressing down so hard it feels like it might crush me. When clarity finds me in the fog, I realize there are motorcycles now parked behind the SUV. I shove the blanket off and stand. One foot in front of the other. That's how I'll survive. Ryder had been patient…so beautifully patient…and I needed to find him and thank him. The amount of grief I've carried this month alone could've killed a person. Hell, it did almost kill me. He is the only reason I'm still breathing. My life-line in all this death.

I follow the faint sound of voices into the kitchen. Kate is prying open cans, her brow furrowed in concentration, probably putting together something that would pass as breakfast. Ryder and Hawthorne lean over the table, studying a paper spread between them. It looks like a small map, its edges frayed and smudged with dirt., I step up behind Ryder, sliding my arms around his waist and letting myself slump against him. The solid weight of him is grounding together. He pivots immediately, and when his eyes land on me, they light up.

"Good morning, gorgeous," he says, his voice low and warm, before leaning in to kiss me. I melted into it.

"Okay, guys, I'm trying to eat here," Kate cuts in, rolling her eyes.

I pull back with a little laugh. "Hey, that wasn't even bad. It was just a kiss."

"Yeah, well," she shoots back, smirking as she cracks another can open, "I know what happens if you two kiss for too long."

She winks at me, reminding me of the stories I'd shared with her about the camp store, the waterfall. Heat creeps up my neck, but I can't help but laugh. Ryder just looks confused and unbearably cute. I steal the can from Kate's hand and grab a spoon to scoop up a bite.

"What else did yah find?" I ask through a mouthful of delicious canned spaghetti and meatballs.

Kate raises a can like a toast, "Good ol' Alphagetti. We've also got a couple cans of chunky soup, some water bottles, and a stash of chocolate bars."

Honestly, not the worst haul we'd scavenged. I joined Kate at the table, chewing steadily. Anything was better than another night choking down seafood. Ryder and Hawthorne sit hunched over the table now, both of them looking like they hadn't slept in days. Their faces are carved out of exhaustion, eyes ringed with shadows. That's when I notice the streak of dried blood matted in Ryder's hair. How the hell had I missed that? My stomach lurches, partly with worry and partly with the messed-up truth that he looks even hotter like that.

Hawthorne drags a map across the table, his voice low but steady. "Kent and I came up with a plan."

I lean in, my spoonful of SpaghettiOs hovering midair as he continues.

"I stole this before we left. Full layout of the compound." Ryder jabs a finger at the paper. "Here's the garage we slipped out of. Those two doors? The right one leads to the corpse dungeon-city, then another hallway takes you to the cafeteria. Down this stretch here, that's the line of rooms I stayed in. Then here…" his finger slides lower, "...pig farm. Canned storage. Electrical. Tompkins' surveillance office. An armory. Two more rooms, unmarked. I'm guessing storage, or maybe the one they first tossed me in."

I stuff the spoon in my mouth, chewing deliberately, watching his lips move as he maps out death and escape like it is second nature.

God, he's so hot when he's assertive.

"Here's where it gets tricky." His voice drops even lower, as if the words themselves are classified. "There's a rooftop helicopter pad and a full second floor I never saw but there's also a back tunnel. Construction access, I think. Big enough to fit a semi. That's how we're getting in."

Kate nearly chokes on her chocolate bar. "Getting in! Getting in? We are not going back there. Are you out of your fucking mind?"

Ryder's head snaps toward her, his eyes flashing that dangerous siren red. "We're definitely going back because Tompkins needs to die."

Kate gawks at him. "Okay, well, we can't kill him if we're dead."

"Yeah, I fucking know that," Ryder snaps again, leaning forward, "Hence the plan."

Kate huffs, muttering something under her breath, and goes back to gnawing her chocolate bar like it is all that stands between her and a meltdown. Even as the anxiety of going back creeps into my veins I know Ryder is right. Tompkins did *need* to die. He'd taken everything from me. My dad, my best friend, my daughter, my little brother, my mom. Everyone I loved. Even the parts of me that still believed in safety, in family. He'd slaughtered all of it. My breaths come too fast, my chest aching.

"Vi?" Kate's voice cuts through, softer than before. "You're breathing pretty heavily."

I blink, shaking myself back into the room. "Oh…yeah. I'm fine. So… what's the plan, babe?"

His eyebrow arches at the word babe, but then his face slides back into that deliciously serious smirk.

"Last night, Hawthorne and I found four motorcycles at some of the nearby houses. I'm ninety-nine percent sure I can hotwire them. Then here's the kicker; you all remember the dead that were in downtown Kelowna? We ride down there at night, rev the engines loud as hell, lead the horde right to the back tunnel entrance. We sneak inside, lock the doors behind us, leave the horde waiting and starving."

He points at Kate and Hawthorne. "You two, go in through the garage, Violet and I will let you in, and you make sure every single door inside that place is open. Including their little undead collection. That way, once the horde gets inside, everyone in that compound dies. *Every. Last. One.*"

Then he glances sideways at me, dragging out each syllable, savoring it. "Me and babe…" he winks, "…we find Tompkins and we don't just kill him; we make him bleed, make him suffer. Then we leave him there with the monsters he created."

He leans back, crossing his arms, his mind already made up.

"When it's done, I'll radio Hawthorne. He opens the horde doors, and we bail out by helicopter. Hawthorne flies it, because he can."

He raises his hand next to his mouth and whispers, "He was a part of the Snowbirds before deployment."

I blink at him, spoon dangling in my hand. Spaghetti Os suddenly taste like gasoline and blood. This is insane. Before I can argue, Ryder leans over, plucks the can straight from my hands, and scoops a bite like it belongs to him.

"Mmm," he says through a mouthful, his voice muffled and smug. "Fuel for war."

I just stare, caught between wanting to laugh and wanting to smack him. Only Ryder could map out the apocalypse, vow to kill a warlord, and then steal my breakfast like it was part of the plan.

"Where do we go after it all?" I ask, my voice quieter than I intend, but heavy.

Ryder leans back in his chair, studying the map like it holds all the answers.

"We can try Vancouver Island, or somewhere that looks safe from the sky. Depends on how much gas we've got in the tank."

"I say we go to Hawaii. I've always wanted to. Who's with me?" Hawthorne chimes in, hand shooting up like we're voting for field trips.

We all just stare at him.

Kate blinks once. "Can you not be stupid for five minutes?"

The laugh breaks out of me before I can stop it, even if the sound is frayed at the edges.

I push the moment aside, spine straightening. "We leave at sundown. What do we have for weapons?"

Ryder's voice drops into that dangerous calm of his, "Two rifles we grabbed off the dead military guys, my knife, Kate's got her bat, Hawthorne's knife, your knife… and I think I dropped my pistol back at the jewelry shop when they took me. So, I could go and grab that."

"Jewelry shop?" I tilt my head.

"Oh, what were you shopping for *necklaces*?" Hawthorne toys in, his grin too wide. "If so, you totally deserved to be kidnapped."

Ryder's hand shoots to the back of his neck, fingers dragging through his hair trying to hide the sudden sweat that appeared there. His eyes dart everywhere but mine.

"Uh…yeah, I saw a chain I… liked," he stuttered, before kicking Hawthorne under the table hard enough to make him grunt.

Ryder clears his throat, tone sharpening again. "Anyway. Let's see what we can scavenge in the next few hours and then go over the plan one more time."

I raise an eyebrow but let it slide, leaning back. "Also, you'd better find me a helmet, or I'm not going anywhere near a motorcycle."

Ryder half smiles, like he'd been waiting for that exact line. He gets up, disappears for a moment, and comes back, swinging four helmets into view. He drops them onto the table with a satisfying thud, eyes locked on me.

"I knew you were going to say that, darlin'."

CHAPTER 35
RYDER

I go back to the jewelry store first to grab my pistol. During the bunker fiasco, I made sure to grab my jacket and when I checked for her ring it was still there, *thank fuck*. Before I go, I scan the cases for a ring of my own. I want her to know I'm hers, just as much as she is mine. I find a silver masculine ring, with a sparkling blue strip down the middle, so we can match. Like my dog tag I'll be buried with it.

Until death do us part.

If the world wants to take everything from me, then I'll take two things for myself, my vow, and my girl. I smirk at the thought, put the new ring in my pocket beside hers and keep searching the streets. The cannabis store is only a block over, and I figure if the end of the world means anything, it's that I get to stock up on what keeps my head from splitting. I grab more weed, a stack of papers, fresh lighters. The backpack I found earlier was filling up quickly, and I liked the weight of it slung over my shoulders. It gives me purpose where I feel powerless to help Violet.

On the way back, I put down maybe ten Dybbuks. Quick kills. A blade through the eye, a round through the skull. Work that's becoming too easy. I'll admit that the guilt does settle in afterward. Not because I give a damn about them, but because every corpse I drop means fewer left to throw at Tompkins. Fewer bodies to watch tear him limb from limb. That was the plan, and every shambling bastard I cut down felt like I was robbing myself of satisfaction.

"Sorry, boys," I state, wiping blood from my knife onto my jeans. "Guess you'll have to miss the party."

I could already see it in my head. Tompkins screaming, ripped apart piece by piece, begging for mercy he'd never get. That was the only music I wanted to hear. I arrive at the military bus and stand in front of the charred wreck, smoke still clinging to the twisted frame like spirits that refuse to leave. I tell myself I came here to scavenge, maybe find something for lunch, something for Violet. She'd be hungry. Perhaps I've just come here to let go, or gather up more rage and fury for the task ahead.

The bodies are blackened, twisted into grotesque shapes that barely resemble the people we'd known. Everyone we'd organized, everyone we'd kept alive this long, reduced to brittle charcoal. Tompkins had done this. *Merciless son of a bitch.* I should've known he was trailing us. Should've been faster, sharper, should've hidden them all better. They didn't deserve to suffer like that. One body still twitched. Skin cracked and split; the face unrecognizable. I put a knife through its skull. My hand stays on the hilt longer than it should have and my head bows over what was left. Grief claws at me, but grief is useless. It doesn't feed Violet. It doesn't put bullets in my gun and it sure as hell isn't going to kill Tompkins.

I lift my head, jaw clenched. The gas station hadn't blown in Tompkins' assault. Finally, some goddamn luck. I told everyone to strip it clean. Dumb move in retrospect now that we need supplies again, but it turns out they'd missed a few things behind the counter. Tucked away on a low shelf, I find some jerky. My lips almost twitch into a smile and right beside it, three packets of Mr. Noodles. Spicy chicken, which is my favorite. A pathetic prize, but in this world, it was a treasure. I shove them into a pack like a thief guarding gold.

My eyes catch the busted chair behind the counter. The leather is cracked, stuffing spilling from the seams. Most would've left it, but not me. Not when I could make it useful. I drag it out, rip the leather free, and set to work with my knife and steady hands. I cut long, clean strips, weaving them tight, threading them together with string from the chair, until they form a crude but strong holster. Something I can sling across my chest, something quick to draw from if the dead or the living come too close for comfort.

It's not my first time doing this. Back in the desert, when command cut me off and left me to rot, I'd used the same ingenuity just to survive. I remembered the heat, the taste of sand in my mouth, the weight of my rifle and the rage that kept me alive. This is no different. By the time the sun began to dip, the air cooling around the ruins of what was, I had what I came for.

Food.

Fire in my chest.

A new weapon slung against me.

Our rings.

I leave the bus and the ashes behind, heading back to the house where Violet is waiting. The first thing I see is the lump of dirt accompanied by a crooked stick-cross jammed into the earth, the word Dad scratched across it in shaky letters. It's small. Too small to hold the life of the man who fills it. My chest tightens, a sharp pain tearing through me like shrapnel. It hurts in a way even bullets never manage to. It's her pain, and I'd take it all if I could. Rip it right out of her chest and stitch it into mine.

Violet sits there, knees pulled in, shoulders heavy like the world decided she's strong enough to carry it. She isn't crying. Not yet. She just stares at the dirt like if she looks long enough, maybe it'll change the final outcome. She's wearing her dad's jean jacket. It hangs off her in a way that makes her look smaller, like she's drowning in his absence while trying to keep what little of him she has left wrapped around her. The sleeves are frayed, collar stained from years of wear, but she holds it close, gripping at the fabric, the only thing anchoring her. A ripple of grief shatters my chest. That jacket is more than cloth, it's the last ghost of him she can touch. She's wrapped herself in memory and loss. I drop down beside her, close enough that our arms touch. I slide my hand behind her back, pulling her against me. She doesn't fight it but she doesn't look at me either. Just accepts it, like she's forgotten how not to. That's all I need. Without a word, I reach into my pack and pull out a strip of jerky, pressing it into her hand. She takes it and chews slowly, eyes still locked on the grave. No taste, no hunger, just going through the motions, just to keep her body from collapsing completely. I lean down, lips close to her ear, my voice low and steady.

"I'm proud of you, Ocean Eyes. He's at rest now. No more running and no more suffering." Her lips tremble, but she doesn't answer. So, I add the part that burns in my gut like fire.

"And Tompkins… Tompkins will pay. I'll make sure he fucking pays for what he did…to him, and to you."

That's when her chest breaks. The sound that comes out of her isn't words, just raw sobbing, tearing from somewhere too deep for me to reach. I wrap my arms around her tighter, pressing her head against my chest. My lips brush her hair, and I kiss the top of her head. I rock her, slow and steady, trying to keep my sweet precious woman from breaking apart. Her tears soak through my shirt, but I don't care. She needs me and a part of me likes that. When the world strips her of everything and she turns to me, I feel alive with purpose. I lift my eyes just long enough to see Kate and Hawthorne returning, packs slung over their shoulders. Hawthorne notices us first. We make eye contact, exchange a nod and a quick flick of hand signals. They read the situation without a word, slipping back into the house, leaving us in silence. Right now, she's mine, and I'm not sharing.

I don't rush her. God knows she deserved every second out here. So, I just sit close enough that she can feel me without me encroaching on her space. I made sure she feels safe. That is my only job. Every time a Dybbuk lurches around the corner, I give a sharp whistle, and like clockwork, Hawthorne or Kate handle it. Clean, fast, no fuss. Then they slip back inside, leaving us in our little bubble of grief and silence.

After some time slowly turns to me, eyes red but steady.

Her voice cracks "Thank you, Ryder… for everything."

I shake my head, about to tell her she doesn't owe me a damn thing, but she doesn't stop. Her hand rises up, trembling, and she presses against the center of my chest.

"I love you. I've always loved you."

Those words nearly undo me. I lean in before I lose the chance, before the world can snatch it away, and kiss her. Soft at first, like I might break her, then harder, because I need her to feel how much she belongs to me. When I finally pull back, I keep my forehead pressed against hers, her breath mixing with mine.

My voice comes out rough, but there is no hesitation.

"I love you, too Violet," I whisper, voice almost breaking. "It's always been you and I thank the universe for bending everything just to make sure we found each other."

Her lips quiver, and I kiss the corner of her mouth just to catch the tremors, to claim them. My chest aches with the truth of it, like my heart is clawing its way out just to prove it to her.

My breath is uneven, but my voice is certain when I whisper against her skin, "Let's go inside, Ocean Eyes. We've got a busy, revengeful night ahead of us."

Her hand tightens on mine.

She loves me. I fucking knew it.

I haven't ridden a motorcycle since I was eighteen. I'm definitely more of a truck guy but I would be lying if I said I didn't feel free with the wind whipping past, the engine roaring under me, and the way Violet leans I get a full view of her ass. *Win.*

I reach into my pocket, feeling the cool edge of the silver band I picked out for her and the blue striped one for me. My plan hasn't changed, once we land the helicopter, I'm going to propose. Officially start our new life together. It's funny… this trip, this insane apocalypse chaos, it's turned into a metaphor for us. Through all the fire, all the dying, all the fucked-up bullshit, our love has been there. It'll always be there.

We tear down the bridge into downtown Kelowna, the moon hitting the lake just right, the smell of the water and the trees filling my lungs. If it weren't for the distant groans of Dybbuks echoing off the buildings, I'd swear we were on vacation. I even let myself smile. We line up, engines growling like hungry beasts. I count down on my fingers, "Three… two… one…"

Burnouts, tires screeching, engines screaming, it's mayhem on wheels. Honestly, it sounds like a frat party where everyone's trying to prove whose dick is bigger. I glance at Hawthorne, who's grinning like an idiot, one hand waving in the air while the other barely keeps his bike steady.

"Hey! Ease up on that burnout, you lunatic!" I yell, squinting through the smoke like I'm about to see a tire fly into orbit.

"Chill, Kent! I'm basically a motorcycle God!" Hawthorne shouts, wobbling like a newborn giraffe almost kissing the asphalt

"Put your helmet back on, you ass!" I bellow, gripping the handlebars so hard my knuckles are about to pop. Violet snorts behind me, and Kate's practically crying from laughing.

"Is this how your army runs?" Violet teases. "A bunch of idiots making tire smoke before battle?"

"Our undead reinforcements are very picky about entertainment."

She giggles and then our first guest arrives. We are the predators now, slow and deliberate, inching forward as if we'd tossed a lure into a pond, waiting for the fish to bite, and bite they did. At first, it is soft groans and scraping feet against concrete, maybe twenty of them shuffling along like drunken men. By the time we reach the far end of the bridge, they have multiplied into hundreds, a limping, moaning tidal wave.

We can't push too fast. Too quick and we'd scatter the growing horde, losing the advantage. Too close and it'd be suicide. One bite, and I'd be one of them. One bite, and I'd never see Violet again. I grit my teeth, my grip tight on the handlebars.

Not today.

Not ever.

I am never leaving her.

Not until we level the playing field, until the world has felt our fire and all the wrath that comes with it. I steal a glance at her, riding beside me, and I swear under my breath. She's the reason I breathe, the reason I kill, and if this horde thought it could get between us, it was about to learn a prime lesson; *you don't fuck with us.* Right before we hit the road to the compound, Hawthorne and Kate peel off to the left, heading toward the garage. Their engines fade into the dark, leaving only me and Violet riding side by side. I'll radio Hawthorne when it's clear. For now, it's just us.

We swing toward the construction access route. Another win for us as the place looks abandoned. I push the throttle, the tunnel swallowing us whole, our headlights cutting through the dust and stale air. The horde isn't far behind, their groans bouncing down the concrete walls, a fucked-up chorus. They're slower now, bottlenecked by the tunnel's walls, but they're still coming.

The steel doors wait at the end. We skid to a stop, rope off the helmets, and I tug at the handle. Locked, because of course it wouldn't be that easy. I glance around, body tight with anxiety.

"Fuck." I say kicking the door." How do we get in?"

Violet tilts her head, scanning the frame. "Probably a secondary latch… here."

She's so smart. We find it, pry it open, and slip inside. One problem down. A million more to go. I follow the map I've memorized, every turn burned into my skull. First stop, the surveillance room. Everyone should be asleep now, but on the off chance someone isn't, I didn't want them seeing us or the horde coming. The hallways are dark, lit only by strips of emergency lights hugging the floor. Each step echoes, my boots too loud, my pulse louder. Finally, we reach the surveillance room. I peek in. Someone's at the desk. If that's Tompkins, our plan's about to die screaming.

I motion for Violet to stay back, hand slicing through the air. Then I ease the door open.

The man swivels in the chair, blinking. "Huh?"

Not Tompkins.

Violet slips inside and shuts the door as the guy fumbles for his radio.

"Nope," I snap, kicking it out of his hands before he can call anyone. He scrambles, going for a gun. My fists aren't Jackie Chan's, but my knife works just fine. I drive the blade into his hand, pinning it to the desk. He screams and I clamp my palm over his mouth as he thrashes, teeth snapping at my fingers.

"Wrong move." I shove the knife into his chest. His body jerks once, then slumps. I let him slide to the floor. He'll come back soon enough to chew on his boss. My eyes flick to Violet. Her mouth is parted, her eyes wide. Shock, yes, but beneath that the protective side of me gives her a thrill.

I wink at her. "One down."

She rolls her eyes and I strip the gun from his holster, pressing it into her hand and she doesn't shy away.

That's my fucking girl.

I turn to the monitors, yank cords, and shut the whole grid down. One by one, the screens die. Darkness replaces the compound's all-seeing eyes.

"They were tracking us?" She holds up the USB stick labeled 'military bus.' It glints under the emergency lights, ugly as a tumor.

"Yeah, the other two cult bastards at the camp talked about it before I gutted them. I'm guessing they planted it. I was a little busy saving the love of my life to notice."

Her lips curve. "You do save me often."

I laugh, plucking the stick from her hand. "Darlin', I'll come for you any day."

I drop it to the ground and crush it under my boot. The plastic snaps like a brittle bone.

She tilts her head, voice low, teasing. "Then let's finish this mission so you can come for me."

I nearly laugh, the tension sharp between us. Instead, I shift my gaze briefly toward her. "Deal."

We leave the room stepping over the soon to be Dybbuk. The next phase of the plan happens in the garage. Voices drift from up ahead and I yank Violet into the nearest doorway. The smell makes me dry heave. Rot, shit, pig feed. Bile rises in my throat.

"A pig farm?" Violet whispers, pinching her nose.

"They're feeding their corpse army with pork scraps."

Disgust crawls over my skin. We hold still as the guard's pass. Their boots fade, and we step out, only to nearly collide with another sentry. His eyes go wide, mouth opening. I grab him by the collar, drag him backward into the farm. My knife flashes once, straight to the throat. I pin him down, watching the light drain from his eyes as blood slicks my hands. The pigs snort and shuffle, restless. I throw him into the pen and let the swine deal with the body. I grab Violet's hand, and keep moving.

At the garage, I raise the radio. "Condor to Slug. Repeat, Condor to Slug."

Static crackles before Hawthorne snaps back, annoyed. "When the fuck did I agree to Slug? I thought I was Hawk."

I grin. "Slug suits you better."

Violet laughs beside me, and the sound makes my chest ache in the best way.

"I'm opening the doors," I say.

"You're an ass but copy that," Hawthorne mutters.

I slam the button. The mountain doors groan open, and two shadows slip inside. Kate pumps her fist in triumph.

"We open every door?" she asks.

"Yeah. But listen," I say, lowering my voice. "Me and Violet are going for Tompkins. If anyone tries to yell or stop you, kill them. I've already put two down. Stay sharp. I'll radio you when we get Tompkins."

Violet grips her new gun like she was born to hold it. They slip through the left door, weapons raised and ready. Violet and I take the right. My pulse quickens. Every door here could hide him. Tompkins had to be in one of these rooms. Our bodies shift in quiet unison, a rhythm of survival and anticipation. I grip the handle of the first door and ease it open. Not Tompkins, just that same scrawny guy from before, sprawled out on the cot, snoring so light it sounds like a wheeze. I keep the door open and motion to Violet to move on.

The second door is occupied by someone who looks like he can bench-press the entire damn bunk. Built like The Rock, arms like tree trunks, head tipped back as he sleeps with his mouth open, rattling the walls with every snore. Definitely not Tompkins. Wrong kind of arrogance. I keep that door open too.

The third room? Bunk-bed setup, four beds all filled. The men are out cold, boots still on, the air thick with sweat and stale breath. A couple shift in their sleep, one stammers nonsense, another drools down his pillow. None of them have that smug bastard's stink. Every door, every room was the same damn thing. Packed with grunts or completely empty. I am starting to feel like I am flipping through a shitty IKEA catalog, one fake room after another.

"This is where you stayed?" Violet asks, her nose wrinkling as she peers inside the room. "Looks like a five-star hotel compared to outside."

I snort. "Yeah, real nice,"

I drag my hand along the edge of a forgotten food tray.

"They even have hot water."

"Lucky duck," she teases.

"Not that lucky. You weren't here."

Her giggle cracks through the tension like sunlight splitting clouds. She leans in and kisses me, soft and quick, but enough to knock me off balance inside.

"You're such a teddy bear with me."

I twirl a lock of her hair around my finger, unable to stop staring at her face even in this hellhole.

"You bring out the best in me," I admit.

She gives a faint smile, glancing at my jeans. "Okay, let's go. Don't want to be fighting Tompkins with an erection, now do ya?"

I look down.

For fuck's sake.

She isn't wrong. I steal my eyes away from her before I embarrass myself further. I storm out of the room with Violet giggling behind me, rolling my eyes and throwing up a hand signal for her to follow. We climb the stairwell and just as we round the landing, a soldier descends from above. A broad frame, with a rifle slung loose. I press myself and Violet against the wall, waiting until his boots nearly hit the bottom, and then spring. My arm wraps tight around his chest, palm clamped hard over his mouth. He thrashes, muffled shouts breaking against my grip.

That's when Violet strikes. She buries her blade in his side repeatedly. The wet squelch of steel punching through flesh fills the stairwell. I lose count, but she doesn't stop, she just keeps stabbing, her face twisted with fury, her whole body moving like every strike is years of rage unleashed.

"I think he's dead, Darlin."

She stops, panting and wiping her forehead with the back of her wrist.

"That's for holding your hand over my mouth, asshole."

She spits on him, her chest rising and falling in hard, furious breaths which is pretty fucking hot.

No, Ryder. Focus. No boner when killing Tompkins.

We leave the body behind, pushing further up the stairwell. I haven't been up here yet, and anything could be waiting. The hall stretches out before us when we reach the top landing lined with four doors. Three on the left, one on the right. The paint is peeling, the concrete walls sweating with the damp, but at the far end a glowing red EXIT sign hums like a beacon. That is where the helicopter is, our way out.

My eyes sweep the hallway, then land on the single door set apart from the others. One big, solitary room. Typical Tompkins. The man can't take a shit without needing it to look like a throne room. Arrogant bastard probably needs a space to match the size of his ego.

I lean close to Violet, my lips brushing her ear, "That's his room. Stay sharp."

Her eyes narrow with focus. I step up to the door, and press the handle.

Locked.

My jaw flexes. The paranoid fuck never leaves anything unsecured. I take a slow breath, glancing at Violet, and then knock three times on the steel.

Lowering my voice, I force out the words "General Tompkins. There's been a breach."

For a beat, there's only silence then a muffled curse shatters it, the voice I'd been straining to catch.

Tompkins.

CHAPTER 36

VIOLET

"I said don't fucking bother me…" Tompkins drawls, his voice thick with irritation as he turns around and is surprised to find Ryder.

He's standing there in a silk zebra-print robe like some sleazy mob boss. His balls hang so low I swear they're nearly dragging across the floor. The sight almost makes me gag. Even Ryder looks stunned for a second but only a second. Then his fist connects with Tompkins's face in a beautiful, bone-crunching punch.

Keep hurting him. Make him fucking bleed for killing my dad.

"Get off of me, you ape!" Tompkins screeches, flailing as he returns Ryder's assault.

I drive my blade straight through his hand, pinning it down.

"Don't fucking touch my man." I snarl.

Ryder only arches an eyebrow, his mouth twitching in that smug almost-smile, before he mirrors me. Stabbing Major Micro Dick on the other hand, pinning it to the floor. The bastard howls, and I feel something darkly satisfying curl inside my chest. My eyes dart around the room, scanning for something heavier, sharper, crueler. My gaze lands on a side table lamp. I rip it off the stand.

"Night night," Ryder says casually, stepping back just as I swing.

The lamp smashes against Tompkins's skull. His eyes roll back and his body goes slack, out cold, but alive.

"Great idea, Ocean Eyes," Ryder says as he yanks the knives free from Tompkins's impaled hands.

My heart flutters every single time he calls me that.

"Thanks, it's what I used for my first Deadhead kill."

"Who knew lamps were such deadly weapons," he hides a laugh, winking at me making murder and mayhem feel like foreplay. "Now let's get this gross-ass cockroach to the place they held me."

He pulls his radio off his belt and calls it in, voice clipped.

"Slug. Upstairs. We've got him."

It takes about ten minutes, but finally Hawthorne and Kate come in, both red-faced and puffing like they just ran a marathon.

"This is why you're a slug. It took you like three to five business days," Ryder snaps.

"Well, I didn't know fucking Bane was sleeping downstairs," Hawthorne shoots back.

Ryder rolls his eyes.

"Yeah, and he decided he needed to pee right when a stranger was passing his door," Kate adds.

"Also," Hawthorne cuts in, "There's a stabbed-up, bloody chomper in the stairwell that I assumed you didn't want me to kill yet. So yeah, I'm fine, thanks for asking." His tone dripping with sarcasm.

"Don't kill any Dybbuks unless it's an emergency," Ryder orders flatly. "Now grab a limb. Violet, you lead us downstairs. Make sure we don't run into anyone or anything."

"Yes, sir." I snap off a mocking salute, earning my own trademark eye-roll.

On three, they lift Tompkins's limp body. His robe shifts open and the room fills with groans of disgust.

"Ew. What the fuck is he wearing and why is his whole tiny package out?" Kate wrinkles her nose, yanking her shirt up over her face.

"Hey. That's average size." Hawthorne says under his breath.

We all freeze and turn to stare at him.

"Shut the fuck up, will ya?" Ryder snarls.

We start moving slowly down the stairs, Tompkins's dead weight pulls at their arms. The air smells of sweat, old blood, and something sour wafting off his robe. I keep my eyes forward, blade in hand, scanning the shadows. The chomper Hawthorne mentioned still twitches on the stairwell, jaw clicking wetly. I don't hesitate, one clean strike through its skull, and it collapses for good. I can't risk anyone dropping Tompkins because of it.

"Oh, so she gets to kill them but I don't?" Hawthorne grumbles, straining against his own frustration.

I hit him with a sarcastic shrug and it earns me a quiet, hidden laugh from Ryder. We keep moving, my steps guiding us toward the room where Ryder had been held captive. The hallways stretch out around us, too quiet, too still.

No patrols.

No guards.

Just silence pressing against the walls but the quiet isn't empty after all. It carries a pulse. A hollow bang, over and over, vibrating through the metal and into my bones. It takes me a second to understand.

The horde.

They've finally caught up to the door.

After we get into the room, I flip the light switch. A harsh, buzzing glow floods the space, illuminating cracked walls and scuffed concrete floors. I shut the door behind us, the echo bouncing in the emptiness. They set Tompkins down on a chair in the middle of the room, his robe hanging in ridiculous disarray, the aftermath of Ryder's punch clear across his bruised face. Rope lies in a neat pile on the floor nearby, frayed but strong. A table with tools on it and two more chairs waits silently; a stage set. I wedge one of the extra chairs against the door, just in case anyone hears his screams and decides to investigate. Turning back to him, I watch as Kate works her magic with the rope. She's precise, methodical and super good with knots, thanks to her scout training. Also, from what she's told me, one of her kinks is shibari.

"Right up your alley," I tease.

Kate shakes her head, a humorless laugh escaping her.

"Yeah, not my type," she mutters as she cinches the final knot.

Ryder tests the ropes, tugging roughly on Tompkins' arms. The chair scrapes across the floor, and I feel my pulse spike, adrenaline and dark satisfaction mixing in my chest. Everything in the room feels charged.

"How long till the fucker wakes up?" Hawthorne asks.

"Twenty minutes… maybe an hour," Kate replies.

I glance around the room, my eyes settling on the tools laid out on the table: a rusted wrench, a jagged screwdriver, and shards of glass from a broken bottle. Our instruments of justice. My fingers twitch, aching to grab something. He deserves every second of what's coming. Tompkins stirs, just a slight twitch at first, then a groan escapes his cracked lips. His bloodshot eyes flutter as he struggles to focus.

I lean forward, letting the full weight of my malice drip into my words. "Good morning, Dick bag. You really fucked with the wrong family."

He thrashes against the ropes, eyes wild, mouth opening to scream. Ryder steps in, hands clamping over his face, silencing him instantly.

He whispers, slow and deliberate, "Shhh… my girl is trying to speak to you."

My hands shake, but the rage in my chest fuels me. I grab the jagged shard of broken glass from the table, pressing it against his thigh. I drag it upward, careful to avoid his gross sack, and watch his muscles twitch at the sting.

"You're going to feel every second of this," I toy, leaning in close. "Do you remember what it's like to be afraid?"

I glance at Kate and Hawthorne. Ryder chuckles low, eyes locked on mine, nodding as if giving me permission to take this as far as I want.

"Let's refresh your memory." I let the shard trace tiny cuts up his thighs again, taunting him. His eyes dart between us, the panic raw.

"Please… stop," he croaks, voice breaking.

I laugh, a low, bitter sound. "Stop? Oh, you should've thought of that before you killed my father."

Ryder leans toward Hawthorne, whispering fast enough that Tompkins can't hear. I catch only pieces.

"The door… ready… now."

Hawthorne's eyes flick to me. Ryder gives me a sharp look, then gestures for Hawthorne. In a fluid motion, they both slip out of the room, leaving me and Kate alone with Tompkins'.

I grin, leaning in close. "Try something smart, and I'll make sure you regret it."

"Fuck you!" He spits.

Kate shakes her head at him, a cold grin spreading. "Shut up. You don't get to have the last word."

She presses her hand over his mouth when he tries again, then, with a weird sort of calculated audacity, slips her socks off and gags him, muffling his voice. The smell is awful, but I don't care. She then crouches in front of him, dark amusement in her eyes.

"You killed my best friend's dad for no reason," She seethes, dragging a small knife along his fingers, slicing the skin just enough to make him flinch and hiss.

"You think you're a wolf, prowling and preying on everyone weaker than you, but the truth? You're just a sheep in wolf's clothing. Bleating, pathetic, pretending to be terrifying while everything real you touch dies anyway."

She lifts the knife, and drags the blade across his face until blood wells up. His muffled scream hits the air as she presses harder, slicing at his cheek, slow and deliberate. The sock gag keeps it soft, but not soft enough to stop the sound from crawling under my skin. Flashbacks hit me.

Me as a little girl, my dad lifting me onto his shoulders at the carnival. Felix laughing so hard his face turns red. Mom swatting Dad for giving us cotton candy before dinner. Jane's first steps. All those memories, bright and golden, pressed up against the nightmare of Dad's face slack with hunger, the way his body fell into the grave. Tompkins' face overlaps it all, his laugh, his voice, his choices.

I grab the screwdriver from the table, pressing it into his thigh. I carve up as his eyes roll white, sweat dripping down his temples, his legs shaking against the chair.

"Scared?" I press the tool deeper. "You should be. My father was worth more in death than you'll ever be worth alive."

Then Kate gets in his face, her voice low and vicious. "You're a coward hiding behind uniforms and chains."

He thrashes, gag muffling his howl, and that's when Ryder returns and goes directly for Tompkins. His hand shoots out, gripping Tompkins' jaw until the man freezes. Ryder leans in close, whispering something sharp and demonic, into his ear.

"I think he's hungry" he murmurs, tilting his head toward the door. "Let's feed him."

The door creaks open and Hawthorne shoves a snarling Deadhead into the room by its shirt collar, its teeth snapping, claws raking the air. Ryder's eyes shift. He doesn't need words.

We step back.

The Deadhead lunges.

Its teeth sink into Tompkins' arm, tearing into muscle. His scream is muted. He writhes, but the ropes hold, and all he can do is choke against Kate's gag while blood soaks his sleeve. Ryder crouches low, voice quiet as poison.

"That's just a taste. Imagine what the horde will do."

Hawthorne and Kate leave the room. Not sure why but I'm enjoying watching Ryder torture him more. Then, with one brutal twist of his blade, he stabs the Deadhead, letting it crumple at Tompkins's feet. He doesn't give General Fuck Face time to breathe. The knife comes up again, and this time Ryder takes his fingers. The knife gleams in his hand, its edge catching the light as he crouches in front of him. My stomach rolls, but I don't look away. I need to see this. Tompkins thrashes weakly against the ropes, his gagged screams spill out in pitiful muffles. Ryder's voice is low.

"This one," he says, "This is for Calloway. Do you remember him? He was my friend… My brother! You let the horde in and left. Leaving all of us to fucking die. All while you took the last helicopter out."

He grips Tompkins' hand, pinning it flat against the armrest. He severs the first finger in one swift slice. Blood spurts, hot and fast. Tompkins howls into the sock. He doesn't pause long before raising the knife again. The second finger hits the floor with a wet smack.

"This one's for hurting someone I love. For murdering Violet's dad. You broke her, like it meant nothing."

I can see the Generals chest heaving, gag muffling every ragged scream. Ryder leans closer, almost whispering as he brings the blade down again. Blood slicks his hand, dripping to the floor.

"This… is for the bus. For every innocent you ordered dead with that fucking kill order. There was a child on that bus, who didn't deserve that. Good people who didn't deserve to die!"

He doesn't stop. He removes the fourth finger, his movements controlled, his eyes flat and merciless.

"And this… this is for hunting us. For tracking that military bus. For watching us and seeing we were driving into a trap."

Tompkins' muffled screaming turns frantic now, his body straining so violently against the chair it nearly tips. Thanks to Kate, the knots hold brilliantly. Ryder's lips curl into something sharp, almost a smile, as he lifts the blade for the last time.

"And this last one…" His voice drops lower and darkness floods it, "This is for all of it. For being one of the bastards who started this nightmare. For unleashing the end of the fucking world."

The fifth finger falls. Blood covers the chair, the floor, and Ryder's hands. Tompkins sags against the ropes, gag soaked with spit and muffled sobs, his eyes wild with a fear I wished I could bottle and feed him on forever. The door opens again. Hawthorne and Kate stagger back in, hauling a heavy black duffel between them. Hawthorne drops it with a grunt, unzipping it wide. Inside it, steel gleams, rifles, pistols, grenades, enough firepower to burn this place to the ground

"Sorry, took us a minute," Hawthorne puffs, flashing a wolfish grin. "We had to stop by the toy store next door."

Kate wipes her bloody hands on her jeans. "Christmas came early."

We are interrupted by the banging. Metal rattling, walls shaking, the compound doors buckling under the horde's weight. It is deafening and relentless. The dead are here and they are hungry.

Ryder straightens, wiping blood off his knife. "They're coming. Time to go. Let the horde do what we don't have time for."

Kate doesn't need more prompting. She bolts for the door, Hawthorne right behind her holding the duffle bag. Ryder turns to leave too, his hand closing around my arm, tugging me with him, but I dig my heels in, my gaze locked on Tompkins, half-naked, bound and pathetic in the chair.

"Wait." My voice cracks like a whip, stopping him in his tracks.

I turn and walk towards Major Dick Chin and lean close, letting my voice lower, each word a blade, "You wore the mask of power, Tompkins, but underneath it's all rot. All fear. You hide behind screams and blood, thinking it makes you a God but you're nothing. Just a shadow of cruelty, and every shadow fades. Remember that."

We leave the door wide open behind us. The plan is simple now. Unlock the Deadhead farm, unleash the horde, and let Tompkins's empire rot from the inside out. Ryder leans close, his voice barely a breath.

"Hawthorne, Kate, you guys take the Farm. Me and Violet will unleash the horde, we meet at the stairs then head to the exit. Be fast and stay alert."

I can feel the ground vibrate beneath my boots; every tremor carries the promise of what waits on the other side. Ryder and I approach the door; he grabs the handle and shoots me a look. The pounding rattles through me, bone-deep, and I start to drift. My mind slips away from the noise, from the chaos pressing in. The sound, the banging. All I want at this moment is the impossible; to be lying in one of these big, fancy beds, Ryder tangled around me, sunlight spilling through glass windows. The smell of bacon frying instead of death pressing at the walls. The ringing grows louder in my ears, sharp and constant, pulling me farther from here.

"Darlin'?"

My gaze snaps up, dragged back by the anchor of his voice. Ryder's hazel eyes are on me, burning steady even with the world breaking around us. I reach up and grab his face, pulling him to me. The kiss is desperate, grounding, a collision of fear and need. He leans into it, then stops, letting our foreheads press together. His breath is warm on my lips.

"You okay, Ocean Eyes?"

I shift slightly, forcing the tears back, trying to make my body believe the lie. "Yeah. I just zoned out, and needed you to remind me of the present moment."

His eyes narrow, sharp and protective, "On the count of three, I'll open this door and we have to run. You remember the way to the exit?"

I shake my head yes quickly.

"Baby. You're so strong. You got this and when we get up there, we start our new life. You and me."

The words crack me open. "Okay. I love you."

His voice is steady, a lifeline. "I love *you*. One… two… three."

The horde spills out, hunger unleashed, centuries of nightmare crashing into Tompkins' kingdom. The sound is thunder and shrieking wind, a thousand mouths tearing into walls and men alike. We run, not stopping for anything or anyone, the screams of his empire trailing us like shadows. We converge at the stairwell, breath ragged, adrenaline sparking through me like lightning in my blood. There's no door here to bar the way, no chance to pause or catch a breath. We're exposed. Ryder and I plant ourselves at the corner, waiting, praying for Kate and Hawthorne.

Shuffling.

Groaning.

The sound of hunger edging closer.

Come on, come on, come on.

Then red hair and a flash of a military shirt. Relief slams through me. Kate's face lights up when she spots us waiting, but my relief curdles fast. Her expression shifts and my smile falters. Behind them, Deadheads flood the hall in a tide of rotting flesh and gnashing teeth.

"Oh fuck!"

We turn, boots pounding against metal steps. My lungs are burning. Ryder reaches the top first, spinning, hand shooting back toward me. His palm finds mine. Warm, steady, grounding amidst the chaos, pulling me forward toward the only future we might have left.

"Up," he says. Just one word, but it carries the weight of everything.

All I can think about is the future clawing its way closer with every stair. This is our chance to burn the past and carve something new. Ryder doesn't let go of me. His hand is calloused, rough, but it fits against mine like it's always belonged there. I squeeze tighter, as if holding on can tether me to this moment, to him, to the promise of more than just survival.

The screams behind us blur into music. Destruction turns into freedom. Each cry is a requiem for the life I lost, for the woman I used to be. And step by step, I feel her peeling away. By the time we reach the final landing, I'm breathless, trembling, alive in a way that I haven't been since this all began. Ryder slams his shoulder into the exit bar, metal shrieking. The door bursts open. Cold night air crashes over us, sweeping the stench of death away. We step out together, hand in hand. Hawthorne and Kate catch up to us with a slam of the exit door. I clutch Ryder's arm, chest heaving looking up to our new way out, our new life only to have my heart shattered.

The pad is empty and there's no helicopter.

CHAPTER 37

RYDER

I've failed us.

The truth hits me like a bullet. There is nothing here, no way out, no miracle escape to be found. Violet drops to her knees beside me, her forehead pressed against the pavement, her shoulders shaking like the weight of the world finally broke her spine. The sight of her like that nearly tears me in half. My hand trembles as I raise my gun, pointing it at the sky. My throat burns as I scream, voice raw and cracked.

"Why?! Why couldn't we get this, huh? What the fuck else do you want from me?"

The gun sags in my grip as I fall to my knees, chest heaving. The concrete bites into my skin, but I barely feel it. My vision swims, my ears roar. Hawthorne tumbles down, slumped against the wall, face pale and tight.

"But… but Hawaii," he mutters.

I want to put my fist through something. Kate shakes her head, pacing like a caged animal.

Her voice is sharp, frantic. "What the fuck do we do now? That door isn't going to hold them! Guy's? Fucking say something!"

My tongue feels heavy and my brain fogs. The world blurs around me until all I can hear is the endless chorus of moans, echoing in my head. The undead are hungry, clawing closer, and we had boxed ourselves in like mice. No escape, no hope, unless… I force my legs under me and stumble toward the edge, searching desperately. A ladder, a fire escape, a hatch, anything to prevent us from becoming Dybbuk chow. My eyes dart everywhere. *Nothing.* Just jagged rock and a hundred-foot drop into nothingness.

"***FUUUUCCCKK!***" I bellow, voice raw, fury ripping out of me like shrapnel. My shout carries over the canyon, echoing back at me. The sound stirs the horde, moans grow louder, sharper, nails scrape metal with renewed frenzy. We are running out of time.

"Screaming isn't fucking helping anything," Kate snaps, her voice cutting through the air.

I whirl on her, heat blazing in my chest, my vision going red. Every nerve in me is coiled tight, ready to unleash. My fists clench, jaw grinding, words forming like knives on my tongue. I'm two seconds away from tearing into her, from letting the fury consume me. Then a hand lands on my chest.

I look down.

She's there.

Violet.

A flash of black hair catches the dim light, framing her face like ink spilled across porcelain. She lifts her head, and her eyes lock onto mine. They stop me cold. Eyes that don't just look at me, but into me, through all the rage and madness clawing inside. The anger drains from me, slow, reluctant, like blood seeping from a wound. My breath catches, chest rising and falling too fast. All I can see is my girl. My anchor in this fucked-up world. I love her more than my own skin, more than the gun in my hand, more than my next breath.

"We can get out of this," she says, her words wrapping around me like a lifeline. "We just have to think. There's always a way."

Something in me shifts. My fury gives way to focus, her voice silencing the storm in my head. For a moment, it's just her and I. The groans of the horde fading, Kate's sharp tongue forgotten, Hawthorne's cries disappear, the hopelessness dulls. Just Ocean Eyes, her voice, and her unshakable faith. I lower my head, taking a breath, grounding myself in her.

"You're right," I sigh.

Her words linger in me. *There's always a way.* I drag my hands through my hair, pulling myself back to reality.

Think, Ryder. Rage doesn't keep anyone alive. Plans do.

That's when my hand brushes against the radio clipped to my side. The plastic is warm from the heat of my body, the faint static whispering, waiting for me to notice. I freeze. Slowly, I lift it, thumb dragging over the knob until the speaker hisses, then clears. A monotone voice breaks through the night air.

This is the Canadian Emergency Broadcast…

The sound spills into the valley, bouncing off the rocks, echoing out into the dark. An idea sparks. I turn to the others.

"We don't fight them head-on. We guide them. We let the broadcast do the work for us."

Hawthorne frowns. "Guide them where?"

I point to the edge. "The noise will pull them like moths to flame. All we got to do is stay out of sight long enough for the whole horde to take the plunge. We get behind that exit door, hold it against the wall. Shut it just enough to shield us."

Kate's brows shoot up. "That's…fucking…. insane."

"Insane works," I released it like a sigh, glancing at Violet, "It has to."

No further words are needed. We move fast. No hesitation, no second guesses. The groans are swelling, building like a tidal wave ready to crash, a wall of death that wants nothing more than to swallow us whole. Hawthorne drops down on one knee at the edge, his hands working fast to set the bait. He cranks his walkie until the static screeches, then twists the dial until the Broadcast blares out loud enough to rattle my teeth.

"Okay," I huff, my eyes wild but steady. "You guys ready?"

He comes running back with the duffel bag of weapons slung across his shoulder. He tosses it down in front of us, the clatter of steel and magazines echoing against the concrete.

"Fuck yeah," he says, sweat slicking his forehead. "This might actually work, Ryder."

We line up tight, shoulder to shoulder, a warped conga line of survivors waiting for the end of the world to pass us by. I lock eyes with Violet, and in that second, it's just her and I. I grab the handle, ready to let hell in. I pull the door and fall back hard against the wall. The hinges whining as the gap yawns open. I nudge the bag forward, steady as a surgeon's hand, every scrape of fabric sounding too loud in the dark. Shoving it into place, a makeshift barricade between us and the flimsy door. I'm frozen in place by the pounding of countless feet, shuffling, scraping, dragging. The sound of a thousand bodies funneling toward the broadcast. The moans rise into a deafening chorus, a storm of hunger and decay pressing against our barricade. The door rattles and shakes. I hold the handle with every fiber of my being.

The first splat is sickening. The second one is worse, bones shattering, meat tearing, the sound ricocheting up the mountain like a grotesque drumbeat. Soon it's a rhythm, steady and merciless, bodies tumbling into the void and breaking on the rocks below. For a split second of foolish hope, it almost feels like it's working, like we've done the impossible. Then the rhythm falters. I hear a metallic scrape. The radio, the lure, teeters on the concrete edge, then tips forward and vanishes into the black. The broadcast echoes, and then drops into the void, silenced. The dead hesitate, and instead of walking off the edge, they start milling, staggering in uneven circles, some colliding into each other, some groaning at the air. A few even start drifting back toward the door.

"Shit," I hiss under my breath, pressing harder against the steel door.

Every nerve in my body screams at me to act, to fix this, to keep everyone safe.

Keep Violet safe.

Hawthorne whispers, "We lost the lure…"

Yeah, no shit.

Kate's breathing sharpens. "They'll find us. We have to do something."

Violet just looks up at me and I hear her voice in my head. *There's always a way.* Slowly, and ever so carefully, I reach for the duffle bag at my feet. The zipper rasps loud in the silence. A Dybbuk groans, shuffling closer. I don't move until they stumble past again, pulled by the phantom of hunger.

Violet squeezes my arm, whispering, "You got this."

Her voice is steady but tight, as if she's holding the terror in her throat with sheer willpower. I nod once. My fingers find cold steel. *A grenade.* Perfect. I curl my hand around it, thumb brushing the pin.

You've done this a million times.

I take a slow breath and meet Violet's eyes. Her pupils are wide, her lips pressed tight. She inclines her head, trusting me without question. That look burns through me, hotter than the fear.

"Brace yourselves," I whisper, more to myself than them.

I pull the pin, feel the metal click free, and in one motion hurl the grenade over the edge. The explosion rattles the pad under our feet, a flash lighting up the valley. The blast echoes for miles, bouncing through the canyon. The Dybbuks freeze, their groans catching like static. Then as if the noise has pulled them by a leash, they surge forward. One by one, they begin to stumble off the edge again, chasing the sound of destruction. The steady beat of bodies falling returns.

Louder.

Fiercer.

Bodies breaking open like rotten fruit against the rocks. I press myself tighter into the corner, jaw locked so hard it aches. Sweat slicking down my back. The steel door is vibrating against my hand, every shove from outside another reminder of what waits if this plan fails. Beside me, Violet presses close. Her shoulder brushing mine, her breath shallow but steady. I feel her tremble, just faintly, but she doesn't break. Doesn't even blink. Her hand finds mine in the dark, and squeezes once. Reminding me she's here, reminding me I'm not doing this alone anymore. I squeeze back, lacing my fingers through hers, holding on like the only thing tethering me to this ruined earth. Minutes pass. Endless, suffocating minutes. I keep counting bodies in my head, counting every sound of something breaking apart, until numbers blur into nothing but noise. Violet tilts her head up, her lips brushing my ear, so soft I almost think I've imagined it.

"We're going to make it," she whispers.

I kiss the top of her head *hard.*

Yes, we are going to make it.

I squeeze her hand harder, silently telling her everything I can't say out loud; *I love you. I'm not letting go. Not now. Not ever.* The sounds of their plummets slow. Fewer groans. Fewer feet. The horde is thinning. The plan *is* working. We stay still, pressed together behind the door, hearts beating in sync, until the silence finally stretches long enough to feel real. Until hope feels closer than death.

"Okay, we go to the garage and take an SUV. Kill every meat bag you see and let's get the fuck out of here."

We get up and close the door, quickly killing the rest of the Dybbuks on the pad. We load the guns and made sure our knives are ready.

"Time to kick some undead ass!" Kate says while cocking her newly found shotgun with that predator's grin she wears when shit gets bad.

Hawthorne grunts, swinging his new rifle over his shoulder. Violet stands closest to me, her father's jacket hanging heavy on her frame. She doesn't need to say anything, her hand brushing mine is enough.

"Ready?"

With a silent agreement, I swing open the door to the stairwell. The groans hit us immediately, echoing up the concrete shaft like a choir of death. Shadows shift below, the shuffle of countless feet dragging closer.

"Here we go," I announce, drawing my knife in one hand and pistol in the other. The first Dybbuk lunges up the stairs, eyes white and mouth wide open. I put a bullet through its brains. It jerks back, slamming into the railing before tumbling down, bowling over two more on the way.

"Keep moving!" I bark.

We charge down the steps two at a time. The stairwell is narrow and claustrophobic, the smell of blood and rot clinging to the concrete walls. More of them surge upward. Hawthorne meets them head-on, his knife splitting a skull clean in two, blood spraying his arms. Kate fires point-blank into another's chest, the shotgun blast echoing like thunder, the recoil almost knocking her back.

"Gross," she exclaims, shaking gore off her sleeve. "Do they ever stop leaking?"

"Nope," I say, shoving my knife under another's chin, twisting until it goes slack in my arms. "That's the fun part."

We keep pushing down. A Dybbuk grabs Violet's arm, teeth snapping inches from her face. My heart stops but she shoves her blade up under its jaw, forcing it back. Blood sprays across her cheek.

"You good?" I ask, grabbing her wrist for half a second.

She shakes her head yes, wiping her face with the back of her hand.

"Yes, I'm okay, thanks babe."

God, I love it when she calls me that.

More are coming, always more. Halfway down, the horde thickens, too many to fight clean. Hawthorne doesn't hesitate, he swings his rifle off his shoulder and braces it against the stair rail.

"Cover your ears!" he warns.

The crack of gunfire explodes in the shaft, deafening in the tight space. Round after round tear into the Dybbuks swarming below, heads snapping back, bodies collapsing into each other. The muzzle flash lights the stairwell in rapid bursts of light, each one carving out a glimpse of blood-slick jaws and clawing hands. Shell casings clatter against the steps, ringing like brass rain.

"Clear a path!" I shout over the gunfire, driving my knife through the skull of one that managed to scramble too close.

Hawthorne keeps firing, every controlled burst hammering the horde back down the stairs, until smoke and the stink of burnt powder thicken the air. The Dybbuks groan, stumbling over their dead, buying us the few precious seconds we needed.

"Move, now!" I shout, pulling Violet forward.

We barrel down, weaving through the blinded horde, stabbing and slashing as we go. My arms burn, my throat raw from shouting, but I don't let go of her hand, not once. We hit the bottom hallway.

"Kate, clear it!"

"Gladly," she says, unloading both barrels of her shotgun.

Two go down in sprays of gore. Hawthorne catches up to us, shooting his rifle while I crush another's skull. Violet slides in low, stabbing one through the gut, twisting upward until it splits open. I shoot the last one through the eye. We don't pause to admire the carnage.

We bolt down the hall, boots pounding on the tile. Through the open doors we pass we catch glimpses of what is left of the *'soldiers.*

Torn apart.

Pieces scattered.

The walls smeared red.

The sound of wet chewing is worse than the sight.

"Eyes ahead. Don't stop." I order.

The other stairwell looms ahead. We sprint for it, boots hammering against concrete, breath tearing in and out of our lungs. The next biter waits right on the landing, head jerking toward us, mouth gaping wide. Not a flicker of fear crosses Kate's face. Just one clean shot, and its skull blows open, brain matter squelching against the walls. Another meat bag flings itself toward me at full tilt, teeth snapping for my face, reeking of rot and bile.

"Oh, you've got to be kidding me," I snarl, grabbing a fistful of its jacket and slamming it so hard against the wall that the plaster spiderwebs. Its growl turns wet and gurgling. I use my fists until its head gives with a sharp, pulpy crack.

"Holy hell, Ryder," Hawthorne mutters, firing past me. "Do you come with a warning label?"

"Yeah," I grin without looking back. "It says don't test me."

I drag Violet gently forward by the elbow as more shadows spill into the stairwell below.

"Sounds kind of like we woke the whole damn building!" Violet shouts, kicking one in the chest as it lunges halfway up the stairs.

"Keep moving!" Hawthorne barks, as I pivot and put a bullet clean through the skull of the next one charging towards us.

"Follow me! SUV… garage doors… now!" I yell.

We barrel down the corridor. A Dybbuk darts forward from a doorway, and Violet twists, driving her blade clean through its temple while Hawthorne shoots another as it tries to flank us. Finally, I slam my shoulder into the steel garage door.

Of course, it's stuck.

"Help me out!" I shout, bracing myself as the growls and scraping claws draw closer.

Hawthorne charges it with me and together we break it open, the hinges screaming as it bursts wide. The garage yawns open before us and the rows of SUVs greet us. Groans rise from the far corners. Shadows stagger between vehicles. The garage isn't empty. The other door is wide open.

"Shit," Kate breathes. "They beat us here."

"They're not beating us out."

We move in formation, backs to each other. The first Dybbuk rounds the hood. Violet shoots it. Kate blows another back into a windshield, glass raining down. Hawthorne tears through two more. A Dybbuk pounces at me from the side, catching me off guard. Its claws rake my shoulder, pain flashing white-hot. I slam my knife into its temple, twisting until it stops moving, then shove it off me. Violet is there instantly, grabbing my arm.

"You're okay, scratches don't kill you" she whispers, panic flanking her voice.

I force a smile, even though the sting.

"I'll live. Just don't leave me behind." I wink.

"Never," she says, eyes smiling, before turning to put another down with brutal precision.

We fight our way toward the nearest SUV. Every step is blood and sweat. My ears ring with gunfire and my arms screams with the weight of every swing, but we keep going. The doors unlock, keys still dangling from the ignition.

"Go, go, go!" I yell, shoving Violet into the passenger seat.

Kate scrambles into the back, Hawthorne piling in behind her. I spin, covering them as more Dybbuks rush us from the far end of the garage. One gets too close so I blow its jaw clean off. Hawthorne reaches out, grabbing my jacket, and yanks me into the driver's seat.

"Drive Kent!"

I slam the door, turn the keys, and the engine roars to life. The sound draws more Dybbuks, their moans rising into a fever pitch.

"Hang on!" I floor it, tires screeching across the concrete. The SUV barrels forward, slamming through the crowd. Bodies hit the hood, cracking glass, rolling off in sprays of blood. The door opens just in time as we drive out of the living nightmare.

"Hell yeah!" Kate whoops, firing out the window at stragglers.

Beside me, Violet grips the dash hard, her eyes steady. I swerve hard, tires screeching, the SUV fishtailing as another pack of corpse's stumbles into the headlights. I plow straight through, the thuds shaking the frame, their rotten bodies breaking across the grille. Violet gasps, but she doesn't look away, she never does. I reach across the console, grab her hand, and squeeze. Her skin is cold, and clammy. She squeezes back, and that's enough to keep me steady.

"We're not safe yet," I breathe, tightening my grip on the wheel as we swerve around an overturned truck. "But we're alive, Darlin'. That's what counts."

"As long as we're together."

From the back seat, Kate groans. "Seriously? We're dodging death and you two are flirting?"

Hawthorne snorts. "Yeah, some of us are trying to survive back here, not choke on secondhand romance."

I look into the rearview mirror, without missing a beat.

"Then look away."

Kate mutters, "Trust me, I am," but there's a smile hiding behind her words.

The road evens out, and as the dark haze thins, a familiar silhouette rises in the distance. The same house we'd used before, still standing, still quiet. I keep one hand near my pistol as I pull up, scanning the tree line, the windows, the roof. Nothing moves except the wind. Inside, the place smells the same like dust and stale air. We settle in, each of us dropping our gear like the weight of it might crush us if we keep carrying it any longer. Kate and Hawthorne head upstairs, I assume to clean all the meat bag blood off of them. Violet lingers in the living room for a while, perched on the edge of the couch. When she notices me watching her, she rises and crosses the room, sitting on the coffee table right in front of me. For a moment she studies me, my bloody knuckles, the grime on my face, the haunted look I know I'm wearing.

"You did good tonight," she says softly, her voice steady even though her hands tremble in her lap.

I let out a short, bitter laugh. "We lost half the plot out there."

Her brows knit, and she leans closer until her knees brush mine, "We're still alive because of you. That's what matters."

Personally, I feel as though it could have gone better.

She reaches out, fingers grazing my jaw, pulling my gaze up to meet hers.

"I'm proud of you, Ryder."

Before I can reply, she leans in and presses a kiss to my cheek.

By the time I manage to breathe again, she's already standing. Kate appears at the foot of the stairs, giving me a look, I can't read, then gestures toward Violet.

"I'm going to try and get some rest, you should too." Violet says gently, and follows Kate upstairs.

Hawthorne walks down and stands near the window, rifle in hand, back straight as ever, but I can see the tension in his jaw. The silence stretches until it's too heavy to breathe.

"You want to say something, say it," I snap finally, throwing myself onto the arm of the couch.

He glances at me, eyes dark. "You almost got us all killed tonight."

I sit forward, elbows on my knees. "You think I don't know that?"

"You think knowing it makes it better?" His voice rises, heated now. "You're supposed to keep your head, Ryder. We were counting on you."

My fist curls on my knee, nails biting into my palm. "You think I knew the helicopter wasn't going to be there? You think I wanted to drag her back here half-dead and bleeding? I'd trade my damn life to keep her safe."

He claps me once on the shoulder and huffs, "You're right you couldn't have known, but we should have checked. Next time we will plan better. Go get some rest."

I wake on the couch. I must have passed out. I grab my pistol and creep upstairs, padding silently toward whichever room Violet is in. I'm just about to open the door when shots shatter the window downstairs.

"Shit!" I hiss, ducking back as the second shot splinters the doorframe.

Glass rains down like knives as I bolt back down the stairs, returning fire blind toward the flashes outside. A white-hot pain blooms in my side, knocking the air out of me, but I keep moving, hand clamped over the wound. Violet bursts out of the bedroom just as I stagger up the last step. Her eyes go wide.

"Ryder!"

"I'm fine, get back!" I grit out.

"No, you're not!" She grabs me, pressing both hands against my side. "You're bleeding."

"We don't have time," I rasp.

The next volley of gunfire punches holes in the wall, plaster spraying the hall. Hawthorne throws himself out of his room, rifle barking as he takes a quick shot toward the muzzle flash outside. A bullet whizzes past his head close enough to shear a lock of his hair.

"Back door!" he shouts.

I move as fast as I can and lean into Violet, her shoulder under my arm as we run for the kitchen. Kate curses, clutching her grazed arm but keeping pace.

Just as I shove Violet toward the door, another shot slams into my shoulder. The force spins me halfway around, vision exploding white. I hit the floor hard, pistol still in my grip.

"RYDER!" Violet's scream cuts through the ringing in my ears.

I push up onto one elbow, blood slick under my hand.

"Go!" I snarl, fumbling for the pistol with my good arm. "Get out of here!"

Another shot grazes my eyebrow, hot blood running down into my eye, blinding me on one side. The world tilts. I fire once, twice, toward the darkness outside, not even sure if I hit anything before the pistol clatters from my fingers. Violet's face swims into view, her hands on my chest, her voice desperate.

"My shoulder hurts."

"Stay with me, Ryder. Don't you dare leave me now."

Her words are the last thing I catch before the black edges close in.

CHAPTER 38

VIOLET

The gunfire stutters to a stop and the air hums with a dull, stunned quiet.

"RYDER!" I scream, fingers digging into his jaw to force his face up. "No…no…NO!"

"We need an intact pharmacy," I tell them between breaths. "I think I saw one on the west side when we came in."

My hands move on their own. I tear a rag from under the sink, and press it to the wound on Ryder's side. Blood soaks through the cloth in a dark fast bloom. He twitches, eyes half-lidded, trying to focus on me. The front door slams open with a percussion that makes everyone flinch. Sinclair appears in the doorway like a ghost, face paper-pale. He looks like he's seen the sky fall.

"I…" he starts, collapsing into words. "I saw the SUV and I thought… I thought you were with them. I thought you were part of the crew that…"

He can't finish; the confession drips off him in a ragged mess.

"Did you do this? Did you fuckin' do this? Why?" I spit, pressing harder on Ryder until he jerks.

Sinclair's hands fly up. "No….no! I didn't mean…."

He swallows like he's choking on guilt.

A small voice cuts through the chaos. "Are you okay, Andrew?"

Little Dion pads in behind Sinclair, cheeks flushed from the cool air. Sinclair snaps at him without thinking. "I told you to stay outside!"

"Thank God you guys are okay!" Kate bursts forward, dropping to her knees and pulling Dion into a hug so tight he squeals. Relief folds her face into something softer for a heartbeat.

Hawthorne leans toward Sinclair, lowering his voice until it's a rough whisper.

"Where's the mom?" He asks.

Sinclair's face goes hard. He meets Hawthorne's look and returns it with something colder. Kate slaps Hawthorne's arm, definitely hard enough to sting.

"Don't you dare," she snaps.

"What? It's a fair question." Hawthorne's voice is flat.

"No. It's a cruel and stupid one." I answer, the heat in my voice evident.

My patience is thin; Ryder's pulse is thudding under the rag. Every second counts.

I shove the rag harder.

"Where's Arthur?" Sinclair asks, scanning the faces for any sign of my dad.

Kate's mouth opens as if to say something, then closes when our eyes lock. She gives me the smallest, almost invisible nod. He doesn't need her to spell it out.

"He's outside in the dirt." I say annoyed and angry. "We don't have time for this…not when Ryder's life is on the line."

"I need all of you," my eyes flick to Dion. "Except you, kid…" Then back to the others. "To shut up and help me lift him…now!"

Kate presses the keys into Dion's small hand.

"Go open the door, sweetheart," she whispers, trying to sound calm.

His fingers shake, but he signals with a small motion and bolts for the SUV.

"Everyone grab a limb!" I demand.

I hook my arm under Ryder's shoulder, pressing down on the wound.

"On three," I breathe. "One…two…three."

He groans, head lolling against my shoulder as we heave him up.

Hawthorne grunts beside me, his voice strained. "Christ, Kent. What the hell do you weigh?"

Ryder doesn't answer. His body feels heavy, like something already slipping away. His skin burns under my fingers, his breath shallow. The man who never stopped moving is fading fast. He's probably starved, exhausted, and to add to the shit pile bleeding out. We stagger across the driveway and lower him into the back seat. The SUV dips under his weight. I climb in after him, knees hitting the seat as I cradle his head. My hands are slick with blood, the rag soaked through, but I don't stop.

I brush his hair off his forehead with trembling fingers and whisper, "You're okay. You're okay."

Hawthorne wedges himself into the trunk space, knees bent awkwardly, one hand gripping the seatback for balance. Kate crouches near Ryder's legs, looping a torn strap around his ankles to keep him from sliding as the vehicle jerks forward.

Up front, Sinclair's knuckles bleach white around the steering wheel. Dion sits beside him, too small in that oversized seat, eyes wide and glassy, trying not to look at the blood pooling beneath Ryder.

"Drive!"

He slams the door and throws the SUV into gear. Dion fumbles with the seatbelt, and Sinclair reaches over to help him before flooring it. The tires scream as we take off. The city blurs past in streaks of grey and red. We loop street after street, but there's no sign of the pharmacy I saw. Just boarded shops, shattered glass, and the shells of what used to be normal life. There's got to be something. I keep scanning the storefronts. My eyes catch on a neon sign with a bright red pill. Hope flickers, until I see the shape properly.

Not a pill.

A bowling pin.

"For fuck's sake, I need medical supplies…"

"What about a hospital?" Kate suggests.

The word hits me like shrapnel. Hospital. My pulse trips. For a second, I'm not here. I'm back there. The smell of smoke and antiseptic. The thunder of gunfire echoing through the halls. People screaming as soldiers fire. The building shaking from the blast. Grace's voice calling my name before…

I blink hard, forcing myself back.

"Shit it's not a hospital, I've only been here a few times, I think it's a doctor's clinic. Next left, it's not a big clinic but it should work!" Kate yells.

I'm not sure how much time passes. I just keep staring at Ryder's face hoping my gaze will heal him.

"Woo!" Hawthorne cheers as we round the corner and see the small clinic is still intact with no Deadheads in sight.

"You boys go and clear it, bring out a wheelchair or something so we can get Ryder in there safely"

"It's good to have yah back." Hawthorne firmly grips Sinclair's shoulder. "Now let's go kick some biter ass."

He smiles deviously and they rush to clear the building.

Dion's voice is barely above a whisper. "Is he… is Ryder gonna die?"

I force myself to look at him, his eyes fixed on Ryder's body sprawled across the backseat.

"No," I say, steady even though my pulse is a thunderstorm. "He's not dying. I'm a paramedic. I can save him."

Kate exhales a shaky breath, pressing her sleeve harder against Ryder's side wound. "Vi, he's lost a lot of blood."

"That's fine," I say quickly. "I'm O-negative. He can take mine."

Dion's eyes go wide. Sinclair and Hawthorne burst open the doors, one pushing a gurney that squeals as if it hasn't moved since the world ended.

"Look what we found!" Hawthorne proudly grins. "Had to wrestle it away from a biter, but hey, it's as good as new."

They load Ryder onto the gurney, metal clanging as Kate and I keep pressure on his wounds. "Kate, grab the med kit, the cleanest one you can find!"

"I got it!" she yells back, skidding around a tipped-over chair.

Sinclair jogs beside me, his hands steady. "I've had medical training," he says, breathless but calm. "Field work, and combat triage. I can help."

Hawthorne and Dion vanish down the hall to block entrances.

The world narrows to blood, breath, and the faint glow of dawn bleeding through the shattered windows. My hands tremble as I press them to Ryder's shoulder. There's no power, no hum of fluorescent lights, no sterile white walls. Just the faint gold of sunrise creeping across the floorboards and catching on the edge of a cracked mirror. I tear through drawers with frantic precision until I find what I need. Rust-flecked surgical scissors, a cracked bottle of iodine, a pack of gauze that might still be clean and a couple pairs of gloves. There's a metal tray overturned on the floor, coated in a film of grime. I wipe it down with the edge of my sleeve and set it beside him. It's not sterile, but it's all I've got.

"This will work…" I stutter to myself.

Kate holds the flashlight steady, the beam flickering from a low battery. It strobes across Ryder's face and then down to the jagged wound on his side. My gloved hands are steady. Somehow, they always are when it's life or death. I take a deep breath, dig in, and find the bullet. It's lodged deep, resisting me like it knows what's at stake. When it finally comes free, it clinks against the tray. I pinch the other bullet free from his shoulder, the metal slick and warm between my fingers. Blood wells up instantly, spilling down my wrist. I press against the wound and glance toward Sinclair, who's standing frozen.

"Sinclair," I rasp. "Find me something to stitch him up with, thread, fishing line, anything."

He blinks, then jolts into motion, boots scuffing across the tile as he tears through drawers and cabinets. The sound of metal clattering and paper ripping fills the silence, the rhythm of desperation echoing off the walls while I keep pressure on Ryder's shoulder, feeling his pulse flutter weakly beneath my hand.

"Come on… come on," I yell.

Then his hand freezes. "Got something!"

He holds up a small sewing kit. A plastic cracked box, and faded red spool rattling inside. The kind of thing someone's grandmother might've kept in a junk drawer. He rips it open and rushes over, the spool unraveling as he moves. I rip it from his hands and start to thread the needle, the thin line of red glinting in the weak light, ready to pull Ryder back from the edge. I start to sew. Kate looks away when the blood splatters her sleeve. I don't have the luxury. By the time I'm done, my arms are soaked, my body shaking from adrenaline and lack of sleep. I throw the gloves and wrap gauze around his wound, winding the bandages tight.

His chest rises.

He's still alive.

"He's lost too much," Kate presses.

I meet her eyes, something fierce burning in me. "Not if we share."

Her brows knit. "Violet…"

I'm already in action. I find an old IV kit in the supply cabinet, the bag yellowed with age but intact. I set it up by instinct, tapping the line to clear the air. Then I slide the needle into my arm, my blood beginning its slow crawl into his veins. Warmth drains from me, the edges of the world softening. My vision swims, but I keep my hand on his chest, feeling for the faint rhythm of his heart.

Sinclair slips out quietly, to check on the others. Kate stays beside me, cross-legged on the floor.

"Come on, Ryder," I sigh out. "Take what you need."

"So… you love him, huh, Vi?" Kate leans back against the wall.

"More than anything," I breathe, my gaze flicking toward Ryder.

Kate exhales softly, the sound almost a sigh. "I'm happy for you."

A small smile tugs at my mouth. "Thanks."

"He's going to make it."

"Damn right he is," I reply, the faintest spark of fire warming my exhaustion. "I'm the best there is."

Kate chuckles under her breath. "You know… from everything I've seen you become, I'm proud to call you my best friend."

"Get over here, you sap," I say, as she drags me into a hug. "You know Kate the last time I was in a hospital, I was admitting Grace because Jeff bit her."

"Jeff bit her? That must've been hard. I was so buried in work; I hadn't seen her for months. How was she?"

"She was happy, healthy, in love. The way most of us hope to go. I mean her arm was bitten but she still had that same spark. I just… hope her soul found rest."

"It did," Kates says confidently. "You did the best you could, Vi and she's probably grateful you found Ryder and I."

I glance toward the ceiling, the cracked tiles above us. "Yeah… I hope she's up there giving Jane a kiss for me and telling my family I miss them."

Kate's hand lands gently on my shoulder, "They know, Vi. Now breathe. You've got a few long hours ahead. I'll go help keep watch."

"Thank you."

She gives a small, warm smile and pulls a blanket from a nearby cupboard, draping it over me.

"You're going to save him."

"Ryder?" My voice cracks as I jolt upright. I drag a trembling hand over my face, blink away the haze, and wince as I slide the needle from my arm. A single bead of crimson wells up before I tie off the tubing. We can't afford to waste a drop. My body feels hollow and drained but I push myself upright anyway.

He stirs, a low groan escapes him.

"Violet…" His hand reaches for me, shaky but sure, fingertips brushing my knee before he squeezes his eyes shut in pain.

"Hey, hey," I soothe, wrapping my fingers around his. "You were shot, had surgery, and a blood transfusion. So maybe… take it slow?"

He exhales, a ghost of a laugh slipping through his teeth. "Where's my jacket?"

I laugh softly. "I had to take it off, silly."

His brow furrows. "Yeah, but where is it?"

I rise, still lightheaded, and grab the jacket from the floor. I hand it to him, and as his fingers close around it, he presses a kiss to my knuckles. Then, with a shaky breath, he reaches into the pocket and my heart stutters.

He pulls out a ring.

Silver.

My favorite.

Its surface glinting with flecks of blue and green that catch the dim light seeping through broken blinds. My body goes still, air trapped somewhere between my throat and my ass.

"Ryder…" The word slips out on a breath.

He looks at me, eyes heavy but blazing with something that burns past the pain.

"Violet, from the moment I saw you all those years ago, I knew you were mine. Our connection…it's rare, something people spend lifetimes chasing and yeah, it scared the hell out of me."

His words come uneven, but his gaze never falters.

"If I could go back, I'd tell you how much I was in love with you sooner. I'd scream it. Now…in this broken world filled with death and silence…I wouldn't trade a single second of it. Because somehow, through all of it, we found us. So… Violet Hayes, my Ocean-Eyed miracle, will you take this ring and be my wife?"

Tears sting my eyes before I can stop them.

"Ryder Kent, you're everything I never thought I'd find again. You're my calm in the dissonance. Thank you for never letting go; even when the world did. I will marry you in this life, and in the next, and in every one that comes after. I love you."

He slips the ring onto my finger. The colors shimmer, tiny galaxies caught in silver. I lean forward to kiss him, but he pauses, rummaging again in his pocket.

"What are you doing?" I ask, half laughing.

He grins faintly and pulls out another ring. A masculine twin, the same silver-blue-green glow.

"Got one for me too," he says teasing.

My heart squeezes. "Well, aren't you the sweetest man alive."

"Alive is a good start," he rasps. "Now we're both bound. Not till death do us part because death doesn't mean shit to us anymore. If I'm a ghost, I'm haunting you and if we're both ghosts, we're flying side by side."

A soft laugh tumbles from my lips. "You're ridiculous."

"Admit it, you love my ridiculousness."

"Always." I trace my thumb along his jaw, memorizing the warmth of his skin. "You're stuck with me, Ryder. On a soul-deep level. Forever."

He cups my cheek, thumb brushing beneath my eye. "Darlin', stuck isn't the word. I'm grateful. Grateful that in this broken, burning world, I still get to love you."

He smiles, that faint, crooked grin that always undoes me.

"I guess this is our wedding," he says softly, eyes flicking between my lips and my eyes like he's memorizing both.

A tear slips free.

"In that case," I whisper, voice trembling, "I do."

A breath of laughter leaves him, both tender and raw. His fingers curl beneath my chin, lifting my face toward his.

"Well then, Mrs. Kent, you better give your husband a kiss."

EPILOGUE

ONE YEAR LATER
RYDER

A Dybbuk lurches out as we are leaving the toy and bookstore, limbs jerking like broken clockwork. I press the barrel to its temple and squeeze. The pop is sharp, sudden, and wet. Its skull caves in with a soft, sickening give, and I step past the body. Violet is beside me, her hair long and wavy, wearing her dads' jacket and the cutest little sundress. She's holding a stack of books we scavenged that had somehow survived the blasts. Things we can use for the newcomers. A wiry boy with too-big glasses who won't shut up about chemistry, a tough-looking girl with a crooked smile, and their mother, the one with bouncing curls who keeps sneaking glances at Kate.

We start loading the loot, stacking battered board games, novels, coloring books, and a few canned goods. Violet puts them into the back of the truck, to make it easier to take back to the compound. We conquered Tompkins' mess of a fortress, and cleaned every corner until it felt like ours. The cafeteria gleams like something out of the Jetsons now, stainless and unnervingly pristine. There's a hidden basement we stumbled on but it's empty. Just more floors we scrubbed and organized, ready for anyone who needs shelter. I glance at Violet as she arranges the books in neat piles.

"Isn't it our anniversary?" she says, tilting her head like she's teasing herself.

"Time's blurry," I admit, shrugging my shoulders. "But yeah… the leaves look the same as last year. Is that why you're all dolled up today?"

We finish loading the truck, shutting the rear doors with a clang. I step around to be a gentleman and open her door. When Violet slides into the cab, I don't close the door. Instead, I pull her toward me, pressing into the warmth of her legs. Her eyes flick up at mine, catching the flare in my chest. I lean close, letting my lips brush her temple as I press against her harder. She looks up at me, a sparkle in her eyes.

"Anniversary, huh? I might need a little… reminder of why I can't keep my hands off you."

She smirks, her eyes dark and mischievous. "Oh? You need me to remind you, huh?"

"Every damn day," I exhale against her skin, grabbing her hips. "But tonight… I want the lesson to last all night."

My fingers drift along the hollow of her back, pressing her near until the heat between us ignites. Her mouth finds mine, soft at first, then insistent, tasting and claiming. Our mouths move like tides colliding. Teasing, circling, and chasing. She bites, I press. She arches, I tilt. Every touch sparks a reckoning, a yearning that's only ours, raw and unyielding, pulling us deeper into the kind of need that doesn't ask permission. I pull away my dick hard now and she starts slowly rubbing me through my pants which means Violet is hot and ready, her whole body on fire with lust. She watches as I move my hands to slide up her bare thighs letting out a small gasp, as she wraps her legs around my waist.

"Fuck, you're so sexy," I speak in a low hunger, flipping up the hem of her dress. "I'm going to eat this sweet pussy until you're dripping all over the seat."

I shove her down and swing her legs up over the headrest putting her into doggy style, forcing her dress up around her waist, exposing her soaked panties.

"Look at you, always so fucking wet for me." I slowly peel off her drenched underwear and toss them aside diving face first, burying my tongue deep in her aching core.

"That feels so good." She says, nails scratching the truck's leather.

I lick and suck at her clit, alternating between broad strokes and teasing flicks that have her squirming. She can feel my fingers digging into the flesh of her ass as I pull her closer, devouring her pussy like a starving man.

Violet's head falls back, a string of moans and curses spilling from her lips.

"That's it baby, fuck my face," I demand before resuming my assault on her sensitive bud. I can feel her walls starting to flutter. Knowing she's close, I plunge two fingers knuckle-deep and pump furiously as I continue my oral onslaught.

"Come on Violet, cum on my tongue. Let me taste you…"

With a keen cry, she obeys, her release flooding my mouth. I lap up every drop, not stopping until she is shaking and gasping. I rise up, licking my lips.

"You taste so fucking good, Mrs. Kent."

In one swift motion, I lift Violet's leg and sink my hard cock deep inside her still spasming pussy.

"Oh, fuck yes," I hiss through clenched teeth.

Violet moans, head falling forward as I begin to pound into her. The new angle allows me to hit that spot inside her that makes stars explode behind her eyes.

"That's it baby, take my cock," I grunt, my hand coming up to rub tight circles on her clit. "You love being stuffed full of my dick, don't you?"

"Yes, yes, fuck me harder!" She begs, rolling her hips to meet my thrusts. The obscene slap of skin fills the cab as I fuck her harder, faster, chasing our releases. I can feel another orgasm building, coiling tighter and tighter in her core.

"Ryder, I'm going to...fuck, I'm coming!" Violet wails as she tumbles over the edge, pussy clamping down on my pistoning cock like a vice. I bury myself to the hilt and empty inside her.

"Take it all Mrs. Kent," I pant, hips jerking as I fill her.

After a few moments, I reach for the cloth we store in the glove compartment, and I carefully clean Violet's thighs and my softening cock. I turn her slowly, feeling the warmth of her body melt into mine. My lips brushing against the curve of her temple, soft but deliberate, as if I can etch this moment into forever.

"I love you so much, baby," I breathe against her skin, letting the words tumble out raw and unrestrained.

Her hands press into my chest, and she tilts her face toward mine, eyes glimmering in the fading light.

"I love you too," she says, and the world narrows until it's just us.

We steal a grin from each other, and decide on a little drive. The world has ended outside, but inside this bubble, it feels like ours.

"You always pick the best spots," Violet says, her voice light, and teasing, as I start the engine.

"Some things stick," I say with one hand on the wheel, the other stealing a glance at her. "Like me, trailing after you."

She cuddles up closer to me in response. The engine hums beneath us as we follow the winding road, each bend unveiling more of the mountains drenched in molten gold. The horizon drips with streaks of amber and crimson melting into soft lavenders and bruised purples. Shadows stretch across valleys, folding into jagged peaks like dark velvet. The sun hovers low, spilling light across ridges, catching on jagged rocks and the glint of distant trees. I can feel her shifting in her seat, the anticipation curling through the air like electricity. We step out, and I sweep her into my arms without a word, carrying her up the trail like she weighs nothing at all, every inch of me tethered to her.

"You know, you make this look way too easy," she breathes, laughing softly against my chest.

"Yeah? I could never get tired of carrying you." I affirm by tightening my hold.

I set her down gently, hands finding hers, fingers intertwining like pieces of a puzzle long missing.

"Good," she says, smirking up at me, punctuating her sentence with a wink. "Because I don't plan on walking back to the truck."

We walk, talking softly about what life might look like together in another year from now, imagining small victories. A garden on the roof of some abandoned building, scavenged books lined up like trophies, and nights by the fire with the stars overhead. She laughs, and it's a sound I want to bottle up and keep close to me. Hours slip by unnoticed, sitting side by side on ancient rock, knees brushing, shoulders leaning. The sky deepens into navy, sprinkled with a million unblinking stars. I trace constellations with my finger, making up stories and watching her face light up in wonder.

"You really think the stars know our story?" she asks, a soft smile playing on her lips.

"I think they've been waiting for us to find it," I reply, brushing a stray strand of hair from her face.

She meets my gaze, eyes glowing in the starlight, "You make me feel safe Ryder."

I lean closer, pressing my forehead to hers, "I love you, Violet. Always have, always will."

Her lips curl into a smile, "I love you too, Ryder. I love you beyond the stars, beyond this world."

We stand shoulder to shoulder, fingers laced like chains that could never break, staring into the vast canvas of stars strewn across the night. The world around us hums with quiet ruin, the echoes of fire and decay lingering in the distance, but here…right here…there is only this. Every heartbeat, every shiver of skin, every stolen breath speaks louder than words ever could. I press closer, letting the warmth of her body tether mine, and she leans in without hesitation, as if we've always been carved from the same shadow. The universe stretches infinitely above us, a dark cathedral of light and void, and I know…without question…that nothing, no fire, no hunger, no hollow-eyed monsters clawing at the world, could ever sever this.

Not now.

Not ever.

In this quiet triumph, this fierce, fragile heartbeat of ours, we belong entirely to each other, together, *Beyond The Dead.*

The End

ABOUT THE AUTHOR

Veronica Talliss is the author of *Beyond the Dead*, her debut novel released in 2025. A lifelong storyteller, she began sharing her writing on Wattpad at a young age, where her passion for dark, character-driven tales took root. When she's not writing, Veronica curate's bookish events that bring stories and readers together, blending her love of community with her love of fiction.

Follow her Instagram for more updates.
@thereallifeveronica

IN LOVING MEMORY OF

Ann Susan Talliss (Gamma)
04/27/1952 - 05/04/2025